GUARDIAN OF DAWN

WORLD WHISPERER BOOK 2

RACHEL DEVENISH FORD

SMALL SEED PRESS

OTHER BOOKS BY RACHEL DEVENISH FORD:

The Eve Tree

Trees Tall as Mountains:

The Journey Mama Writings- Book One

Oceans Bright With Stars:

The Journey Mama Writings- Book Two

A Home as Wide as the Earth:

The Journey Mama Writings- Book Three

A Traveler's Guide to Belonging

World Whisperer

First published in 2016

Copyright © 2016 Rachel Devenish Ford

For Kai, who is finding his path of springs.

1

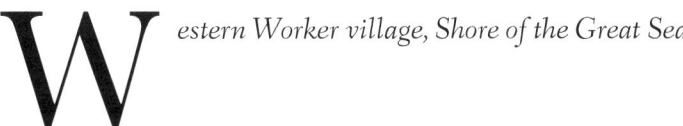
estern Worker village, Shore of the Great Sea

THE FIRST TIME she saw the giant bird was the day she gave birth to her baby boy. Jerutha paced, gasping for air, while pain like hot knives spread from the lowest part of her belly to the very tips of her fingers. She walked the small birthing room wildly, shoulders held against the pain, and took a deep breath.

She tried humming as the spasm subsided. The birthing room she had prepared was peaceful at least. The herbs she had tied to the doorway released their gentle scent into the air. The walls were white and clean, and a few squares of sunshine fell across the simple mattress on the floor. She breathed. The ache in her heart hurt more than anything. She wanted her stepdaughter, Isika. She wanted her mother.

She couldn't have either of them, and the old midwife wouldn't be much comfort, coming only at the end of her labor to help the baby into the world. *Focus on the baby,* she told herself. When she had her child in her arms, she wouldn't be so lonely. Now, though, she had no one except her husband, Nirloth, the old village priest. Not so long ago, the house had been full of life. But Nirloth's stepchildren—Isika, Benayeem, Ibba, and Kital—were gone, and she missed them desperately. Since they left, a gray haze had covered the house as Nirloth grew sicker. His death seemed imminent. He skipped many days of temple work, and the villagers grew nervous that the goddesses would retaliate in anger.

Jerutha paced and swung her arms, preparing herself for the next wave of pain. What she would really like was to go into the forest to have her baby. Or to the sea. She could sit on its shores and let the pain drift out into the water. But she must stay in this room, alone until the midwife came. Another pain ripped through her and she gasped. She fumbled for the birthing ropes she had tied to the rafters, gripping them until her knuckles were white. The pain subsided, and she exhaled. The spasms were coming more quickly now. She whimpered, afraid. How could she do this alone? No one had ever told her just how much it would hurt.

Just when her terror felt unbearable, there was a breath of sweet-smelling air and a bird landed in the birthing room doorway. Jerutha froze. The bird was massive, as black as midnight, though when it lifted its wings, its feathers gleamed like jewels, purple and red in the light. She couldn't move from fear. A strange sound, a hum overlaid with words, came from the bird, though Jerutha could not say how.

"Don't be afraid," the bird said. "Rest."

It sang a low, quiet song, and Jerutha's terror and loneliness eased until she was filled with warmth and comfort. She lay on the mattress and dozed between pains. When she woke, the bird was gone. The midwife arrived and she rose to grasp the birthing ropes and deliver her son into the world.

THE MIDWIFE CHECKED the baby over silently. She bathed him, then Jerutha held her baby in her arms for the first time. A son. He moved his little mouth, searching for food, so she held him to her breast and he moved his face back and forth until he found her and latched on. She nursed him a long time, and when he seemed satisfied, she held him out in front of her. He opened his eyes and looked at her—a little mouse-bright creature, soft and new. She kissed him all over his face and marveled over his tiny body, his miniature hands and feet. A fleeting thought drifted through her mind. Who was the bird? How had he granted her this strange peace?

Jerutha and her newborn son lay curled together for hours, feeding and sleeping. The old midwife went home after she brought Jerutha the day's food; a weak porridge, filled today with chopped green vegetables for strength. She was staring at the baby's perfect, sleeping face again when a shadow fell over her. She looked up, expecting to see Nirloth, but was startled to see four strange men, dressed in the robes of priests, standing on the ground of their courtyard. It was unspeakably rude to tread on another family's grounds except for extreme circumstances. Jerutha's heart beat rapidly as she covered herself.

"Woman," one of the men said, and she shivered at the sound of his voice. "Dress yourself and attend us."

"Lord," she said, because though she didn't know who he was, he was clearly a man of great power. "I have given birth to a new son, not five hours ago."

"We have grave business with your husband and it cannot wait," the man said.

"Oh, but he is very sick," Jerutha replied, her heart still tapping a rapid, terrified rhythm.

"We know, and that is why it cannot wait. Please dress and attend us."

THEY TURNED and walked toward the house, and Jerutha knew they would go to Nirloth whether or not she was there. Wanting to spare him, she sat up and pulled her heavy outer dress over her head, wincing at the stiffness in her muscles, the pain in her abdomen. She may not have felt much love for the old man, but pity twisted in her gut as she thought of him lying alone in his bed. She picked up her baby and held him close, tucking his soft head under her chin. She felt the fierceness of her love for the tiny creature, the way it was already forming her, shaping her into something stronger than she had ever been, yet helpless to save them from whatever would happen next.

The men stood around Nirloth's sleeping pallet in the dim room. Their faces looked repulsed as they stared down at the old man. He sat up and shifted so his back leaned against the wall.

"Jerutha," he said, as she entered. "Prepare some tea for these men." His voice was weak.

She stared at him, but he didn't look at her again. Surely he hadn't missed seeing the baby in her arms. She bowed her head and went to the kitchen, anger sparking deep within her. Who were these other priests? She wouldn't have lost her stepchildren if it wasn't for the ways of priest and goddess.

Isika, Ben, Ibba and Kital were considered outsiders because they had walked out of the desert from an unknown place with skin as richly black as the losh trees that surrounded the Worker village. The Workers had finally succeeded in driving the children away, even if by accident. Jerutha felt her anger flame higher, remembering. Isika and Ben had fled to rescue their brother when Nirloth, in the way of the Workers, had sacrificed him to the goddesses, sending him out to the deep ocean in a tiny boat. Had they succeeded in rescuing him? Where were they now? Were they safe? She laid her baby in a nest of blankets and bent to revive the fire, then filled the kettle and put it over the flames for tea.

Her mind raced. Who were these men? She had heard rumors, only whispers, really, of other villages, other Workers, but she had never seen one before. They seemed like priests, they were dressed like priests, but she had never before considered that Nirloth might have men to answer to. She stood frozen as she listened to what the men were saying.

"Nirloth, you have allowed too many cracks to enter the structure of this village," the man who had spoken to Jerutha said. "You haven't made the required sacrifices, the temple is filthy, and, worst of all, you brought black outsiders to work in the temple. You have ruined this village, its power is diminished and the favor of the goddesses is no longer upon it."

Jerutha heard her husband gasp, his breath becoming jagged and choked. Her heart caught in her chest and she scooped up her baby and ran into the room. He sat, clutching at his chest, and she rushed to him and helped him lie on his side. The man droned on, heedless of Nirloth's distress. Jerutha stared up at the strange priest. His face was a shadow in the darkness of the room.

"The goddesses are angry. You are no longer priest of this place, Nirloth. Hakar will take your place here and you will be his servant."

Nirloth continued to gasp for breath. He turned away from Jerutha without even glancing at the baby in her arms, and pressed his face to the wall. Jerutha looked up at the men.

"Please," she said. "You have said what you came to say. Please let him rest."

They looked at her and slowly one of the men, who hadn't yet spoken, nodded. He put his hand on the arm of the spokesman, and the four of them turned to leave. Jerutha nestled the sleeping baby beside her and turned to put an arm around Nirloth, who was shaking, his face still pressed to the wall.

He didn't live through the night. The only thing he said to Jerutha was something she barely heard.

"Tell Isika I'm sorry," he whispered. A few hours later, she stood and left the shell of her husband, walking out to the birthing room in shock. She lay on the mattress and nursed her new son. Nothing felt real and she was afraid.

She watched, numb, as over the next days, the strange priests performed the funeral rituals. She worried about what would become of her and her son. Even in her grief and fear, the tiny boy was clutching at her heart, a perfect being who comforted in the endless nights of worry.

The priests left the village without saying when the new priest would come back. During the weeks that followed, Jerutha settled into a kind of life that was hard and lonely, but peaceful; making porridge in the morning, tying the little baby to her so she could work in the garden. She began selling her vegetables in the market, leaving herself only the ones that were misshapen or overripe. The coins she gained helped her to buy grain for the porridge.

The baby was remarkably good. He blinked at her when she bathed him in the warmth of midday, and he grew more solid as the days went on, smiling at her when her heart felt unbearably lonely. The people of the village complained and muttered because there was no priest, and Jerutha felt as though she was always looking over her shoulder, waiting for more trouble to appear. She didn't know what would happen when the new priest arrived. She supposed she would move into her brother's house, though it was too small. She thought often of her mother in those days. Jerutha's mother had wandered into the desert, insane, when Jerutha was young. She had never recovered from her first daughter being given over, sacrificed to the sea long before Jerutha was born. Jerutha missed her and wished hopelessly for a familiar hand on her shoulder on the loneliest days. Sometimes when she felt the most despair, she smelled a fragrance like the one the bird had brought with it, and she looked up, but didn't see anything.

The moon grew and shrank four times and the baby could laugh, but Jerutha didn't see the bird again. She wondered about it often. Was it the result of a labor dream, or had it been real?

The priests finally came back on an afternoon when the sun had leached the color out of the sky. Three this time. One marched straight into the temple and began to ring the bells and burn the incense. The other two strode into the house, going from room to room, muttering to each other. Jerutha tried to make herself small, but she couldn't help overhearing what they said.

"We will take the widow to Batta," one said to the other. "The high priest wants her. She is young and already has a baby, perhaps he will marry her. If not, another priest will."

Jerutha felt the blood leave her face. She stumbled out to the garden. She fell to her knees on the ground, the baby banging against her ribcage, tied to her front with a long strip of cloth. He made a tiny sound of protest, and she sobbed. What were they bringing her to? How could she protect her son? She looked around wildly, thinking of running out into the wilderness, away from priests and men. But she sat back in the dust, knowing she wouldn't survive alone with a baby. She cried until she couldn't cry anymore and sat staring without seeing.

A shadow crossed the golden afternoon light in the vegetable garden she had planted with Isika, many months before. She felt a stirring of air and smelled the sweet breeze from her birthing day. Despite itself, her heart lifted. She looked up to see the bird standing before her. It was not as large as she remembered. It was taller than her as she sat there, but her memory had made it taller than a standing man. The colors rippled through its feathers as it opened and closed its wings once. Jerutha felt a strange rush of hope as the bird spoke.

"Isika gave you a promise before she left," the bird said, once again making its words flow into the air around Jerutha in a way she couldn't see. "She told you she would help you if you called for her. Tell me, young one. I will pass on your message."

Jerutha gasped as hope blazed up in her heart. And then she began to speak.

 zariyah, Royal City of Maween

Isika sat at the pottery wheel, wrapping both hands around the wet lump of clay in front of her. She pressed down on the clay to make a platform, moving the wheel's pedal with her foot to keep it spinning.

"Perfect," said Tomas, the master potter. "Now pull your elbows in to center it."

She did as he told her, anchoring her elbows beside her to bring greater stability to her arms. The clay followed her wish and became a perfectly centered cone on the wheel. She felt a flash of satisfaction as she watched her hands, black against the light clay, which felt almost alive as she worked with it.

"Make your indent," Tomas said. He was about the same

age as Isika's Auntie Teru, gray hair showing at his temples.
One day she had asked him how many pots he had made. He
snorted. "Enough," he had said.

"Thousands," one of the other apprentices had mouthed
at her when he turned his back.

Isika kept her hands on the cone of clay and placed her
thumb on the top center, pushing it down to make a deep
hole, then, before Tomas could give her further instructions,
she dipped her fingers in the water and put her hand into the
hole she had made. It felt like she had been waiting forever to
actually make something with clay.

She was fifteen years old, well into her apprenticeship in
her new home; Azariyah, the city of the Maweel. For six
months, she had done the grunt work in the workshop. She
had kneaded stacks of clay, driving out the bubbles so the
other apprentices could use it. She had mixed glazes for the
master potter and swept the floors of the workshop every day.
She cleaned baked clay from the kiln, she built up the fires
every firing morning. But today was the first time Tomas had
allowed her to sit at the foot-powered wheel.

The other potters had already gone home for the day and
Isika had been sweeping, as usual, when Tomas asked if she
wanted to try the wheel, his voice light, as though it was
merely a passing thought. Isika leapt at the chance, dropping
her broom and practically running to the wheel.

Now she leaned in without being told, delicately molding
the shape she was making, pulling the edge of the bowl up
and thinning it so that it flared into a shape like a flower just
opening. She hummed to herself as she did it, Tomas silent

beside her. She did what she had seen the potters do many times before, and she did what seemed right, what felt natural. When she was done, a perfect bowl sat on the wheel before her. It was beautiful, she thought, as she sat back to look at it. The angle was delicate, the arch of the clay gentle and graceful.

She looked up at Tomas and he stared back at her for a moment, his face slack with shock, finally breaking into a huge laugh that filled the workshop.

"I had a hunch," he said. "And Ivram warned me. So I waited until the other potters were gone. Apparently being World Whisperer gives you many talents, young one."

Isika scowled. She still didn't feel like the term World Whisperer belonged to her, so when people called her that, it was as though they were talking about someone else, not her, Isika, the girl who had just thrown her first pot on the wheel.

World Whisperer was the title of the person who had the direct connection between the Shaper and the Maweel people, the one who protected them, went before them, and healed them. Isika didn't feel like that, even if she could make a pot on the first try.

"It's just clay," she said.

"It takes months," Tomas said, his voice thoughtful. "Years, sometimes, before apprentices can make a bowl like that. But never mind. Let's get it off the wheel and into the drying room. I'll try to stamp my jealousy down and you still have to finish sweeping. Teru will have my head if I keep you too much later."

Isika cut the bowl off the wheel and set it on a tray, which she carefully carried to the drying room to add to the other pieces that had been made that day. She allowed herself to feel proud of finally making her first wheel pot. The feeling spread into her arms and legs, so that she was nearly dancing as she finished sweeping the dusty workplace.

SHE HUNG up her apron before she left, calling out a farewell to Tomas as she stepped out into the early evening light, drawing in a breath. Tomas's workshop sat at the bottom of a valley clustered with trees and houses, now glowing in the beautiful light. The green and golden light streamed through the leaves of the trees. It was soothing to Isika's eyes after the hours she had spent in the studio, and she walked home in a kind of reverie, letting her eyes rest on the lovely earth walls of the homes, the patterns the owners had painted on the outsides, the climbing flowers that spilled over the arbors and rooftops. She stood for a moment under her favorite tree; a giant, sprawling, gnarled thing with ridged leaves. It spread its branches over the marketplace she passed on her way home, bustling at this time of day. Isika lay her hand on the trunk and felt the tree's life rush through her, causing her to stand a bit straighter for the last climb up the hill to Auntie's house, her home now, for five months.

Isika had grown up as a black-skinned outsider in the Worker village after her mother died. She, her brother, Benayeem, and her sister, Ibba, had fled the village by boat, to rescue Isika's youngest brother, Kital, who had been sent out as a sacrifice to the four goddesses the Workers served. When they met Jabari and Gavi, two boys from the Maween, they discovered that all the sacrificed children had been rescued from the waves by the Maweel: a dark-skinned people now scattered with pale-skinned rescued ones, who were adopted into families.

They had journeyed together to Azariyah, only to make the discovery that their younger sister, Aria, was alive, and that Isika and her siblings were direct descendants of Maween's stolen queen, which made Isika heir. They also found that Kital and his rescuers had been imprisoned by the sea people, leading to a struggle where Isika fought, retrieving Kital and the rescuers, revealing herself as World Whisperer when she went head to head with one of the Worker goddesses, Fate. When they came back to the city, the elders decreed that she would live in Azariyah for a year, and at the end of that year, they would discuss the future again.

Living in Azariyah, Isika and her siblings had been transformed by a new life. They lived with Auntie Teru and Uncle Dawit—the new parents who had adopted them—learning to be a family in a place that filled her heart with light. Growing up in the harsh Worker village, she hadn't known life could be so beautiful. Teru's home was built on trust and care. Isika had learned so many new things: the six gifts of magic, the singing of stories—which Ben excelled at—more about how to use numbers, reading and writing. Auntie was teaching them gathering magic, which she said everyone possessed in some small degree. They grew food and took care of the gardens.

They were slowly getting to know their sister, Aria, who

had been given over to the goddesses as a sacrifice when she was nearly eight years old, rescued by the Maweel, and raised here ever since. When Isika had first arrived, four years after Aria, she had asked Aria to move in with them, fully expecting that her sister would be happy to be reunited. She was stunned when Aria, now twelve years old, laughed at her and told her she had a new family, one she wasn't going to leave.

Isika had hidden her hurt. *She* was Aria's family. She crept away and cried about it to Auntie, but Auntie had seen it the same way Aria did.

"Give her time," she said. "It's a lot of change for her. She had a place here. She found a way to relate with herself as an outcast, a rescued one, and then you four walked in. Her world is shaken."

Isika saw it differently. Aria was their sister. Their sister should be with them, restored to them. But it seemed that reunions were much more complicated in real life than in dreams. Life, even in a nearly perfect place like Azariyah, was full of complications, like the sorrow she still felt over her mother, or guilt she fought every day.

She woke up with a start sometimes, in the middle of a bad dream about Jerutha, her stepmother, left behind in the Worker village. Sometimes it felt to Isika that she wouldn't be able to enjoy her life here at all, if Jerutha couldn't be here. And then there were days when she didn't think about Jerutha, but lived as though she had been one of the Maweel all her life, as though she had never come from a barren, dusty place on the edge of the desert. And when she eventually remembered that she had a stepfather and stepmother somewhere, it was like a pail of cold water on her head. She wanted to shrug it off, to not think about it anymore, to be free of her past. But she loved her stepmother and she often missed her, often thought of how much she would like Auntie and Uncle, or how she would love the food here, the flowers that spilled from every surface. Isika and Jerutha had fought so hard for every blossom in their garden in the Worker village.

On her way up the hill, many people met Isika's eyes and nodded as she passed, but she knew they discussed her when she was gone. People were interested in her, confused by her, overwhelmed by her abilities. Somehow she found herself in the center of the tapestry of this beautiful city, occasionally attending meals at the palace, taught personally by Ivram, the second elder: a rare privilege. She was in the center, but she was also on the outside, as she had been all her life. She was a newcomer who was the heir of their stolen queen. They had become used to having regents, and knowing that Isika could become their queen unbalanced their world.

Isika knew she wouldn't become queen if she could help it. She had no interest in ruling over anything, wearing fancy robes at the palace, or presiding over dinners. She wanted to make thousands of cups and bowls, as many as Tomas had made, to learn how to use her bow, to learn to run as fast as Jabari could. These were the things she wanted.

She shrugged the thoughts away and looked up at the sky, the clouds that were edged in fire as the sun prepared for its descent. Adjusting to life here wasn't easy. But, she thought, as she walked up the final steps to get to Auntie's house at the top of the hill, it was life. She felt more alive than she had ever felt before, brimming with life; sadness and joy and pain and longing. And it hurt sometimes but it was good. It was better than her previous life in the Worker village—work that never ended, work without joy.

A small shape barreled out of the house's front door and launched itself at her. She caught her five-year-old brother's small body and held him close. Kital stayed in her arms for only a moment before he wriggled back to the ground, hopping from one leg to the other, skipping beside her as she walked into the house and set her pack on the table beside the door.

"I missed you!" he announced, as he always did. She sometimes wondered if he only said it to please her. He was happy here, with Auntie and Uncle, shadowing Uncle in his workshop, playing with the kittens in the garden.

"I missed you too," she told him, but he was already gone, flying outdoors where he would find something to get his hands in, whether it was dirt, the pond with its brilliant fish, or maybe the sawdust piles in Uncle's workshop. Uncle Dawit was a palace guard, but he was semi-retired and spent the rest of his hours in his wood-working shop, a tiny building behind the house. Kital thought the shop was magic itself. He wasn't wrong—one of the gifts was Building magic; the ability to call the shape out of things, to put things in their right places and keep them there, whispering to the edges, the beams, the grains of wood. Or a lump of clay that became a bowl.

The house smelled wonderful. Isika took her soft leather shoes off and walked through the entryway into the house, breathing deeply. She smelled cinnamon and pepper—Auntie was making spice tea—and she smelled the beginnings of dinner as she stepped into the large room at the center of the house. To her left was the kitchen, open to the rest of the room but separated by a long, curving countertop that had been built with earth and topped by a huge slab of wood. To the right, the table; beyond, the low seating area covered with pillows and cushions. There were also two elaborately carved lounging chairs. Auntie said she and Uncle had a hard time getting all the way to the floor these days. Ben sat on a cushion, his face hidden behind a book. The last rays of sunlight streamed through the windows, lighting up Auntie's curtains.

The people of Maween made a kind of fuel that was not wood. It was clean to burn and left no smoke or smell, a kind of magic. The fuel looked like small cubes of red rock, and burned for a long time. A large metal pot sat on the top of the stove, now alight with the fuel, which the Maweel simply called red rock. Auntie stood at the countertop, chopping vegetables furiously. She smiled as Isika walked in.

"There's spice tea in the pot," she said. Isika smiled and

took her favorite mug from the earth shelf. She gazed at it for a moment, trying to imagine how she would pull the clay up to make a shape like this, and blinked when she realized that Auntie had spoken to her.

"What?" she said. "I'm sorry, I didn't hear."

"Did you do much beyond sweeping today?" Auntie repeated. She gathered the tomatoes she had been chopping and threw them in the pot of water on the stove.

"I did, actually," Isika said. She poured herself some tea and pulled up a tall chair to sit at the countertop. "Tomas let me try the wheel after everyone left." She closed her eyes as she took a sip of the hot tea, pepper heating the back of her throat, remembering the feeling of the clay in her hands.

"How did you like it?" Auntie asked. Isika opened her eyes. Ben put his book down to listen to her.

"I don't have words. It was as amazing as I thought it would be. Tomas said I did well."

Auntie snorted. "Of course you did. You have every gift."

Isika smiled. She didn't mind when Auntie boasted about her because she did it in the way she did everything, fiercely protective of her new family, puffing up about every accomplishment.

"We had a visit from Teacher Leila," Auntie said. "She says that Ben shows more promise in the singing stories than any student she has ever had."

Isika turned to look at her brother. He stood slowly, stretching and carefully putting the book back on the shelf that was built into the wall. He was taller than he had been a few months ago, taller than Isika now. His long, dark brown limbs and shoulders were filling out. He smiled at her.

"I don't think she used those exact words," he said, his voice wry.

Auntie snorted again. "Sometimes you have to read between the lines."

"The singing stories, hmm?" Isika asked.

"How much time have you spent on them with Ivram?" Ben asked.

"Not much. We've been focused on the life gifting."

"They're so beautiful," Ben said. "And they calm the noises I always hear. They settle everything into its right place."

Benayeem was still figuring out his own gifting. He had the magic of justice; the discerning magic, and it had driven him nearly crazy when he was younger and didn't know why he heard horrible music that no one else could hear. Now he studied justice in the regular school, not with Ivram like Isika.

She didn't like that they were learning in different places, but Ben didn't seem to mind. He accepted the fact that she was World Whisperer, not him. He had never wanted to be noticed. It wasn't his way. In a way, she wished she could be like him. It was terrible to be whispered about. People talked about him, too, of course, but in the same way they talked about all of the outcasts, the rescued ones; with curiosity and pity, not wonder.

They all had their own gifts. Aria was clearly gifted in protection, and was training to be a seeker. Ibba, their eight-year-old sister, was showing strong leanings toward the gathering gift; the kind of magic that brought plants out of the earth and enabled the Maweel to eat well. On their journey together from the Worker village, Ibba had shown strong signs of having a healing gift, something she might develop in the future. For now, she spent hours in the garden. Isika had found her murmuring over a handful of dirt one day, and had backed away slowly, trying not to laugh. Her little sister hadn't even noticed her.

Ibba came in from the back garden now, carrying herbs in a little hammock she had made with her tunic.

"Here Auntie!" she sang out. "Are these the ones you wanted?"

"Perfect, dearie," Auntie told her, taking the herbs from her and rinsing them in a small bowl of water.

Sometimes Isika envied her smallest sister and brother. They hadn't experienced the terrible weight of their mother's death, just two weeks after Kital was born, in the same way Isika had. And they hadn't been old enough to understand the looming threat of the sending out: without warning, someone you loved could be sacrificed. Because of this, they seemed more ready to love, sunnier and more cheerful, less afraid. Isika couldn't let go and fully sink into her new life. She brooded over it as she helped prepare for dinner, changing out of her apprentice clothes and lighting the lamps as the sun sank behind the mountains. It was a flaw deep inside her, and she didn't know how to change it. She always felt prepared for something horrible, ready to run or flee at a moment's notice. She couldn't quite believe that this safety and peace was their life now.

They sat at the table and sang the eating song of gratitude to the Shaper. Auntie served up bowls of spicy vegetable soup and Uncle and Kital chatted about the boat they were making between building shelves and cupboards for all the new people in their house. Teru and Dawit had lost a son, a Ranger, in a rescue journey gone wrong, so there was pain that would never leave their faces, but they were the kindest people Isika had ever met.

As they began to eat, Dawit looked up.

"I almost forgot to tell you," he said. "Aria will be going out on her first seeking journey next week. Jabari has just been named a master, so he will be taking her on as an apprentice."

Isika felt a sudden flash of pain that seemed to come from nowhere. She was secure, she had a family; why this hurt over Aria going on a journey? She looked up to find Ben looking at her with concern. Maybe it was only that Aria was fully accepted here, without any of the suspicion that a possible future queen seemed to bring out in people, and Jabari had spent his whole life as the son of the high elders. Why should she be sad that they were going on a journey together? She was happy to stay here and make pots. It was what she had chosen, out of all the apprenticeships she could have taken.

But traveling with Jabari and Gavi had been wonderful. She remembered Lake Ayo with its waters that seemed to take all fear and pain away. Sitting around the fire every night as Gavi cooked what he had managed to find. There were bad memories too; Jabari's anger when Isika had broken down the poison walls around a house by herself, the horrible evil of the goddess, Fate, that Isika had faced at the end of their second journey. But the life that coursed through Maween was beautiful and her friendship with Jabari and Gavi was new and fragile. She felt left out. That was all. She swallowed and remembered the clay responding to her hand in the workshop, the delicate flare of the bowl.

"When is the sending?" she asked.

"A week from today," Uncle said.

"How good for Aria," she replied, and took another spoonful of soup.

She ignored the concerned glances sent her way and focused on trying to swallow the potato that was suddenly lodged in her throat.

J abari jumped up from his cushion and started pacing, shaking his head against the tirade of words coming from his mother's mouth.

"...must accept the wisdom of the collective elders," she was saying. "Things cannot go on as they have."

He sighed and sank down to sit directly on the cold tiles of the floor, ignoring the cushions that were scattered throughout the room. His family was gathered in the small room they used for private discussion, off to the side of the throne room. The floor tiles were colorful and intricately painted, the palace walls were white. There were hanging lamps that were not yet lit, since twilight had not yet fallen. He looked through a window with longing. It was a waste to be indoors on a day like this.

Jabari's father, Andar, First elder of Maween, lounged on his cushions, a slight frown on his face, while Jabari's mother, Laylit, sat regally on one cushion, her back straight and rigid.

"Things have been fine," Jabari said. "We had one difficult journey."

From the corner of his eye he saw his brother, Gavi, turn to look at him. Okay, maybe he was stretching things a bit. It was true that on their latest Seeking journeys things had been strenuous even for Jabari and Gavi, experienced seekers. They were used to walls from the Great Waste. The walls grew magically, formed of poison, infecting the people within them with isolation and despair. But the walls had started to become taller and they came back quickly, even after the seekers tore them down. He knew things were different, that somehow Mugunta was stronger. But his parent's solution was too much; it threatened everything he loved about his life: the open road, he and Gavi running along, quiet and free.

He and Gavi had been close since Gavi was rescued and adopted into Jabari's family when he was two years old. Though they were exactly the same age, they were very different, not only to look at—Gavi, a rescued Worker, was pale-skinned and broad, while Jabari was black like his parents and as lean as a running cat—but in personality as well. Jabari was quick-tempered and impulsive, while Gavi was wry and not easily ruffled. But as different as they were, they knew each other so well they were like twins.

Jabari loved wildness and solitude. He loved the wilderness for its silence and for the fact that it was away from the complicated relationships and politics of the palace where he had lived all his life. In the wilderness, he and Gavi were just boys, surviving and protecting their land.

The seeking journeys were regular treks into Maween outside the city of Azariyah. Their purpose was to seek out poison and destroy it, healing people and the land when they could. The poison came from Mugunta and the Great Waste, the evil that wanted to destroy the Maweel's link to the Uncreated One, Nenyi, the great Shaper of the world. Before the queen of the Maweel people had been stolen, the poison was mild, easy to send away even for the people themselves. But these days there were always seekers needed to rid the land of poison.

Isika had introduced a lot of complications when Jabari and Gavi found her and her siblings on the last trip, though Jabari did have to admit they had become friends by the end of the journey. But Jabari had been looking forward to things returning to normal, the way they had been before Isika came, when he and Gavi traveled long roads by themselves. And then his parents had sent down their decision; his seeking group was going to triple in size. This meeting was one last attempt to change their minds.

"How will people take us in when we heal their homes?" he asked, his voice a barely masked growl. He knew he sounded like a frustrated child, and tried to calm down. "We can't expect people to host so many of us, but you know it's essential to their healing."

His father shrugged. "Send two people in and the rest of you can sleep outside. You can figure it out. What you need to understand, Jabari, is that you are a master now. Gavi will be a master soon. As such, as leaders of the Maweel, things won't be the same. You need to accept your responsibility."

The room seemed to be closing in on him. Jabari dropped his head into his hands.

"So is it decided then?" Gavi asked.

"Yes," Andar said. "We don't understand why things have become more difficult in Maween. If Isika truly is the queen's granddaughter, things should be easier now that she is restored, but they are worse than they have been in years. We, the elders, don't want any more seeking or rescuing treks to go wrong. You will be teaming up, and it is up to you to make sure this journey goes well. I don't want our seekers in more danger than they need to be."

"It has always been dangerous," Jabari said. "That's what seeking is."

His mother stood. She was very beautiful, standing there, her robe a midnight blue shot through with silver sequins. She looked like the night sky; a very angry sky, though. Her lovely dark face was scowling at him. He flinched and Gavi shot him a warning look. The look said, *tone it down, Mom's mad.* It was a look Gavi had been giving him since they were young boys.

"Jabari, elder's Son, you don't seem to understand the danger. For the security of Maween and the surrounding lands, we as regents must remain in command of the country. We have a young heir to the throne living among us. If things become unstable, people in Maween could easily demand that she sit on the throne. We need peace in the land so this won't happen." She sat back down with a huff.

"A fifteen-year-old poison-lander is not a good queen for

this land, no matter how powerful or whose granddaughter she is," Andar said.

Put like that, Jabari didn't feel he could argue, but something about what they said didn't feel right to him. His brother spoke before he could.

"Isika doesn't even want to be queen," he said. "At least not now."

Andar nodded, his hand on his wife's arm. His voice, when he spoke, was soothing. "Of course she doesn't, and we aren't accusing her, but the truth remains that we are in need of safety and peace more than ever. You are not to do anything to endanger the apprentices or other seekers on this journey. Including Aria is an expression of goodwill toward their family." He didn't add *a safe one* but he didn't need to.

Jabari knew that his parents considered Isika a wild card. To be honest, he did too. She was too powerful, with no experience of life with them. She was dangerous for everyone. Aria, on the other hand, seemed to have a very simple protection gift and showed no signs of getting crazy ideas. She'd also lived with the Maweel for four years.

Andar looked at a piece of paper in front of him and went on. "You will take Aria, Ivy, Deto, and Brigid."

"That's only two apprentices," Gavi said. Ivy and Deto were skilled rescuers, and they had gone on seeking journeys as well.

"Yes, that's true. Well that should turn out all right," their mother said.

Jabari tried to shake off the feeling that this was all just an elaborate way of showing goodwill to Isika's family under the guise of bringing apprentices into the seeking. He and Gavi rose and bowed to their parents.

"Come back for dinner tonight," their mother said, as they turned to leave. "I'm talking to you, Jabari."

"Yes, Mother," he said, and bowed again.

They pushed through the big doors and Gavi nodded at the guards the way he always did. He was the good son, there was no doubt of it. He had the thankful, gracious bearing that so many rescued ones did, full of gratitude for his place in the Maweel. Sometimes Jabari wanted to punch it out of him. He didn't want his brother to believe he needed to behave well to make sure that people were happy they had rescued him. Sometimes he did try to punch it out of him, just to try to rile him up. But his brother was amazing and funny and sweet, genuinely good. Jabari knew he was not. The raw energy, almost anger, that sometimes welled up inside him was not appropriate for palace dinners. It was best in the wilderness, where he could get away from the clatter and buzz of voices and be in pure, blue space, lying in a field, gazing at the sky.

THEY HAD TAKEN ONLY a few steps down the hall when they ran into Isika. Or rather, she ran into them. She was coming from the upper floor of the palace, skipping down the stairs, and she stumbled right into Jabari and Gavi.

Gavi laughed, but Jabari straightened and frowned. There was that small shiver he always felt when he and Isika bumped into each other or touched hands. It was her magic, he thought, too deep and strong, sizzling like lightning. There was no doubt that she was dangerous. He looked at her as she stood biting her lip. She didn't look dangerous; she seemed innocent, and she was beautiful. She was tall, like a queen, her skin dark as black coffee, her eyes wide set, tilting up in a face that was all curved lines and high cheekbones and lips that swept up at the corners. Her hair was braided away from her face today. She stuck out her chin at them now.

"You're taking Aria," she said, her voice an accusation, and Jabari bristled.

"Hi, Isika," Gavi said softly, and her eyelids fluttered as she looked down at the ground.

"Sorry," she said, her voice softer. "I'm a little upset today. I don't understand why she has to go already. We've only been here for a few months and I want her to stay."

"She's been waiting for this a long time," Gavi said.

Isika crossed her arms in front of her, as though she wanted to hold onto herself. "How are you two, anyway? I barely see you anymore."

Jabari's face softened. Her voice sounded sad and a bit overwhelmed. Sometimes he tried to put himself in her place, understand what this was all like for her. It was hard. He couldn't imagine life without his parents, his role, all his responsibilities.

"We're well," he answered. "I'm not too excited about taking so many people on this journey." He surprised himself with his honesty.

A glimmer of a smile crossed her face as she met his eyes. "I can imagine. I almost wish I could go with you, though."

"Have you thought about becoming a seeker?" Gavi asked.

Jabari could have kicked him. That was the last thing they needed.

"No, I'm going to be a potter," Isika said, her voice bright and determined. Jabari blinked in surprise. He knew that she was an apprentice, but had assumed it was only to make the time pass during her trial. His parents should be hearing this. Not a queen, but a potter, sitting in a workshop, making pots that would collect dust on people's shelves.

"Where are you going now?" he asked.

"Home. I've been studying with Ivram."

"Is he being hard on you?" Gavi asked.

Gavi and Jabari, as sons of the First elder, had also studied with Ivram, and Gavi was still tentative around the Second elder, who could deliver blistering remarks when he thought you were being stupid. He was also standing at the top of the stairs and had heard Gavi's unfortunately timed question.

"I'm not hard on Isika," Ivram said as he walked down the stairs. He looked like a king himself, with his gray hair and silverwood staff in hand, prowling down the stairs like a lion. Ivram went on as he reached the bottom of the stairs. "She listens well and is exceptionally smart, so I've never had to be as hard on her as I have on some others."

Ouch. Ivram gave them all a benign smile and left, heading in the direction of the throne room. Gavi widened his eyes at Jabari.

"You deserved that," Jabari said. "You know you can't talk about him. He's everywhere."

Isika looked like she was trying not to smile, but now

laughter burst out of her, and her face changed completely, full of joy. Gavi pretended to scowl.

"What's so funny?" he asked.

"You two don't do a very good job of being regal and proper," she said.

"Me?" Gavi asked, pointing at his chest. "I have the manners of a prince."

They started walking toward the door. Though their banter had taken the sting out of the discussion with his parents, Jabari felt like he couldn't get outside fast enough. He was going to run up a mountain, to a nearby waterfall, and let the crashing sound of the water ease his frustration.

"You know all about us," he told Isika, his voice serious. "The boys you journeyed with are the real us. This palace thing is not really real."

Her face grew serious again. "That's why I want to be a potter," she said, and he felt a flash of pity mixed with something sweet. Understanding? Care?

She turned to walk up the hill that led to her house.

"Tell Auntie Teru hello," Jabari called after her, and she waved briefly, then turned and kept walking. Jabari looked away to find Gavi smiling at him.

"What?" he said, his voice annoyed.

"Nothing," Gavi said, and his voice was deceptively light, but he was still smiling.

Gavi went off to his gardens to check on his tomato plants, and Jabari did what he had been thinking about all day. He ran. He ran through a forest of large trees with branches reaching to the sky, and as he ran his heartbeat sped up. He felt his muscles loosening. There, that was what he needed. His feet pounded the ground as he ran up the paths of the forest, heading higher and higher, leaving behind all the questions and muttering that had followed Isika's arrival.

The truth was that Jabari was torn. He had a tentative friendship with Isika, and his relationship with his parents, who tried to protect the people, was deep and true. And then people were always asking him if he really thought she was the lost queen's granddaughter, was she really the World Whisperer, come to put things to rights, what was she like? It was all very boring and complicated.

He just wanted to run. He wanted to be out in the air, feeling the breeze on his skin, damp now with sweat. He ran up, the forest growing thicker so that less light fell on him and he felt the cool breath of the forest. He ran up and up, until he could hear the roar of the waterfall and finally it was in front of him and he stripped off his clothes and dove into the pool at the bottom of the falls. He let the water beat at him and tumble him over until thoughts of the palace had left him completely and he was in that quiet, happy state where he felt most unified with Creation magic, with the Shaper. He knew then, finally, that it would all sort itself out.

Benayeem sat very still as Uncle cut his hair, turning the scissors so they came close to his head. The haircut was taking forever, but Ben had learned that rushing Uncle Dawit would only make him go slower, so he waited, holding his body still though he wanted to jump off his stool. Today was the first day he would be with the singers for a ceremony, a journey day.

Last week Ben's teacher had put a hand on his shoulder and told him that he could join the other singers for this journey day. Hundreds of Maweel would meet in the meadow at the banks of the river, just beyond the palace, for the travel ceremony. A thrill had run over him at his teacher's words. Singing the stories with all the other singers!

Ben had seen only two of the travel ceremonies. One was during his own journey: a short, emergency ceremony when they had gone to find Kital, after he had been captured by the sea people. The next had been when two sets of seekers had set off a few months ago, Gavi and Jabari and Ivy and Deto. The music was so beautiful that his heart had nearly stopped beating, and his gift shouted like a wild thing, telling him how right and good the songs were.

This time, he would sing, and as a singer, he knew he could bring his gift under control. He had been studying the songs for all these months, and he had also taken every chance to ask his teachers about his peculiar gifting. Benayeem's own body was like a tuning fork, he had discovered, now that he lived in Azariyah and knew what a tuning fork was. He heard sounds, songs, music, voices. He was learning to interpret them. He could hear beyond the sounds that people normally heard, into the spirit of people and events. His teachers were puzzled by his gifting. Justice was usually general: a faint understanding of which way to move, rather than a solid YES ringing out over the whole body, musical notes ringing through the inner being. Or a NO. The no's were the worst, the beating, doom-filled music and drums. Life had been better since he had come to Azariyah, where there weren't as many terrible things as the Worker village had held.

Uncle finished with his hair, squeezing his shoulder and sending him toward the bathing room to clean up. Ben took his clothes off and immersed himself in the pool of water that he had already poured from the hot faucets that were made from a kind of building magic.

Ben had spent the first years of his life believing that he was crazy, so sensitive that all he could do was escape and find quiet places where he was free of the constant torment of horrible sounds. He felt more sane now, as he wrestled his gift under his control. He could quiet it sometimes, say if he was in a big group of people and didn't want to hear all the little threads of rightness and wrongness in each person. He could shush it, tell it to sleep. He no longer believed that he was crazy.

He put on a green tunic and brown pants, charging out of the bathing room, nearly knocking Ibba over in the hallway.

"Whoops! Sorry, little sister," he said.

"It's okay," she said, regaining her balance. She held something out to him. "I picked some honey berries for you. They'll help your voice."

Ibba was spending so much time in the gardens that Jabari thought she would become a plant. As soon as she could be free of studying numbers, reading, and writing at school, she came home and spent her afternoons among the plants of Auntie's garden, helping the beans by building them trellises, pouring water on their roots, singing to the soil. She was the most careful eight-year-old gardener Ben could imagine, though Auntie and Uncle didn't think it strange that she was so careful and so young. This was giftedness, they told him. This strange care. A soft way of moving. He was still learning to understand it all.

He took the berries and tossed them into his mouth. They burst between his teeth with the taste of honey and something like crushed mint, soothing and awakening his throat.

"Thank you, little flower," he said to her. "I'll see you down there, okay?"

"Okay," she said, giving him a hug.

He waved at Auntie, who grinned at him, then left to walk down the hill to the meadow. The light of the morning was gentle, turning the stones beneath his feet to a warm brown color, touching the flowers that grew beside the path. A slight breeze whispered beside him.

People were already gathering in the meadow, milling around, laughing and talking. Ben scanned the crowd, looking for the other singers, and found them quickly, dressed in green and brown, as he was. The group of singers included black Maweel, with their dark skin and tightly curling hair, cut close or braided, or felted into long locks, and the Rescued with their pale skin and hair, or black, straight hair and long eyes. A garden of people, Ben thought as he waved hello to the other singers.

Ben headed toward Deto. Ben had first met Deto when they rescued Kital. Deto would be going out with the seekers on this journey. Deto was a rescued one, with long black hair, skin the color of sand, and long eyes that tilted up. The rangers, the bravest of the Maweel, had rescued him after he had been sold to slave sellers when he was four years old. Rangers fought groups of children-catchers and rescued children who had been sold by their people for money or good luck from the goddesses.

Deto had told Ben that he still dreamed about his people, who came from the high desert of the mountains. He missed his mother. But he was brave and funny, and his long hair, always pulled into a braid, set him apart from the crowd so that Ben found him easily. When he wasn't on seeking journeys, Deto was a singer. He held the lowest notes in the group, with a surprisingly deep voice rumbling out of his thin frame.

"Nervous?" Deto asked as Ben caught up to him now.

"A little," Ben said. "What about you?"

"Yes, but not about singing. I'm nervous about the journey for some reason. Maybe it's the apprentices."

Benayeem frowned. He and Isika thought it was too soon to send Aria on a seeking journey, but her adoptive parents were fine with it, and it wasn't really his place to say anything.

THE MEADOW WAS SHAPED like a bowl, surrounded by trees, with one side curving down toward the river. The grass was spongy and short under their feet, clustered with tiny, star-like flowers that let out a spicy, minty fragrance when they were crushed. People drifted in, walking in small groups to attend the travel ceremony. Ben joined the cluster of singers and they began the wordless welcome song, a melody for peace and beauty, the notes of the high singers floating up and the low singers making a firm base underneath. Ben gave himself over to the song; when he sang, his body was an instrument that finally made sense.

The people came and stood in a large circle. Ben and the singers began the first of the thankful songs. This was a direct song to the Shaper, and it listed the many ways the creation sustained the Maweel, the Rescued, and the world. Benayeem shivered as the words washed over him.

LINE OF STARS
> Highest mountain
> You bring the morning
> The sun beginning
> The waves restoring
> food from the earth
> Eyes that open, feet that run
> The perfect light of the dawn
> The day in all its brightness
> You bring the rain
> You bring the rain
> You bring the rain
> Quiet twilight
> The rich black night
> A line of stars
> A line of stars
> It leads to you.

THEY STOPPED SINGING when it seemed as though everyone who would come had arrived. Andar stood on a bench in the middle of the circle.

"This travel ceremony is the time when we bless our seekers and send them out into our lands for the protection of Maween, the healing of the lands and the restoration of peace."

He gestured for the seekers to come forward. Ben saw Jabari and Gavi, Ivy, Deto, a girl he didn't know very well named Brigid, and last, his sister, Aria, step into the center of the circle. The singers began to sing a low note, almost a drone, that built into different harmonies. This was Ben's favorite part of the ceremony, and the reason was a secret.

He hadn't told anyone that the notes of this song were an exact match for the music he heard in his head when good things happened. This was the song of blessing, to bestow power on the seekers, who represented the Maweel along all the small road and paths of the land. The song of blessing had come to him before he ever heard it sung, and he treasured the knowledge, because it made his gift feel right.

Ben looked around for Isika in the crowd. After a minute he saw her behind Dawit, nearly out of the circle. Her hands were in fists. She wasn't happy about Aria journeying as a seeker.

The song grew louder and louder, then Andar held out his hands and spoke the words of the traveler's blessing:

"Go well, with speed,
    The road be smooth
    The trees give their bounty
    Your hearts thankful and brave
    Come back to us quickly."

After the blessing, the others melted back into the circle and Benayeem and the other singers began the story singing, weaving their voices as each one took a turn to tell a part of the story. They were telling the saddest story, the one about the queen being stolen. Ben thought back to the first time he had heard the story, when he was still a Worker, half-starved and weary, sitting on the road while Jabari sang.

He put more strength behind his voice and began his solo. His voice flowed out over the circle as the Maweel listened. His part was the part when the queen was taken.

BUT HEARTS BREAK *and the Great Waste*
    Moved against us
    Thieves, they wanted her,
    They took our queen
    she was gone and her baby with her
    we wailed to the heavens,
    but the grasp of the cruel was strong,
    the Great Waste didn't give her up to us.
    Still we search,
    Still we search
    Still we search.

HIS VOICE nearly broke as the sorrow of the real thing crashed over him, but he kept the sound strong and rich, and around the circle people wiped tears from their faces.

A thought pricked at him. Isika was the found queen. She should be in the circle, right in the center, rather than huddled off to one side. Finding her should have been the beautiful ending to the sad story he was telling in the song.

He didn't understand why there wasn't more rejoicing over finding her. Instead, it was as though she was suspect, because she had come from the Workers. But that wasn't her fault.

A WIND ROSE UP. There was a shift in the sounds in Ben's head. He stopped singing and the other singers turned to stare at him. A few moments later, they too stopped singing, because the whirr of many wings filled the meadow as four giant Othra swooped from overhead and dropped into the middle of the circle.

Ben knew three of the giant birds from his journey to the city: Efir, Nirral, and Eemia. He had never seen the fourth, though he knew there were Othra deep in the mountains who rarely came to Azariyah. The Othra were birds half the size of a grown person. Eemia was the smallest of the group. She was an ancient Othra, quiet and wise. He thought she was Efir's mother, though he had never asked. Their black wings were shot through with jeweled colors that flashed in the sunlight, and they brought a feeling of deep peace with them. When the Othra were around, Ben heard the most soothing music he could imagine. Isika told him that for her it was more like a warm feeling in her heart, as though she knew without any doubt that all would be well. And Gavi said they brought the fragrances of the most beautiful days with them. Ben saw Gavi lifting his face now, breathing deeply.

Andar held his hands in the gesture of welcome, though

the look on his face was surprised. This wasn't planned, Ben realized. Andar spoke.

"Welcome, wise ones. What do you have for us, or is it only your company?"

Eemia stepped forward, her eyes alight.

"I have a message for the World Whisperer."

Across the circle, Ben saw Isika's head shoot up.

Andar's face clouded and he took a small step backward, staring at the bird. Then slowly, he turned and beckoned Isika to come. Isika made her way through the crowd until she was in the center of the circle. She bowed to Eemia.

"Peace, Eemia," she said.

"Peace in your heart," the bird said.

The way the birds talked without moving their mouths was always startling. From his sister, Ben knew that the birds could also talk somewhere in the mind, so that only someone who understood animal speech, like Jabari and Isika, could hear, and even then, they could choose to talk to only Isika, or only Jabari. But now the bird was talking so everyone could hear.

"Do you remember the promise you made to one of the poison-landers?" Eemia asked.

Isika froze, then nodded slowly, her eyes wide.

"The poison-lander is calling for you to fulfill that promise now. The woman is in need. She wanted me to tell you that Nirloth is dead. Others have come. The baby is born. She is afraid of what will happen and she has no hope for mercy. She doesn't read her future, doesn't know what will come, but she believes it won't be kind to her."

Ben took a deep breath to calm his racing heart. It was jarring to hear that his stepfather was dead in this way. He sat down quickly, watching Isika to see what she would do. She was very still, her face stricken. Benayeem never, ever wanted to return to the Worker village, and he knew that the words that came out of her mouth next would change everything.

Isika took a deep breath and straightened her shoulders so she was standing very tall. She had the bearing of a queen, and Benayeem watched her with awe and fear of what she would say.

"We will go," she said. She turned and searched for him, finding him sitting in front of the other singers. She looked at him as she spoke, pulling him into her answer. "We will go to help Jerutha."

6

As she stood in the meadow, Isika watched her brother sing, trying to untangle the threads of voices to hear his voice more clearly. She was proud of him. Not long ago, he was a shrinking, terrified boy, certain the voices in his head were his own insanity. He fled people and difficult situations. Now she was the one having a hard time and he was in the center of the ceremony, singing the old stories. Her soul leapt up as she listened. A humming inside told her that, though she had never learned the song, she would be able to sing every word perfectly if she tried, but she kept her mouth tightly closed, and her fists too, wishing she could disappear.

People had whispered as she and Uncle approached the meadow. They made a wide space around her, *trying not to touch me*, she thought miserably, as she stood with her shoulders hunched and her fists clenched tight. But despite her efforts to make herself small, Gavi had found her, he'd caught her eye from where he stood, close to the center of the circle with the other seekers going on the journey. He'd winked. Jabari saw her as well, smiling at her.. She felt a little better. Her stomach hurt less.

But then, without Isika asking for it, while she was doing her best to be small and unimportant, Eemia, the Othra revered because of her age, came and called Isika out as World Whisperer. As soon as Isika heard the title, dread shot up her spine. Something had happened, she could feel it from the birds. She reached out with her mind, touching theirs. No one else could hear.

What is it? she asked.

You are needed, daughter, Efir told her in response.

Does it have to be me? she wailed to them.

It can only be you.

Well then, she would listen to what Eemia had to say, even in front of all the people. When Andar gestured to her, she walked into the circle, her knees shaking, to hear what the bird would tell her. Eemia spoke so everyone could hear, and they heard of Isika's father's death and the danger her step-mother was in. As Eemia spoke, Isika's magic stirred and boiled, as though it would lift her off her feet; a strong response from her gift. She felt it gather, a stream of aware-ness, flowing through her body. As it did, she straightened to give her answer.

Jerutha had helped them escape. She had given them a boat, she had resigned herself to being all alone in the house with Nirloth, and there wasn't one single day that Isika didn't think of her, wonder about her. Of course she would go. She would go even if her gift wasn't doing the equivalent of shouting at her.

"We will go," she said, looking at Ben. "We will go to help Jerutha."

At her words, it was though a blanket of silence was lifted. A clamor of words came from every direction. Isika saw Ben cover his ears as he sat on the ground. People shouted, turning to speak to each other, and the noise felt hostile. Andar strode into the clearing and held his hands up. Quiet fell. Jabari stood scowling at the ground, and Gavi was staring at Isika, pity on his face. Isika's face ached with threatening tears.

"There will be no decision now," Andar said. "But we do not meddle in the lives of the Poison-landers. Their village is not on our lands. They have not invited us."

"But," Isika began to protest but Andar's eyes flashed and he held out his hand for her to stop.

"The elders and I will confer and give you our decision.You and Ben may attend dinner at the palace tomorrow night, Isika. The journey will be postponed until we have decided what to do. Go now, and be at peace, all of you."

He dropped his hands and strode toward the Othra across the circle. Isika reached out with her mind again, but the birds were closed to her now, busy with Andar and Ivram, who had a concerned frown on his face as he joined the huddle of Othra.

She sighed in frustration. Gavi and Jabari stood talking with Deto. She walked toward them, careful to keep her head high, thinking rapidly of what she would say, what she would ask.

"Please help me," was what came out without any decision on her part. She looked up at Jabari and he looked back. His eyes were serious, troubled. "We can go together again," she went on. "You're about to go out on a journey anyway. This will be perfect. Just bring me and Benayeem along and we'll travel swiftly to the village. We'll take the river, like last time—"

"No," Jabari interrupted. His eyes were hard. "No, Isika, we don't meddle with them. Remember how I told you that, long ago? We don't cross the boundary into the Worker village. And I can't take anyone else with me on this journey, we are too big already. And anyway, you are not ready for seeking, you have had no training..."

Isika stared into his face. She tried to put all of herself into the gaze, reminding him of what they had been through together, what they had seen and done, the fragile friendship they had made. He looked away.

She looked at Gavi. Him then, the more reasonable of the two. But he shook his head sadly.

"The elders will discuss it," he said. "And we'll do what they decide."

She shook her head, anger rising up behind her teeth.

"It is the way of the Maweel," Gavi said, his voice very gentle. "You are one of us now, you have to come to an understanding of our ways."

SHE CROSSED HER ARMS, not backing down, then finally growled in frustration and turned to walk away. She looked for Uncle in the crowd and saw his high, graying head bent toward Ibba. She went to him, ignoring all the curious and even sympathetic looks she was receiving.

"Can we go?" she asked. Her voice was tight with tears and she needed to get away before she started crying.

"Of course, young one," he said. He put a hand on her shoulder and squeezed. They walked home together. Auntie hadn't come to the travel ceremony. She didn't leave the house much these days. Her son had been killed while on a ranger mission, and the announcement to the people of Maween had been made in a circle like this one. Since then, Auntie kept away from large gatherings. She preferred to sing the ceremony songs in her own garden.

Ibba slipped a hand into Isika's as they walked, and Isika kept herself together until she reached the threshold of their little house. At its familiar smell and warmth, as the house reached out and welcomed her, grief welled within her and she fled to her room, falling on her bed and sobbing until she thought she might die. She cried for Jerutha, for her confusion, but most of all, for the mother she had already lost. She missed her own mother, who had died after Kital was born. She longed for her gentle eyes and soft brown skin more than seemed bearable. Would she lose Jerutha forever as well? How much loss could one girl handle?

After some time she felt a familiar weight settle on the bed, and a soft hand touched her back, rubbing between her shoulder blades until her sobs slowed and finally stopped.

She sat up and buried her face in Auntie's shoulder. Auntie held her tight. She was strong and warm and soft. Isika stopped crying. She sat back and looked at Auntie, swiping at her own swollen, wet face.

"What is the point?" she said, "Of being the World Whisperer if they won't trust me or listen to me when I need them?"

Auntie sighed. Her face was dark and lovely against the red of the scarf she had wrapped around her hair. She was still beautiful. Isika thought she must have been extremely beautiful when she was a young woman. Her eyes were a deep, clear brown, wide set, with a delicate tilt. She looked fierce now, as she struggled to find words.

"They try, young one. This is all so sudden. But take heart. You will know what to do when the time comes."

The words were so simple, but Isika felt them enter her soul and strengthen her bones. She looked at her hands and gathered herself. The hurt of being mistrusted, suspected and ignored, eased as she dwelled on the words Auntie spoke to her. You will know what to do when the time comes.

SHE WASN'T any less determined, as she walked down the hill to the pottery workshop that afternoon, hand in hand with Kital, but she was at peace. Jerutha needed her. The stepmother who was like an older sister to Isika had been through so much in her life. Something terrible must have happened, if Jerutha had sent for her. It wouldn't be something small.

The thought sent a shiver through her and she tightened her hand on Kital's. He looked up, a slight frown on his face. She smiled at him. He had turned five a couple months ago, and nearly all the baby roundness was gone from his face, but he still had those dimples. His skin was much lighter than hers, because pale-skinned Nirloth was his father. Her heart fell as she looked at her little brother, because though he didn't really understand, Kital had lost his father a second time today. The first time was the day Nirloth chose to give him over as a sacrifice, pushing him out to sea to die in a little boat.

Jerutha had called her. Jerutha had helped save Kital, by sending Isika, and Jerutha needed her. Isika had to find a way to help her.

They reached the workshop door and walked in. The kiln hadn't been fired today, so the air was cool and smelled of earth and clay. Tomas bent over one of the wheels, though today was not a work day. Isika wasn't surprised. There wasn't much in the master potter's life beside pottery. He ate, drank, and slept pots, sometimes even staying over instead of going home. She had come to the workshop on more than a few mornings to find him wrapped in a blanket on the floor of the workshop.

He looked up and she nodded a greeting at him.

"Come for your gift?" he asked.

"Yes," she said. "How did it come out?" He had fired the kiln after she left, the day before.

He tilted his head toward the storage room. "See for yourself."

She left Kital watching Tomas expertly shaping a bowl on the wheel, walking into the storage room beside the kiln. She found her gift immediately. Four cups, glazed in a perfect sky blue: one for each elder. The cups were delicate, wider on the bottom than the top. She let a breath out. They were lovely. She placed her hands around each one, feeling the cup's weight and softness on her palms. They would be a good gift.

She had been planning to give a gift to the elders for a long time, as thanks for the time they had generously given her family. She hoped it would be seen as only gratitude, after the events of the day, and nothing more.

She took the cups, two at a time, out to the outer workshop, and found one of the small wooden boxes that Tomas used to pack the dishes he made. She packed the cups in sawdust and put a lid on the box, tying it together with twine. When she looked up, he was watching her.

"You heard, then," she said.

"Of course I did," he said. "Everyone did. And Teru might have made her way down here as well. My ears still hurt."

Isika smiled. One of the best things about her new life was the protectiveness Auntie had for her. Anyone who got in Isika's way had better watch out, and that included the elders. Though Auntie wouldn't go against them, Isika could well imagine the blistering account she had for her old friend Tomas.

"She's incredible," she said.

"Don't I know it," Tomas said. He sighed. "Saddest day of

my life when she decided to marry my best friend instead of me."

Isika grinned at him. She didn't believe for a moment that he had ever wanted to be married to anything other than his pottery.

"Good thing she did," she said, picking up her box and holding a hand out for Kital. "Or she would have been a pottery widow."

She called an airy goodbye out to Tomas as she left, feeling better from the earthy workshop air.

As she and Ben walked up to the steps of the palace the next night, Isika let her eyes rest on its beauty. She felt the familiar way it reached out to her, settling around her in contentment as she walked up the steps. At first she hadn't understood why the palace responded to her this way. Now she knew it recognized her.

She was the oldest grandchild of the beloved stolen queen. At the end of the hall, she paused to look at the huge portrait of the queen who had been kidnapped, eventually perishing in the Desert King's city. The Desert King's demon magic had made his city invisible to all who had searched for the queen, and the Maweel never found her, though they searched for many years. The face of the queen in the portrait was warm but stern. She was so familiar to Isika, because she looked like Isika's mother, but her mother had been softer. If this woman was a thorny rose, Isika's mother was a meadow flower.

Ben waited for her, and when she was ready, she walked on, toward the banquet room. She held her gift close to her side, and though one of the servants offered to take it, she smiled at him and shook her head. She wanted to put the box straight into Karah's hands.

Isika wore a brilliant blue tunic, shot through with golden thread. Auntie had braided her hair into a crown, and her skin glowed with oil. She wore gold earrings in her ears, and a thin gold chain around her neck. The pants under her tunic were a deep, midnight blue, nearly black, and the neckline of the tunic was elegant, dotted with tiny jewels. She had felt, looking at her reflection in the mirror as she dabbed a flower-scented oil on her wrists, as though she was beautiful. And Ben beside her was handsome in a white shirt and pants of the deepest green. But as she stood at the door to the huge dining room, she knew she wouldn't even be visible amid the beauty within.

People wore robes and tunics of every color. Some wore head wraps, sweeping their hair up and away from their necks. There were feathers in some of the women's ears, or dangling jewels of every color. The room was a sparkling, shimmering sea that Isika made her way through, nodding to the people who greeted her. She tried to be polite, but she didn't love the palace dinners. She worried that the elders didn't actually enjoy her company. It seemed as though they invited her out of pity, not knowing what else to do with the lost queen's heir. She would rather be in the pottery workshop or outside in a tree. She continued across the room. She did love the palace food. There was that.

Ben left her side when he spotted Aria. Isika continued alone. She came to a corner where Karah sat with the other three elders, on colorful cushions and low platforms scattered to make a pleasant place to sit and talk. Isika smiled to see them together. She could give her gift to all of them at once. She stood and watched them, waiting for them to see her.

Karah had been the very first rescued one, thirty-five years ago. She had married the much older Ivram—Ivy, their daughter and one of the seekers, told Isika it had been a whirlwind of a love story. Karah's robe today was a deep, sea green. She often wore green; it seemed to be her favorite color. Her flaming red hair was tied into hundreds of braids, some with tiny jewels woven onto the ends. They sparkled when she moved.

Next to her was Laylit, Jabari's mother. Laylit was so beautiful that sometimes Isika couldn't stop staring at her. She had black skin, the color of night with no moon, and long, graceful hands. She wore a golden robe today, shot through with red thread. Next to the two of them, Isika and her best tunic were starting to look very plain.

Karah looked up, and Isika held the box out before her.

"Peace on you, Elders," she said. "I have a gift for you."

Karah took the box. "Thank you Isika," she said with her soft voice. She loosened the twine and pulled the lid off, reaching a hand into the box and taking out a cup. She held it carefully in both hands.

"There's one for each of you," Isika said, feeling awkward and embarrassed, now that her work was on display. She hadn't thought this part through. "I made them."

"They're lovely," Karah said, her voice warm. Beside her, Laylit nodded, her eyes warming. Isika nodded and turned to go, giving Ivram a tiny smile. Though they spent hours together in the classroom, she always felt shy around him when they weren't in class.

"Wait," Andar said, as Isika began to walk away.

She turned back. Jabari arrived and sank onto a cushion, his long legs taking up half the little corner. Isika met his eyes briefly, then looked away. She was still frustrated that he hadn't taken her side and agreed to accompany her to find Jerutha. But she waited, a knot growing in her stomach. She knew she was about to hear their verdict.

"We have discussed the news the Othra put before us," Andar continued, and Isika stood with her head bowed slightly, waiting. "The Othra are wise, they are ancient and some of our oldest allies, but they are messengers, and they do not always understand the ways of our people." Out of the corner of her eye, Isika saw Jabari's head pop up, surprise on his face.

"We will not change our ways to meddle with the Poison-landers," Andar said. "I'm sorry, Isika, you will not be able to help your friend, though we can offer up prayers for Nenyi to send help from a different direction."

Isika told herself she had been expecting it. She took a shaky breath, trying to still her racing heart. She wanted to run, but she took a moment to look at each person. Ivram and Jabari looked back at her, troubled. Andar and Laylit looked determined, but didn't meet her eyes. Karah looked at Isika with questions in her eyes. None of them had any malice, but the result was the same. Jerutha would go without any help from the city of Azariyah. Isika bowed her head in response and turned to go, blinking back tears as she walked out of the room, then out of the palace. Help from a different direction? She was the help. The Othra had made that clear. She felt helpless, confined by the traditions of a people who were so new to her. She pressed her palms hard against her eyes, trying not to cry again.

When she reached the soothing black of the open sky, the stars and the gentle branches of the trees, she breathed a deep, deep breath. She wouldn't give up. There must be a way to help Jerutha. She just needed to find it.

7

J abari finished tying on his travel boots and jumped to his feet. He picked up his traveling sack, settling the familiar weight onto his back, and slung his bow and arrows across his chest so they rested over one shoulder. It was the day after the palace dinner and they were ready to leave again. Jabari hoped there wouldn't be any additional announcements from the Othra.

He took a moment to look into his mirror. No matter how many times he set the thing in the hallway for the palace servants to take away, he always came back to find it on its place on the wall. He grinned at his reflection, feeling lighter than air. The road waited. He could leave the palace and the smothering sense of moving slowly, as though through water, that he felt here.

He loved Azariyah, his city; a beautiful jewel that he would protect with his life if it came to it. But he knew he was born for trees and open sky, and he was somehow less alive in the city. His waist belt held his water flask, his large knife was slung at his side, ready for danger or overgrown plants. His clothes were loose, for the heat and rain, made of cloth that dried quickly. He carried only one extra set of clothes in his pack, as well as a smaller knife, kitchen supplies, a light blanket, a book to write in, and some soap. It was all he needed.

He looked closer at the mirror, feeling as though the reflection was almost a stranger. He had felt like a man for a long time, but now, at sixteen, he looked like one. He picked up his *ser,* his light scarf, and slung it around his neck. All Maweel carried one when they traveled, to tie on their heads under the hot sun.

He gave his room a parting glance, then strode down the hallway of the palace, running down the stairs three steps at a time, and nearly crashing into his brother, who stood waiting at the bottom. Gavi had a slightly larger traveling sack, which they argued about sometimes because Jabari wanted to carry equal weight. Gavi, however, didn't trust Jabari to carry his precious cooking pots. Gavi's light blond hair was sticking up like a sea plant as usual.

"Finally ready, Yab?" he asked, grinning. Gavi used Jabari's nickname, the brother name he had for him ever since they were both two years old and Gavi couldn't pronounce Jabari's name.

"I've been ready forever. Are they going to make us do the thing? After we already did the other ceremony?"

"You know they will. It's only a few minutes."

Jabari frowned. Through the open door he saw people clustered on the steps of the palace, which meant they were going to do a proper travel blessing. Again. He sighed. The two of them walked into the brightness of the morning. It would be scorching by midday, but now the air was still fresh and cool.

His parents were there. Ivram, Karah, and Ivy stood nearby, and Jabari spotted Aria standing with her parents, dressed for travel. Isika and Benayeem hovered not too far away. Deto smiled at him from where he stood with Brigid. Hopefully they could get this out of the way quickly.

His father spoke the words of the travel blessing, and the seekers were embraced a hundred times. Jabari gave his father a quick hug. His father looked at him with stern eyes that glinted with emotion..

"Remember what I said, son. On the surface, it is a simple seeking journey, but the currents underneath are deep and serious."

Well, no pressure then. Jabari held his tongue, nodding at his father and giving his mother a hug. She dashed quick tears from her eyes as she hugged him and Gavi, and he gave her an extra squeeze on her shoulder. She always cried when they went out seeking, though she tried to hide it.

Through the crowd he saw Isika again. She stood very still and tall, her hair braided up around her head from the night before. He read sadness, clear as water in her face and the way she held herself. Without thinking, he went to her. She smiled at him, her face tentative.

"No hard feelings?" he asked. He saw understanding in her face. She knew what he was asking.

Isika wanted him to take her side in the battle to help Jerutha, and he hadn't. He didn't tell her there were other ways to make things happen. Fighting stubborn elders wasted time when you could go to the problem without troubling them with requests for permission.

"No, of course not," she said, her voice soft and her eyes wistful. "I kind of wish I was going with you."

He smiled. He knew how she felt. The urge to walk down long paths could overtake him at any time, prompted by a cool breeze or a certain scent in the air, or just the sun rising as it did every day. "Don't worry, you'll have more journeys."

Gavi joined them and grabbed Isika for a big hug. She spoke to Jabari again as soon as she extricated herself, reaching up to mess up Gavi's hair.

"I'm happy here for now," she said, looking over at Aria, who stood with her parents.

"You should go to her," Gavi said. "Say your goodbyes."

Isika bit her lip. Gavi looped an arm through hers. "Come little sister. We'll go together."

Jabari watched them approach Aria, who kept her face blank. Isika spoke to her sister, then reached forward to pull her into a hug. Aria stood stiffly for a moment but finally hugged Isika gently. Jabari would have to try to figure out what was going on there. It was important that Aria feel safe around Isika in the future, they needed her as an ally, not a potential problem for the throne. He blinked, surprised at himself. Despite what his parents said, he was certain Isika would become queen.

AFTER THE BLESSING, Jabari set off with the other seekers. The road that led out of the city was lined with tall trees, a long ribbon of them that filed down the hill and into the next valley. There were silverwood trees, their gleaming trunks tall and faintly shining in the morning sunlight; hoona trees with their yellow bark; and eveningstar trees that dripped with purple flowers.

The paving stones ended and became hard packed dirt, held together with magic that kept it from flooding and becoming mud when rain fell. The dirt felt better than stone under Jabari's soft-soled boots, and he grinned.

"Let's start with a run!" he called. "To the first well!" He jogged forward, leading them down the road, feeling the Maweel lands helping them, boosting them, the air sparking with life around them. Traveling joy entered his heart and he took deep, burning breaths of it.

He stopped at the first well, barely winded, and they all drank and refilled their flasks. He noticed that some of them looked worn out already, especially Brigid and Aria. He would go slower for them today, but they would soon learn to run. He and Gavi spent a lot of their days running.

"First lesson, Aria and Brigid: At every well, drink and fill your flask, even if it already has water in it. You never know when the next well will turn out to be poisoned or dried by demon magic."

Aria's eyes widened slightly and she nodded. She wasn't as tall as Ben or Isika. Her face gleamed with perspiration and she took off her *ser* and wiped at her face. She wore small gold earrings in her ears as well as a gold nose ring that gleamed against her dark skin. She was prettier than Isika, certainly, but without the same wildness of magic about her. She was sweet. She had always been sweet, ever since he had met her when she was rescued at the unheard of age of eight, four years ago.

He was twelve, nearly thirteen when it happened. He still remembered. She was the oldest child they had ever rescued—normally they were two or three years old—and the only black child they had ever found in the sea outside the poison-lander village. She was a mystery, so traumatized by her sending that she couldn't give them answers. The sending tea—for sleep—that the poison-landers usually gave to the cast-off children had worn off Aria quickly because she was so much older. She had curled up in the tiny boat, awake, wrapped in her sending cloths, waiting for death. When the rescuers reached her, she was mute with fear.

Jabari remembered the thin, traumatized girl who had come into the village with the rescuers. She hadn't been able to speak for nearly a year after she arrived, and by the time she did, they didn't ask her any questions about how she came to be in the Worker village. Jabari frowned, remembering. He supposed they had forgotten to ask. By then she was one of them.

She was so different now, feisty and glowing with health, laughing with the others as they stood by the well, teasing

Deto mercilessly. But sometimes Jabari still glimpsed that tiny, terrified girl inside her eyes.

He looked at Gavi, who nodded. Jabari's brother often knew what Jabari was thinking, and this time was no different. The way they could speak without words was almost a gift, or perhaps just the intuition of brothers. It didn't matter. Gavi would look out for Aria on this journey. He was a gentle person; she would feel safe with him. It was clear to both brothers that she needed someone to look out for her.

The other apprentice, Brigid, was also a Rescued, also from the Worker village, but she had been the normal age, two years old, when they found her. Though she had the familiar bearing of the rescued, she didn't seem fragile, the way Aria did. Brigid was tall, with pale skin, bright blue eyes, and long brown hair that she kept in two long braids. She was dreamy, a little clumsy, and distracted easily, by flowers and trees or the sounds of birds chirping in bushes. Her adopted parents were weavers, and Jabari wasn't sure why she wanted to be a seeker. He was exasperated with her already, but not worried the way he was with Aria. He gulped more water, fighting frustration at the way this journey had turned out. Apprentices. He sighed.

Ivy approached and put her hands on her hips, leveling a stare at him that could wither leaves. Her father said she was like a crane, her long arms and legs, graceful neck, skin the color of coffee with milk. She was wiry and graceful. Also terrifying. She was like a sister to him; Jabari, Ivy and Gavi had grown up fighting over dessert under the tables in the banquet room. Or Jabari and Ivy would fight, Gavi would just sit and ponder how the dessert had been made, then find a way into the kitchen and make some for himself. Jabari knew their parents hoped that that he and Ivy would marry one day, but Jabari couldn't imagine it. They were too much like brother and sister.

She continued to glare at him and he kept himself perfectly still, refusing to look away. Then she grinned. "Do you want to tell us the real plan now?"

Everyone stopped talking, their attention caught. Too much like brother and sister. Only Gavi and Ivy would be able to tell that Jabari had another plan. He narrowed his eyes. Deserts and spines! How could they always tell when he was thinking? He had tried to appear as though he was following orders exactly.

He hesitated, looking around at his five companions.

"Well," he started, and they broke into smiles.

"I knew it!" Ivy crowed, and she reached over and smacked Gavi on the shoulder.

"Do you want to hear the plan?" he asked, a fake scowl on his face, "Or do you want to keep talking about how you knew I had it?"

"Okay, okay," she said. "I'll be quiet now."

"Well," he said again. "I thought that since the Worker village is on our way... we might have a quick look... see if there is anything we can do."

There was silence. Aria's eyes were huge in her face. Then, slowly, she nodded, and the others did as well, Ivy and Deto with huge grins on their faces. Gavi was shaking his head, looking at the sky. Jabari crossed his arms and leaned against the well with satisfaction, happy that his plan had gone over without a hitch so far. And the elders didn't suspect a thing. If they had, they would never have let the seekers go. He felt a twinge of guilt, but shrugged it away. It would only be a little look. They wouldn't have to do anything.

8

When the priests arrived, Jerutha had nearly resigned herself to the fact that they would come. She watched for Isika daily, but Isika hadn't appeared, and as Jerutha sat in her garden, surrounded by the green of the plants she had cared for, she thought she had no room for fear. The days had been reduced to a fever of hope that was crushed every evening. No Isika. She was still alone with her baby.

Because she was bad luck, the villagers she had known her whole life barely acknowledged her now. Except for one. Faiza still cared for Jerutha, chin jutted out as she ignored the hisses from the stalls nearby. Faiza bought food for Jerutha from the stall owners who wouldn't sell to Jerutha. She gathered it all and gave it to Jerutha with a soft look on her face. The look said everything, and Jerutha found that she couldn't look at Faiza too long or her own face would fall from its set, brave expression.

Even her brother was wary of her, especially after she had given his boat away. But she still went to visit her grandmother in the evenings, and her grandmother was always kind. She loved the baby, cackling while she played with him in her bed, while Faiza's brother and wife pretended Jerutha wasn't in the room.

"What is his name?" Jerutha's grandmother asked, every time, as though Jerutha hadn't told her already.

"Mesu," Jerutha told her softly again, holding the old woman's frail hand gently in her own.

"Mesu, Mesu," her grandmother sang. "And are you drinking the tea for good milk?"

"Yes," Jerutha lied, because she had no one to gather the bark for her, so how could she make the tea?

Her sister-in-law avoided her eyes as she left. She walked home in the dark of evening, pain so large in her heart she didn't know if she would die from it. It wasn't only her loneliness that gave her pain. It was all of it, she could sense the larger pain of people being cruel to one another, abandoning each other to protect themselves from the wrath of the goddesses.

So when the priests came, she had nearly resigned herself, and her heart was so full of pain and crushed hope that she believed there wasn't any more room for fear.

She was wrong, she knew as she watched them approach the house across the market square, black robes flapping around them, hoods over their faces. She was so wrong. Fear could swallow everything, even pain, even hope.

The new priest moved in quickly, throwing Jerutha's

things out of her room while she scrambled to pick them up. She found a travel sack that had belonged to Nirloth and put her things inside while the priests roamed the village, looking for food and transgressors. They slept scattered throughout the house that night, while Jerutha locked herself in the birthing room with Mesu, nursing him to sleep, wiping away the tears that sometimes fell on his head.

In the morning, they left. There was nothing to do. She had no way to escape and Isika hadn't come. As the four priests marched through the market square, Faiza ran out to give Jerutha a hug, but the priests pushed her back.

"Back! She is bad luck and she must be cleansed!" the tallest priest barked.

Faiza stopped, but she gave a small wave and Jerutha held her eyes as long as she could. Then they left the gate and all that was before them was a bit of straggly forest and the endless desert. Jerutha had never dreamed that she would cross it.

She knew the stories, though. Isika's mother, Amani, had crossed the desert, pregnant, with three small children at her side. She stood straighter. She needed to be strong, like the stories of Amani, gaunt and determined, striding across the sand forever.

In the forest, the priests had three mules, and Jerutha's heart lifted at the thought that maybe she could ride, but the tall priest laughed at her when she asked.

"They carry our water and supplies," he said. "Not women."

"Where are we going?" she asked, desperate, her voice catching.

"To Batta," he told her, his heavy-lidded eyes cold on her face. "To the head priest."

"But sir," she said, keeping her eyes on his shoulder. "I am nursing my son and it will be hard for me to walk so far."

She glanced at him and saw him regarding her. One of the other priests, this one thin with a high voice, joined them.

"Perhaps we should leave the baby behind," he said to the taller priest, and Jerutha shook her head wildly.

"No," the tall priest said. "I don't think his holiness would like that. But if it gets too hard for you, perhaps we will have to do so."

Jerutha bit down hard on her lip to keep from crying, and the tears that stung her eyes then were angry, not broken-hearted. She straightened and hardened herself. Well, then, she would be like stone. She would not complain.

THE JOURNEY WAS a long waking nightmare. They walked in the afternoons, evenings, and early nights, sleeping at middle night and waking after the noonday sun had begun its descent. The beginning of each afternoon's walk was torture to Jerutha. Her legs hurt, the sun beat down on her bare head, and her mouth was always dry. She drank and drank, but it seemed that her thirst couldn't be quenched.

But she was thankful. She had milk for Mesu. Her body continued to make milk, enough milk, and her heart beat with a storm of love for him as they walked. It was what she put all of her focus into, this fierce love for her baby. She despaired that Isika hadn't come to her after all. She was resigned to it now, but she had Mesu, and she loved him until her vision swam with tears and she forced them back because they were precious water.

She focused on him as she fed him, his tiny precious face close to her. She focused on him as he smiled at her in the middle of the night when they stopped to sleep. She focused on him when the priests jerked her up by the elbow, just to be mean, or left her the smallest portion of water. They wanted to keep her alive, but they didn't show her any kindness.

As she walked she pondered Nirloth. He had seemed so stern, but he must have been soft for a priest. He certainly had been kind compared to these men who drove her on and on, who seemed like the monsters from Jerutha's mother's nightmares. Perhaps that was why he had been put in the tiny village on the western coast. Nirloth was too soft. Then again, she supposed she couldn't judge based on four priests.

Sometimes as they walked in the afternoons, she saw specks in the sky, flying high, high above them, so high that Jerutha didn't know whether she was seeing things that weren't there. The sun was merciless, even in the afternoon, and her head always felt hot. She might be dreaming heat dreams. But she stared at the specks and found that hope wasn't quite dead in her.

And then there was an afternoon when they walked on and on, and she fell to her knees. She tried to get up and found that she couldn't. She had reached the end of whatever reserve of strength she had, and there was nothing at the bottom but despair.

"Get up," she whispered, but her body wouldn't listen and the sun was so hot. With all her heart she wished for the sea, her sea. She was a fisherman's daughter. What was she doing in this horrible place? Sand and sand for miles, nothing but dry, dead beige. No green, no blue. The sky was white, drained of color by the sun.

"Get up, woman," the tall priest told her. He handed her a water flask and stood there while she drank.

"I can't," she told him. Her voice was flat, not begging, not defiant. Flat like the sand that stretched in every direction.

The priests exchanged glances.

One of them, a man who rarely spoke and seemed to hate the journey, approached, shaking his head.

"A short rest," he said. "This tree is giving some shade. Let her sit there for a few minutes. Then she must walk." He took the flask and refilled it from the water skin on the mule's back, handing it to Jerutha again when he was done. The "shade" from the stunted tree nearby was more like a few lines in the sand, but Jerutha was grateful. She clutched her sleeping baby to her and wept. She tried not to cry, the water was too precious, but it had been too long and hope was fading. Her weakness overcame her.

Why? she thought, as though the bird who had come, all those days ago, could hear her. *Why make me hope? It only makes it worse that she didn't come.*

High in the sky she saw the specks that had followed them since the first day. Flying, circling, diving. Then quickly she dried her tears and sat up, because clouds were forming. She watched the sky while the priests muttered to each other near the mules and she saw clouds racing toward each other, meeting in the middle, gray and majestic. Eventually, one crossed the sun and the priests looked up as well.

They muttered exclamations, glaring darkly at the specks that were quite clearly birds, closer now, still circling, circling. One bird gave a low cry that raised the flesh on Jerutha's arms, and at the same moment, rain fell from the sky.

The storm was quick, strong, and over within minutes. But Jerutha would never forget those minutes, some of the most beautiful of her life. The rain fell and she lifted her face to it, sheltering Mesu but wiping his hot head with her wet hands. She was soaked, and when lightning flashed and the thunder roared moments later, she felt the exhilaration of the water.

It made her think of her favorite moments on the shore when she was a small girl, before her mother left. Playing in the shallows, feet wet, the breeze across the water bringing ideas of playful things, dancing sun on the waves.

The rain stopped and she sighed. She bowed her head to keep the moment away from the priests, and was jerked out of her reverie by the tall priest pulling her roughly to her feet by the elbow. He glared down at her from beneath his heavy brows. Instead of shrinking, she pulled her arm away from him. For the moment, anyway, the glare couldn't reach her.

"What have you done?" he demanded.

"Nothing," she answered honestly. "What, you think I can

control the weather? I am only a small woman, at the mercy of the weather, as we all are."

The priest ground his teeth, looming over her. For a moment, Jerutha thought he would hit her, but the priest with the high, thin voice spoke up.

"Let's go," he said. "Before there is any more... interference."

And Jerutha found she could walk again. She looked at the distant specks and breathed, "Thank you," at the sky.

THAT NIGHT, she dreamed soft dreams of the shore when she was a girl, dabbling her feet in the water. But she looked down at her arms and she was a grown woman, holding Mesu. The birds came to her then, three of them, taller than her as she sat, their black feathers flashing with red, purple, blue. She was dazzled by them and held up her hand to block the light.

Her heart was full of sweetness and hope. What was the feeling she had? She felt as though the birds looked at her with tenderness. The kindness of a mother's eyes, something she had only known a few times before her mother went mad and wandered into the wilderness to die.

Why are you being so kind to me? she asked.

Suddenly, light, on her, all around. Tears sprang to her eyes. The sky shifted and colors raced across it. She felt weight, as though someone draped a blanket around her shoulders. She leaned into it.

You helped the World Whisperer, she heard. And the sky

cracked with light and colors and there were thousands of the birds, everywhere she looked.

She woke to the tall priest shaking her, and she smiled at him.

He looked briefly stunned. "Get up, woman," he said.

She sat, the feeling of the dream still with her. The stars filled the huge desert sky, glittering, far away and impossibly lovely. How could she have thought the desert was a dead place? She picked her baby up and kissed him all over his face.

As they began walking, the priests argued. She tried to listen but they were too quiet for her to understand. Finally, one of them turned to her and pointed at her, speaking to the other priests. She caught his voice on the wind and shivered.

"It's her," he said. "She's a witch. We should leave her here. We shouldn't bring something like her into the city."

The tall priest slowly nodded.

Fear clutched at Jerutha's arms and legs. If they left her here, Mesu would die.

"No," she said. "But the high priest! He wants me. Wouldn't he be angry if you left me?"

The tall priest stared at her for a moment, then laughed.

"He would indeed be angry with us, but not because you matter to him. Is that what you think? Don't flatter yourself, girl. You're nothing but bait for the one he really wants, that outsider who defied the goddesses. You're a fisherman's daughter, right?"

Jerutha nodded, numb with horror that he knew anything about her life, her past.

" The worm, on the hook?" he went on. "When men want to catch a fish? That's you. You're the trap," he repeated. "Nothing else." He turned back to the other priests.

"We bring her," he said. "Stop being superstitious. It was just rain. You've all felt rain before, it won't melt you."

They walked on, and after a moment, Jerutha stumbled after them, feeling as though she'd been struck in the face.

Isika. This was all a trap for Isika. And she was part of it. She had sent Isika a message, caring nothing for Isika's own safety. Her heart ached as she walked and even memories of her dream couldn't help her.

9

On the morning after the sending, Ivram showed up on Auntie's doorstep. Isika was at the table drinking her morning coffee, when she heard a knock. Normally, Teru and Dawit kept their front door wide open, but it was still early, and they hadn't yet opened it to let in the day. Auntie Teru looked up from the stove, where she stood cooking breakfast in her night robe.

"Answer it Ibba, will you? Perhaps someone has smelled my morning flat cakes and followed his nose to our house."

As Ibba ran toward the door, Isika pulled her wrap around her, stretching and inhaling the scents of coffee and flat cakes. She loved mornings in her new home; the slow start, the light gradually brightening until everyone in the house went off to different workplaces or schools for the day. In the morning they were still all together. Ben and Uncle read in the corner; Kital played with a wooden toy on the floor.

Ibba skipped back toward them, and Isika's eyes grew wide as she sat up straighter. The visitor wasn't a neighbor who had smelled breakfast. It was Ivram. He seemed very large and regal as he walked after little Ibba; so tall he had to bend to fit under the arched doorway that led from the entrance to the living space. He held the silverwood staff that would one day be Isika's. As usual, it drew her attention, pulling at her, the bulb glowing softly in her presence.

Dawit stood, going to Ivram with his hands outstretched.

"Ivram! Welcome in my home! Are you hungry?"

With a rush of emotion, Isika felt again the difference between her old village, where one person was not allowed to tread on another person's ground, and the homes of the Maweel, open to friends and neighbors, even strangers. She blinked tears away, thankful for her new home here. The feeling of being watched or not fitting in didn't matter. She loved it here. She would make herself fit in if it killed her, just so she could stay in this beautiful land.

Ivram looked around the room, his smile taking them all in. His gray hair gave him a look of wisdom. Isika thought it matched his true heart—he was the wisest person she had ever met. She felt a sudden desire to join in the welcome, and jumped up to pull out a chair for him.

"Please, Uncle," she said. "Eat with us. Do you know how divine Auntie Teru's flat cakes are?"

He nodded and smiled, sitting where she beckoned him. "Yes, I do know. I have tasted them many times. Only a few, Teru, and I mean it. I've already eaten at the palace."

A FEW PLATES LATER, he leaned back and patted his stomach, groaning.

"This is why I don't come here, as much as I love you, Teru and Dawit. In this house I somehow become a small boy again, and lose my guard, stuffing my face with too much food."

Teru laughed and sat back in her own chair. "Is there a reason you came here today, Brother?"

"Besides your food? Well, let's see. Yes, there is." He looked at Isika and Benayeem.

"These two have done good work in adjusting to our ways. They have shown themselves to be diligent, working with kindness and thankfulness."

Isika felt a rush of pleasure at his words, her face growing hot. She was still getting used to being praised. Since her mother died, there hadn't been many kind words for her from anyone other than a younger sibling.

"What about me?" Kital said. "Have I been doing a good job?"

They all laughed. "Yes, young one," Ivram said. "You've been doing the most excellent job of all. But you're too young for the reward I have in mind."

"Reward?" Isika couldn't help herself. She clapped a hand over her mouth, and Ivram laughed again, the rich, deep sound filling the house.

"Yes. I think it's time you two met the horses."

A SHORT TIME LATER, Ivram, Ben, and Isika walked down

the mountain together, heading for a field just beyond Isika's pottery workshop. Isika could barely keep calm, her heart leaping inside her. She had glimpsed the horses from afar and knew they were ridden for short messages or special occasions. Students generally didn't learn to ride until they were sixteen. The Maweel took good treatment of animals very seriously. But there were exceptions, and Ivram was making one for Isika and Ben.

Isika could sense the horses as they drew closer. The sun was higher in the sky, and Isika used her *ser* to wipe sweat from her face. She squinted, trying to spot the horses.

"Where are they?" she asked.

The horses were kept in a pasture and barn at the far end of the little valley that also held the pottery workshop and wood mill. Forest surrounded three sides. One side opened on a wide field.

"They're under the trees in the shade," Ivram said, planting the staff beside him.

Isika looked again. Now she saw them. Slight movements and twitching told her exactly where they were. As they drew near, some of the horses drifted over to the fence, curious about the people approaching them. They came slowly. Isika's stomach felt as though it was full of tiny birds, she was so excited and nervous.

"Hold your hand out like this," Ivram instructed, and Isika did as he said, her hand shaking. "They will breathe your scent and learn whether you are safe."

As she and Ben held out their hands, the horses walked closer and sniffed at them, then drew near, nickering softly.

Ivram nodded. "It is as I thought," he said. "They recognize you."

Isika drew in a breath, surrounded by warmth as they welcomed her. She reached out with her thoughts and they answered her in their gentle way.

Welcome young one, they said to her.

Thank you, she said in return. She was overwhelmed by the kind thoughts they sent, streams of welcome, love, and hope. Ivram looked at her closely.

"Can you speak with them?" he asked, and she nodded, speechless. He smiled. "I thought so. I'm glad to have my hunch confirmed. Are you ready to learn the art of riding?" He leaned over the fence and called out. "Little sister!"

In answer, a tall woman strode around the corner of the barn, smiling as she recognized Ivram.

"This is Bara," Ivram said. "Bara, these are our newest riders, Benayeem and Isika." Bara nodded and said hello, a pleasant look on her face. As she opened the gate, a thought popped into Isika's mind.

"Why don't the seekers ride horses?" she asked. "Wouldn't it be faster?"

Ivram shook his head. "It would indeed be faster, but the horses respond badly to the poison. It terrifies them. They tend to throw their riders and flee, or go mad entirely. We keep them close to the city so they will be safe and sound in mind."

Isika looked at the beautiful creatures, struck by their vulnerability. It was sad. The poison that came from the great waste did so much harm. Ivram gazed at the sky, continuing to speak. His voice was different, strangely light, and Isika paid attention.

"During the time of the queen, there were more Maweel who could speak to animals. The hearts of those people calmed the horses in the presence of poison, so we could take them far out of the city, even into fights if we needed to."

Isika drew in a breath, thinking for the first time that Ivram's timing in introducing them to the horses wasn't coincidental. She waited for him to say more. His face grew sad.

"It was the undoing of our land. Because when the queen was captured, most of the magic of animal speech went with her, and when our king took horses to look for her, one threw him and became his end. He died by a horse he had loved."

Isika swallowed. They walked faster to catch up to Ben and the woman, who stood looking at four saddled horses. A crazy idea had come to Isika, as sudden as the first star on a black night. The idea was quickly joined by a rush of fear. Isika bit her lip, staring at the horses, wondering if she could ever be brave enough.

The morning was long and impossibly beautiful. Ivram left them after the first hour, and Bara continued to lead Isika and Benayeem through the pasture on their horses, teaching them the basics of riding. Isika was in heaven. The horse she rode sent her little inquisitive thoughts and floods of excitement and welcome, so that Isika's experience was packed with sensation: the smell of the pasture, the horse's voice in her mind, the sun and the feel of riding swiftly through the grass.

When the sun was high, Bara declared that the two of them had done enough for the day. Isika climbed off of her horse, and for a wild moment she thought her legs wouldn't hold her. She limped over to the gate, where Bara and her brother stood. Bara laughed as Isika reached them.

"Yes, you'll be sore for a day or so. It gets better."

Isika smiled. "I don't even care. I don't think I've ever had such a beautiful day. How many horses do you have?"

"Come and see," Bara said. "Almost all of the horses are stabled here, including the palace horses. Some of the farmers have their horses on farms in the valley."

They walked across the meadow and through the grove trees on its edge. The grove opened up onto another field, dotted with wildflowers. Isika drew in a breath. The hills rose up around them, the field was ringed with silverwood trees. Bara cried a sharp, long call, and as Isika watched, a whirl of activity came from across the length of the field, soon revealing itself to be a hundred or so horses galloping toward them. Isika put her hand over her mouth.

"They pasture here and in nearby fields," Bara explained. "The poison doesn't reach them in this valley, protected as it is by our hills." She sighed. "I hate that Great Waste makes it so the horses can't roam free anymore." She shook her head, then turned and smiled at them. "But here is your true gift from the elders."

Benayeem looked at Isika, so she asked the question. "Our gift?"

"Two of these horses are yours. Ivram picked them out. You will need to care for them and ride them, get to know them in the coming weeks."

Isika put a hand to her mouth. "Ours?" she asked. "But why?"

"The children of the elders all have horses of their own," Bara said, "though they don't come here often, since they are seekers and are often on foot. I suppose Ivram believes that the least he can do for you... is give you horses."

Isika heard the unspoken words. The least he could do for heirs of the queen who were on probation in their own city. But this was no small thing. She bit her lip as the horses slowed to a walk and came languidly toward the fence. One horse stood out to her, gray and very tall, its shoulders rising above the shoulders of the other horses. The tips of the hairs on its coat shone like silver, it had a long black mane and tail, and a star on its face. Isika walked toward it, drawn to it, and the horse lifted its head and whinnied at her.

Hello beautiful, she said to it, reaching with her mind.

Today... the horse breathed back to her. She reached out and cupped her hands around its muzzle, stroking the soft hair under its eyes.

Oh, this one, Isika thought, her heart yearning back toward him.

Behind her, Bara laughed. "His name is Wind. And he is yours. How beautiful that you found each other."

Isika felt a wild leap in her heart and turned toward Ben. He was watching her with a strange expression on his face and she knew he was hearing some kind of music.

She looked at him with a question in her eyes and he smiled. "It's beautiful," he said. "Wild and beautiful, like nothing I've ever heard before." Dimly, Isika heard and saw Ben receiving his horse, a wiry black gelding named Night. But it washed over her like a dream, because she was too busy talking to her new horse, who told her of sunshine smelling fields and rain on the trees, the beauty of running, the way birds looked when they rose up suddenly from the grass. She loved him.

Isika didn't know what to do about Jerutha, so she waited for something to happen, going back and forth between the pottery workshop and the horse meadow, home only for sleep and meals. After she finished with her apprentice chores, Tomas let her help him with his newest commission; throwing a new set of plates for the palace. It was a huge job, and she could see that Tomas was exhausted and happy. They made plate after plate, cutting them off the wheel with thread, setting them in the drying room to get ready for the kiln. Tomas had mixed a deep red glaze for the plates. Because the palace paid well, he could try things he never had before, like layering the red with an overglaze that turned out to be silvery in the light, causing Tomas to shout as they pulled the first load out of the kiln and saw how lovely it looked.

The other workers and apprentices had gotten used to Isika's new role as Tomas's assistant in the workshop. Sometimes she felt a presence and looked up to see two or three apprentices watching her at the wheel. She was uncomfortable with the wonder in their faces, but fine with it, because others were suspicious. She was second only to Tomas now in her ability, and not everyone was happy about it. She began to try to get to know the other apprentices, with varying degrees of success. One handsome boy smiled at her every morning when she came in. He was eighteen, a young apprentice on the verge of becoming a journeyman, and she liked him, but not that way, she told Tomas when he tried to tease her about it.

As soon as she was done at the workshop, she tore off her apron and ran to the horse barn. Wind always greeted her at the door. He could tell when she was coming, and she often called to him in her mind along the way, testing how near she had to be for him to hear her. She saddled him quickly and they tore off through the fields together. Sometimes Benayeem came after his classes and the two of them raced, late afternoon sun turning the grasses golden, making their shadows stretch over the meadow, and highlighting every curve and dimple in the hills around the valley until Isika felt a wild, almost painful joy, wishing she could launch herself into the hills, or break off a piece of the highest and take it home with her.

Twice that week, she had lessons with Ivram, who sometimes looked at her with a strange look on his face, though he wouldn't tell her what he was thinking when she asked. Both days, the lesson was about healing. Some things she already knew, but one point confused her. On the second day she asked him about it.

"Uncle, you said that healers can only send the sickness somewhere else, right? And they normally send it into the ground."

He looked at her, and she saw the barest glimmer of a smile before his face went back to its normal dark stillness, like water in a pond. They sat facing each other on short stools, in the corner of the palace library, where many books were stacked in rows and columns. Isika ran her hand down the rough page of a book that she held in her lap.

"Yes," he said, "because the earth can absorb and cleanse any amount of disease. This is why we house our sick in tents, moving every year, so the earth can recover. We plant restorative herbs and give it a few years to rejuvenate."

"Yes, but... when I was with Jabari and Gavi, I healed Ben... and I took the sickness into myself."

Ivram smiled and sighed again. "Yes, child, I heard about that. It is a deep and old kind of magic, one that only the World Whisperer has. When you healed Ivy, did you bring her sickness into yourself?"

Isika frowned, remembering. "No. No, it was too much. I sent it into the earth."

He looked at her, his eyes kind. Light streamed through the windows, onto the book of healing and herbs in Isika's lap, and onto Ivram's staff. "It is an incredible thing that you do by instinct what many of us have to learn."

Isika shook her head, but he thumped his staff lightly on the ground. "You should trust yourself, daughter. Have faith in your abilities and your understanding. Your gifting and your blood will not serve you wrong."

AFTER THE SEEKERS had been gone for seven days, Isika was more restless than ever. She tore across the fields on Wind, comfortable now with high speeds, trying to rid herself of the image of Jerutha alone and scared, when a sudden gust wind hit her. It made the hair on her arms stand on end and brought the horse to a stop. Isika stayed on his back only by instinct; the horse shifted sideways to help her. She looked up to see what had caused the strange gust of wind, and saw the Othra descending, large black phantoms plummeting out of a stormy sky that had been blue moments before. She waited for them. Her horse's heart was beating wildly, his eyes rolling back at her, and she automatically sent a surge of peace toward him. He slowly calmed and began eating grass.

The three Othra drew close. Eemia left the others and flew straight to Isika, dropping to the ground just in front of the horse, who was still busy tearing mouthfuls of grass. Isika didn't like looking so far down on the ancient bird, so she slid off of her horse and stood, wobbly in the knees but keeping her feet.

"Young one," Eemia said, and there was sadness and reproach in her voice. It curled around Isika and she gasped and bowed her head.

"You have not done anything about the message we sent you," the Othra said.

Isika looked up, stung. Dark gray clouds swirled in the sky behind Eemia. "I wanted to help, but the elders forbade it!"

"The elders are more important than your word?"

Isika felt a stab of pain and regret. She held her hands up, open to the raindrops that splattered on her now. The other two Othra came closer.

"They don't see any worth in the Worker village," Isika told them, furious despite the reproach.

"Do you?" Nirral asked, the voice in her head deep and sad.

"Of course I do," she said. Tears joined the rain on her face.

"Then why do you remain here, leaving her to fight alone?"

"How can I go when they have told me not to?"

"That is yours to decide," Eemia said. "We can only warn you that if you continue to ignore your heart, it will wither and no longer speak to you. Is that who you want to be, World Whisperer? A queen who cannot hear her heart?"

Isika wanted to retort that she didn't want to be queen at all, but the Othra didn't give her time. The rain was coming down in sheets, and the birds lifted as one and disappeared into the clouds. Isika scowled. Not only was she blocked from helping her friend, it seemed she was going to be blamed for it. Argh. Jerutha. She buried her face in her horse's wet shoulder and he sent a questioning thought toward her.

"I don't know what to do," she said aloud.

Go? He asked, and she looked at his calm brown eye. She clambered back onto him, gripping the saddle hard, and galloped back across the wet field to find Ben. As they ran, the rain slowed and stopped, one ray of light breaking through to light up the meadow in front of her.

"Okay, okay, birds," she muttered. "I get it." And though she felt the sorrow and responsibility crashing over her, she couldn't help smiling.

"What do you think?" Isika asked Ben, after she had told him her idea. They sat in their courtyard, near the grass that ran down to the garden. Ben fiddled with the grass, picking small bits and laying them on the stone of the courtyard.

"I don't want to be cast out of Azariyah," he said.

Isika sighed. "I agree. But if we do nothing—nothing, Ben —we will have to bear it forever."

He was silent. Isika could hear Ibba singing in the kitchen as she helped Auntie wash the dishes. Isika wanted to be here, never to leave the home she had come to love. But she couldn't ignore Jerutha, who was like a sister to her, who had helped her find Kital, who was alone now, and afraid. After she had given them the boat and the plan, they had left her. Isika's heart ached, thinking about it, and she felt her resolve grow stronger.

Auntie walked outside with a towel in her hand, and

Isika swallowed what she had been about to say to Ben. Auntie's face was troubled as she sank into a chair. She wore her normal housedress, a simple, long, cool garment. This one was red with tiny yellow lines that hatched across the fabric on the sleeves and several inches above the hem. Her plump, dark brown arms glowed, and she wore soft bracelets of leather. Dawit had told them that back when Auntie left the house more often, she had been known for her stunning dresses and jewelry. But now she stayed home, wearing house dresses. She still looked beautiful, her thick hair braided and tucked on top of her head. The frown on her face was unfamiliar, and Isika watched her with concern. After a moment, her face cleared, and she spoke.

"I want to tell you something, daughter," she said, leaning forward.

"What is it, Auntie?"

"Just this: I trust you and believe in you, no matter what. No matter what you do or decide in this life, no matter who it *goes against.*" She paused, then went on. "I believe in you. You are led by deep, ancient forces, and we all believe in you."

Ben looked up at Auntie, and slowly he nodded.

"I believe in you too," he said, "and I'll never leave you alone."

Thankfulness and pain twined together in Isika's heart. She dreaded returning to the Worker village. What if they were captured and kept there? But she knew she couldn't leave Jerutha there, alone and afraid. Auntie had helped her decide. They would go.

THAT NIGHT she dreamed of her stepmother and a baby, asleep, lying side by side on a pile of rocks, next to the ocean that Isika had healed once before. The ocean was poisoned again, sluggish and green. An evil vapor hissed out of it, and it ate away at the rocks. Slow, sulky waves hit the shore, and Isika could see every poisoned drop lifting and falling. The sky was gray, without color. The waves landed closer and closer to Jerutha and the baby, inching up the beach toward them, until Isika woke, sitting bolt upright in her bed. She was damp with sweat, her sheets twisted into knots, tears running down her face.

She went into the boys' room and woke Ben. "We need to leave now," she said, softly so Kital wouldn't wake. Back in her room, she dressed quickly in her travel clothes; a green tunic and loose brown pants, her *ser* and the soft leather boots that laced up to her knees. She picked up her travel satchel and bow, leaving her room with a last glance at Ibba. She would have kissed her, but Ibba was a light sleeper. Out in the living space, she nearly shrieked when she bumped into someone, but bit back the scream at the last second. The someone was Auntie Teru. She placed a sack of food in Isika's hands and gave her a fierce kiss on the cheek. Auntie's cheeks were wet.

"Don't worry about us," Isika whispered into Teru's ear. "We will come back. And perhaps we will bring another part of our family with us."

"I know you will," Auntie whispered back. "Nenyi goes with you. You will be well, and you will come back to me."

They stared at each other for a long moment, then Ben came out and Auntie hugged him too, before they went off into the night.

THEY STUCK to the shadows to keep from being seen. The sun would not be up for another two hours and they needed to be well away from the city by then, so they moved quickly. Before they got to the horse pen, Isika reached out for Wind. *Must be quiet,* she said. *Tell others.*

"What about the poison, the effect it has on the horses?" Ben had asked as they left the house.

"I think I can protect them," Isika told him, fully aware of how crazy it sounded. "Ivram hinted at it the other day." She remembered how he told them about the days of the queen, when the horses could be taken safely over long distances. And how, after the queen was taken, the king had been thrown from his horse and killed. She took a shaky breath, but after a moment Ben nodded and said no more.

The horses were silent as they arrived, without even a whicker, and Isika patted her horse on the nose. "Thank you," she breathed.

Ben went for the saddles, moving like a shadow past the small room where Bara slept. They saddled the two horses and mounted. Wind was slightly taller than Night, but Night was faster, always winning the races Ben and Isika ran in the meadow.

Quiet, Isika told the horses again, and she and Ben rode

their horses away at a walk, as silently as they could. Ben's horse faded into the shadows, barely visible. But Wind gleamed faintly in the moonlight.

She looked back, once, as they crossed the valley just before the forest, and saw Bara standing at the horse gate. Bara raised a hand, and Isika's heartbeat quickened. Bara turned and silently went back to her room. Isika felt as though her heart would leap out of her chest, with love and fear. She had offerings of faith from Bara, from Auntie, and a subtle one from Ivram, in the gift of horses and the hints he had passed their way. Maybe the support of these three would be enough to get them through. She clucked her tongue at her horse, laying the reins lightly on his back, and they galloped out of the forest and onto the road.

By the time the sun rose, they were far from the City, retracing their steps, going back to the Worker village the same way they had come, all those long months ago. Except this time, on horses, they went nearly three times as fast. The sun rimmed the earth as they left the City and its mountains behind, coming out onto the plains that led to the desert. The fields were newly planted. All the young green filled her eyes and her heart. If it wasn't for the fact that she was headed the wrong way, she would have been full of happiness. The horse beneath her, muscles springing with every step, the wind on her face, whipping through her braids, the clouds as they scudded across the sky. They rode until midday, then stopped to rest.

Opening the bag that Auntie had given her, Isika found

bread and meat, vegetables and fruit. They ate slowly, saving some of the food for later.

"What made you decide to leave so quickly?" Ben asked.

"I had a dream," Isika said. He nodded simply as she told him about the dream. He knew about the things that dreams and feelings could tell. "They're in danger," she said.

"So we go back to the village?"

She hesitated, thinking. "Yes." Ben squinted at the sky and nodded. When he spoke again Isika heard the new deepness in his voice. They had both changed since they arrived in the City, taller and stronger than they had been on their last journey, their arms and legs filling out after months of Auntie's good food.

"Do you think we should do anything for Father?" Ben asked, and Isika thought of the only father she remembered, Nirloth. The last time she had seen him, he had beaten her, severe in his anger, but she felt only pity for him now. He had died a bitter, burdened old man, tied to the poison of the Great Waste by the four goddesses he served, Fate, Power, Wealth, and Independence. There was nothing they could really do for him, but they made a small fire to honor him and sang a Maweel mourning song, then scattered the ashes and continued on their way.

They crossed the rivers on the horses, the water reaching the horses' knees, or less often, their shoulders. Isika wondered how they would cross the one river that was very deep, that they had crossed in Jabari's little boat. It wasn't long before they arrived at the large river. The horses danced along the edge, too nervous to go in. Isika reached out to Wind with her mind.

We need to cross, she said. *What can we do?*

She heard them speak together, in a nearly unintelligible horse speak that was full of words she didn't understand, though she saw images of swimming things and felt tendrils of fear. Finally Night bowed his head and Wind spoke to Isika.

We swim together, he said. *But you have to climb off and swim beside.*

We can do that, she said.

They dismounted and took off their boots, tying their bundles to the tops of the horse's saddles. They waded in, and as the water rose to their necks, Isika remembered Gavi, and how afraid he was of the water, so nervous that he could barely control it, after being set adrift in a little boat when he was a child. She wondered if Aria felt the same way about water.

The water wasn't too cold, and Isika relaxed as she felt its friendly approach. It was clear of even traces of poison, a good thing, because she didn't know what she would do if the horses panicked in water. They swam quickly, resting by draping their arms over the horses when they had to.

As they neared the opposite bank, Isika saw Jabari's boat tied with another, and smiled. The seekers had gone before them. It explained the fact that every place had been clear of poison so far. But then she frowned. They would have to find a different road, if they didn't want to run into the seekers. And that road might be poisoned. She weighed the worry of poison against the fight she would have with Jabari if she ran into him. He would discourage her and try to send her back. She believed she could handle the poison, but how to find another way? They didn't have to decide now. They had been riding since before sunrise and they were both exhausted and sore from being in the saddle longer than she was used to.

They found a forest grove and unsaddled the horses, rubbing them down with handfuls of soft leaves to dry them. Then they changed into dry clothing. Ben built a fire and they hung their wet clothing near, sharing more of the bread and cheese that Auntie had sent. They would have to use their bow to find food the next day, with only enough of Auntie's food to feed them for the morning meal. They unrolled their blankets next to the fire. The night air was chilly, but the blankets from the city had a special magic woven into them and kept them very warm.

After a while, Ben spoke.

"Do you think the elders will send us away?" His voice was brave in the darkness, but Isika could hear the fear underneath.

She thought, weighing the possibilities, trying to imagine what would happen, what the result of their running would be. She didn't know, in the end. She didn't know the elders well enough to know what they would do. In going to save Jerutha, would she lose the only home she had ever really loved?

"Auntie won't let that happen," she said finally. Her voice was much more sure than she felt, but it must have satisfied Ben, because he laughed.

"I didn't think of that," he said. "She'd tear them apart. Well, that's comforting."

They both lay in the dark a long time before falling asleep, though.

IN THE MORNING they set out again. The horses were happy after eating the lush grass at the river side. Isika knew that at the speed they were traveling, it wouldn't be long before they ran into the seekers. If the seekers had been pulling down walls, they would have taken time in people's homes, and she didn't know, honestly, how much farther along the road they were. Isika and Ben continued on their horses until Isika spotted a crossroad.

"Let's turn," she said to Ben.

"What if we get lost?" he asked. "We don't know another way."

"I don't want to run into the seekers," she responded.

He shrugged, though his face was worried, and they turned the horses and cantered down the road, side by side. As soon as they left the path the seekers had taken, Isika could feel it. Little nudges of poison, tendrils, like a bad taste in the mouth.

"Isika," Ben warned. She knew he would be able to hear a great deal of poison at a distance, and then they saw it; a house with a poisoned wall around it. Suddenly Wind reared up on his hind legs, and it was all Isika could do to hold on. This was what Ivram meant; the sensitive animals couldn't stand the poison. She sent waves of calming thoughts to both the horses. Ben's horse had been neighing in terror, but it quieted at the touch of her mind.

Bad taste, Wind told her. *Fire eyes.*

It's okay, she said. *There will be wide fields. Grass on the road. I will keep you safe.*

They calmed entirely after a few minutes, enough that Isika felt that they could keep walking. After that, she kept her senses awake and open, ready to feel if the horses got nervous. If they did, she sent the calming magic out to them again. She told them stories of the best oats, of ripe apples, of sleepy evenings spent under trees.

Shadows passed overhead as they walked the horses, and because Isika had her senses thrown open, she felt the friendly breeze of the Othra. She looked up to see Nirral and Efir.

Hello, she told them. *I listened.*

She felt something like a laugh come from Efir, Eemia's daughter.

You are off the familiar road, young one, Efir said into her mind. *How will you find your way?*

Isika had a thought. *Can you show me?*

This time Efir definitely laughed. *You are learning to ask, daughter.*

Suddenly, Isika was out of her own body, seeing through their eyes. She saw herself and Ben on Wind and Night, and she saw the road stretching out before them. She went up higher, perhaps in Efir's memory, and saw where their path would take them. One way glimmered softly, outlined in light, and as she looked closer, Isika saw that it led to a grove not far from the Worker village. As she looked at the glimmering road, it lifted and entered her eyes, wrapping itself into her mind. And she found, as she came back to her own eyes and Wind's ears in front of her, that the road glimmered as the one in her vision had. She would not lose the way.

11

J abari felt the wall before he saw it. He closed his eyes to sense its size, then strode forward, the others following him. He shook his head as they rounded the corner. Since they left home they couldn't take five steps without needing to restore a home. Or it seemed that way. He glanced at Gavi, who widened his eyes at Jabari. They'd never had a journey so steeped in poison.

Mugunta, the Evil One, boiled over in a never-ending flow of poison from the Great Waste. The poison collected in malicious streams, much of it gathering into poison walls around the homes of unsuspecting people. Without realizing what was happening, the people became suspicious, angry, and, when the walls were at their highest, completely isolated. The walls cut them off from neighbors and friends. A person with a poison wall around his house would fight a friend who came to help. The seekers roamed the country-side, looking for walls like these. Normally they found walls that were still quite small since they went on frequent journeys. But this seeking journey had been unlike any other, with high walls around every bend in the road.

Jabari took a long look at the house on the other side of the wall. The wall came to his shoulder; he could still look past it, but the house was hard to see, wrapped in haze, a poison that kept people who passed from seeing the house. Jabari squinted and saw toys scattered along the porch.

"All right, birdies," he said. "This one is larger but I think we can take it together."

"Of course we can," Ivy said beside him. Jabari smiled at her, but noticed that Aria looked worried.

"You okay, Aria?" he asked. She jumped when he said her name, and smiled, but there wasn't any real happiness in her smile.

"I'm fine," she said. "Let's take this wall."

He stared at her a moment longer, but shrugged it off. They approached the wall and he held his hands over it to test the poison. Suspicion, fear, isolation. The usual. "Should be easy," he said. "Let's go."

They broke pieces of the wall away. The pieces came apart like bread, crumbling in their hands, turning to dust that would soon disappear completely. The dust rose up around them, and Jabari worked to disperse it with his mind, so it couldn't choke the others while they worked. The tendrils of fear, isolation, and suspicion could cloud even the most trusting mind if its owner wasn't careful. It was the most insidious of the poison from the Great Waste. It was also the easiest to heal.

He put his hands around a really large section of wall and pulled, watching the rock crumble under his hands. It was perfectly satisfying, a destruction that healed. All boys like knocking towers of blocks over, and his work called for it. He laughed, exhilarated. The walls were real enough; they would feel solid to any regular person, but to those with the restoration magic they were like paper.

"Yab!" Gavi shouted. Jabari looked up and saw Gavi pointing at a section of wall they had already taken down. The wall was back in place, regrown as if they hadn't taken it down. Jabari froze. *What?* He walked toward the new wall, and saw that actually it looked as though it was formed of one smooth stone, half the width and half the height of the previous wall.

He and Gavi stood and stared for a moment before Jabari leaned forward and crumbled the new wall. The dust from the wall had a new potency. He spit it away as he tasted it, his gift telling him what kind of poison it was. *Shame.* The walls usually reeked of isolation and fear, but now the sickly scent of shame was everywhere, coating his face, his hands, his mouth. A dangerous poison, undoubtedly attacking the people in the house, even as the seekers worked to free them. The wall was springy under his hands, too, elastic and harder to crumble.

"Look," Gavi said, pointing. Jabari straightened and saw that all along the sections of wall that they had already broken, the same smooth stone was erupting. Only half the height again, but that same springy substance. He frowned. This shouldn't happen.

"These are strange days," Gavi said. "But we can't leave a wall standing."

Jabari shook his head slowly, trying to come to terms with something he had never seen before. "No, we can't," he said, collecting himself. "Twice the speed, mob! Let's free this family from this poison. Get the walls as fast as they come!"

He heard Ivy laughing as she attacked the wall, and her glee in the battle with the wall fed his own. He grinned as well. Mugunta wanted to make them discouraged, wanted them to lose hope and fight with one another. But they wouldn't give in.

THE SUN WAS high in the sky before they were done. Jabari took a moment to catch his breath, then followed Gavi onto the porch, where they sent the haze away from the house, revealing a lovely earth home with blue designs painted on its doorways, a dusty woven mat in place outside the door. They touched the lintel of the doorway before stepping into the house, the others coming quickly behind. Jabari turned.

"It will be overwhelming for the family if we all go in. Ivy and Aria, you come. Deto and Brigid, stay here for now." Deto and Brigid settled on the porch to wait. Brigid looked a little gray around the mouth, and not sad to stay behind, Jabari noticed. Aria had shadows under her eyes. He needed to take better care of his apprentices.

He turned to assess the room. Gavi walked the circumference of the room, gently touching the walls and humming songs of healing. Jabari breathed a sigh of relief. After the second wall, he had worried that they had approached a wall that contained poison too potent for their healing skills, that the people who lived here would be sick beyond Gavi and Jabari's ability to heal. But the owners of the house were all up and working at tasks, though they kept their eyes away from the newcomers.

This was part of Mugunta's poison. In Maween, even strangers walking along a path would be cause for people of the house to call out welcome and offer food. But these people acted as though they couldn't see their visitors.

Jabari approached the old grandmother, who rocked in a worn wooden chair, murmuring to a cat in her lap. Her dark face was heavily wrinkled and her eyes remained on the cat as he approached, as though he wasn't there. He squatted down and carefully placed his hands on her hands, feeling the magic leap out of him and flow into her, pushing the poison out of her, replacing it with warmth, care, and affection. After a moment, she looked up at him. Her eyes were very bright. She couldn't speak yet, so he didn't take his hands away, but continued to send Nenyi's magic, reassuring her as he did.

"It's all right, Grandmother. I'm a seeker. We found your walls and tore them down."

After a moment, tears trickled from her eyes and she opened her mouth to speak. Her voice was rusty.

"Bless you, son. I didn't think the poison would ever come to this house."

"It can come to anyone," Jabari said. "Don't worry."

He straightened and looked around. Ivy and Aria were

with a pair of children in the corner, and Gavi stood next to a tall man. The room was dark, so he went to the windows and threw the shutters open. When people were poisoned, they tended to give attention only to the most basic things. They ate and slept, but barely cared about anything, so they might go weeks without sweeping or opening the windows to let the air in. They let their gardens go, they stopped seeing neighbors. The neighbors could only wait for the seekers. It was why Jabari never wanted to stop, never wanted to spend too much time in the city. People might be stuck behind their walls, lost in a poison haze, with no one to help them. But it was frustrating because it had only been half a year since he was last down this road. Why were the walls growing so quickly? And what was that new kind of wall?

He spotted a woman sitting on the floor of the kitchen, her head on her hands, and he walked to her, his feet making hardly any noise on the dirt floor. She was rocking from side to side. He reached out and touched her hands, but she looked straight at him and hissed. He jumped back, shocked.

"Go where you came from," she said, her voice echoing unnaturally. "You are not welcome here."

He had been wrong. The poison was strong, horribly strong, but somehow it had all concentrated into this woman. She pushed at him, but he didn't move away.

"It's all right," he said, though he was afraid. They didn't have a skilled healer, only their own basic healing abilities. "It's all right. Give me your hands. I can help you."

"No," she said. "I know who you are and I don't like you. Young upstart, desiring the throne. You'll be kicked to the edge of your world, you'll have a boot on your throat, you'll be dead soon."

He moved away slightly, startled by the venom in her words. She would have been beautiful if she hadn't been covered in soot and grime, her hair wild and untamed. For a moment he considered leaving her, but he saw the tiniest glimmer of fear in her eyes, as something behind the hostility pleaded with him. He caught one of her flailing hands and held it fast, even as she tried to pull it away. He sent wave after wave of restoring magic toward her, and her hand grew still. She shook her head from side to side, but as the warmth coursed through her she stopped flailing and curled up on the ground. Jabari held her hand more gently as she began to weep. He took her other hand in his.

Ivy approached and put her hands on the woman's face, pulling them back with a sharp gasp.

"So much shame," she said. Then she reached out again and began to sing. The magic curled around the three of them, and peace drifted through Jabari's body at the sound of Ivy's voice, rich and pure. After a moment, the woman stopped weeping, and her little sighs and sobs slowly eased.

They let her go and her husband immediately swooped in and picked her up, carrying her into another room. Jabari followed and watched for a moment as the man settled her on the bed and lay down beside her. He backed away to give them space to reconnect. He suspected they had been estranged for many months.

BACK IN THE LARGE ROOM, the kids played with the cat and the old woman had a broom out, sweeping at the thick layer of dust on the stone floor. Gavi looked as though he hadn't slept in a month. He had dark circles under his eyes, sharp against his pale face. Ivy leaned against a wall of the house. Aria sat on her hands on a bed in the corner, rocking slightly and watching the kids play. Jabari felt as exhausted as they looked. He made a motion with his chin and they went out on the porch to sit with Deto and Brigid.

"What was that?" Ivy asked.

"I don't know," Jabari said. "I think it was more insidious than slow poison, though. She had been listening to something, believing it. It gripped her."

"Why are things getting harder?" Deto asked. He leaned against the wall of the house, his long braid pulled to one side so he wouldn't sit on it. He looked at Jabari as though he would have answers, but Jabari had none. Again, he wrestled with questions. When the Maweel had the World Whisperer, everything was supposed to be better. But instead of growing easier, more pure and less poisoned, things had gotten worse. If she really was the World Whisperer, shouldn't Maween be returning to the way it was when they had their queen? At the same time, Jabari wished he had Isika's knack of restoring without being completely drained afterward. And he hoped things wouldn't get much harder, or they wouldn't have the smooth, uncomplicated trip his father had ordered him to have. He laughed to himself. Not that it had ever been likely.

"I don't know what's going on," he said. "But we have to

continue. We're needed now more than ever." There was a chorus of soft sighs from his very tired seekers. Then Gavi stood up.

"Okay, troop," he said. "Let's pitch in with cleaning. I think they need our help."

12

When Aria woke up, her back ached. For a moment she didn't know where she was. But then she heard whispered voices in the kitchen and remembered the poisoned house and the events of the day before. She ached from pulling the wall apart and from so much work afterward. They had scrubbed the house from top to bottom, with the help of the children and grandmother, who directed from her chair. When the mother and father of the house finally came out of their sleeping room that evening, they had found their house sparkling again. The woman stood up straight and blinked tears back.

"Thank you," she said. "I don't deserve your help, but thank you."

Aria had listened as Jabari told the woman that part of the healing was to cook for the seekers and allow them to stay in her house. She nodded.

"I know we are a big group of seekers," Jabari said. "So

you're welcome to invite only a couple of us and the rest will sleep in your barn. I'm sure it's warm enough there."

She wouldn't hear of it, so Aria and Deto helped chop vegetables while Gavi, Brigid and Ivy played a tile game with the kids and Jabari carved a new arrow on the porch. Aria had noticed that he worked with his arrows more than seemed necessary. Maybe it helped him think. She knew cleaning and taking care of her arrows helped her think.

She stretched on her mat and sat up. Across the room, Jabari was still sleeping. She watched him for a moment, then looked away when she realized she was staring. She didn't really want to have the feelings she had for the older boy, but her thoughts had taken over. She couldn't fight it. He was the most beautiful boy she had ever seen, strong and wide in the shoulders. His face looked like the paintings of the mythological spirits who used to roam the earth before the Great Waste sent them fleeing to another world. He had skin nearly the same color as hers, dark and rich as earth, wide-set eyes that always seemed kind when he looked at her, and his mouth... she looked away again. Gavi watched her, smiling knowingly from where he sat, cross-legged, rolling up his sleeping blanket. She glared at him, but it didn't have any effect on him.

"Glorious, isn't he? Even when he's snoring."

"Stop it," she said, but she couldn't help smiling. If she had a paralyzing crush on one brother, she felt absolutely comfortable with the other, and that was reassuring, especially on a journey like this. She felt like she would trip on the flat ground when Jabari looked at her, but she could always spend a little time with Gavi and Ivy if she wanted to put herself at ease. Deto and Brigid were fine. She had grown up with them, after she came to the City. And Deto, more than any other person she knew, understood what it was like to be someone like Aria. He had been older when he was rescued, too, though he was only four years old, and she had been nearly eight. He knew what it was like to remember *before*. And he had been sold. Sometimes she wondered how he dealt with it. To be sold was almost worse than being given over, sacrificed to goddesses by people who knew you would drown. The anger came back, sharp-edged and hot, so she jumped to her feet and rolled her sleeping blanket up.

It had happened a long time ago. She had worked through it for years with her adopted mother. She had believed she was completely over it, but that was before Isika came and brought it all flooding back to the surface.

Aria walked into the kitchen and saw Deto and Brigid chopping fruit. The woman who had been so badly poisoned yesterday looked like a new person today. She was wearing a long house dress, with flowers in her braided hair. Her face was lovely; oval, dark brown, with wide cheekbones and lips. Aria felt her anger disintegrate at the sight of the woman they had healed. She smiled to see her rolling dough on the stone countertop.

"Good morning," the woman said. "Aria, is it? I'm making a fruit pie for breakfast. Would you like to gather some eggs?"

Aria's mouth had already begun watering. Her stomach growled. Brigid grinned at her as she took the basket the woman gave her and went to gather eggs from the hen house, one of the children with her to show her the way. Her anger had dissolved for now, in the radiance of the healed woman, the beauty of the house without poison. She remembered why she was here, remembered the true enemy, Mugunta, and the way he distorted everything. It was why she had always wanted to be a seeker. She smiled as she put eggs in the basket, the little boy handing her two for every one she found.

THEY ATE BREAKFAST TOGETHER, sitting on the earth floor of the house. Jabari had been the last to wake up, and his sleepy face made Aria's heart ping. She had taken him a piece of pie herself, and he thanked her, though he seemed distracted and worried. They didn't linger long before they set off, touching the house's corners to seal it with protection magic before they left.

Aria walked for a while almost without knowing where she was going, she was so deep in thought. After a while, she looked up to see Gavi beside her. He grinned at her.

"You're somewhere else today," he said.

"Yes," she replied.

"Tell me about your thoughts," he said.

She considered it. Perhaps he would understand.

"I guess I just haven't ever seen this much poison before, at least since I was a child."

"You're still a child, little Aria."

She punched his arm lightly. "I'm nearly thirteen. Not a child anymore. You're only three years older than me."

"Three years at our age is a world apart."

"Well, time goes fast." She stuck her chin out. She didn't like being reminded of how much older Gavi and Jabari were.

"It is strange when you see the poison for the first time. After the safety of home."

"It makes me feel... unprotected. Like I might be forced to go back to the old village."

She hadn't meant to say that out loud. She always talked too much to Gavi; something about him made her share what she normally hid from people. But at first Gavi didn't say anything in response. He whistled for a while with a thoughtful frown on his face. Then he looked at her.

"It can't touch you, you know. You're still safe."

Aria felt tears rising and fought her emotions. The reason she wanted to be a seeker was to protect people from the kind of evil that had hurt her when she was young. She wanted to stop the poison, maybe end it. But she hadn't known how unprotected the unchecked poison would make her feel. As though she was looking out for others, but no one was looking out for her. Fear rolled over her while they journeyed, and she felt powerless to stop it.

And all the while anger lingered just below the surface, waiting. She hated it. She wanted to be free of it, to be normal, to be free of resentment over what had happened when Isika sent her out. No. She shook her head. She was thinking confused thoughts again. That wasn't right; Isika hadn't sent her out, it was her stepfather, Nirloth, who had pushed her out in the boat. But no matter how many times she told herself that, it didn't seem true. It felt to her as though she needed to become friends with the person who had sent her out to die.

At noon they stopped to eat. The woman of the house had packed them flat bread, cheese, and fruit. Aria ate quickly, then lay back in the grass under a tree and stared at the sky. It was beautiful, a clear, radiant blue. She felt the tension drain out of her as she let the warmth of the day soak into her arms and legs. And then the sky seemed to be filled with iridescent birds and she sat up as four of the Othra descended among them.

They brought their beautiful sense of well-being with them and Aria opened her heart to let it come in. She had never talked with them directly. It bothered her a little, if she thought about it, because wasn't she also a descendant of the queen? But they had spoken only to Isika. And there it was again, the anger. She pushed it down and breathed the air that followed the birds, spicy and sweet.

The seekers blinked at the birds, sleepy after their lunch. Jabari waited for the birds to speak, but the birds also seemed to be waiting for him.

"Greetings," he said finally. "Do you have a message for me?"

The birds shook their feathers and seemed to laugh.

"Don't be angry with us," the tallest one, Nirral, said, speaking so they all could hear him. "Our very work in life is to aid the World Whisperer."

"At a cost to the Maweel?" Jabari asked.

"There will be no aid to the World Whisperer that will block the eventual well-being of the Maweel."

Jabari snorted. "It's that one word, *eventual* that worries me. But I am not angry. Maybe a little worried. Please tell me what you want to tell me."

"It is the World Whisperer," the fourth bird said. Aria didn't think she had ever seen him before. His voice was grave and hoarse. He seemed older than the others, though Aria didn't know how she could tell. "We wish to tell you that she and her brother are on their way to the Worker village."

"*What?*" Jabari jumped up from where he sat on the grass. "*Isika*, deserts and thorns, why can't you stay put?" He looked at the birds, his face a storm. "When did they leave? They will arrive long after us, will they not?"

Aria held herself very still, trying to understand what the bird was saying. Isika had gone back to the Worker village? With Ben?

"They will arrive before you," the bird said. "They have horses."

"Horses?" Jabari whipped his head around to pop his eyes at Gavi, then turned back to the bird. "They took horses? Of all the... And I'm sorry, Honored One, I don't know your name."

"I am Keethior," the bird said. "Protector of the World Whisperer from the beginning of time."

Jabari stared and Gavi jumped. They looked at each other, then bowed to the bird, gesturing for the others to bow as well. This bird was almost as tall as Nirral, and his feathers glowed a deep blue, even when the sun wasn't shining on him. Aria bowed, feeling stunned. Isika had her own *Othra?*

"They were given horses by the elder, Ivram," the bird went on. "If you want to help them at the village, you will need to hurry." The birds clicked at each other, then rose as one and left.

"Wait!" Jabari said as they lifted into the sky, but they were already gone. He sighed. "Why do they always do that?"

Aria felt a flash of hope that they might not have to go to the Worker village, but Jabari stood up and put his fists on his hips.

"Oh, argh, Isika. So frustrating!" He counted on his fingers as he spoke. "She's stubborn, uncaring of our Maweel ways, annoying, too sure of herself." He shook his head, dropping his hand. "But... we need to help her. We'll have to move quickly, if Isika and Ben are on horses. She may get there first but we can still meet her there. Let's run."

Gavi and Ivy grinned at each other, and together, the seekers stood and pulled their bags together, preparing for another long run.

As Aria jogged after the others, she seethed. Isika had inserted herself into this trip almost without effort. Despite the fact that Isika had been left at home, Aria's first seeking journey was turning out to be all about her older sister, who had a dedicated Othra and horses. Horses? And yet she could be in terrible danger. Aria hated the thought of her sister being stuck back in the Worker village. She couldn't tell if what she felt for Isika was love or hate. It was strong, though. And painful.

Ben's heart was light as he and Isika rode the horses hard down an unknown road, fields of flowering plants stretching to the horizon on either side. He and Isika had stopped to talk to a farmer half a day-ride back, and he told them that in another month, the plants would be heavy with beans. The old farmer, who had sweet, sad music within him, wore a heavy work tunic and a sturdy *ser* wrapped around his wrinkled forehead. He had forked piles of grass out of his weeds for their horses to eat. Then he shared nut-filled loaves of bread with Isika and Ben. Almost all the other houses they passed had poison walls, and Isika had asked the man how he kept the poison away, and whether it was always this bad.

He looked at them, his eyes bright in his dark face, then shrugged and smiled a tired smile.

"I'm gifted. I am old now, and I prefer farming to protection, with the bad sense of poison in my ears and behind my knees. I can protect my house and barn, and in previous times I kept Mugunta's poison from the homes of my neighbors as well, but the days have turned bad." He squinted down the road as though he watched something approaching, and Ben glanced over his shoulder. Nothing was there.

"Can't keep it away anymore," he said. "And the seekers were here not so long ago. Ah. What will become of us? Why does the Great Waste grow stronger?"

He looked at Ben and then at Isika, standing beside their horses. "And you two. How is it that you can ride horses through these poisoned lands?"

Isika looked at the ground, so Ben answered for her.

"She speaks to them," he said. "She tells them they don't need to be afraid."

The old farmer stood very still, moving nothing but his eyes, which roamed over Isika's face until he must have seen something he recognized. He bowed his head for a long moment. When he looked back up at them, he wiped tears from his cheeks with a gnarled hand.

"I heard rumors you had come," he said. "But we hear so many rumors out here, I didn't know whether to believe them." He went into his house and returned with a sack full of food, which he handed to them despite their protests. When they rode off, he stood at the fence and watched. Ben looked back after a while and saw him standing there still, a speck in the distance.

Isika had told Ben that she saw the path glittering with light, after the Othra showed her the way. He couldn't see anything so he had to trust her word, but if he had learned anything in the months since they left the Worker village, it was to trust Isika. So they rode fast down the road, and the horses had power because Isika told them that all would be well. She was tired, Ben knew, because she was doing so much magic, whispering to the horses and following the lights all the while. But she sat straight on the horse and Ben knew he would follow his sister anywhere. She might be impulsive, but her path was always true.

They stopped under a large tree for the night, and after tying the horses in a patch of clover, Isika sank to the base of the tree with a sigh. She closed her eyes. She had told Ben about trees' strength flowing through her, and he had secretly tried touching the trees around their house, but nothing happened. His sister was connected to the world in a way that Ben wasn't, but it was just as well, because he had enough to think about, with his wild internal music. He shrugged off his satchel, bow, and quiver, and bent to build a small fire, leaning his face to the ground to blow on the flames. It took a while. He knew that Isika would have done it in moments; fire was one of the things that listened to her, and as if to prove his point, she spoke.

"Do you want me to do that?" she asked. He scowled in her direction, but then his face softened as he registered how tired she looked.

"No, you rest," he said. He was still leaning to blow into the dried grasses he had laid on the fire, and his voice was muffled. He sat up and smiled at her. She couldn't help her gift any more than he could help his.

"I hate to say it," she said. "But I wish Jabari and Gavi were here. They could tear all these walls down."

Ben didn't wish they were here. Well, maybe Gavi, but he was conflicted about Jabari. On one hand, he was a friend. On the other, he was years older, and he had been the most gifted child the Maweel had seen in decades before Isika popped up. Ben couldn't help wishing he was the one with all those gifts, especially after his own magic had let him know, rather forcefully, that his purpose was to support his sister. It would help to have more to offer. But Jabari was the one with all the magic, and sometimes it seemed that he didn't even support Isika. He could have spoken up for her, asked his parents to allow her to accompany the seekers on their journey. They could have gone to find Jerutha together. But Jabari hadn't said anything, and now Ben and Isika journeyed alone.

Ben sighed, feeling a flash of pity for his sister. He had seen the way people looked at her. The way Jabari looked at her. Jabari had seen her in action, he knew who she was, but he still didn't seem to have a clear mind toward her. And there was the smallest part of Ben, okay, not always small, that wondered whether supporting Isika, the World Whisperer, was going to be his only purpose. Or would he have a purpose of his own? He pushed the question away once again.

"Isn't that what they're doing already?" he asked his sister. The fire was up and going now. Dusk had fallen, the last of the pinks and purples of sunset fading out of the sky. "They'll get here eventually."

"Yes, I guess so," she said. "I just hate riding by people's homes and leaving them like that. But we need to hurry."

Ben knew how she felt. Whenever they passed a house that had walls up around it, demon magic woven into stone, isolating the people in the house from other people, he heard the loud, crushing sounds of bells that clanged and rang wrong notes, sounds of grinding teeth and yells. He hated riding by without trying to help. He tried to shove the sounds back in his mind whenever he couldn't do anything about them. He used the curtain his teachers had showed him. But what use was a gift you were always shoving away?

He dug around in his pack and found the small water pot, filling it in the nearby stream, then setting it on the fire to make tea. They wouldn't need to hunt tonight, after the food the farmer had given them, but they could drink something hot.

"I wish Gavi was here for his food," he remarked, and his sister smiled, her eyes still shut as she sat at the base of the tree. She opened them.

"Come here, Benayeem," she said. "Try this again."

He shook his head.

She insisted. "No, this time, instead of trying to feel something, try to listen. Your magic speaks to you in sound, maybe you'll be able to *hear* the tree."

He stood and looked at her, unmoved. "Then why wouldn't I have been able to hear the last time I tried?"

She shrugged. "Maybe it takes practice. I wouldn't imagine trees would be very loud."

He almost laughed. As though she knew anything about

the sounds things made, whispering and shrieking and howling, sometimes making impossibly beautiful music.

He sighed. He may as well try. Then maybe she would leave him alone. He walked around the fire, to her tree. The first stars were out. The tree was tall, with giant, gnarled branches that pointed in every direction, black against the dark blue sky. He sat two hands-breadths from his sister and leaned against the large trunk. He sighed. It felt good just to lean against something after a long day of riding his horse.

He quieted all his thoughts, turning his mind to listen. He couldn't hear anything and he almost jumped up to get away from the feeling of failure. But then everything became still and somewhere in the quiet, he heard it. He knew immediately that it was the tree's life song, like the blood of a person, the life that flowed from the earth to the tree's farthest branches. The song was light, peaceful, piercing his heart with sweetness. He sat up straighter, listening harder.

"Do you hear it?" Isika asked.

"Shhhhh, yes," he said. They sat like that until they realized the water was boiling, and then, in silence, they ate and drank silently, perfectly content.

The bird woke them. Ben sat up as he felt a rush of wings. He knew that feeling and sound, even half asleep. He recognized the Othra. The rising sun's light dazzled him, and he squinted and held up a hand to block the light and see which bird had come to them. He rubbed at his eyes. He had never seen this bird before. But wait, maybe the fourth bird? Four birds had come to give Isika Jerutha's message, when they had only ever known three. Ben couldn't be sure, but he thought this might be the extra. On the other side of the fire pit, Isika sat up. Her braids were heading in several different directions and she looked half asleep.

"Collect yourselves, young ones. I will come back later," the bird said, before either of them could speak. The giant bird flew off and Ben heard the familiar strains of Othra music. The melody of each was slightly different. This bird's sound was rich, old, and lovely.

He met his sister's eyes across the cold ashes of the night's fire. "That is an ancient bird," he said. She nodded, shaking her head as though to clear it. They stood. Isika silently used water from the stream to wash her face and Ben did the same. Isika pulled food out of the farmer's sack and Ben put water in the kettle. While they waited for the water to boil, they rolled their sleeping blankets up and tied them to the outside of their packs.

"I wonder what he wants," Isika said finally, taking a seat on a large stone with a cup of spice tea in her hand. Ben put his face over the steam coming from his cup. The morning was chilly and washing in the cold stream water hadn't helped. The tea was hot and woke his throat up. He felt strangely at peace, though his shoulders were sore from sleeping on the ground.

They didn't have to wait long to find out what the bird wanted, because he came back when they were finishing their simple breakfast. He dropped out of the sky to land on a tree stump not far from the little camping site. Ben took an involuntary breath, hearing the bird's song again. He knew from studying that what he heard was each bird's lifesong. This bird's lifesong resonated with sacred magic. The Othra brought a clear stream of well-being with him. Isika smiled at the bird.

"Do you have a message for me?" she asked, bowing her head slightly as she spoke.

The giant bird ruffled its feathers and Ben watched the light making patterns in his feathers, different from the three Othra he knew.

"Not a message, young one," he said. "I bring a door. A welcome. I come to tell you that I am Keethior, Protector of the World Whisperer from the beginning of time."

The bird's music became deeper, more haunting. Isika's mouth dropped open.

"What does that mean?" she asked.

"It means that I will be with you. Where you go I will go. I am in your service as long as you live. I will go where you send me, I will attack what you tell me, I will sing over you when you are in need." The bird hopped three steps sideways and tilted his head. "So, yes, anyway. Here I am."

14

K eethior flew above them as they galloped the last half-day ride before the Worker village. Every once in a while Ben saw Isika look up at the sky from her horse, as though to check whether the bird was still there. Ben grinned to himself. The look on her face, after the bird announced himself as her private servant, had been amazing. He only wished more people had been there to see it. Surely the elders would have to accept Isika now that the World Whisperer's own Othra was flying around after her.

Night, Ben's horse, was faster than Wind, but Ben kept his horse at a slower pace because Isika knew the way; it was lined with lights for her, and they had taken many turns to reach the village.

Isika had asked Keethior where Jabari, Gavi, and the others were. He told her that the seekers were somewhere behind them, waving one wing vaguely, and Isika was satisfied that she and Ben could charge ahead and find Jerutha, without being intercepted.

They were drawing near to the Worker village. Ben's stomach felt tight with nerves. Night's muscles flexed and smoothed, flexed and smoothed, under his black coat as he took great, leaping strides.

And then Ben heard the horrible grinding that meant there was demon magic nearby.

"Isika!" he shouted. She pulled her horse up quickly, and Wind danced from side to side, unhappy with such a sudden stop. She walked the horse back to Ben, her face open but impatient.

"Yes?"

"We're here. This is the losh forest on the north side of the village. The gate should be just... over there." He pointed. They couldn't see the walls yet, but he could hear them. He heard the clanging of bells, the dissonance of whispers and teeth grinding. He pushed the sound carefully to the back of his mind so that he could concentrate on what Isika would say next.

"What do you think we should do?" she asked. He glanced at her, surprised that she was asking him, and saw fear in her face. Of course. In this place she had been so low, nearly a prisoner. She had not been World Whisperer, she had been weak, not strong. The horses danced, eyes rolling, afraid of the poison they sensed, and Ben saw the very moment that Isika calmed them, their faces as they breathed her comfort and relaxed. She was still strong, even if she was doubting herself.

"I think we should leave the horses and go on foot. The closer they get to the walls, the harder it will be for them, and we need to focus on finding Jerutha."

Isika nodded, furrowing her brow in the way she did when she was mind-speaking with the horses. They left Wind and Night under a tree that gave more shade than most of the spindly losh trees. Isika put her hand lightly on each horse's neck for a moment, and this time Ben could hear music as she sent soothing words toward them.

She adjusted her satchel and arrows, falling into step beside him. As they walked through the forest, the sounds in Ben's head grew louder, squealing at him, insisting on his attention. He pushed them back again, sensing nothing worse than the sounds of poison he had heard all his life. Being here reminded him of all those years, when he had felt terrified and insane. He had been a prisoner as well, very small, hiding in the shadows. He took a deep breath. He knew who he was, he didn't need to be afraid. But he was scared, and so was his sister. She took his hand and squeezed it. The wall appeared between the trees in front of them.

"I think..." he had a hard time speaking around the noise. "I think we should very carefully walk around to the gate to see what we can."

She nodded and gripped his hand harder. "I want to get Jerutha out of this place so badly," she whispered. "Where's Keethior?" she asked, looking up and scowling. "He could tell us what's ahead, but he's nowhere to be seen."

"He may be your protector, but he's still an Othra," Ben said, smiling.

Isika smiled back at him and laughed softly, the worry in her face easing. "True," she said.

On their last journey, the Othra had come and gone on their own whims, often disappearing just when they were needed most. Ben thought they did it on purpose. Protector in an Othra's mind didn't necessarily mean protection from all danger. Perhaps it was only danger that the Othra deemed important, or disastrous.

They came to the part of the wall where the main gates started, and the drums and clanging in Ben's head intensified so much and so suddenly that he threw his arms over his head and sank to the ground. It was excruciating—the poison was pointed and vicious.

"Ben!" his sister cried, as he fell. He pressed his face deeper into his arms, trying to control the pain. Stars flashed behind his eyes with the mind piercing sounds. He breathed, struggling to get a grip on his thoughts. Slowly, slowly he pushed at the noise until it retreated. He sat up slowly, his eyes shut tight.

"What's happening?" Isika whispered, panic in her voice.

"Just… one moment…" he said. There was… something. He waded through the sounds, trying to distinguish what he was hearing. The noises were like pointed daggers, sharp knives, not the usual dull hatred and poison of apathy that he was used to in the village. He isolated the sounds that felt sharp to him, and listened to the message it was sending to him. A cry for the blood of their family. Some new kind of poison was holding the gate, aimed at him and Isika.

He opened his eyes. "I don't think we can go in there," he told his sister. She stared at him, her mouth open.

"But how are we supposed to find Jerutha?"

He shook his head back and forth, slowly, then more firmly. "No, no, Isika. We have to find another way. Something terrible will happen if we go into the village."

She watched him with serious eyes. Now that he had told her of the danger, the noise in his head subsided somewhat. There was a dull roar at the back of his skull, but he was able to pull the curtain closed and focus on his surroundings. He was crouched in the dust, his sister sitting in front of him. He was surprised to find sweat trickling down his face, and he wiped at it with his *ser*. The heat was intense in this dry wasteland.

"Okay, Ben. I trust your magic. What do we do?"

"Let's go to the gate and call someone out to talk with us."

She sighed. "This just got scarier and more complicated. All right, let's find someone."

He stood and brushed off his pants. His knees hurt from falling so heavily on the spiky weeds and small rocks. He reached a hand out to his sister and helped her up, and the two of them walked to the large main gate of the village, close to the market square.

They peered inside, trying to keep hidden around the corner of the gate. The market wasn't busy; it was midday, when the sun was hot and people stayed in the shade. Ben saw people he had known for more than half his life, milling around, dressed in long sleeves and pants, guarding their pale skin from the sun. An old man who had chased him away every time he tried to shop at his stall was asleep in the chair behind his very pricy oranges, his mouth hanging open.

It didn't take long for people to notice them. Workers clustered and began pointing at them, fear in their eyes, and before long they were buzzing. It didn't seem like a friendly buzz. Isika moved closer to Ben and grabbed his hand. He watched in disbelief as two men picked up large stones.

"Are they going to stone us?" Isika whispered in horror. Ben's stomach dropped. He pointed to the one friendly face, a red-headed woman who had a hand over her mouth.

"Faiza!" Isika yelled. "Faiza, we only want to talk."

The muttering turned to a furor at the sound of Isika's voice. Ben heard many things like "Demon magic!" and "Go away! There's nothing here for you anymore." One man hurled the rock he was holding, and it hit the wall they were standing next to with a crash. Small pieces of rock and dust broke away and fell into the sand.

"She has to come," Isika whispered. She clutched Ben's arm. Another rock sailed through the air and this time it struck Isika on the shoulder. She yelped and Ben got angry.

"We only want to ask a question!" he shouted. "Faiza, please!"

As though she was in a dream, Faiza pulled herself away from her stall and held up a hand. Faintly, Ben heard her speak to the others, drowning out their protests. "I will speak to them so they will leave," she said. "We don't want any more deaths on our hands—it will bring more bad luck on us."

She walked toward them, her eyes wide and her face pale, and stopped about two strides from the open gate.

"You need to go now," she said in a low voice. "I wish I could give you a hug, Isika, but they will kill you. Things have been so hard, the priests are asking for more taxes, Nirloth is dead, and they say you brought it all upon us."

Isika's eyes were wounded.

"We... we didn't mean to bring anything on you..."

"Never mind. Why did you come?" Faiza asked. Her eyes were hard as she glanced at them, then looked at the ground.

"We need to find Jerutha. Where is she?"

Faiza was shaking her head while Isika was still asking the question. "She's not here. The head priest demanded that she come to Batta, and they came for her and the baby. You should go. It will be bad for you if the new priest comes. They say this village is cursed because of you."

"Batta? Head priest? What are you talking about?" Isika asked. Ben felt sick to his stomach. He knew of Batta. Nirloth had been teaching him the work of a priest, so he knew the levels of priesthood. Nirloth, though he had seemed big to them, was a low level priest in one of many tiny Worker villages. Ben had sworn not to talk of it. He saw now that Isika had no idea of the bigger world of the Workers.

"Batta is the Worker capital," he said. "A big city where the high priest has his temple."

Isika gaped at him. "You knew about this? Why didn't I?"

Faiza scowled. "It is a long-held secret, apparently," she said. "It's out now, though, and there was nearly a rebellion here until the priests who came struck it down by cursing some of the men. It's why they are so angry with you now. Just go—perhaps Benayeem can explain it to you. They took

Jerutha and the baby—that way." She pointed to the other side of the village, toward the desert that Isika and her mother had crossed so many years ago.

"And the baby?" Isika asked, her voice breaking on a sob.

"He is well," Faiza said, and her eyes held something, the tiniest bit of kindness, before she looked away. "May your eyes be guarded," she said.

"And your speech kept safe," Isika responded automatically, and then Faiza turned and walked toward what was now a great crowd of people. Ben tugged at Isika's hand and they walked back into the losh forest. He tried not to look behind them, though he felt the Workers' eyes on his back.

"We can't go to Batta," he said to Isika, as soon as they were back in the cover of the forest.

She turned to him, tears on her face, her eyes wide, her face stunned, from Faiza's news, he thought. Around them the losh trees pointed at the sky, tall with black bark, the trees that had caused the children of the village to call Ben and his siblings Loshy, back when they had been the strange outsiders who lived with the priest.

"We have to, Benayeem!" she said. "How can you say that?"

"It's a terrible place, Isika."

"All the more reason to go. We have to get Jerutha away from there," she said, her voice so full of tears it sounded like she was gulping her words. She put her face in her hands and cried.

Ben's heart sank. He didn't want to go into the desert. Nightmares from the desert still plagued his sleep. And he didn't want to go to the city that Nirloth had told him about with something like fear in his eyes. Benayeem knew the music of demons would be terrible, that he might not be able to stand it. But he looked at Isika standing there, her wet eyes flashing, and he thought of the kindness and softness of Jerutha, their stepmother. He thought of the way Jerutha had risked her own life to help them save their brother. He knew, with a sick feeling in his stomach, that Isika was right. Jerutha wouldn't last long in a place like Batta.

"Okay," he said, swallowing hard. "Let's go to the horses. They'll need you to soothe them again. There's too much poison around here for anyone to feel safe."

"Do you mean we'll go?" she asked.

"We'll go, sister," he said. "But I don't know whether we'll come back. Batta is rumored to be a terrible place, and we may not make it out alive."

"I believe in us, Ben. We're gifted. And," she added, "we have Keethior," Isika said, smiling slightly through her tears. She gestured at the empty sky. "Wherever he is."

15

Jabari and the others ran all that day and all the next, trying to reach the Worker village before Isika did. Bursts of frustration gave Jabari speed as he thought about Isika going back to her old home like she didn't know any better, and he tore ahead of the group, taking the lead to set the pace. Ivy was right behind him, and Gavi ran at the back of the group, keeping an eye on everyone. Every once in a while, Gavi yelped, "Yab, hold up!" and Jabari knew someone was falling behind and he needed to slow his pace.

He glanced behind him the second time it happened. Sure enough, it was Aria, holding her side and gasping. He scowled. She really was too young and inexperienced to be out here. What had his parents been thinking? No, he knew what they had been thinking. It was all political, a gesture of good thought toward Isika's family, but politics didn't matter when they were seeking, and especially when Isika, the most frustrating girl alive, had simply run off herself.

Over years of running, he and Gavi had learned to match their pace exactly, despite the difference in their bodies. Jabari was sinewy and energetic, Gavi well built and powerful, a little slower to start but able to run extremely long distances. With practice they had learned to run in step for hours, in forests and along dirt roads. But he wasn't only with Gavi, so he slowed down. It wasn't Aria's fault the elders had sent her. Stupid politics. Jabari wanted nothing to do with any of it. He only wanted to restore the brokenness of his land, maybe even find a way to eradicate poison forever.

Right now, though, he had to reach the village before Isika. He had started to think that the message about her step-mother was really a trap, a ploy to get her back in the prison of her old life. His heart raced as fear for her and Ben flooded his mind. They ran and ran, finally reaching the walls in the late afternoon. He stopped in the forest before the walls.

"Losh trees," Aria said, putting her hand on the trunk of a tree as she bent over to catch her breath. Her eyes were wide and she looked exhausted and jittery. Jabari watched her with concern, getting an inkling of how strange this would be for her. The Worker village had been her home before she was cast out. Aria was the oldest child the rescuers had ever discovered in one of the little boats the Workers pushed out into the sea. A sacrifice to the goddesses. Jabari frowned as a new concern made itself known.

"Ivy, Gavi, I need to talk with you," he said. "Alone."

They walked away away from everyone else, squatting among piles of fallen leaves to talk.

"You called, little brother?" Gavi said. Jabari smiled at him. Jabari was the older sibling, and when Gavi called him little brother, it was code that he needed to lighten up a bit. Jabari was intense and rebellious. Gavi was easy-going and had difficulty taking things seriously. It made them a good match for each other.

"I did, big brother."

"You're awfully serious on this trip, Yab. Could it be that you're taking our dear parents' words to heart more than usual?"

Jabari blinked. His brother was right. Normally he let his parents' advice roll over him, measuring and following through on exactly what he needed to, out in the real world, far away from the comfort of the palace. But this journey was laboring under a heavy burden of expectations. He nodded.

"Thanks. You're right. I am."

"Gavi's always right," Ivy said.

Jabari grinned and rolled his shoulders. "Okay, turning over a new leaf."

Gavi smiled and reached out to punch him lightly on the arm. "If it's not fun, it's not..."

"Worth it," he and Ivy finished. Their motto, even when their work was serious and dangerous. They had learned it in school, actually, when a wise teacher whose name happened to be Ivram taught them that one of Mugunta's intentions was to rob them of joy, to make everything serious, tedious, and desperate.

Ivy laughed. "We're Dad's best students. What did you need to talk to us about? We need to go find Isika's step-mother, don't we?"

"It's something else," Jabari said, lowering himself from a squat until he was sitting directly on the forest floor. He picked up a handful of old leaves. "I don't know what to do about Aria. She was sent out. If the Workers see her, they'll know she didn't die in the sea, but that will lead them to question their other children, and as much as I'd like to bear the good news that everyone is safe, will that just lead them to kill their children in a way we can't rescue? It seems we need to get rid of the poison that makes them sacrifice their children before we let them know that we rescue the kids."

They both stared at him. For a moment he smiled, not believing he had thought of this before them.

"It's a flaw in the plan, isn't it?" Ivy said, her voice shaken. "Simply rescuing children and not interfering?"

Jabari stared at her. He had always upheld the elders' decisions not to get involved in the Worker villages. But it was true, their plan was flawed. Because the Workers kept sending children out.

Gavi cleared his throat. "What about me?" he asked.

Jabari blinked, aghast. "That's right, what about you?" His brother had also been rescued, though he was only two years old when he was sent out. What if he was recognized? But Jabari couldn't imagine going in without Gavi. They always worked together. "For that matter, what about Brigid?"

"Brigid was rescued from the southern Worker village," Gavi said.

"I think you should stay out here," Ivy told Gavi, her voice firm.

"That's not happening," Gavi said. "We're here to rescue Isika's stepmother—let's focus on that problem. I don't think we should split up. We'll deal with the fallout after. Who knows, maybe they won't recognize either of us. We all look so different from one another—they'll be shocked to see us at all."

"So we all go in?"

Gavi nodded, and after a moment, Ivy nodded as well. Jabari looked at the two of them and felt a rush of affection. Many, many days of playing hide and seek in the palace as young children, and here they were, about to rush into a Worker village for the first time.

"Okay," he said. "Let's go."

THEY WENT BACK to the others. Aria looked more and more distant, staring off into the sky. She barely acknowledged anyone else as they went over the plan, which was simple. They would walk into the marketplace and ask for Jerutha.

Ivy walked over to Aria and put a hand on her arm. After a moment Aria blinked, seemed to come back to herself with an effort, and smiled, straightening up.

Deto and Brigid went first. The two of them seemed unconcerned and cheerful. Deto had never seen the Worker village before, and he was full of questions.

"So they just leave their walls?" Deto asked.

"They revere their walls," Aria said in a soft voice. "The walls are sacred."

"How are you doing?" Ivy asked her, turning and catching her hand. They were nearly to the gate.

"The walls feel... heavy... to me. As though they could crush us."

"It must be your past here," Jabari said, and after a moment, Aria nodded, biting her lip.

"Yes, it must be that."

They reached the gate quickly. It was open. They looked at each other and then Jabari took a breath and strode into the village with Gavi at his side. The market was full of people, and as the first people noticed them, there were shrieks from some of the children. The Workers were not used to strangers coming to their village, which sat on the edge of the barren desert. People ran from nearby stalls to form a cluster. A few men broke off and shouted to them to stay away.

Jabari slowed and stopped walking.

"Welcoming bunch, aren't they?" he said under his breath. Ivy snorted. Jabari looked around. There were six seekers, and perhaps they looked menacing. He couldn't tell what the problem was. He held up his hands.

"We have peace in our hearts toward you," he called across the village square. "We only need to ask some questions."

"Ghosts!" one woman called out, pointing at Gavi. Jabari frowned. They had already recognized his brother. Another person took up the cry: "Ghosts! Ghosts!" Jabari told another step forward, opening his mouth to ask for help finding Jerutha, but then a rumble began. Beside him, he sensed Gavi preparing himself for attack. Jabari stood up straighter and reached for his bow. The rumble went on, turning into a roar that grew louder and louder. What was it?

Panic hit the people in the square. He notched an arrow and looked around for the threat. He couldn't see anything, but the roaring grew louder and louder until it was all he could hear, and the villagers clung to each other, covering their ears. The sound was unbearable. The ground started to shake. He saw the villagers screaming but couldn't hear them in the noise. Then the sound suddenly cut out and the shaking stopped, so that the screams were audible. There was a pause, and he heard women and children sobbing.

"What was that?" Brigid asked, her face even paler than normal, her hands shaking as she held her staff out in front of her. Jabari shook his head, looking around wildly, mystified.

Then the roaring started again, but this time there was a sharp whine and then water poured out of the walls in great sheets, like Jabari's mountain waterfall, but sinister and in the wrong place. For a moment, the villagers were frozen, and then the wailing began as the people ran from the walls, toward the center of the village. Still the water came. It poured and poured, and rather than seeping into the dry desert floor, it gathered and pooled up quickly. Soon Jabari's feet were covered and still the water came.

Jabari thought quickly. The village was chaos. People shrieked and ran in every direction, trampling each other.

They ran into their houses and onto their rooftops. He turned and looked at his friends. Behind them, the gates to the village swung shut with a huge, resounding clang. Jabari felt a sudden exhaustion, as though he had climbed a mountain. He met Gavi's eyes. This was a very sudden and malicious poison. What on earth was it, and what did they need to do?

16

Think! Jabari told himself. How could they fight this poison? He ran through several possibilities in his mind, discarding them as they came to him. Then he nodded as an idea slowly made itself known.

They would have to try a restoration similar to healing a diseased forest or river. It was chancy and difficult and normally rangers would be the ones fighting something like this, older than seekers and more experienced with the more volatile poisons that came from the Great Waste. All these thoughts were whirling through Jabari's head almost as quickly as the water was flowing out of the walls.

The poison seemed so pointed, as though there were thousands of arrows directed toward them. Which of the villagers had the power to trigger something like this?

He held out his hands on either side of him, yelling to be heard over the roar of the water.

"We need to form a circle, quickly!" he shouted. The

water was lapping at their thighs and didn't appear to be slowing. On either side, Gavi and Ivy were already gripping onto his hands. They had done high level restoration before, but never without a ranger or two, and never in such immediate danger. But they were calm, though Gavi had the tense look he always got near water. Aria's eyes were wild with fear. She had also been sent out in a boat, and she had been much older; her memories traumatized her.

"What is happening?" she screamed at him.

"I don't have time to explain right now!" he shouted. "Grab hands. When I say, do as you've been taught with the restoration of the forest and drive all the poison back into the earth. This water comes from somewhere, Mugunta is terrifying it and misdirecting it—we need to send it back where it belongs!"

"How do we do it?" Aria asked.

"The same way we do other sending restoration. Pretend it's a wall and you're leaning on it."

Ivy called it before he could. "One, two, three," she shouted, and together, holding hands, they leaned into the circle. "Push!" she screamed. "And when I say the word, run to the far corners of the walls. First we need to send the waters back, then we need to be sure the sources are sealed off!"

They leaned in. Jabari pushed with his mind and his heart. He worked at it with everything he had, pushing the water back into the deep recesses of the earth. At first it seemed to rise higher, and he felt the arrows sharpen, but then a glow emerged from their circle and the water shrieked and began to disappear, sinking into the earth.

On the rooftops, people had been shrieking for them to leave the village, but when they saw the waters receding, their clamoring changed. Their anger lessened, they waited with pale, tense faces. Jabari kept pushing at the water until all that was left was a sheen on the ground, and then Ivy broke away, gasping.

"Run!" she shouted. "Seal the walls off. The water is still coming!" It wasn't pouring out anymore, but dribbles leaked down the uneven surfaces of the ugly walls.

"I don't know how to do that!" Brigid cried, and Aria shook her head as well. Aria looked as though she was barely standing.

"Come with me," Jabari called to Brigid, and as they turned and ran, he saw Aria trailing after Gavi.

They scattered toward the walls. Jabari hated touching walls as deeply poisoned as the walls of the Worker village. It was why, despite the fact that he had come close to this Worker village a thousand times or more, he had never come in. That, and it was forbidden. Oh, he was in all kinds of trouble now.

But he told Brigid what they needed to do, and then he laid his hands and even his face right on the walls, pulling protection magic from the earth, sealing the walls, stopping the gushing with a thought. They ran from corner to corner, closing the water off. It was horrible to work with the poison of the walls, but strength from the earth rose up and helped.

The walls were cracked in many places, held together by bits of metal, old nails, and even slabs of wood.

It took them a long time to seal all the walls around the village. By the time they were done, there was almost no trace of the flood that had risen to their thighs, except for the red mud that smeared the bottoms of the buildings. The dirt itself was as hard and dry as a bone, as though it had never been wet. Jabari felt a brief longing for the friendly soil of Maween. All those fields with rich, soft earth. He shouldn't take his lands for granted. He walked with Brigid to the main gates and found them open again.

Good. Isika wasn't here and it was time for the seekers to leave; they had been delayed far too long.

He walked with Brigid, who was limping, and found his brother sitting beside a wall, Aria asleep beside him, her head lying on his shoulder.

"She's exhausted," Gavi replied to Jabari's questioning look. "We need to get her somewhere safe, so she can rest."

"You both need to get out of here," Jabari answered. "I want to talk with the people here and we may need to do some healing. I don't like how they were shouting at the two of you. Who knows what they'll do, especially after this little water incident?" He glanced at Brigid. "You should go too. Lie down in the forest and rest for a while." Brigid nodded, her face worried as she looked at Aria.

"She's sleeping so deeply," she said, pulling her hair off her neck. "Will she wake up?"

"Of course she will," Jabari said, and smiled to soften his voice. Brigid nodded.

Gavi looked at Aria, crashed on his shoulder. "How do I get her out of here?"

"The way you get me around when I'm taking a nap. Carry her."

Gavi snorted with laughter, and Jabari smiled, relieved. Aria wasn't the only one who looked exhausted. The shadows under Gavi's eyes were as dark as losh trees, and Brigid's face was drawn and even paler than normal. After he pulled Aria into his arms, Gavi turned and raised an eyebrow at Jabari.

"Somehow I think this 'water incident' will qualify as 'meddling' to Dad."

"One thing at a time, little brother."

Gavi pulled Aria a little closer, making sure her head was leaning against his shoulder, then walked quickly toward the gate, Brigid close on his heels. Jabari sighed as some of his anxiety lifted, seeing them leave the village. He was more worried about the villagers than he had let on. A stoning would be very inconvenient, especially after a flood.

HE WENT to look for Ivy and the others, locating her and Deto in the middle of trying to help a banana seller put his bananas back on his cart. The poor man was shaking with fear. He was short, with thinning hair, and he looked like he could have used a lot more food at his daily meal. Jabari scowled. The Worker practice of eating only one meal a day made him angry. He hated the thought of hunger, especially of any child going hungry, and the memory of all the children they had rescued, the way their bones jutted out, bothered him more than almost anything else the Workers did. Even Isika and Ben had been terribly thin before they started eating enough food every day. He felt a sudden urge to flee, to get out of the horrible village. But first he needed to find Jerutha.

He strode through the square, noticing that many people limped as they walked. One small boy caught his attention. He had hair like Gavi's, sticking up on his head like golden grass in late summer. Jabari put a hand on him and felt the way the water had weakened him. Jabari wasn't a healer, but he had a little healing skill. He gathered some strength and sent healing into the boy. The boy straightened, and looked at him, eyes wide.

"Thank you," he said, in a voice that reminded Jabari so much of Gavi's little boy voice that he had to blink back a sudden ache behind his eyes.

He stood staring at the boy, his hand still on the boy's shoulder, shocked by the sudden thought that the only difference between this boy and his brother was where they had been raised. He stood there, a blinding question hitting him on all sides: was it right not to interfere? Was his father right to leave the Workers alone?

Or was Isika right, with her desire to help the Workers, to save her stepmother. Jabari knew she was deeply disturbed about the fact that the Workers still labored for the goddesses. He had shrugged her worries away before.

The boy ran away, but Jabari was frozen by the traitorous thought, a deeper questioning of the ways of his people than he had ever allowed himself. He was bumped out of his reverie by motion in his side vision. It was a woman piling tomatoes back on her cart, taking time to lift them and arrange them one by one, after wiping them carefully on her dress. She looked up and saw him watching her, then, after shaking her head and glaring at him, she barked an order at a nearby child and walked toward Jabari. The child began picking up the tomatoes, piling them on the cart less carefully than his mother.

The woman had dull copper hair, not as brilliant as Karah's hair, but still brighter than most hair Jabari had seen in the village. He watched her as she approached in her heavy dress, wondering how she stood the heat in all that clothing. When she reached him, she looked into his eyes once, swiftly, and he felt the intelligence of her gaze. Then she looked down, in the way of the Workers. The adopted families of rescued Worker children had to spend hours training the children to make eye contact. It was forbidden by the goddesses, the small children told them. Jabari felt another flash of anger, following by a sick feeling at the fact that they didn't do anything to stop it.

"What are you seeking?" she asked. "Your presence here is disturbing my people, and we have no priest to protect us at the moment. So tell me what you want, so you will go away again."

Jabari thought he knew what he was going to ask, but he surprised himself with his first question. It burst out of his mouth before his head had a chance to catch up with his fear.

"Have you seen Isika?"

Surprised, the woman met his eyes again for a second, before squinting up at the sky. She drew a breath.

"She was here, briefly, a day ago. She stood outside the walls with her brother. She didn't come in."

A rush of understanding came to Jabari. The poison of the flood was meant for Isika. But she hadn't entered, and it had found Aria instead. He wondered what it had done to Aria, how much it had hurt her, directed toward her the way it had been, seeking someone of their family. He had led her straight into it. He wondered what wisdom had kept Isika outside.

"What about Jerutha?" he asked now. "We have come seeking Isika's stepmother."

"I'll tell you the same thing I told Isika," the woman said, still squinting at the sky. "Jerutha has been taken away, across the desert. That way." She gestured with an arm swathed in the stiff cloth of her dress. "The priests took her to Batta." The woman wiped sweat off her head.

Jabari drew in a breath.

"You know of Batta?" the woman asked. Jabari could only nod. Yes he knew of the city that thoroughly belonged to Mugunta.

"Come," he said. "I'll bother you only a little longer, but you should sit in the shade. You look tired." For the third time, the woman was startled into looking at him, and this time her eyes were incredulous and then angry.

She turned swiftly and stalked back to her stall, scolding the child for not stacking the tomatoes evenly. Jabari looked at the child again and saw that it was actually a girl. A thin girl, with big eyes and tufted red hair cut about an inch from her head. She looked as though she was about six.

The shade of the stall made little difference in the heat.

"What is your name?" Jabari asked. The woman polished a tomato, then threw another one into a bin of rejects. The girl reached into the bin and bit into a tomato. Juice dribbled down her chin.

"Are you asking me? Or her?" the woman asked, jerking her chin toward the little girl.

"You, but you can tell me her name too, if you like."

"I'm Faiza. This is Lora." Her face softened. "She's eight. I was friends with Isika, you know. She was always kind to Lora. And I was friends with her mother before her."

Jabari felt the blood leave his face. He wondered what the woman would think if he told her that Isika's mother had been the daughter of a lost queen. He didn't say it, though. He asked the woman if he could buy a bag of tomatoes and asked one last question.

"What will happen to you now? Will you get a new priest?"

The woman's face clouded, and for a moment it seemed like she might cry.

"They say we'll get a new one. Heaven knows what he will be like. May your eyes be guarded," she said to Jabari. He nodded and left her, letting his hand rest briefly on the little girl's head for a moment before he left.

He found Ivy and Deto at the gate, waiting for him.

"Is the woman here?" Deto asked. His long eyes didn't flinch away from Jabari's, and Jabari felt a very particular kind of relief at this. People should never be prohibited from meeting one another's eyes. Love was communicated through eyes. Affection, kindness. Anger, true, but even emotions like anger should be open, expressed, communicated. Magunta wanted to cut the Workers off from one another and he had found so many ways to do it.

"No," he said. "We must cross the desert to find her. And the wily World Whisperer, who has undoubtedly followed her to Batta."

Oh Isika, he thought, while the others exclaimed over his words. He looked in the direction of the cursed city. Be careful.

17

They rode hard through the night, because Isika didn't want to cross the desert during the scorching day. They needed to find shelter before morning, to be out of the sun when the heat was at its worst. She worried about water. She and Ben had filled up their flasks at the last stream, but that was nearly a full night's ride behind them. She hadn't seen water since.

The desert spread out to the horizon on either side. In the dark of night Isika couldn't see the landscape, but the stars told her where the sky began and the earth ended, flat on every side, hard, packed sand that was easy terrain for the horses. Their hooves fell with dull thuds as they walked and cantered, the only sound Isika heard in the quiet night.

Something seemed to be wrong with her eyes, but she rubbed them hard and the feeling persisted. After a moment she saw it was only the sky changing color before dawn. The sky slowly grew purple, then gray, and she realized that

Keethior was flying high above them, just a speck in the great bowl of sky.

Keethior, she called to him. *Come down. Lend me your eyes*. Right away, she sensed his attention on her and then she saw herself from above, a strange feeling. She followed the thread of his sight until she spotted exactly what she needed: an old ruin of a building. The roof was broken, but it should still provide enough shade. She looked as far as she could in each direction from Keethior's perspective, but still she didn't see water anywhere.

"Up ahead," she yelled back to her brother. Benayeem looked exhausted, and she slowed so his horse could catch up with hers. She wondered if she looked anywhere near as terrible as he did, with shadows under his eyes and a pinched, gaunt face. "Shelter up ahead," she repeated. He nodded, just a quick jerk of the chin.

The horses sailed into a gallop, Wind's muscles bunching and smoothing underneath her. *We'll stop soon,* she told him.

Thirsty, he said. Isika gripped the reins until her hands hurt. How was she going to find water? The first blinding rays of the sun rushed over the earth from the horizon. They needed to get to shelter.

A little way longer she told her horse, though it felt like a lie, because she had no ideas, no way of finding them water. Her hands shook as desperation grew inside her. Had they come to the desert to die? Wind sped up, running with longer strides, eager to be done with the night's ride. Isika hadn't needed to calm either horse for some time. This part of the desert was as barren with poison as everything else.

Up ahead, a speck in the distance, and as the horses thundered toward it, the speck became a blob, then a square shape, and then a building. The roof was fallen half in, the walls made of the same sandstone as the houses in the Worker village. She caught herself thinking, "in my village," and shook her head quickly, forcing the thought away. She belonged to the City of the Maweel now, to Azariyah, where one day she would be queen. She couldn't let the Great Waste throw its claim over her, just because she had come so far away.

The horses pulled to a stop, panting, and Isika gingerly dismounted, sliding down Wind's flank and leaning against him for a moment.

Okay? She asked.

Thirsty, he told her. Night agreed. *Thirsty, sister.*

She would have known that they were thirsty even if they hadn't told her, by her own thirst and by the way their sides were heaving as they panted. She looked up at Benayeem.

"Will you search for water nearby?" she asked in a low voice. He turned and surveyed the area around them, the cracked, dry ground, layers of sand beneath her feet. There were a few scraggly bushes and a twisted tree, as well as some prickly, oddly shaped trees that Isika didn't know. They were far into the desert, now. Ben met her eyes and she knew she was only asking him to go as a show of trying to do something. There would be no water here.

With a gust of wind, Keethior landed on the ground beside her, and Isika turned to him in despair, speaking only to him with her mind so she wouldn't alarm the horses. *We don't have water,* she said. *Can you bring us water somehow? We won't survive without it.*

He flapped his wings at her and she flinched a little at the wave of reproach she felt coming from him.

You are the World Whisperer, he said. *The link to the Uncreated One. Call the water and it will listen to you.*

"What?" she said aloud. "Call it?"

"Yes," he said, also speaking aloud so Ben could hear. "Call it. It will know your voice and listen."

Isika stared at the blowing sand under her feet. She looked at Ben and he looked back at her, his face blank. She thought for a minute, then began to walk, wondering how one *called water.* But she remembered the trees. When she leaned against them, she felt their life. Maybe if she lay on the earth, she would be able to feel its life in the same way. So she stretched out there, on the sand, touching the earth from her head to her boots. The sand was cool; the heat of the day had not yet made it burn like fire, the way it would later. Isika pressed her face to the earth and listened for it.

There it was, the earth's life, like a giant, humming stone, filled with cracks of light and rivers of gushing water, and somewhere deep inside, heat, raw heat that burned her face, though when she touched her forehead, it was cool. The earth was strong and ancient. She worked through the feelings that came, the ways that she felt so small, as the huge rock power hummed beneath her. Somehow it listened, waiting for her to speak. So she did. She leaned harder and reached out to it with her mind.

We need water, she said. *Please send water.*

She felt a surge of power and then she scrambled backward because her face was getting wet. The sand dampened quickly and before her eyes turned to a basin of rock. A pool of clean water, about the width of one of her arms, formed in the rock basin as the water bubbled out of the spring. As she watched, small plants grew alongside the pool.

She stared for a few moments, then thirst drove her forward. She scooped a handful of water and put it to her mouth. The water was clear and sweet, and she drank again before she turned to her brother. She had nearly forgotten he was there.

He stared at her, his face slack with shock. She smiled tentatively and gestured at the pool with one hand.

"You have become incredibly weird," he said, then stooped and drank out of his hands as well. Isika laughed.

"Wait until Jabari sees water coming out of the ground," she said. "He'll be so jealous."

"Is making the elder's son jealous a good aim for the World Whisperer?" Keethior asked. He had been standing and watching silently. He slowly flapped his wings now, and his feathers shone in shifting patterns of blue.

Isika winced. She supposed it wasn't very dignified. But Jabari... he made her crazy.

"Do you know him?" she asked. "Because if you did, you would understand."

Ben just shook his head and then led Night toward the water. Night bent his head and drank and drank.

Isika looked for her horse and didn't see him. *Wind!* she called. *Where are you? Come. We have water.* There was no answer, so she went to find him. He stood at the other side of the building, facing the strong, sandy, wind that came from the west, the way they traveled.

We'll reach the city in two more nights, he said, and Isika stared at him. What kind of horse had they given her? Could animals be gifted?

She didn't realize she had thought into his mind until he snorted a horse laugh. *Animals are always gifted,* he said.

She laid her hand on his neck. *Come,* she said. *Drink.*

She rubbed the horses down with sand. It was all they had to dry their sweaty hides. When she was done they were sandy but content. Then she and Ben slept until sunset, and woke hungry.

"Have you ever eaten snake?" Keethior asked, before lifting off into the sky with a few strokes of his powerful wings.

Isika shuddered. "I suppose there's a first time for everything," she said to Ben. But they didn't have to eat snake, because Keethior caught them a rabbit.

"I could get used to this," Ben said. "Othra hunting for our meals."

The bird flapped his giant wings again, and beside the blue, all the lights of the sunset seemed to be reflected in them. He hissed.

"Othra do what they want to do," he said. "I wanted to find food."

It was like having the grumpiest person in the world declare himself your servant and then state he would only do what he wanted. Isika thought about it for a minute, then happened to meet Ben's eyes and she dissolved into laughter. They both laughed for a long time, and their laughter was a relief, on this long, lonely trip.

They saddled the horses to move on. Isika studied her *ser* for a moment, then tied it so it looped around her head, then over her nose and mouth as well. She could breathe better when she wasn't choking down the fine grains of sand that flew constantly in the wind. She showed Ben and he raised his eyebrows and laughed at how she looked, but he followed her lead and tied his *ser* the same way.

Keethior showed Isika a map the way he had done before, a golden line that ran ahead of them, across the desert, tracing the path they needed to follow. The last of the sun disappeared and they mounted and galloped across the sand. The night was bright with a nearly full moon and the sand stretched in all directions, broken only by the curiously bent trees.

Half the night was over when, without warning, shapes loomed up out of the rippling sand. Animals of some kind, six of them, and before Isika could see them properly, she had reached for her bow and notched an arrow, but Keethior flew down and landed on the sand between her and the creatures.

No weapon! he cried, and his voice was angry in her mind. She blinked and put her bow away, confused and frustrated. She was the last to know everything, and now she had committed some grave wrong.

Keerza he breathed at her, and she reached out with her senses and felt a strong hum, like the *naia*, the dolfina, but stronger, deeper, earthier. She dismounted and left Wind to walk toward the creatures slowly. They were delicate, like the gazelles that the Workers sometimes hunted on the edge of the desert, but their hides were a rich purple that glowed in the moonlight, striped with fine white lines. They had large white rings around their eyes. Two had silver antlers like tree branches.

They stood silently as she walked to them as if in a dream. Carefully, she laid her hand on the head of the largest one, who had a set of antlers that shone in the moonlight. His life glow hummed into her. He was like deep, rich earth, as old as the stars. He was completely pure; he had done no wrong in his long life. The purity of his eyes was almost too much for her, but she held herself still and looked into them, and he spoke to her.

Welcome, child, he said. *We have been waiting for you.*

A female approached and put her nose on Isika's arm. The humming grew, and she felt sparkling, sparking energy like fire, or stars, moving in and around her. She stood straighter, felt much, much stronger.

She felt suddenly as though she shouldn't be touching them, taking all this strength, as though it was all too much for any person to touch such a pure being. She drew her hand back, but all six of them crowded around her and pressed their heads against her arms.

We come to warn you, the largest one said. *You are sought by the man who leads the city, Batta. Young one, evil is revered in that place. You are sought and you will be trapped if you go there.*

"But we need to find our stepmother," Isika said aloud,

aware that Ben had come to stand beside her. "She is part of our family, we can't abandon her."

She glanced at Ben, and he smiled at her. She knew he heard their song, and that he also felt how good and pure they were.

We will come with you, young one. We cannot go into the city; it is poison to us, but if there is a way, we will help you.

The first female that had touched Isika nudged her arm again. *You will have to be very strong, child, because they will try to hurt you. Their magic hurts and enslaves. If you go into the city, we won't be able to protect you.*

Isika felt a painful rush of fear, but she shook her head. "Then we have to go! If it is a hurting magic, we must get Jerutha and her baby out." She turned to look at Ben again. He stared at the Keerza, then slowly nodded, but his face was tense.

They remounted. Wind and Night cantered through the desert, the Keerza flanking them, as sure and quick-footed as the gazelles they resembled. Tiny lights glittered from their hides as they ran, like lights that Isika could sometimes see on the *naia*, or trees. They were so full of pure life that they shimmered always. Having them beside and Keethior overhead made Isika feel magical and strong, and she tried to hold onto that feeling as she grew more and more afraid, bracing herself for the walls she knew would appear before them in less than two nights time.

18

Gavi filled every seeker's flask with water at the well outside the Worker village, then he found the extra flasks that he had in his own pack and filled them too. Jabari was unshakable in his plan to run across the desert to find Isika, but Gavi knew it was madness.

Gavi had spent his life supporting his brother's schemes; he wouldn't even know what it was like to refuse them. And he knew Jabari was right. Isika and Ben needed them. Even so, running across the desert was madness. When he put the extra flasks in his pack, it weighed as much as a house. He groaned and took some out to give away, one flask for each person.

"Don't you dare drink it until I tell you to," he said with his sternest voice. "This is your extra water, for desperation only. Small sips everyone. Running across the desert will kill us if we don't have water."

He ran his hands through his hair, which already stood

on end, the color of wheat bleached in the sun. He looked at Aria, messing with his hair until he realized what he was doing. He fiddled with his pack. Did Aria have it in her to run? He worried about her every second that she was out here. They had been friends for a long time; she sometimes worked in the gardens as an extra school activity. But lately, since Isika had come back, she was like a different person. He shook his head. She shouldn't have come.

The seekers sat on the ground near the well, repacking for a run, distributing the weight the way seekers were taught. They had eaten rabbit stew, cleaned the dishes; any minute they would start. Gavi stretched his arms over his head and glanced at Aria again. She was fragile, and the Maweel were a running people. Jabari and Gavi ran almost all the time when they were on seeking journeys. And of course they needed to run if they were ever going to get to the city in time to help Isika and Ben. Horses! He shook his head. He couldn't shake the feeling that this was not going to go well for Aria.

He stood and went to sit beside her, holding the last of the extra flasks out for her. She took it silently. She hadn't said a word since he carried her, asleep, out of the village.

"How are you feeling?" he asked her. "Can you sleep more? We have a long night of running ahead of us."

She sat for a while before answering, as though she was sifting words, choosing them carefully.

"I'm tired," she said. "I feel... I don't know how to describe it...a little bit dead inside. I don't think this place is good for me."

Gavi knew what she meant. He had also been outcast from this very Worker village, sacrificed by his own parents, laid in a little boat to die in the waves. Things had turned out well, but it was no thanks to his father and mother. He had been rescued and raised in a palace. He was endlessly thankful to the Maweel, and he also carried around a little pocket of hurt, the place that still felt betrayed. He looked up at the walls of the village, white and cracked with time and heat. He sighed.

"Do you want me to try a healing?" he asked. "You need strength before you can run all night, like Jabari is planning to make us do."

She looked up at him, alarmed. "All night?"

"If we can, yes, to catch Isika."

She held her hands out in front of her, staring at them, dark brown and slender.

"Yes," she said, and he caught his breath at the frightened look on her face. "If that's what Jabari's planning, I suppose you should try. I feel like I could sleep for a month."

He placed his hand gently on her forehead and closed his eyes. She was still young, only twelve, such a child in some ways, a strong woman in others. He felt her deep exhaustion and pulled it away from her, sending it into the ground the way they had learned. Then he sensed something that wasn't tiredness or sickness. It was a little like an arrow, and though he tugged at it, he couldn't get it to budge. There were more, all poisoned, malicious and sharp. They felt like the poison that had caused the flood in the village. What? Where had they come from? He shuddered and opened his eyes, staring at her. No wonder she was exhausted. He couldn't believe she was still conscious, injured the way she was.

She smiled at him.

"I feel much better," she said. "Almost like I could run all night."

He smiled back at her with gentle eyes, but inwardly he was troubled. As long as the arrows were there, she wouldn't be able to sustain energy, and they would eventually kill her. They needed a skilled healer. An idea struck him and he wondered if Isika could get the arrows out. She had shown herself to have an amazing healing gifting, back on their last journey, when she healed rescuers who would have died without her. One more reason to get to her quickly.

Jabari walked over with his long-legged stride.

"Let's go," he said.

Gavi raised his eyebrows at Aria.

"This guy," he said, "thinks we're horses."

"I think you're a donkey," Jabari said. "Thanks for all the extra weight."

"You'll thank me when it saves your life," Gavi said, grabbing Jabari's ankle and pulling so he stumbled.

"Don't start that. If I beat you up you'll whine the whole time you're running."

"Boys!" Ivy called. "Enough! Let's go. We need to run while it's dark, and we need every minute."

They tied their *sers* over their faces to keep out the dust and began jogging. It didn't take long for Gavi to see that it was going to be a long, torturous run. The sand was difficult to run through, though thankfully Jabari found places where it wasn't too deep. He hung back beside Aria. They ran silently, under the moon, which hung in the sky, so big that it seemed it could fall and roll away. The moonlight on the sand shone silver, and Gavi soaked in the beauty of night, even as his lungs screamed at him.

"Break!" he called, when he thought Aria couldn't run anymore.

They stood around, swinging their arms, catching their breath, taking sips of water. Gavi noticed something odd; a glittering line on the sand. It disappeared if he focused on it directly, but when he looked away, it was there again.

"Yab, do you see that?" Gavi asked his brother.

Jabari nodded. "An Othra trail."

"What does that mean?" Brigid wanted to know. She stood bent in half with her hands on her knees, catching her breath.

"It means Isika and Ben have an Othra with them," Jabari said.

"Where do you see the trail?" she asked, turning her head to look all around.

"It's right there, on the ground, stretching ahead. Like small lights. Do you see it?" Jabari asked.

"No, I can't see anything."

"Who can see it?" Jabari asked. Only Gavi and Ivy said they could. "That makes sense, though I'm surprised you can't, Deto. But you have to learn to see them. It takes a long time of seeking, and especially seeking with Othra." He frowned. "Of course, the fact that it's here means that Isika can already see them. Like with everything else, she doesn't need to work to learn it."

Aria stood up and walked away.

"It's a good thing," Gavi said, the mildest hint of reproach in his voice. Perhaps Jabari didn't realize how bitter he sounded. "It means they'll be safer than if they were alone, and it means that we'll be able to follow their exact trail." The trail looked like a line of glowing stars, flickering against the sand. He was glad to see it. Glad that Isika and Ben weren't alone. "Of course," he added. "Their Othra is probably the ancient one we met. The one dedicated to the World Whisperer. That's even better."

They rested a while. They were all weary. Ivy walked around rubbing each person's shoulders.

"The worst thing about running is the way people hold their shoulders. Try to relax your shoulders when you run, or you'll get more tired than you need to," she said.

"We'll stop for the night when we find a clump of trees big enough to rest under," Jabari said. "I'm pretty sure there's one up ahead."

Gavi remembered too, from a trip the two of them had taken, long ago, when they were on a seeking journey and had decided to see as much of the desert as they could. They had nearly collapsed of thirst, and they never told their parents. It was why Gavi had given everyone extra water. But as they began to run again, he knew the water they had wasn't going to be enough. He made calculations, thought about how there was supposed to be water inside some desert plants. He turned it over in his mind until he thought he would go crazy.

They stopped for the day at the clump of trees he remembered. This point was as far in the desert as he and Jabari had ever been. From now on, they would be winging it.

"Do you think Isika and Ben stopped here?" Ivy asked, as they lay in a circle on their sleeping mats. Dinner had been bread and cheese. There wasn't enough wood for a fire and Gavi hadn't brought any. When he said this, the others gave him looks as though he had betrayed them.

"What?" he said. "I brought water."

"No," Aria said suddenly. "I don't feel her here."

They all stared at her. "What do you mean?" Ivy finally asked.

Aria shrugged. "I can feel her. If Isika has been somewhere, if she is somewhere, I always know. I can also sort of tell whether she was in a place a long time ago or recently. It's part of my gift, I guess. Though why my magic should want to figure out where my sister is, I have no idea." She took another bite of bread, and chewed it, then spoke up again. "It's especially strong if she's done any magic."

Jabari met Gavi's eyes, and Gavi knew what his brother was thinking. Aria's gift could be useful when they got to the Worker city. Otherwise, finding Isika was going to be like finding a needle in a haystack.

In the morning they each had one flask of water left. Gavi's stomach hurt, thinking about the water problem. The flask would last through another night, but what then? Still, they ran. They ran all night, stopping for sips of water and more chunks of bread from the food sack. Jabari told them that if they kept going, they might find Isika and Ben's shelter for the night, since the pair would have been able to travel twice as fast on horses. They followed the trail of sparks that lit the way, mostly silent. Gavi could almost taste his fear of thirst. Thirst was a terrible thing. It made you something less than human.

When the sky grew light and they were nearly spent, they still hadn't found shelter. Gavi pulled Jabari aside.

"What now, little brother?" he asked, choking on his words. "Are you leading us to our deaths?"

Jabari scowled at him. "You know I'm trying my best."

"We have no shelter from the midday sun and no water. It sure seems like a recipe for a horrible death."

Aria sat up. She had been lying on the sand, gasping, but now she stood and limped to them, calling as she came, "Jabari!"

He turned to her, still scowling, and she stopped and flinched. Gavi elbowed his brother and he calmed his face and put his hands out.

"No, no, it's okay, Aria. My brother is just being a pest."

Gavi took a deep breath.

Aria spoke. "They stopped ahead. In shelter. And I feel a huge amount of Isika's magic. Larger than anything else on this journey."

They stared at her. Jabari moved first.

"Aria! You're amazing. Good news, Gavi, good news will get you anywhere," he said, and Gavi suddenly felt actual, hot anger toward his brother's flippancy. He breathed for a minute, bit his tongue, heaved his pack onto his back, and prepared to run again.

It was harder this time. His worry about water made him even more thirsty. He knew his brother. Jabari was hiding his concern under nonchalance, but it didn't make it any less annoying. For once, he wanted Jabari to just say, "You're right, Gavi, I didn't think this through." He snorted. He would be waiting forever for that.

They ran and ran, and after a while, a shape appeared on the horizon. He supposed it was the shelter that Aria had felt. He glanced at her and saw a look of relief on her face. She looked as though she was putting all her strength into not collapsing, but it didn't matter because they were... there.

Deto and Ivy each flopped onto the sand and Gavi bent over with his hands on his knees. Brigid, surprisingly, was turning out to be an excellent runner. She walked in circles this time, raising her arms over her head, and flashed Gavi a grin when she met his eyes.

And Gavi turned to look at Aria, but she wasn't laying on the ground like he expected, or even paying attention to any of them. She stood, her thin chest heaving, but still, as though she was listening. After a moment, she turned and walked to the other side of the building.

Not sure what was there, or whether it was safe, Gavi followed her, only to nearly crash into her when she stopped short.

"That's what she did here," she said, and her voice was full of part awe and part frustration. Gavi moved around her and blinked back sudden tears as he saw the most beautiful thing he had ever seen in his life: clear water, bubbling out of the ground into a rock basin, forming a crystalline pool. It was clearly magic; there was nothing but barren desert on every side for days and days of running. He swallowed. They wouldn't die.

"Thank the Shaper," he breathed, and then he called to the others while Aria bent to drink at the spring her sister had called out of the earth.

19

J erutha sat against the wall in the tiny room they kept her in. Since the priests marched her in here, she had alternated between two states: a stupor of sadness in the day, and the sweetness of her dreams while she slept.

She barely remembered reaching the city. By then she was exhausted and nearly starving from the effort of walking so far while breastfeeding a baby. Her memories of the arrival were hazy, a blur of buildings and faces.

It wasn't as though they fed her a lot now, but she slowly regained a bit of strength now that she wasn't walking in the desert sun. Her face was peeling, but it didn't feel as hot. She wasn't thirsty anymore—they did give her a lot of water.

She spent her days caring for her baby and singing to him. She changed him and washed him, using the water they brought daily. There was just the one tiny room and an outdoor latrine that was attached to the room by a door. The latrine had bars everywhere, like a cage.

She grieved because she had failed. She had sent the message that would lead Isika into this trap, and now that she knew the truth, that she was there only to lead Isika to the priests, her stepdaughter would come. She felt it in her bones.

From hope that her stepdaughter would come, she turned to the tiny possibility that she wouldn't. She could live here, with Mesu. Surely they would give them some sort of life in this place, once it was clear that Isika wasn't coming. Jerutha's son would grow up away from the sea and the thought made her sad, but there would be something here they could do. If only Isika would stay away.

At night, though, her dreams were always beautiful. She sang and swam and played. She sat by the shore and talked with Isika for hours. Jerutha always meant to tell Isika not to come, but in the dreams she forgot about the need to warn her. They sat by the shore or in the garden together, whispering among the bean plants the way they used to. Sometimes Ibba and Kital were near, playing like puppies.

Nirloth was close by in her dreams, and his nearness felt comforting. And Jerutha's mother was always there. In the dreams, Jerutha's sister hadn't been sent out and her mother's mind stayed orderly and full of love. She never saw her sister in the dreams; she was a shadow that sparkled at the edges of Jerutha's vision.

But the strongest thing in the dreams was her sense of well being, the knowledge that all would be well. She awoke each morning with the feeling lingering in her mind, spreading its flavor through her weakened body. As the day went on, it slowly escaped her. She remembered where she truly was, and that she was honey in a trap for a girl she loved. By the afternoon, she was full of grief again.

Still, she couldn't help feeling that the dreams were a gift. She wished she knew who sent them, so she could express her thanks. She developed a habit of simply saying "Thank you," when she woke up, in case the god or goddess responsible for the dreams could hear her.

Maybe the birds sent her? The birds were another bright spot. Every once in a while, she would see one perched on the sill of her tiny square window, outside the bars. They never spoke to her. There were two, or maybe three of them— she couldn't tell, they were so similar. But the fact that they were there made her feel as though all was not lost.

At first, she pleaded with them to keep Isika away. But they never answered, so she stopped begging. Whenever they were there, the room filled with well being like the feelings in her dreams. Once she realized they wouldn't respond to her pleading, she stopped and soaked the feelings in, like sunshine on a cold day, back in the village. There wasn't much else. The room didn't have a stick of furniture in it, and her back ached constantly. She comforted herself with the knowledge that there was softness and warmth for her baby, he had what he needed. She drove panic about the future down.

There was one other bright point in her capture and imprisonment, and it was a servant. Servants came to bring food, or clean the room, or take away Mesu's dirty diaper cloths and bring her new ones. At first she tried to speak to these people, but most were surly and tight-lipped. Some seemed afraid. They wouldn't speak to her. So she became silent. But there was one servant, one man who spoke to her. He was a sweeper.

The first time he had come was three days after she arrived. The room was dirty then, so when she saw him come in with his bucket of water and broom, she was glad. His appearance alarmed her; he was so tall, taller than anyone she had ever seen, with long black hair tied in a braid, and skin the color of tea with a tiny bit of milk. When he turned his head, she saw that he had tiny gold rings in his ears. She stared, which was rude, but he didn't seem to mind, and he smiled at her.

She turned her attention to her baby, rattled by him. Maybe it was the smile. No one else had smiled at her. Or maybe it was that nothing about him seemed servant-like. The others had been almost transparent with servility.

"How old is he?" the man asked, and she jumped at the sound of his voice. He spoke from his throat, and his accent was thick and curved.

She counted. "A little more than four turns of the moon," she said.

"So happy," the man said, carefully sweeping the dust from the corners of the room.

Mesu gurgled and played with Jerutha's hair. Yes, he was happy. His eyes were wider now, turning a brilliant blue. His shock of reddish brown hair curled up from his head with a life of its own. He was the most beautiful thing she had ever seen, but it felt strangely wonderful for someone else to notice him, say something kind about him. It made her feel less alone.

It was all the man said. He finished cleaning and left. The days passed, Jerutha dreamed beautiful dreams, and sometimes one of the large birds from her dreams came and sat at her window, making the atmosphere in her prison lighter but refusing to talk to her.

Three days later the man came again, and this time, when he was finished with his cleaning, he gave her an orange, pulling it from the pocket of his robe and offering it on the palm of his hand with a small bow. She took it so quickly, she almost snatched it from him. Oranges were a rare treat in the Worker village, only available for a very short season. Her mouth watered as she remembered the flavor; bright and juicy, like a day outside.

The servant bowed again, then left the room, closing the door behind him. Jerutha sat against the wall and peeled her orange. The room was transformed by the smell of the oils in the peel. She ate the orange, piece by piece, then lay down and slept, though it was midday. She dreamed of home, and of Isika, back in the garden, whole and free.

That afternoon there were two birds at her window. She gazed up at them, then spoke, though she knew it was no use.

"Tell her not to come," she said. They flapped their wings, clicking at her, but didn't reply. After a few more moments, they flew away. She wondered if she had only dreamed that the bird had spoken to her. That would be good, because perhaps it wouldn't be able to tell Isika to come to this horrible place.

Three days later, there was a scraping sound at her door and when it opened, two servants carried a heavy mattress, red-faced with the effort. One was the tall servant with the long braid. She watched, open-mouthed, as they hauled it over to the corner and set it down. Soon after, a small woman in a gray dress fitted sheets over the mattress and laid a small pillow on it.

They left, the tall man bowing once again. Jerutha stood, stiff and aching as usual, and laid her sleeping baby on the bed. As she stood without him in her arms for the first time in days, she felt so light that she could skip. So she did. A couple practice skips around the room, and then she whirled, arms out, till she was dizzy.

The door opened. She turned, hoping it was the man, hoping he was truly responsible for this, but three priests walked into the room, the tall priest, another of the priests from the desert, and one she had never seen. The new priest wore black robes edged in red. His face was pale and stern, and she reflexively cringed away from him, ducking over to the bed in the corner and sitting in front of Mesu to keep him out of sight.

The priest with the red-edged robes stared at the mattress.

"What is this?" he asked. His voice was smooth and cultured, but Jerutha hated it immediately. "I gave no instructions for a bed. Where did this come from?"

Jerutha couldn't explain the sudden relief at the fact that

the unexpected kindness hadn't come from the priests. She wanted it to be pure, somehow, without double intent.

The priest seemed to be asking her. She cleared her voice and spoke, unsure if sound would actually come out. Her stomach was tight with fear.

"I don't know," she said. "They brought it today."

"Probably some confusion with the palace staff, your eminence," said the shorter priest, the only one who had ever shown Jerutha even the tiniest bit of understanding in the desert. She took comfort in his presence. "It's probably better. We don't want the boy to get sick from the cold floor."

Jerutha looked at him then, meeting his eyes for the briefest moment, and she couldn't say quite what she saw there, but it was unexpected.

She waited for them to tell her what they wanted, but they continued to speak to each other as though she wasn't there.

"She's unimpressive. Do you think the girl will even bother?" the priest with the red-edged robes said, but he answered his own question. "But who knows why the weak do what they do? Dragged around by their foolish concepts of loyalty and *love*. She'll come."

"And what will you do with this one after?" the tall priest gestured to Jerutha with his foot.

Her face burned with the indignity of being discussed like a mule or a piece of rug. *I'm right here!* she wanted to say. But she didn't want to draw attention to herself. Or Mesu. So she kept silent. *I may be a fisherman's daughter,* she wanted to say, *but no one has ever treated me this way before.*

I don't think I deserve it. She felt better, after saying it in her mind.

She felt the head priest—for that was what he must be—eying her for a long moment.

"She's devout enough, I'm sure. She was married to that weak old priest, anyway. She'll do for a lower wife. We'll leave the baby with her for a while, then maybe she'll have more."

Jerutha bit her lip to keep from shouting at him. Disgusting man, did he really think she would ever marry him? She looked up briefly, then back down at Mesu, determined to be invisible, until... what? What could she do? How could she get away?

They muttered for a few more moments, then left without saying a word. Jerutha lay down beside her baby and sobbed into her hands. Many minutes passed before she was able to stop crying. She wiped tears away from her eyes and cheeks and chin, taking long, deep breaths. If she waited for Isika to come, the priests would have Isika in their trap. But if Isika didn't come, Jerutha would be forced into a life she couldn't bear. There was no way out.

She sat up as the door opened again. If it was the priests, this time she would not be invisible. This time she would scream and scream. But it was the man who had given her the orange. After the pale, angry faces of the priests, his tea-colored skin glowed in the white room. He held his usual bucket and broom, but he also held out a folded piece of cloth that unraveled to become a clean dress, the same gray dress of the servants.

"I will take you to the bathing room," he said. She must have flinched, because he added, "It will be private. I will wait for you outside."

He led the way to the bathing room and gestured for her to go ahead. She went in, locking the door behind her, and lay Mesu on a little nest of towels she made on the floor. She quickly bathed in the warm water from the pipes in the middle of the room, scrubbing herself raw to get the feel of the desert off her skin. She washed her hair, as well, with soap she found on a small table in the corner of the room. And there was hair oil, which she pulled through her tangled hair and rinsed out afterward. She felt like herself again, when she was through, though the gray dress was unfamiliar. Mesu was fussing in the nest of towels so she picked him up, scanning the room for possible escape routes. Nothing. There was one high window, much like the one in her room, barred and entirely too small.

There was a mirror. If she was weak, like her mother, if she didn't mind leaving her child, she could break it, end her life. But she looked at Mesu and knew she would never, ever leave him.

The man waited outside the room, and when she emerged, he nodded and walked back with her. She stared longingly down the hallway, measuring the distance she could run before he caught her. Probably two steps, she thought, looking at him again. He towered over her, and besides, she was still weak from her journey. They went back into her prison room and she sat cross-legged on the bed while he began to sweep.

"Help me," she said, surprising herself. "Help me escape."

He glanced at her once, his eyebrows high. His eyes became sad.

"I cannot," he said. "I am sorry."

She didn't ask him again. Before he left, he put a hand in a pocket of his clothes and brought out a tiny paper package, offering it to her with a bow, like he had the orange. She took it and held it as he left the room, and when she opened the parcel, she found nuts and figs. She ate them all, bite by bite, making them last as long as she could.

The birds came.

"Tell her not to come," Jerutha said, once again driving away her only hope.

20

Ben heard the city before he saw it.

"Isika," he called, his voice sharp, but a crippling sense of doom overwhelmed him, and he couldn't go on. He curled half over on his horse, holding his ribcage. Wave after wave of discordant sound pushed into his thoughts, tapping on his senses, pulling him apart, until he was a horrified, shaking witness, locked inside while he watched himself unravel. This was too big. He couldn't fight the horror he was hearing, the shrieking, grating, terrifying music.

He was only vaguely aware of Isika riding alongside and reaching over to stop his horse. Somehow he slid down onto the sand and collapsed on his side, curling his legs up and hugging them. He tried to block the sounds, but everything went fuzzy at the edges, then black...

When he came back to himself, he heard singing, but not inside; inside was quiet for the moment. The voice he heard was Isika's. She was singing one of the songs of the Maweel, and she was doing it wrong. He tried to tell her the notes were out of order, but his mouth was full of sand and he couldn't get his throat to work. He waited a moment longer, trying to pull himself together enough to tell her the right way to sing the song, and then he realized that her hand was on his shoulder. It was so quiet in his head. The only thing he could hear was the song of her magic. She was holding the horror of the city away from him.

He sat up slowly, and she moved so her hand stayed on his shoulder. They sat there like that, side by side, facing a dim, distant shadow that he knew must be the city.

She stopped singing. He sighed.

"That bad?" she asked.

"That bad. I think this is way beyond the poison we're used to, Isika."

She got the flinty look that meant she was ready to argue.

"All the more reason we need to go," she said. But then her face softened. "But first, Ben, you need to pull it together. You can't collapse like that again."

"What use is this gift?" he asked, his voice bitter.

Isika sat for a while, her chin in the hand that wasn't holding him together.

"I can see a lot of power in it," she said finally, "if you can learn to use it without being sat upon by it." Ben couldn't help smiling. He looked up and saw Keethior and the Keerza standing a few feet away, forming a loose circle around the two of them. He took a deep breath.

"Okay," he said. "Ease your hand away from me, I'm going to practice."

Slowly, bit by bit, she lifted her hand. A thousand shrieking voices broke into Ben's mind, drums beating a wrong, dangerous rhythm, teeth grinding and crying, wrong notes. Pain stabbed his temples and tears flooded his eyes. Keethior flew over to stand in front of Ben, huge, flapping his wings gently.

"You have learned about the curtain, right?" the bird said, his voice faint through the noise. "This is bigger. It needs a door. Form a room in your mind and send it to the room. All of it."

Ivram had told Ben about the room: a place where he could send the warnings his gift was perceiving, shut them away, so he wouldn't be incapacitated. He had been progressing in lessons about shutting a curtain on the small life songs he heard all around him every day, the small petty grievances and wrongs, but this was different, a mountain of sadness, sickness, oppression. How could he take in so much evil committed against many thousands of people? This mountain would collapse on him, smother him.

"How am I supposed to do that?" he gasped, nearly sobbing.

"You can do it Ben," his sister said. "I know it."

He took a shaky breath and focused on constructing the room: strong walls, jars for sadness to pour into, basins and beds and curtains for the windows. He gasped; the room was taking shape, it was working. He pushed the sounds—the yelling and growling and horrible music—into the room, and leaned on the door with all his might until the door was shut. There was sudden quiet. He sat with his head down on his knees, panting with the effort.

"Good," Keethior said. "When the Great Waste makes itself known to you, push its presence into the room. Keep your mind clear."

The bird opened and closed his giant wings. He was taller than the two of them as they sat on the ground.

"It is a good gift, young one, an ancient one not known by many from the beginning of the world. The World Whisperer is right, for you cannot be fooled by smooth words or false promises. But if you cannot control it, you will go insane. It is good that you came to Azariyah, young one. You need their guidance. I have only met one other person like this. Your grandmother's father's grandfather." He cocked his head and peered at them with one eye, suddenly looking so much like a common bird that Ben held back a laugh. Isika smiled as well.

"Two things, Keethior. One, do you think you can call me by my name? It's Isika, not World Whisperer. We're friends, right? And two, how old are you, anyway?"

The bird made an Othra snort. "Old enough, World Whisperer."

Ben looked toward the distant city. "I'm about to get a lot of practice controlling my 'gift,' if I can sense the Great Waste from this far away."

"We can barely see the walls!" Isika said. "Why is the poison affecting him like this?"

Keethior flapped his wings open again, blowing grains of

sand into the air. Ben blew sand away. "The city is full of evil, unchecked by any power but a stronger man's greed. Of course there are many good people there, but they are usually preyed on by those who have no desire for good. It is power and power alone that rules this city. You will need to be careful, children."

"Aren't you coming?" Isika asked.

"We will be near, but soon we can go no farther. We will not be able to blend into the city, where there are no beings like us and the animals are poorly treated. Your healthy horses would give too much away also. Let's walk now. We'll show you the place where you need to leave us."

THEY REMOUNTED. Ben kept careful control of his mind, holding the door to the room shut tightly. He could still hear and feel, faintly, the clamor of the room, but it was separated from him, fuzzy and indistinct; it didn't take over. The desert changed to a straggly forest of losh trees, their tall black branches lacing patterns of shadow on the ground as the sun came up. Ben could not believe they were still walking the horses toward the horrible city; going to it, rather than running away.

When he thought of his stepmother in there, though, in that Great Waste, alone and maybe hurt, he set his face and didn't question his sister.

He looked at her. She was quiet and focused, sitting tall on Wind, like the queen she really was. They came to a small copse where the trees were thicker. A few round-leaved trees gave good shade. Isika dismounted and quickly knelt and put her face on the ground, calling up a small spring. She stood, after drinking, gesturing for him to drink as well. The horses pulled at the leaves on the low hanging branches. The Keerza settled in loose ring, and a low, lovely hum came from them.

"The horses like these trees," Isika said. "They can wait here."

Ben understood that there had been some kind of unheard communication between her and Keethior or perhaps the Keerza or the horses. He felt the lost, unmoored feeling he got when he realized he was on the outside of a conversation. It didn't matter though, because Isika was settling her satchel over one shoulder and her bow and arrows over the other.

"In Batta the people wrap their faces often, especially travelers or traders. You can use it to blend in," Keethior said.

"We'll need to use our cloaks as well," Isika said. Ben untied his cloth and rewrapped his face, tucking the ends of his *ser* under each other. He then pulled his long, brown cloak out of his satchel. It was made of fine, strong material that rolled up tightly, keeping him warm at night, but cool and breezy in the sun. He looked at the cloth for a moment. A lot of shaping magic had gone into it, from one of the cloth masters in Azariyah. He would have to ask Uncle which one, if they got back. He thought about the possibility of not making it back, and swallowed hard, throwing the cloak around his shoulders and pulling up his hood. He turned and looked at Isika. They were mirrors of each other. She was also draped in a cloak, though hers was midnight blue. Her face was wrapped so he could barely recognize her. He smiled under his *ser*.

"Who are we supposed to be?" he asked Keethior.

"Pilgrims, come to worship at the temple," the Othra replied. "In Batta there are many pilgrims who come from faraway lands. You won't seem out of place."

Ben frowned. He didn't want to go anywhere near the temple. But of course that was where they were headed. Jerutha had been taken by priests. He sighed.

"Will they let us through the city gate?" he asked.

The bird's feathers trembled, and Ben realized he was laughing. "Yes. You'll see. This isn't like your Worker village."

Ben had more questions. Why hadn't they ever met another priest, in the Worker village? Why all the secrecy? Nirloth had given him hints, but who decided what Nirloth should tell?

Isika looked at him. "Ready?" she asked.

He nodded, putting his questions aside for now. It wasn't the right time.

Before they could walk away, though, the Keerza circled them and came very close, touching Ben and Isika's arms and shoulders with their noses. A wild, haunting music sprang from them, though it was muffled behind the door in Ben's mind. He stood perfectly still as wave after wave of encouragement and peace washed over him. When at last, the Keerza backed away, he felt as though he had slept soundly, in his bed at home. Everything looked brighter and more beautiful.

"They say they can only give this gift for now," Isika murmured. Her eyes behind her *ser* were bright.

"Thank you," Ben said to the graceful animals. Even behind the door in his mind, the pressure had lessened with their presence.

They set off, giving one last glance to the little stand of trees and the horses and Keerza waiting there. They trudged across the loose sand, trying to march on a surface that slid sideways underneath them. The sun was rising, the sand was heating up in the morning light. Ben had to admit that the great expanse of the desert was beautiful in a way that was totally different from the beauty of the forests and mountains around Azariyah.

Once they were away from the Keerza, the feeling of well being left, though he was still more energized than he had been. In the room in his mind, the voices screamed at one another, drums beating wildly as they approached the gates of the City. His heart sped up until it seemed it would shake him apart. It was a terrible idea to walk toward the place that filled his head with screaming, rather than running in the opposite direction. His was a warning gift. But they were not heeding the warning.

Jerutha, Ben thought, as the gates became more clear. He kept putting one foot in front of the other, though his mind screamed at him to leave. He said her name over and over in his head. *Jerutha*, and a step, *Jerutha*, and another step.

It wasn't long before they were near the city gate and Ben saw why Keethior had laughed at him. A steady stream of people moved through the gates, without anyone watching all that carefully. Ben and Isika would be able to wander right through. Isika reached out and grabbed Ben's hand, and she didn't let go. Hand in hand, they joined the mass of people trying to get into the city and out of the brilliant, deadly sun. The sand was hot underfoot, scorching even through the soft leather of Ben's boots.

He tried to look at the people around him without staring, darting quick glances from under his hood. There were pale-skinned Workers in the clothes he was accustomed to: the long dresses and jackets that covered them from head to toe. There were people with light brown skin and long black hair, braided, like Deto's. They wore straight-brimmed hats with bright ribbons wound around the crown. Their clothes were loose and robe-like, with wide pants similar to the Maweel, but less colorful and with more embroidery.

Ben realized that despite his efforts, he was staring, when a woman with braided hair and rings in her ears looked at him, then made a dreadful face, contorting her mouth so she looked like a monster. He looked away quickly as her friend laughed. In the opposite direction, he noted with alarm, six people stood, chained together. He stepped closer to Isika, a flash of fear moving through him even as the voices behind the door shrieked louder. This was some great evil. A man held an end of the chain in one hand, and a whip in the other. He grunted at the people to go forward, then shouted when they didn't respond.

"Move up or I'll make you move," he shouted. They shuffled ahead, the chain pulling and relaxing as they attempted to move together. The slaves, or prisoners, or whatever they were, all looked different. There were two old people, with skin as papery and white as Nirloth's had been before he died. And there were two small children with black skin. They looked the way Isika and Benayeem had looked as children, holding hands, their heads down. Ben drew in a breath. His throat was tight.

The two last people stood straight and tall, gazing around fearlessly, occasionally glancing at the man who held the chain. They looked at him with pure hatred, as though they would kill him if they could. One was a man and one a woman: they had jet black hair and piercing, deep-set eyes. Their skin was the color of sand, and they had chiseled faces. The way their eyes glittered when they looked around reminded Ben of the young hawks in Azariyah's rookery.

Ben was fascinated, caught between wonder and fear. The woman saw him staring and winked at him. When she shifted from one foot to another, Ben saw a glint of silver in her closed fist.

Just then, one of the children stumbled and fell. The man with the whip was beside the child in a second, hitting her with the blunt end of the whip. There were yells and Benayeem found himself running toward him, but the woman with the hawk-like face got there first and the glint in her fist flashed out into the open air: a knife.

She stabbed at the man holding the whip, the knife a whir of light in the bright sun. The man fell, heavily, and within seconds, he was dead or dying on the ground. There was blood everywhere. Each of the chained hawk people scooped up one of the black-skinned children, the woman put the knife in her waistband and hissed at the old people, who stood slack-jawed.

"Run!" she said. Her accent was thick and curved, her eyes deadly. The old man and woman seemed to wake up and the four of them ran, carrying the children, chains clinking, away from the gate and into the forest.

21

The guards at the gate tried to get to the runaway slaves but the mass of people closed in and suddenly no one knew enough to get out of the way. Ben wouldn't have believed that people chained with heavy iron could run so fast, but they were among the trees, out of sight within minutes.

A guard finally pushed his way out. He looked at the dead man on the ground, then scowled at the surrounding crowd.

"You saw what happened. Where did they go?"

Somehow, no one had seen the slaves go, people looked back at him with blank faces, refusing to answer. He frowned and sighed, then shook his head, shrugging.

"Good riddance," he said. "Filthy foreign slaves." His gaze landed on Isika, and he jabbed a finger at her.

"Pull your cloak back!" he barked. "Show your face!"

Ben's heart sped up as Isika pulled her cloak back, but her

ser revealed only her eyes. The guard's own eyes narrowed as he saw the strip of black skin that was showing.

"Pilgrims from the Desert City?" he asked, glancing at Ben.

The Desert City? Ben pushed hard on the door so it wouldn't pop open with the force of the horrible music that pulsed at the name, unknown and familiar at the same time.

Isika nodded. "Making an offering on behalf of our master," she said, and the guard grunted, satisfied.

"This temple sees a lot of pilgrims," he said. "Better get through before there's more trouble."

They glanced at each other, then scurried through the gates, leaving the crowd and other guards to deal with the body of the slave-driver.

Ben followed Isika as she ran through the streets toward the towering shape of the temple. They whirled into a narrow alleyway and she stopped, pulling back her cloak and unwinding the cloth around her face. Ben put his hands on his knees, feeling as though he would throw up. He kept seeing the man hitting the little girl, then the man's blood, so much red running into the sand. He took deep breaths and heard Isika panting beside him.

"This is a horrible place," she said at last. "People owning each other."

"Were those Maweel children?" Ben asked. "What were they doing here?"

"Remember the sea people? They steal children from villages for the Desert King. Maybe those were children that they had stolen and sold." They were silent, and the bleakness that fell over Ben felt thick, as though light couldn't cut through.

"Have you ever seen anyone who looked like the woman who killed that man?" he asked eventually. "She wasn't from Maween or the Worker village."

Isika stared at the alley wall, her face blank. The music coming from her sounded like fear. She looked over her shoulder every so often to make sure no one had followed them.

"Yes," she said. "In Azariyah. One of the apprentices at the pottery workshop was rescued from a gang of slave sellers from the Desert City. He looked like that woman. They're called Gariah. The Desert people. They're fierce and strong, and Tomas said they used to be artisans who made things more beautiful than anyone in any kingdom could imagine, but their king has taken everything from them. His father is the one who took our grandmother, Ben."

Ben stared at her, his body ringing with horror. "I remember," he said. "I think we used to live in the Desert City, Isika," he whispered. "Before our mother took us away. When we were very small."

He watched as Isika's face closed, slowly, he could almost watch it shutting him away.

"Let's go," she said sharply, and fear was stronger in her music. They turned to look down the narrow alley. The temple rose up, a white hulk of a building, sharp cornered and tall. It was still far off, but wouldn't be hard to find. Ben imagined you would be able to see it from anywhere in the city.

They walked along the alley. Now that his stomach had calmed down, Ben could look around and take in their surroundings. The buildings were all made of sandstone. They were tall and sometimes crooked, with roofs made of interwoven branches or sometimes metal. Homes were close together, squashed-looking, and Ben could hear people quarreling inside. A gutter ran along the street, emitting a stench that hit them in the face mercilessly. As they rounded a corner, they saw an old man squatting and relieving himself. He cackled at them as they passed, his toothless mouth agape. Ben looked away quickly, making sure to shove the dissonant noises back in his mind. The noises sounded like madness.

They came out into a large market square and looked around with curiosity. In every direction, people shouted and haggled. There were colorful cloths draped over one stall, oranges stacked high on another. The mass of things, colors, and people was overwhelming. Ben felt a rumble of hunger, but they couldn't risk being noticed, so he put his head down as they hurried past the roasting meat. He breathed in deeply, missing Auntie's table.

They needed to find Jerutha and bring her home.

They drew closer to the palace, leaving the market square and finding themselves in a narrower alley than before. At the end of it, Ben saw the temple walls rising up, pure white marble with no windows on the outside walls. They stopped. Ben glanced at his sister and saw that she was staring as well, biting her lower lip. She walked on again, Ben following, and turned at the end of the alley. The temple complex rose like a mountain out of the city, a mass of towers and sheer, unscalable walls.

Stalls selling food and goods surrounded the temple and after a moment of gaping, Isika turned to Ben.

"It's a bit much, isn't it? These priests must be rich." Around them the chaos and filth of the city roiled and buzzed, contrasted sharply by the walled-in grandeur of the temple.

Isika walked toward a tomato cart. Ben couldn't think why she chose that cart except that Faiza sold tomatoes and Isika might be heading for the person who reminded her most of a friend. This tomato seller was no relative of Faiza's, though, because when Isika started to ask a question, he spit on the ground and told her to go ask questions of someone who had time to talk to dirty foreigners.

She turned back to Ben, making a face.

"We need to find someone who will give us information about the temple and how we can get in," she said. She looked at him. He could see the wheels turning in her mind.

"What?" he asked, suspicious.

"Can you isolate your gift and hear what one person sounds like?" she asked.

He understood her meaning immediately, and thought about it, surprised. It was a strange idea.

His gift had always been so frustrating. The great grandfather of the queen who was the last known person who had it hadn't left any instructions. Could using it actually be so simple?

"Put your hand on my arm again," he said. She did, and in

the quiet, he opened up the room in his mind. This time he could hear only her, and he realized that she held back the cacophony of the city with her own quiet music, something like stringed instruments, deep and rich and a little sad.

"I might be able to do it," he said.

He shoved everything back into the room in his mind, to separate it from him, then moved away from Isika's hand and turned toward the market sellers. He looked at the tomato seller and carefully opened the door a tiny crack, focusing on the man. Sure enough, he heard what he realized was the sound of the man's thoughts and feelings. Harsh, discordant, sad, suspicious. Not him.

He needed to find someone who might talk to them. Next he looked at a woman selling fruit, straining to hear her, but she sounded disappointed, sad, and closed. He heard wailing in her music. He frowned, flinching. This was hard. Next was a cloth seller he shut out very quickly, disturbed by the anger and sickness in his music.

He turned again to a woman selling fresh vegetables. She looked old and tired, so he nearly skipped over her, but when he paused to listen, he heard horns and strings, mixed with bright drums. The music coming from her was a song of sadness mixed with small glimmers of beauty.

"Her," he breathed to Isika, and she nodded, then walked toward the woman. Ben held his breath as he followed her, wondering if the gift would come through, do something good for once.

"Sister, I'm wondering if you know anything about how pilgrims might get into the palace," Isika said to the woman, who was busy rearranging her meager selection of vegetables. The woman had skin that was tanned and wrinkled. When she looked up at Isika, her eyes were brilliant blue in her face.

"Pilgrims, are you?" the woman muttered. "You can get into the temple in the same way as the others. Up through the main gate. They'll only let you in the front courtyard for the briefest of seconds, though. And you need to give money for the priests."

Isika and Ben looked at each other, dismayed. They needed to get farther in, all the way to the head priest's living space, where Jerutha might be.

"Is there any way to see the high priest?" Isika asked. "We need to make a petition. We're desperate."

She did look desperate, Ben thought, watching her plead with the seller. The woman looked at her more closely.

"They do make it hard to do the normal things," she said, tutting.

"In my village," she said, her voice low, "there wasn't all this fuss around seeing the priest. But the king has made it very hard. And if you ask me," she said, and leaning close, she finished her thought with a whisper, "the priest is the king's puppet."

"The king?" Ben asked. "Do you mean the Desert King?"

The woman looked at him as though he was crazy, blinking rapidly. "Of course. What other king is there? Unless you go across the sea, of course."

"But here? He rules here?"

"Of course, since the war twenty years ago. Where are

you from, anyway? You didn't know that the Desert King rules over the Worker city? Goodness, child."

"They didn't tell us in my village."

"Oh, a villager. Well, then, that's to be expected. They do keep it secret from the villages. Eventually, though, when they have soldiers to watch every village, everyone will know."

Ben shook his head, this information scrambling everything he had ever known about the Worker village. He didn't like any of it. He wanted to go back to Azariyah, to get out of this horrible place. But the woman was speaking again.

"I like you two, and I want you to be able to make your petition. All people are supposed to be able to make a petition to the goddesses. That is the way, even I know that, though I'm a silly old woman. I'm supposed to make a delivery to the temple kitchens, but I'll send you instead. Here, I'll write you a note. I'm friends with one of the guards. I let him take from my gardens for free, and he doesn't charge me for deliveries. We all know where that money goes. Straight to the guards' pockets, that's where. As though they don't have sufficient pay already."

"You grow all this?" Ben asked. What had seemed scarce looked bountiful, if she had grown it with her own hands.

"Yes." She said. She loaded a sack with several bunches of salad greens and spinach, as well as some herbs that Ben didn't recognize. He could place her music now. It was the music of the tired earth. It seemed to be waiting. The vegetable seller had her hands in the dirt. Perhaps it kept her mind hopeful.

She handed him the sack. "Okay, go that way, pilgrims," she said, pointing. "At the end of the wall, turn left and walk to the back wall door."

"Thank you. May your eyes be guarded," Isika said.

"And your soul kept safe," the woman answered. They had taken about a dozen steps when Isika turned to Ben and grabbed his arm, grinning at him, her eyes sparkling.

"We found a use for your gift!" she said.

He thought about that. It was true. He smiled at her, his heart growing lighter. His gift had helped them and maybe it would turn out to be useful after all. Useful for drawing them closer to danger, he thought then, wryly. But Isika kept her arm tucked in his as they walked and his smile didn't falter.

22

They carried the sacks of vegetables on their heads, in the way of market sellers. Isika felt herself sway with exhaustion as they walked down the alley, spotting the door the woman had described.

"Can you tell if one of the guards is friendly?" she asked her brother in a whisper.

He frowned at the four guards, concentrating.

"None of them are friendly," he said, after a moment. "But that one is the least angry." He used his chin to gesture at a man who was as thick and tall as a tree, with enormous hands and a huge brown beard. His eyes were like pieces of coal in his pale face.

Isika took a shaky breath. "Are you sure?" she asked. He was the last guard she would have picked.

"As sure as I can be, trying to gauge people by the music only I can hear," he said dryly, and she smiled at him. Their lives had turned very strange very quickly.

"Okay," she said. "I trust you."

They walked to the man, handing him the note from the vegetable seller. His eyebrows rose as his eyes ran down the page, and he glanced at them before turning back to the note.

"The old woman's back troubling her again, eh?" he remarked, his voice mild. He stepped back and jerked his chin toward the door. "Go on then. Be quick about it."

Another man, this one thin with a sweet face, stepped forward.

"What? Are you sure, Griffin?" His voice was flinty. He was the one Isika would have picked. She would have been wrong.

"Yeah, yeah, it's fine." The big man said, waving him off. "I've known Essa all my life." Isika looked at him one last time as they passed, and was shocked when he gave her a tiny wink. This was a strange place to find an ally.

They walked up the steps, the vegetables still on their heads. Walking through the door, they entered the solid white walls of the compound and found the richest world they had ever seen. It was the size of a city, laid out on a square with the grand temple on one side. The temple was massive, built with the same white marble walls and gold trim, and a gold, flat roof. Straight ahead was another building, even more opulent, with gems laid into the walls themselves, swirls of reds and greens, trimmed in gold. There were large square windows and open doors. Isika could see hallways and rooms inside.

Someone bumped into her from behind.

"Oy, merchants!" she heard a voice say. "If you're looking

for the priests' kitchens, they're that way." She turned to see a skinny arm gesturing toward the large, gem encrusted building before them, and the person whirled off in another direction.

Isika looked at Ben. He shrugged, so she started toward the colorful building, which she supposed was the head priest's house.

"It's so colorful," she said to her brother under her breath as they crossed the threshold into the grand building. They walked toward the smell of food frying and what sounded like cooks yelling.

"It is," Ben agreed. "But it feels horrible, and the sounds are from nightmares."

"I can't help thinking all the money the Workers gave to the goddesses in our village found its way here. Did Nirloth know about this place?" she asked, but even as she wondered, she knew. She remembered the pilgrimages he made, to pray in the desert, he told them. But why so much secrecy? Why would it be kept from the Workers in the village?

"He did," Benayeem said, confirming what she already knew. "But I had no idea it was like this."

They arrived at the kitchens: huge rooms that bustled with people scurrying around, wearing the standard dress of the Workers, but in a deep shade of gray, like a uniform. A short woman came and took the sacks of vegetables from them, then put a piece of bread in each of their hands and shooed them away. They didn't ask questions, just ate the bread, which was soft and buttery, nothing like the thin porridge that was the staple of the Worker village. Isika raised her eyebrows and looked at Ben again, full of questions.

"We need to focus, Isika," he told her. "We can't solve every mystery. Let's just find Jerutha, then leave this place forever."

His eyes were large and fearful as he scanned the hallway. Isika didn't sense danger the same way he did—to her the place seemed sleepy and busy all at once, but not something to fear. The buildings felt dead and cold, not alive the way buildings in Azariyah did, sighing in response when she walked through them. She noticed a guard staring at them.

"We'd better walk," she said. "Try to look as though you know where you're going."

They turned and walked away from the guard, deeper into the house of the priest. The walls were tall, sheer marble, cold to the touch, with torches lighting the way to the high roof.

"Where would Jerutha be?" Isika asked.

"In this building somewhere, surely," he answered. "Didn't she say in her message that she was being taken to be the wife of the head priest? They would keep her here."

Isika felt a rush of fear. What if they had forced her to marry him already? But then she remembered the appropriate mourning time. The head priest wouldn't marry her until three months had passed. Maybe they weren't too late. As long as he followed the rules.

They walked and walked, deeper and deeper into a maze of hallways. Through doorways they saw people cleaning, washing walls or floors. Everyone seemed to be a servant or a guard. They didn't see anyone in the black robes of the priests, and it struck Isika as odd. Ben was still wild-eyed and jumpy as they walked deeper into the palace—it couldn't be called anything else—winding their way farther and farther in. Isika started to feel frightened as well, for though she couldn't hear the undercurrents of the palace, she could sense that it seemed unnaturally still, that it was strange not to come across a priest.

She remembered the words of the Keerza: *"You are sought and you will be trapped if you go in there."* But they needed to find Jerutha. She wished for Keethior or Jabari with a sudden longing that made her catch her breath. Just being World Whisperer didn't make her smart enough for this.

She heard something that made her jump.

"What is that?" she asked, gripping Ben's arm.

"You hear it too?" he asked, and she nodded, concentrating on the faint sound.

"It's a baby crying," she said. "They're this way." She pointed down a long hallway that was arched overhead, edged in gold trim where the walls met the ceiling. It was fancier than the other hallways and she realized that these were the rooms of the head priest. Terror washed over her like cold water at the idea of walking any closer to him, but the baby wailed again, and she took a deep breath, grabbed Ben's hand and plowed forward.

They walked toward the sound, hand in hand, turning at the end of the hallway. Up ahead, the hallway ended, turning to the right, and it sounded like the baby was just around that curve. Isika walked quickly forward. Ben said, "Isika! No, we

—" but before he finished, three priests, dressed in black, turned the corner and walked toward them, taking up the hallway so there was no space to go by.

Isika and Ben turned and ran the other way, but three more priests appeared. It was as the Keerza had said. They were trapped. Isika tried to calm her heart, which beat as wildly as a bird's, as the priests came slowly toward them, stopping when they were only an arm's distance away. She bit back a whimper.

They were all men of different heights and ages. There were two that were quite old, and four that were middle aged, not yet white-haired. Isika felt faint, and beside her, she felt Ben sinking, losing his battle with his mind and the sounds. She squeezed his hand hard, putting her thoughts toward calming him, and he straightened. One man with hair like straw, and a long, pointed nose, spoke.

"The head priest was right," he said. "She did come straight to us."

"Of course he was right," another man replied. This one had thick eyebrows, no hair, and a scowl on his face, his hands clenched into fists. Isika was instantly terrified of him. "He is always right, let him live forever." He smiled, and it was horrible, Isika wished he would stop. "It is a strange thing, *loyalty*." He sneered. "Leading people into places where they are in the most danger."

"Yes, how odd," another man said in a high, thin voice. "It brought the downfall of their *stepfather* as well. Loyalty to the foreign witch."

Isika had to break in. She couldn't stand there and listen to them any longer. "Well?" she demanded. "What now?"

"What now?" the man with the high, thin voice, repeated. "You never leave this building again, that's what now. The king wants you here, where he can watch you, forever."

"What king?" Isika shrieked, but Ben turned and ran, dragging Isika with him. He tried to barrel through the space between two of the shorter men, but they closed in quickly, and the big man with the horrible smile reached out and hit Ben on the side of the head, hard, so that Ben fell, his hand leaving Isika's abruptly. He crumpled and didn't get up.

Isika roared and flew at the man, hitting at him, and he slapped her, hard. Pain. She saw lights and nearly fell, but she pushed forward, trying to reach him as he grabbed her and held her arm behind her back until it hurt so badly that she froze.

"You're a bully," she spat at him. "Hitting a child."

"I would never hit a child," he said, smiling his horrible smile again. "A demon, though, is another matter."

He started walking, pulling her alongside. Two men picked Ben up and dragged him between them. Isika didn't know if it was the blow or his gift that had incapacitated him, but as she twisted to try to see her brother, the man gave her arm a savage twist, and she cried out in pain. She couldn't break away and run again, not while Ben was unconscious, so she walked, head down, tears of pain streaming from her eyes. Trapped. She felt panic rising and breathed to calm herself down.

"Arl, tell the head priest we have them," the big man said.

They came to a open door and Isika was pushed in quickly, Ben tossed in afterward, like a sack. The room was a simple, square cube, with a torch in each corner, and one small, impossibly high window. The door slammed shut behind them. Isika fell on the door and pushed at it, beating it with her hands, but it didn't move. There was no handle, and the door was made of smooth marble, flush with the wall, so close that they were nearly one thing. She couldn't grip anything to pull. She slid down the wall, holding her head in her hands.

On the floor, Ben stirred. Isika jumped up and ran to him, gently touching his forehead. A large lump was already forming over his temple. She moved him so his head was at a more comfortable angle, and his eyes fluttered open.

He sat up. "We have to get out of here!" he gasped. "This place, Isika, I've never felt such evil."

"Shhh," she said. The sound of his voice echoed in the marble room, hurting her head, which she realized was also bruised from the man's heavy hand. "We have to think. We have to think."

Panic was just under the surface, but she needed to stay calm. Caught in this room, in the Worker city, oh, it was so terrible that she couldn't think about it, couldn't think of staying here.

"They said the king wanted us, why would they say that?" Ben asked.

Isika swiftly shook her head. "Which king? I don't understand. But never mind. We can't waste time thinking about their reasons. We need to get away, quickly!"

She stood and ran her hands over the door again, looking for a way to catch an edge of it, but there was barely a crack to put a fingernail into. She switched to the window, trying to climb the wall to get to it. She couldn't make it up the slippery wall, and she could see only a tiny piece of sky through the metal bars. A crow passed, and she gasped as an idea came to her.

"Keethior!" she exclaimed.

"Where?" asked Ben, who was sitting against the wall with his head in his hands. He winced as though speaking hurt.

"Nowhere, but I could try to call him."

"What could he do?" Ben asked.

"I don't know, but it's all I can think of."

Keethior. Please come. We need you.

Nothing. She paced, then tried again, focusing on the outside of the walls, imagining her mind flying, flying out of this prison and reaching all the way to the bird.

Keethior. Come to me. We are in need.

Silence. Then the sweetest sound. Keethior's voice in her mind. *Child? I told you I can't come into the Worker city. Did you already forget?*

She laughed under her breath with relief.

Keethior! They have caught us and put us in a room with no exit.

He didn't respond with words, but she felt a flood of indignation and scolding both for their captors and for them for being caught.

Yes, I know. Please come, and you can tell me all the

things I have done wrong.

There was a sound at the door and as she turned, it scraped open. She heard just the faintest sound of agreement from Keethior before she let go of her connection with the bird. She moved until she was standing over Ben, her hands in fists. Three people came into the room and shut the door behind them. One was obviously the head priest. He had the black robes of a priest, but edged in red, with a tall hat also edged in red. Then there was the man with the ugly smile, the one who had hit Ben and twisted her arm. And the third man wore white robes. He had a strange look on his face, almost as though he was listening. His eyes flashed onto hers.

"Were you speaking to someone?" he asked. His eyes were blue and angry. He had a slight lisp, and his voice was high and cold, like the priest Isika had noticed before. She briefly wondered whether they were related.

"Only to my brother," she said. She tilted her chin up and leaned forward, her hands in fists at her sides. "Let us go."

The head priest laughed lightly, his voice a soft tinkle. At her feet, Isika saw Ben cringe away from the sound. She placed a hand on his head, lightly, and some of the tension left his shoulders. He had to keep it together. She couldn't do this alone.

"Let you go," the head priest said. "That's very cute. For a demon, you're adorable."

"I'm not a demon."

"No? The king says you're a demon, therefore you are a demon. It is decreed. Helar, show the demon what happens to people who contradict the king."

The big man moved so swiftly that Isika couldn't even flinch away. A sudden blow on her cheek made her stumble and brought tears to her eyes. He wore rings. She raised a hand to her cheek and brought it away to stare at the blood on her fingers. Ben scrambled to his feet and stood beside her.

"There's no need to hurt her," he said. "You have us. What do you want? What do you have to do with the Desert King?"

Yes, Isika thought. What did he want with them?

"Only everything," the head priest said. "I don't know what he wants with two demon children, weak and pitiful as you are, but we are only his servants. We do as he says."

"What about Jerutha? You have our stepmother."

The head priest laughed again. "It is amazing, how predictable people are, even demons. The goddesses know all, they tell all. Jerutha is here, with her child. She will make a good wife, easily controlled by her emotions. We'll allow the baby to stay with her until he is weaned and then he will serve as a temple boy. Don't worry," he said, and his eyes flashed at Isika. She thought she might throw up. "They're perfectly safe. And you're here together forever. You will never see each other, but you'll always know she's here."

He turned to the white-robed man. "Show her."

The man took a step forward and stared at them, until everything faded from view and Isika was watching Jerutha, who sat on the ground in a tiny room that looked a lot like theirs, crying softly. She held her baby close and tried to sing through her tears. As the picture faded, Isika shook her head. It was horrible.

"You are a monster!" she shrieked. "Is that how you treat

your wives?"

He laughed. "No, I give my wives everything. But she was showing a lot of ... reluctance. She needs to learn first, and then she will be ready to serve in the highest capacity allowed to a child of the goddesses. The wife of the head priest! Most would be leaping at the prospect."

"You are nothing but evil," Isika said, nearly spitting in rage, "controlling a woman you want to be your wife! Jerutha will never love you."

The priest regarded her with heavy-lidded eyes for a moment, no longer laughing. Then a single word. "Helar," he said, quietly. Isika stood her ground as the big man came forward, but she fell on the fourth blow.

A WHILE LATER, she opened her eyes. They were alone again. She was crying, but as she came back to herself, she heard Ben singing softly. His pure voice was the most beautiful sound she had ever heard. It was deeper now than it had been when he was a child, but he could still reach the high notes. She closed her eyes and let the music wash over her. She hurt everywhere, and she lay with her eyes closed until she felt another presence.

She opened her eyes again, though they were so swollen she could barely see.

"Keethior!" she said, as she saw the bird sitting behind the bars at the window, looking down at her.

"Oh, young ones," the bird said, sighing. "How are we going to get you out?"

23

Jabari and the other seekers ran for six nights, stopping just before dawn each day to make camp where they could find shelter in small groves of trees or beside buildings. They found springs all along the way, small pools of crystal clear water that nearly glowed with the magic of the World Whisperer.

They hunted in the early morning, eating rabbit, snake, lizard, and edible cactus that Gavi carved and salted, until it was a salad worthy of a palace table, or so Jabari thought. He had to tie his pants a little tighter though. They didn't get huge amounts of food to eat and all the running was beginning to show.

On the sixth night, the landscape changed. There were losh trees in the spaces between cacti, and then the trees moved closer together and became groves, and then even a sparse forest. He stopped and everyone pattered to a halt around him, panting and walking in circles until their breathing slowed.

Jabari thought they were only a few days behind Isika. The springs were fresh, and they had found the remains of Ben and Isika's camp spots. He squinted into the distance as Gavi handed him a water flask. A smudge stretched across the horizon. The smudge could be city walls. Batta. He frowned. He could never have imagined that he would walk willingly into Batta.

They were so far outside Maweel that he was still shocked at himself for even considering coming here. But Isika was somewhere in that poisoned city. Deep within him, something had been changing, something strong and sure. He didn't only feel angry with her, though he did feel that, angry that she had put him in this position. But he had become aware, as he ran by spring after spring that she had called out of the earth, that his strongest sense of loyalty was for Isika, not his father. And it had nothing to do with anything he felt or did not feel for her.

She was the heir to the queen of the Maweel, the World Whisperer. As one of the Maweel, he was compelled to serve her with his life. And there was no longer any doubt in his mind that she was the World Whisperer. Keethior had come to her. And Jabari's own magic was strong, perhaps the strongest in generations, but even he couldn't call springs out of the desert.

The others began to lay out mats for sleeping. Aria didn't get winded as quickly as she had been at the beginning of the trip, though every day Gavi used his healing gift to take out the poison of the arrows in her spirit. One of the strengths the Maweel took pride in was the ability to run for long journeys, and the rescued ones had to learn it from the time that they were very small, so Gavi and Brigid could run as well as the others. Aria hadn't had as much practice, however. This trip was training her quickly.

"Not much longer now," Jabari said, pointing at the smudge in the distance. There was a chorus of weak cheers and sighs. The journey had been difficult, even for seekers of the Maweel. They were away from the healing air of their lands, for one thing, so every step took more effort, and they took longer to recover after a long run. They didn't feel sudden energy in the morning the way they did in Maween. Jabari allowed his thoughts to rest on his land for a moment, dreaming of good food and a swim in a river or Lake Ayo. But there was no use dwelling on what he couldn't have now. He walked to a tree and used it for balance while he stretched his aching calf muscles.

He let his gaze wander through the losh forest, which grew lighter as the sun came close to rising. Then he dropped the leg he was stretching, giving a particular group of shadows a second look. He saw movement, then a vague shape. Something was there, in the forest. His hand went to his bow. The thing came forward. He stood straighter, watching the apparition. It looked like a bundle of cloths with many legs, moving with a metallic rattle. He felt a shiver of fear.

"Gavi," he said sharply, drawing his bow and notching an arrow, and Gavi was instantly on his feet beside him, staff in hand. The others stood as well, standing quietly, waiting. As the thing came closer, Jabari's eyes adjusted and it separated into six people who walked slowly through the forest, chained together, two by two. Jabari felt relief slide over him as the monster of his imagination disappeared. The two at the front saw the seekers first, and held up their hands to show they meant no harm. Jabari let his bow drop to his side, but his awareness, his scouting sense for danger was thrown wide open, and he kept himself straight and alert.

"Oh, Nenyi, help us," Ivy whispered beside him, and Jabari agreed with her silently. The sight of the exhausted, bound people was wreaking havoc with his mind. Who could chain a person to another person? What evil was this?

There were three pairs of matching people; including two dark-skinned young ones who looked like Maweel children. Jabari's gaze landed on them immediately. They were much younger than the others, and were clearly hungry and thirsty; they could barely stay on their feet. The two adults in the front were more alert—Gariah, Jabari thought. And then there were two elderly Workers, a man and a woman, shuffling at the back of the strange line.

He walked forward with his water flask, offering it to the smallest child, a little girl. She took it from him without hesitation, almost snatching it out of his hands.

"Slowly, slowly," he said, and she glanced at him for a moment, her eyes wide, before taking a few gulps and handing it to the boy beside her. From the corner of his eye, Jabari saw Deto and Gavi giving water to the other prisoners. They all drank, and then the Gariah woman spoke, her strange accent curving and looping around the words. She was obviously exhausted, but she held herself tall.

"Do you have anything for these chains?" she asked.

"I may," Jabari replied. "Let us sit and talk. You look very tired."

"Yab," Gavi said. "I'll go hunt. Looks like we could use a meal." Jabari smiled into his brother's eyes, thankful for his constant cheerfulness. His stomach felt a little better. Maybe there were people in the world who had been chained together, but Gavi would still find food and cook it while he hummed off-key songs.

Ivy sat forward. "I'll come with you," she said, but Jabari shook his head. "I want you here, Ivy. Aria, you go with Gavi."

The woman had been watching all of this with her eyes narrowed. "What do you mean, you may have something for the chains? You either have something or you don't. Or are you going to force us to bargain for our freedom? I should warn you that we have already killed a man to get free."

At her words, the small girl turned and hid her face in the boy's shoulder. The boy stared at Jabari with wide eyes.

"Don't kill him, Leela," the boy said. "Please, I think he is a good man."

"Quiet, little one," the woman said, not unkindly. "You don't know of what you speak."

"Who are these children?" Jabari asked, keeping his face stern, though he felt more trusting of the woman now that he saw a glimmer of gentleness in her.

"I have no idea," the woman replied. "We are all slaves, as you can see. Or we were. Now we escape, unless you will try to enslave us again. We have been walking slowly, to keep from being seen. And the old ones cannot walk far without needing rest. It would be good for us to walk by ourselves. We could get much farther that way."

The Workers stared at Jabari without much hope, as though they fully expected him to take charge and whip them forward again. The Gariah man was silent but watchful. Seeing Jabari's gaze on the man, the woman spoke again.

"He cannot speak, but he can hear. His was a punishment for speaking against the king."

Beside Jabari, Deto put a hand over his mouth, and Ivy gasped. Brigid let out a little shriek.

"I've never heard of such brutality," Jabari said. "What king would do this?"

"The Desert King, of course," the woman said, her voice scornful, as though she couldn't believe Jabari was so stupid.

"You come from the Desert City?" Jabari asked.

"Yes, but we are criminals. I stole, and it earned me a life of slavery. He spoke against the king and it earned him a wound which will keep him from speaking, or singing, forever. He was a bard, a songmaker, before. But he sang too many hopeful songs in public places."

It was so sad that Jabari took a jagged breath and Ivy cried out this time. Brigid was crying softly into her hands. The man's eyes were wide as he watched them, as though he was used to his punishment and surprised by their reactions.

"What kind of a man is this? How can he be so cruel?" Jabari asked.

"He is very, very cruel, and his weight upon our people is

heavy." She paused. "You must be very soft, if you do not know of these things."

Jabari had always believed that the Gariah and their king moved as one. The words she said were turning his beliefs inside out.

"Are there many like him?" he asked. "Many who see and resist the cruelty of the king?"

The woman named Leela laughed, bitterly. "More than you can count," she said. "But many also who strive to gain wealth and favor with him. They will turn the other kind over, to gain a few coins or a brief audience with a cruel king." She gazed beyond him for a moment, remembering, her eyes bleak.

"I will help you get out of your chains," Jabari said. "But we will take the Maweel children with us." He turned to them. "Were you taken from your village?" he asked.

The little girl shook her head and the boy bit his fingertips. "We were on a boat," the little girl said. "And it stopped and people took us. I don't remember anything more than that, except that our mother and father were still on the boat. They couldn't get to us."

"We'll try to find their parents," he said, turning back to Leela.

The woman looked hard at him, then turned to the mute man who had been a song maker. He nodded, and she turned back to stare at Jabari again.

"Do you want to go with these people?" she asked the children. They were wide-eyed and frozen for a moment, then the tiny girl nodded, slowly. The boy squeezed closer to her and took her hand.

Leela sighed. "Yes, you can take them. It would be hard for us to keep them alive anyway."

"What about you? What will you do?" Ivy asked.

"Find a wandering tribe, try to get them to take us in," the woman said. Jabari didn't know if it was hopelessness or exhaustion that made her sound like she didn't believe in her own words.

"You could come back to Maweel with us," he said, the offer leaving his mouth before he had time to think it over. Beside him, Ivy jumped.

The woman smiled. "You Maweel are as kind as they whisper about you. Thank you, but the desert is our home." Jabari couldn't imagine calling this bleak place home, but he nodded in acceptance. He moved toward them and put his hands on the shackles on Leela's legs. He pulled at the magic he used to break poisoned things. He hurled it out and sent the poison into the ground. The shackles dissolved. He did the same for everyone until all the cruel shackles were gone.

The two elderly Workers stood up and bowed to Jabari, then turned toward the desert and began to walk away. Jabari watched in surprise, turning to look at the Gariah man and woman, and the children. They stayed where they were, in no apparent rush to leave. But the Workers kept walking.

"Wait! Don't you want to eat?" Ivy called after them.

The old man turned to look at her with a tired face. "No thank you. We will go back to our village now."

"Uncle!" Jabari called. "The way will be hard! Eat before you go."

He shook his head. "No, it is not far. We will go."

Jabari watched until they were blurs in the distance.

"I worry that they won't make it," Ivy whispered.

"You can't make their choice for them," Leela said.

"How did they end up as slaves?" Ivy asked her.

She shrugged. "They would never say. But sometimes the Workers send their old people out, if the village doesn't have enough food. Maybe they were sold, instead."

It was so horrifying that Jabari's stomach dropped three inches and turned over. Just then, Gavi came back with a rabbit in his hand. Aria, behind him, carried a large desert lizard.

"It's desert stew for breakfast," Gavi sang out, bending to start a fire with sticks that Deto had gathered. Jabari saw Aria walk over to the children and squat down beside them. At first, they cringed away from her, but she showed them that she could juggle three small sticks, and soon the tension had gone out of their shoulders and they were laughing as she pretended to drop the sticks. Brigid chopped the last onion from Gavi's food sack, gently asking Leela questions. After a while, she reached into her own sack and pulled out one of her most treasured possessions, her silver flute. She offered it to the mute man, who turned it over in his hands a few times before lifting it to his mouth and beginning a song of such sad sweetness that Jabari had to swallow hard.

That was when the Keerza came.

24

I t happened while they were sitting around the fire, eating the desert stew that Gavi had wrangled into actually tasting good. Jabari had never loved lizard, but his brother had a way with spices that was undeniable. Just as Jabari was sighing with contentment and leaning back on his elbows, his gift told him something was in the trees and he was on his feet with his staff in his hand.

The something that he sensed was several four-footed creatures, and Jabari blinked as they became emerged from the scraggly forest. It took him a minute to realize what he was seeing, but once he did, he gasped and threw his staff on the ground, bowing deeply.

"Keerza," Ivy breathed beside him.

They were radiant as they came into the sunlight, deep purple, with delicate faces and silver streaks through their hides.

"What are they?" Aria whispered, her eyes wide.

"Some of the oldest creatures that exist," Ivy murmured. "Very rare, now, and special, like the Othra. I've never seen them in real life, though they are in many of our stories and paintings."

"And they can understand you, so you can address your questions to them," Gavi added, also bowing his head toward the silent creatures.

Welcome Keerza, Jabari was busy saying with his mind speech, while the vocal conversation was going on.

Hello, young animal speaker, replied the Keerza with the largest antlers. Jabari counted six of the animals. The lines on their faces were graceful, curling around their eyes. Their heads were narrow and their eyes were strong and wild. Looking at them, Jabari felt the thrill he got when he ran as fast as was physically possible, or when he saw trees shaking with wind, or sandstorms, or great ocean waves. He realized his hands were shaking.

You are needed, young one, the Keerza continued. *Your friends need you badly. They have been trapped, imprisoned, and beaten.*

Jabari drew in a breath. *How do you know this?* he asked, and his voice in his head was shaky. A hot wave of anger washed over him at the thought of anyone hurting Isika and Benayeem.

Keethior, servant to the World Whisperer, came and told us, the Keerza said. *He is trying to find a way to help your friends, but he is only one Othra. You must go swiftly. The gate is not yet open. Can you climb the walls?*

"I can do better than that," Jabari said, his voice like steel, he was so angry. He was furious with the priests of Batta, as well as the stubborn, gifted girl who had run straight into their arms, putting herself back in danger as though her safety didn't matter to her or the people of Maween.

"What is it, Yab?" Gavi asked, putting a hand on Jabari's shoulder.

Jabari told them what the Keerza had said, and saw the effect of the words striking them, Aria's eyes growing wide and terrified, Deto's mouth drawing into a thin line, Ivy putting her head in her hands, perhaps reliving her own imprisonment from the year before.

Keethior? He asked the Keerza with the large antlers. *He has declared himself to her?*

Yes, the Keerza answered. *As is right. We also will support her in any way we can. But we cannot go into the city without being captured.*

Jabari felt shy talking to such an ancient creature. He didn't know what else to say. *Thank you for coming to us,* he said finally.

The Keerza bowed, quiet and solemn.

Keethior had declared himself to Isika. The protector of the World Whisperer, one of the oldest and most powerful Othra. Jabari had a thousand emotions going through him. A girl, a young girl with no respect for the wisdom of the elders had the loyalty of one of the most powerful ancient creatures known to man. And yet she didn't have the full support of her own people. Everything was backward and upside down. Nothing was easy or neat.

"Who is staying with the children?" Gavi asked, eying Ivy.

Her head was still in her hands. Jabari knew what Gavi was saying, and he knew his brother was right. Ivy and Deto had recently been imprisoned and didn't need to put themselves in a position that would remind them of being tied up on the horrible boat last year.

"Ivy," Jabari said. "Will you please stay and protect the children until we get back?"

She lifted her head out of her hands and nodded at him.

"Deto?" Jabari said. "You too." Deto didn't say anything, just flicked his braid over his shoulder and blinked out of the daze he was in. He winked at the kids, who giggled.

The Gariah woman, Leela, stood up and walked forward, holding her hands out in front of her.

"I don't really understand what is happening," she said, "but you have been very kind to us. Can we help?"

Jabari saw a complicated tangle of emotions playing in her face. She was bound by honor to help him because he had dissolved her chains, but it cost her, because her freedom was so recent and she wanted to go.

"No," Jabari said. "But perhaps I will have a chance to ask you for help in the future."

She smiled, and it brought unexpected beauty to her strong face. "Thank you, brother," she said. "We will go. Thank you for feeding us and helping us. Here." She pressed something into his hand. "This is old magic, from before the present King, before the poison ruined our land. Wear one and give the other to someone you want to call if you need them. You can touch the stone with the question in your heart and you will feel the answer in your mind."

Jabari opened his hand to look at what she had given him, and found two necklaces. He prodded them warily, but the magic within them was pure and strong, not poisoned.

"Are you sure about this gift? It seems valuable. You could sell them—you'll need money. And should you leave in the sun?"

She scoffed. "We won't walk long, and we are used to desert heat. And we would not sell the stones. They are passed from my own grandmother. Our owners didn't recognize them or they would have robbed them off our necks. But they are not as valuable as our freedom. Thank you."

She and the mute man picked up their sacks, and after bowing to each of them, walked away, out into the desert, holding hands. Jabari gazed at the stones on the necklaces. They were a creamy blue color, like the sky, with light glinting within. He offered one to Deto.

"In case of trouble," he said. He looked at Aria, Brigid, and Gavi. "We leave now."

They pulled their things together and left Ivy and Deto and the two children with the bows, which would be no use to them in the city, and the food. Jabari squeezed his near-sister, Ivy, on the shoulder.

"Be well. Use the necklace if you need to," he said, and then he and Brigid walked toward the city, Aria and Gavi coming behind.

"I think I know what you're planning," Brigid said, tossing her long brown braids behind her. "You don't think it's too dangerous?"

Jabari looked at her, wondering how it had come to pass

that he and Gavi were entering the Worker city with two apprentices. This wasn't what his father had meant by an "uneventful journey."

"No more dangerous than trying to walk through the front gate in the day."

"What if the whole thing collapses?" she asked.

"I work with walls," Jabari said. "I know how much is safe."

She shrugged. "Walls are fickle things," she said, and though Jabari waited for her to explain, it seemed it was all she had to say on the subject.

The high outer walls of the city rose in front of them, and they approached quietly, flitting from shadow to shadow to avoid the eyes of the guards. Jabari pushed some of his magic into hiding them, and the shadows grew thicker around the group of seekers. He was careful with how much magic he used. The wall would take a lot of energy from him soon. They reached it without being seen. Jabari counted stones to find the safest place.

"Okay," he said. "I can't take too many bricks because I don't want the wall to collapse, as Brigid reminded me." Brigid looked up dreamily. "And also I hope it won't be noticed anytime soon. So we have to squeeze through. Easy enough for me, Brigid, and Aria. But you, Gavi. Suck your stomach in."

Gavi threw his arms around Jabari and picked him off the ground. Jabari squirmed away, laughing.

He put his hands on the wall and felt for the weakness, pushing at the stone with his magic. These walls had been built of real stone, but they held the intention of keeping bad things inside, hiding and covering. He sensed secret, untold sadness and oppression, and he wanted to drop his hands and get far away from the evil within the city, but he stayed. He found the spaces woven between and the bricks began to dissolve in his hands. He took out as few as he thought they could manage. Just enough for them to get through, but not too few, or they would move slowly and be caught struggling through the wall.

He held his breath, but the wall seemed fine, strong and solid enough to be able to take a small hole. He kept going until the hole was big enough for a person to climb through, and held his breath again. The wall held. He sighed in relief, and then there was a flash and a loud crack and all around them, pieces of the wall began to shiver away. He had barely even taken note of the danger they were in when Brigid held up her hand and whistled a song, the same song she had been whistling for days. Instantly, the cracks in the walls filled with blue light and the crumbling stopped.

They all stared at her. She smiled. "I have a way with walls too," she said, her voice serene. Jabari popped his eyes at Gavi and made a note to talk with Ivram about her building gift when they got back.

He went through the hole first, climbing into a well-shadowed area on the other side. He worried that the sound of the wall cracking would bring someone running, but no one came, and he pressed himself to the wall, signaling for the others to come through. Aria came next, then Brigid, and

Gavi. They stood quietly while Jabari worked out distances between shadows and came up with a route.

"This should be easy" he whispered. "It's so quiet and we only need to get into the temple courtyard without being seen, through a back door, if possible."

"Oh," said Gavi. "Is that all?"

"That and turn into Keerza," Brigid said, and she and Gavi laughed softly. Aria was very quiet.

"Hush, stupids," Jabari said. "You okay, Aria?"

She appeared to shake herself awake, and looked at him, her eyes large in her face.

"She's here," she whispered. "I can feel her. She's in pain. What have they done to her?"

Jabari felt his face hardening. He couldn't bear the idea of Isika in pain. He put a hand on Aria's shoulder.

"Time to go." he said. "Follow me and stay right on each other's heels, but don't step on each other. Gavi, I'm talking to you."

Gavi gave him the barest glimmer of a smile, and they ran, dodging from shadow to shadow, heading for the back wall to find a way in to their friends.

25

Ben hovered over Isika, who slept with her less sore cheek cushioned on his knee. They had been captive for three days, and Isika was only a little better. Her head was cushioned on his knee and he sat with his back against the wall of the small, white marble room he had come to detest. There was nothing soft here, and the air was stuffy. The food they had been given was nearly rotting, the water was tepid and dirty. It wasn't a good place to heal, and Isika wasn't healing well.

Benayeem had never felt more tender toward his sister than he did in the last three days, as she lay sleeping, blood still on her cheeks and hands, one eye swollen completely shut, her lip split and bruised.

The day that they beat her, he had lunged at the priest who struck his sister, desperate to stop him, but the magician held him back without even touching him and Ben could do nothing but watch. Now, when he managed to drop off to sleep, he had nightmares of Isika being beaten, himself unable to stop it, again and again.

How strange that the temple had a magician. Nothing in his previous life made sense anymore. He had believed that he was part of a small, nonmagical village that served goddesses he didn't appreciate or love. But here was this huge, twisted mess. A large city, a head priest, other villages, and practicers of magic that he had never known existed. And this king who wanted them imprisoned.

He focused on singing to block out thoughts of imprisonment and priests. During the last days of imprisonment in this palace, the music he heard was more ominous, more twisted and evil than ever before, but he kept it locked away in the room in his head. He sang song after song of the Maweel to his sister. The songs calmed his own panicky heart, and it ached less.

So many times he had watched or heard his sister being beaten and he hadn't been able to do anything about it. Even now, his gift threatened to incapacitate him more than it ever seemed to help him. But he sang the songs and felt calm enter the room, felt the sad, helpless part of him grow smaller. The beautiful music of Maween pushed back despair, tying him and Isika to creation despite the fact that they could only see one tiny piece of sky through the window. The songs rang off the walls and filled the space so that there wasn't room for the hatred of the priests, or the hopelessness of the people.

"Water flowing between earth and sky
Bright day, old night, gentle and wise
Birds on the wing, fire in the stars

Oh high one, earth is in your hands
Oh true one, we are in your hands."

He paused, wishing again for water, so he could wipe his sister's face. He glanced up at the window. Keethior wasn't back. The bird had flown off with a haunting, chilling cry, soon after Isika had gone back to sleep, the night she had been beaten. Ben hoped the Othra had gone to find a miracle, and that the miracle would come on quick feet. As he stared at the morning sky through the window, the huge bird flapped into view and gave a low cry, settling on the windowsill outside.

"Keethior!" Ben cried, shaky with relief. He felt the calm the Othra carried, and he closed his eyes, drinking it in.

"No time for rest, young one," Keethior said. "We have work to do."

Ben's eyes flew open. "What do we do?" he asked. He meant it genuinely, and the bird seemed to understand. The Othra could hear the words behind words.

"I have looked for help and found nothing near enough to save you. But I have spoken with the Keerza," the bird said. "And they have an idea that might work. The idea depends on you, young one, so you must stay alert. I have been watching and listening since yesterday. Three people will come to the door this morning. One to deliver water for washing. Another to give food. And yet another to sweep and clean the room. Our only chance is to convince one of these people to help us."

Ben felt strong disappointment, thinking of the sullen

people who had come each day since they arrived. This was the miracle?

"No one will help us here," he said.

The bird flapped his large wings from his perch, and clicked angrily at him. "How can you be so sure? Has no one ever helped you in dark places?"

Ben remembered the woman in the market who had shown them the way to get in. He thought of the guard who had let them past.

"I guess so," he said. And then it hit him. Keethior had gone to look for help, and had decided who would be most likely to save them: it was Ben. No one else. This was how his gifting was meant to be used. To weigh and see. To find lies or kindness or the tiniest bit of compassion that might help them escape.

"Are all three servants?"

"Yes," the bird answered. "And young one. Music is healing, but it also softens the heart." With that cryptic statement, the bird flew away again.

The first person to come to the room brought water. He carried a pail in one hand and a basin in the other. He walked into the room, looked at them warily, then poured some of the water into the basin and offered a cup to Ben for the pail. Ben stooped and dipped the cup in the pail, and as he drank, he concentrated, focusing on the music that came from the man. It was not good. The sounds Ben heard were dark with despair, and worse, utterly empty of hope. Not this one.

After the man left, Ben cleaned Isika's face, angry that the priests had made them wait so long before giving them sufficient water to wash. The priests wanted their prisoners worn down and hopeless. He waited for the next person to come, his heart beating hard. Keethior had been sure that someone would help them, but perhaps Keethior didn't know humans as well as Ben did, and in Ben's experience, in a place like this, there weren't many helpful people. Isika murmured in her sleep as Ben gently dabbed at the blood on her face. He didn't clean it completely, not wanting to wake her.

He heard the second person while she was still outside the room. She marched in with a tray of food, and Ben shrank back from the proud, angry, taunting sounds that came from her. She had dark brown hair and pale skin, and she crossed her arms and looked at him from heavy lidded eyes. She had sneered at him when she brought food the last two days as well.

"Are you a demon?" she asked.

"No," he said. She smiled, but it wasn't a kind smile.

"Demons always lie."

"So why did you ask?" he said, frustrated. She stood there, though the tray with its unappetizing gruel was already delivered. He wanted her to leave, so he could wait for the third and final person. Their last hope. He didn't know where Keethior was.

"Are you a slave?" he asked the woman, and her lips tightened.

"No," she spat. "I serve the goddesses willingly."

"That's too bad," he said, and she moved toward him forcefully, as though she would kick him, but at the last minute, she turned and left, slamming the door shut behind her. He couldn't help himself, he moved Isika's head, then jumped up and felt for the cracks at the edges of the door again. The door was made with magic; no normal door could seal itself that way.

He ate a little of the gruel, and finally woke Isika to eat. She needed strength if they were going to escape. If Keethior's crazy plan worked. He filled her in while she ate the larger portion of gruel, making faces as she did so.

"I've gotten used to good food," she said. "This would have tasted excellent a few months ago." She swallowed and reached up to touch her swollen eye. "Keethior has a lot of faith in us. It seems crazy to think that a slave would help us, but maybe he's right. Who is coming last?"

"The sweeper," Ben said, and they looked at each other without much hope. Sweepers were the lowest kind of slaves, and it was unlikely that kindness or boldness existed in a sweeper, a victim to the utter disdain of others. There had only been one sweeper in the Worker village, a disabled man enslaved to sweep for all of his days.

They waited in silence, their tension growing, until finally Ben felt him coming.

"It's a man," he whispered, as they heard the door click open. He reached out to listen to the man's music, then sat up quickly. The music was... interesting. Not what Ben would expect from a sweeper. He listened harder. The man who entered was a tall Gariah man with long black hair tied behind him, and gold rings in his ears. He didn't look like a sweeper. He smiled at them as he entered the room and gestured at his broom apologetically.

As if in a trance, Ben watched the man bend and begin to sweep, gently coaxing dirt out of the corners of the room. The music coming from him was sad, and kind, and... hopeful. Was it possible? He listened longer, his heart beating faster. There was a certain sound, a repeated sound, and he realized it was a song, one with words that he understood. Keethior's meaning came to him, that music could soften as well as inform, and, knowing he was was diving into an unfamiliar abyss, Ben closed his eyes and began singing the song.

He sang a few lines of the haunting song, wordless, in a minor key, and stopped when he heard wonder pouring off the man. He opened his eyes. The sweeper was standing straight, staring at Ben, his broom loose in his hand. Beside Ben, Isika was very still.

"How do you know that?" the man asked in his thick accent. "It is a lullaby my mother sang to me, from our tribe."

"I heard it, in your mind." Ben said, honestly.

The man recoiled for a moment, then took a step closer. "You don't look evil," he whispered.

"We are not evil. Isika is the one who will make the world right again," Ben answered, speaking into the deepest place he knew. "The Desert King wants to keep us here forever, so she cannot heal broken things." He swallowed, summoning courage. If the man wasn't sympathetic, he might tell the priests what Ben asked him, prompting another beating, or worse.

"Can you help us escape?" he asked simply.

The man looked at him, his strong face full of pain.

"I'm a slave because I resisted the Desert King's iron grip on my people. But if I help you I will die. How do I choose between my life and yours?"

"Come with us," Isika burst out. It was the first thing she had said. Ben stared at her. "Come with us and then you won't have to choose. If they catch us, they'll catch us all together. And you won't be a slave anymore, if we escape."

The man put a hand to his forehead, staring at the broom in his hand. He stood a little straighter, and in his wide shoulders Ben could see that he was actually a warrior, that the broom would look more at home if it was a spear or a bow.

"I will come. Where do you want to go?" he asked. Ben's heart felt as though it would leap out of his chest.

"We need to find our stepmother," Isika told him, "Ben can listen for her if we can find a way to get around unseen."

"We should flee immediately," the man said. "They will know that we are gone, and they will search. We should be far away by then."

"You don't understand," Isika said, standing with effort. A flicker of pain crossed her face, but she faced him without fear. "They have imprisoned our bodies, but if I leave a member of my family behind, they will have taken my soul. I will never be able to stand properly again."

The man looked at her, his face twisted with emotion. Then he nodded, slowly.

Ben let a breath out.

"Your stepmother. Where does she live?"

Isika shook her head. "We don't know. But she is a prisoner here, like us."

The man looked at her more closely, emotion passing over his face like a cloud.

"She is a Worker," he said. "She doesn't look like you. And she has a baby."

Isika and Ben both nodded breathlessly.

"I know where she is," the man said. "Follow me. Quickly and silently."

He opened the door and looked out. Ben saw him bring his arm down in a swift motion, then he gestured for them to follow.

Isika went out first, then Ben. Next to the door lay an unconscious guard.

"Did you kill him?" Ben hissed.

The man shook his head. "No. Hush," he said. "This way. Absolute silence."

They ran down a corridor to a set of stairs. The stairs led them down into a dark room filled with vegetables. Ben sighed and tried to feel relieved, but danger pounded through the walls at them. Surely if the priests could see Jerutha in her room, they could find the fugitives as well.

He asked the sweeper. "Can they see us wherever we go? The way they showed us our stepmother in her room?"

The sweeper shook his head. "I don't know a lot, but I can listen." His accent was melodic and rough at the same time. "Sweepers are nearly invisible. I know that they cannot watch everywhere all the time. The magicians can see certain rooms they choose to see. They will almost certainly have been watching the room you were in. So they know we've left, but they don't know where we are now. We need to keep moving, or they'll find us for sure. Now, I need to think about the layout of the palace above, to find her."

Isika looked at Ben. "Do you think you can feel Jerutha's specific sounds? Can you find her from down here? Through the ceiling?"

Ben stared at her. "You mean...?"

"If we walk through the cellar, will you know where she is?"

Ben listened to the floor above them. He heard music, very faint, unfamiliar and unpleasant. He thought of Jerutha's calming music, music he had known for years.

"I think so," he said. "But we should stop every so often, because I'll have to focus."

They walked through room after room, following the direction the sweeper believed was the right way, and in every room they stopped to listen to the floor above. Ben shook his head each time. It was hard work, listening for sounds, trying to make sure he really heard everything. He quickly became tired, but he pushed on. He wanted to find Jerutha.

As they walked, Isika spoke to the man who guided them. "What is your name?" she asked.

"Abbas," he said. "And what are your names?"

"I'm Isika, and my brother is Benayeem."

"How old are you two?" he asked.

"I'm fifteen and my brother is fourteen." She was quiet for

a moment. "Why, if you could have knocked out the guards at any time...why have you never escaped?"

He glanced back at her, his face mild.

"I supposed I was waiting for a good reason," he said. "They made me a sweeper because I was leader of a tribal resistance army and they wanted to humiliate me. At first they bound me, but when I was well behaved for a long time, they figured they had broken my spirit and they wanted me to sweep faster, so they doubled my quota and took off my bindings." He laughed. "Stupid of them. Sweeping is easy. But they are blind and stupid."

Ben had many more questions for Abbas, but a bigger problem came toward them.

"Isika!" he breathed. "I hear someone, many someones... I—"

But it was too late, because there was a crashing sound in front of them, and a door burst open suddenly with a lot of noise. They were caught.

26

"We'll have to make a diversion," Jabari said, "to get that guard away from the door." They were clustered together in the shadow of a tall building, staring at the jeweled palace that seemed to be the rooms of the high priest. Brigid stood next to him, her eyes moving from the tall walls of the compound to the shadows at the foot of the massive, unfriendly building.

"What about that door?" she asked. "Could we make it in through there?"

Jabari looked where Brigid was pointing. At the base of the palace was a short, wood door, likely leading to the kitchen cellars. He rubbed one cheek, thinking.

"We're still going to have to get the guard away from this side of the wall, but we'll probably have better luck on the other side of the door, if there are nothing but potatoes to greet us."

"Mmm, potatoes," Gavi said. "Good thinking, Brigid."

They watched the guard, who was slumped against the wall, nearly asleep. Jabari struggled to come up with a good diversion. He wasn't thinking as quickly as usual; his mind was cloudy and tired from the thick, unfriendly air of the city.

Then, shouts erupted from another side of the temple compound and the guard stood and ran. Jabari's mouth fell open, then he shook himself.

"Looks like our diversion has been created for us!" he said. "Let's go!"

As they ran from shadow to shadow to get to the wall, he wondered what the commotion was, whether it had anything to do with Isika, and just how much trouble they were running into. They should be running away from that kind of trouble, not straight into trouble's arms. He was seriously going to kill Isika.

The door didn't prove to be a problem; poison held it together. He used his magic to dissolve the poison in the handle and the lock sprang open. They hurried into a dark room filled with radishes and turnips.

"No potatoes," Gavi said. "Think we'll still be okay, Yab?"

"We'll see," Jabari said, scanning the room for possible traps or people in hiding. It looked clear.

He led the way, Brigid behind him, Aria next, and Gavi behind her. They moved from cellar to cellar, going from radishes to cabbages, then to a stock of firewood, then to carrots.

"Awfully organized, these priests," Gavi said.

"They have a lot of food for people who only eat once a day," Brigid said with her soft voice.

"Oh, I don't think the priests eat once a day," Jabari told her. Anger burned inside him, but he was breaking every rule of the Maweel. He shouldn't be here, in this place that was riddled with oppression. It wasn't his job. It made him want to fight, and his job was protection, not going into enemy territory and bringing wrath down on the stupid oppressive ways of priests who cheated their people. He took a deep breath.

"I feel her so close," Aria said, her voice nearly a whisper.

Jabari looked back at her. "Maybe she's being kept in a room above," he said.

"We should try to find some stairs," Gavi said.

"What do you think I've been looking for?" Jabari asked.

"All right all right," Gavi said. "You're always so touchy when we're in Worker temple cellars."

Jabari couldn't help grinning, then his grin disappeared.

"There are people in the next room," he said.

"We don't even have any weapons," Aria breathed.

Jabari had his staff, but he didn't correct her. She was shaking. He should have left her with Ivy and Gavi, even if she *could* feel her sister's presence.

"We need the upper hand," he said to Gavi. "We're going to charge through this door before they know we're here. Hopefully surprise will be enough, and you and I can knock them out before they set off an alarm."

Gavi nodded. He was strong and capable of delivering the kind of solid blows they would need. Jabari took a deep breath and felt the readiness for fighting, the adrenalin surge.

He leapt at the door and it fell away from him, surprisingly weak. He lifted his staff above the man in the next room, ready to bring it down, and vaguely he heard Gavi shout, "Yab! No!" just as he spotted Ben in the corner of his vision. His staff came down on the man but the man put up a hand and caught the blow, turning the momentum of Jabari's swing against him, and jabbed Jabari hard in the stomach with the end of his own staff. The room turned all shades of purple and red as Jabari lost his air and crumpled in a pile of boxes. He lay twitching, trying to get air back into his lungs, listening with half an ear to the commotion.

"Don't hit him again!" he heard someone say with Benayeem's voice. "He's our friend!"

"Do your friends always come charging into rooms, hitting people with sticks?" an unfamiliar voice asked, the voice rough and heavy with a Gariah accent.

Jabari had his eyes squeezed shut as he tried to get his lungs to bring in air. When he opened them, he found that Isika's face was very near, or what seemed to be Isika's face. It was hard to tell under the swelling. She had cuts along an eye that was nearly shut, and a jagged gash from the outer corner of her other eye, down her cheek. Her lip was swollen and split, too. She blinked as he met her eyes and smiled. It looked painful.

He couldn't stop himself from reaching up to gently touch her face. "What happened?" he whispered, finally managing to get a breath.

Her face fell, and she turned and lay her face against his shoulder briefly. There was a slight shock, like two magics meeting, and she pulled away. "The usual," she said, her mouth twisting down. "He's alive!" she called out to the others. "No harm done!"

Jabari managed to sit up. "Some harm done," he said. "But I'm glad you weren't in front, Isika. You can get yourself killed sneaking around like this!"

She stared at him. "What are you doing here?"

"Rescuing you, you ridiculous girl! What do you think?"

"We've rescued ourselves, as you can see," she said, "or rather, we found ourselves a rescuer. This is Abbas. Abbas, Jabari."

Jabari narrowed his eyes at the man with the staff.

"If you two are finished with your lover's quarrel," Gavi said, "we should really get out of here."

Jabari scowled at his brother and Isika looked embarrassed, but Ben broke in.

"Not until we find Jerutha and the baby," he said.

Jabari groaned. "Not this again."

Isika's flinty look grew flintier. "We came all this way to get her. We're not leaving until we do."

Jabari shook his head, but Gavi shrugged. "Sounds reasonable," he said.

"I wouldn't say reasonable," Jabari said. "At the very least, we need to get your wounded self to the healers, Isika. But I guess we have to honor your whims, since you are the subject of our grand rescue. How were you planning to find her?"

"Ben can hear her through the floor," Isika said. "And

Abbas knows the general direction of her room. We're going to keep walking until we find her."

"Ben can what? Never mind, tell me later. There's some kind of furor outside and I have the sinking feeling it's about your disappearance. We need to get out of this city as soon as we can. Lead the way."

They walked back through the cellars, the way Jabari and the others had come; first carrots, then wood. The Gariah man was at the lead and Jabari itched at the annoyance of following someone he knew nothing about. Who was this guy? But they didn't have far to go because Ben spoke when they reached the cabbage cellar.

"Here," he said, pointing to the ceiling. "She's up there."

"Good," Jabari said. "There's a set of stairs right over there, and the door out of this horrible place is in the next cellar. This is turning out to be a very convenient inconvenient rescue." Beside him, Isika sighed.

"Does Jerutha seem to be okay?" she asked her brother.

"I can hear a lot of sadness in her. But I think she's okay. Her baby is with her."

"Now's the time. Let's go," Isika said.

"Nope!" Jabari said. "You're not going anywhere. Gavi, Brigid, and your rescuer..." he looked at the new man.

"Abbas," the man reminded him in his deep accented voice.

"Abbas," Jabari agreed. "And I. We'll go. You're staying here."

"Absolutely not!" Isika said, her face furious.

"Sit your wounded self down and be quiet," Jabari said.

"You can't go charging up there to get hurt even more. We ran all the way here to help. Let us help."

"It's a good idea, Isika," Benayeem said, and Jabari slung an arm around his shoulders.

"Oh, you guys are such...," Isika couldn't even finish the sentence. She sighed heavily. "Fine, I'll just sit and *wait* then, on this pile of cabbages. But please tell her we're down here. She won't even know who you are."

"I don't think she'll have a hard time believing me. She sent a message with the Othra, after all, and you can't make stuff like this up: 'Hi, Jerutha, is it? Isika's waiting for you in the cabbage room.'

The barest glimmer of a smile crossed Isika's face. Jabari turned away, smiling himself.

"Come, rescue delegation," he said. "Staffs at the ready, if you have one. If not, pick up a cabbage."

Gavi caught up with him at the stairs. "You're awfully cheerful all of a sudden, Yab. Any reason for that?" Jabari ignored him.

They crept up the stairs, Abbas at the lead. At the top there was a large, imposing door, but Abbas merely put a hand on one section of the door for a moment. There was a faint click and he pushed it until it opened about half an arms length.

"The cabbage cellar is not as well guarded as it should be. How does it look out there?" Jabari whispered.

"It is clear," Abbas said. "It is far too quiet. This is the hall-way. They keep her in the southwest prison." He frowned. "A strange home for the future wife of the high priest. We will go to her. But be alert. I do not like this quiet. This hallway is usually guarded."

They crept into the hall and followed Abbas to another tall, imposing door which he merely brushed again. This time, Jabari saw a small stone that brushed against the door and heard a sharp click. He craned his neck to see exactly how the lock worked, but the door was already open.

The room was bare, with one small barred window. A woman sat in one corner with her head bowed. She had long reddish brown hair that pooled around her as she sat. After a moment, Jabari realized that her head was bowed over a tiny sleeping baby. She looked up wearily, and alarm flashed in her eyes as she saw them. Then she saw Abbas.

"It's you," she whispered. "But who are these others?"

"Don't worry," Jabari said. "We're friends. It's time to go."

"He means that Isika sent us," Gavi added. "She's downstairs waiting in the cabbage room."

At Isika's name, the woman gasped and her eyes flooded with tears. She blinked them back, dashing them off her cheeks with the back of her hand.

"Oh, Isika. With the cabbages? I'm ready, of course. And I have nothing to carry other than my son," she said with a shaky laugh. "But I'm afraid I'm very weak and I'm not sure I'll be able to travel. They haven't been feeding me much and I'm nursing my son."

Jabari said a not-nice word under his breath and strode into the room.

"Just when I think these Worker priests can't get much

worse," he said, "they surprise me again. We don't have much time, I think."

Abbas rushed to Jerutha and held his arm out for her to pull herself up.

"Lady," he said. "Would you permit me to assist you?"

Jerutha gazed at Abbas with level eyes. He was a striking contrast to her, with his light brown skin, midnight black hair and gold rings in his ears. She must have seen something she trusted, because she slowly stood and nodded, and he came closer. Jabari reached for the baby and after a moment's hesitation, Jerutha handed the infant to him. The baby didn't wake, his face smushed against one closed fist. Abbas lifted Jerutha's arm and settled it around his shoulders. She leaned heavily on him. Jabari worried about how they would get away when she was so weak. One step at a time, he thought. Just get back to Isika.

"Ready?" Gavi asked from the doorway, where he was watching. "We shouldn't expect this luck to hold."

Jerutha laughed under her breath. "Look at me," she said. "I go with strangers right away, without even questioning that you're really from Isika." She looked at Jabari, taking in his black skin, he assumed, matching it to the way her step-daughter looked. "I feel that you are telling the truth. Yes. Let's go. They see everything. We need to move quickly; they will know you are here."

27

Isika sat gingerly on a pile of cabbages, vibrating with impatience. Ben and Brigid sat nearby, filling each other in on what had been going on since they left Azariyah. She heard snippets, but couldn't follow everything. She had nearly forgotten her injuries, focused on getting away and finding Jerutha, but now, sitting still, she had time to realize that her whole body ached. It hurt even to blink. She sighed.

Aria sat a little way away, on the floor beside a wooden box, but at Isika's sigh, she stood and walked to sit beside her sister, looking into her face. Isika felt her own face soften, looking back at the sister she had believed dead for so many years. Aria's brown eyes were familiar. They looked just like Isika's mother's eyes: deep, soft brown, tilted up at the corners.

"Does it hurt?" Aria asked. "I mean, it looks like it hurts, but does it hurt a lot?"

"Not too much," Isika said. Her sister shrugged and looked away. Isika put a hand on her arm.

"That's not really true. It hurts like crazy."

Aria looked up at her again. "It's been hard."

"What has?"

"Seeing all of this. We were in the village again. I saw people I recognized."

Isika watched her. Something was wrong. Aria seemed tired and defeated. She seemed more tired than Isika felt, which couldn't be right.

"That must have been sad," she said.

"Yes," Aria said. She picked up a cabbage and turned it over and over in her hands. "But I've never been beaten or hit, Isika. Never in my life. You've always had a harder time. I see that now."

It felt like a thousand emotions flowed through Isika, and her hands shook. It was the first time Aria had admitted that Isika's life had been hard. She felt thankful for the understanding. She hoped that Aria could see that Isika wasn't the enemy who had abandoned her. But what she really wanted wasn't Aria's sympathy. She wanted Aria to accept her, to let her into the world she had created since she was cast out and adopted by the Maweel. She didn't want to stand on the outside anymore, and suddenly her longing for that acceptance was so strong she could hardly breathe.

"Thank you," she finally said. "But there's no way to compare being hurt. Everybody feels things differently." She watched Aria for a little while longer, still worried about the gray cast to her sister's skin and the way she seemed to be breathing too quickly.

"Can I try something?" she asked her little sister.

Aria looked at her. She shrugged, her shoulder barely lifting. A single tear escaped the corner of her eye. Alarmed now, Isika put her hands on either side of her sister's face and leaned forward, wincing slightly because the cuts on her face hurt, until her forehead touched Aria's forehead. She could feel a gray, swirling cloud inside Aria right away, and tried to pull it out, but immediately she sensed resistance. There were sharp barbs in Aria's heart. Arrows. Lies. Poison. Isika took a deep breath and tried to reach into the earth to heal her sister's wounds and pull the poison out, but she couldn't reach anything deep or substantial. All the same, she pulled a few of the poison arrows out and sent them into the ground beneath her feet, with great effort. She pulled away from her sister, alarmed.

"What happened to you?" she breathed, dizzy from the effort.

Aria shrugged again. "I overheard something about poison in the Worker village. Poison meant for you."

Isika felt the blood leave her face, and Aria leaned forward at her expression.

"It's okay!" she said. "Gavi's been working on healing me every day, but it doesn't seem to last."

"We need to get you to a skilled healer," Isika said. "You have these arrows... I don't think they should stay there long." She swallowed. "I'm so sorry."

"No, it's fine." Aria put the cabbage back on the pile. "You are the World Whisperer. Of course they will try to poison you."

Isika was trying to think of what to say in response when Abbas walked through the doorway with Jerutha leaning on his arm. Jabari was just behind them, holding a tiny baby.

Isika jumped up and rushed over to her stepmother, trying to hide her limp. Jerutha opened her arms and Isika fell into them.

"Whoa," Abbas murmured, as he kept the two of them from toppling over. Jerutha's face was wet, and Isika found she was crying too.

"I knew you would come," Jerutha said. "But oh, what have they done to you? Your face!"

"Don't worry about that," Isika said. "And I promised I would come." She looked at the baby. "Can I see him? What is his name?"

"Mesu," Jerutha said. "His name is Mesu."

Jabari cleared his throat. "We'll have time for reunions when we are safely out of the city walls," he said. "We need to move swiftly. By now, the high priest certainly knows that he has lost all of you, and somehow I don't think he's particularly happy about it. I mean, I would be ecstatic if I didn't have to feed you, Isika, but you never know with these evil priests."

He frowned and pulled back his shirt, peering at a necklace he was wearing. "Plus, there's the fact that this stone has been glowing since we found Jerutha's room. It's warm, too. I don't really know how it works, but I'd guess that Deto is trying to call us."

"What does that mean?" Brigid asked.

"Either that they miss us, or that something bad has happened, so I suggest we part with this temple complex, no matter how much it breaks our hearts."

Isika shook her head at him. It seemed like no amount of danger could make him completely serious, but fighting back smiles was good, no matter how much it made her face hurt. She felt real hope, back with Gavi and Jabari. They made her feel as though a good meal and a swim in the sea were just around the corner. And this time, she would know that Jerutha was safe and happy too. As soon as they got away from this horrible desert.

She walked after the others in a fog of pain and happiness. Gavi and Jabari had some way of sensing whether the guard was at the door. He hadn't returned, and Isika had an uneasy feeling in her stomach as they continued, undiscovered, running across the empty square. Abbas half carried Jerutha and Isika limped along at the back.

There wasn't a soul around. Isika's right leg felt like it was going to break in half where the priest had hit her the hardest, but she bit back the pain and ran. A deep sense of foreboding grew stronger.

They found Jabari's crack in the wall and slipped through. Once everyone was outside, they stood and looked at each other. By the looks of the others, Isika thought she wasn't the only one who was worried. Brigid chewed her lip and Ben kept staring off into the sky, listening. He shook his head when she looked at him. Nothing useful then.

"That was fortunate," Gavi said.

"Or?" Jabari asked.

"Or ominous," Isika said.

"Never mind. Let's find the others and get away from this place as quickly as we can."

"The others? How many others?" Ben asked.

Jabari exchanged a glance with Gavi. "Um, a few more than we intended."

Isika smiled. "Your favorite, Jabari." She knew how much he hated to travel in large groups.

He winked at her and her face grew hot, so she looked away.

They walked in the direction of the same grove where Isika had left the Keerza and the horses.

Jerutha spoke up, still leaning on Abbas. "I'm not sure I'm able to travel," she said. "Maybe you should take Mesu and leave me somewhere peaceful. I'm not so well, I won't linger long."

Isika stared at her. "What?" she yelped. "What do you mean, leave you? You mean, to die here in the desert? That's ridiculous. Absolutely not. Besides, we have horses."

But when they got to the grove, they didn't see any horses. They found Ivy and Deto, who ran to them and hugged Isika and Ben, clucking over Isika's wounds. There were also two small children, and the Keerza, standing silent, but the horses were gone.

"Did you sense something from the necklace?" Deto asked.

"Yes, it worked," Jabari said. "Why did you call?"

Deto shook his head. "Something changed in the air... the horses got nervous.."

"They bolted," Ivy interrupted. "I'm sorry, I couldn't keep them."

"What?" Isika said. "Why would they do that?"

Lady, they felt a strange, strong wind, the leader of the Keerza said, only for her mind to hear. *It came upon all of us and went right under our skin. We had the presence of mind to withstand it, but the horses are more simple. Everything in them told them to run, so they did.*

Isika told the others what the Keerza said, and they looked at each another in dismay.

"Well, all I know is that Ivram is going to kill you two for stealing horses and then losing them," Jabari muttered.

"If we get close enough to Ivram to be killed by him, I won't complain," Ben said, and everyone laughed.

"Never mind," Jabari said. "All we can do is start. Jerutha, Sister, we'll help you. Please tell us if you need to stop."

Isika's heart warmed at his courtesy toward her step-mother, her dear friend, and she met Jerutha's eyes. Jerutha stared at her, obviously overwhelmed and exhausted, but Isika smiled, trying to encourage her. After a moment, Jerutha dipped her chin, then squared her shoulders for the journey.

With the two children and Abbas, they were a traveling company of thirteen, including Mesu, Jerutha's tiny son. It was a large unwieldy group with injured people, and they needed to make it all the way across the scorching desert. Isika could barely stand the idea. She focused on thinking about each step. They filled their flasks with water from Isika's spring. Gavi looked at her with questions in his eyes as she bent to fill her flask, but she shrugged him off. Of course he wanted to know how she had made the springs, but how could she explain what she herself didn't understand?

"We still have some food in our packs," Jabari said. "Let the hungry ones eat and we must begin our journey. Where is Keethior, anyway?" he asked Isika.

She reached for the bird with her mind, but found only emptiness. She shook her head. "I can't feel him anywhere. He's elusive even for an Othra, isn't he?"

"Yes, you're welcome to him," Jabari said.

"Yab," Gavi said reproachfully.

"Sorry," Jabari muttered. "I'm sure he's a perfectly helpful servant. When he wants to be."

"I would never call him a servant," Isika flashed back at him. She stared at the clear sky, willing the bird to come.

"But he declared himself to you, didn't he?" Jabari asked. His voice was sharp.

Isika nodded without looked away from the endless blue. Why must they always point out how different she was? She didn't ask for her own personal Othra, not even one who was grumpy and independent.

THEY LEFT AFTER JERUTHA, Isika, and Ben had eaten. Jerutha fed the baby at her breast. The wind felt unfriendly to Isika. Was it only the Keerza's doleful words, or was there some evil magic at work? She looked at the gentle animals, somehow knowing that no matter how badly her leg hurt or how weak Jerutha was, she couldn't ask to ride on their backs.

It would be wrong. They walked for a long while, until they were out of sight of the city. Once the city was just a smudge on the horizon, they all began to relax. Maybe the sense of something evil had been nothing but the bad air of the city, maybe they would walk away without trouble. But still, the wind pulled at them and sucked their laughter away.

As they walked, the ground grew increasingly dry. They weren't in the deep sand of the desert yet, but the hard ground looked even dryer than it had on their way into the city. Isika looked around, frowning. The trees, also, seemed more withered. Cracks began to appear in the earth, running in every direction.

"Stop!" Isika called.

Jabari whirled to face her, and she stared in horror. His face looked dry and old, as though he had aged years. The cracks in the ground grew and spread.

"What is this?" Aria cried. The wind rose to a howl, and the inside of Isika's mouth grew dry, drier than the earth. The cracks widened, the trees shriveled and shrank. The children shrieked in terror and Abbas roared at the sky.

"I want to fight this!" he said. "But how can I fight what I cannot see?"

Jabari bent to the ground and placed a hand on it. "Horrible poison," he said. "I have never felt anything like this before." It sounded as though he was having a hard time catching his breath. Bits of skin flaked away from his face; he was drying up before Isika's eyes.

Jerutha fainted, her eyes rolling back in her head, and Gavi caught her before she hit the ground. The baby gave a thin wail from where he lay in Benayeem's arms. Terror stabbed Isika's heart as she looked down at her hands. They were cracked like a dry earth wall. She was desperately thirsty. She tipped her water flask and took another sip of water, but still she felt parched. Abbas whirled in circles, staff in hand, slashing at the sky.

"You don't have to look any farther," Gavi said, his voice a wheeze. He knelt on the ground, clutching Jerutha. Beside him, Aria sank to her knees, her face as withered as an old lady's. Gavi took a strained breath and continued. "Here is the enemy now."

Six figures, robed in black, emerged from the direction of the city. They came up out of the desert like an apparition, heat forming waves in front of them. Isika blinked, looking around for the Keerza, but the gentle animals had disappeared. Deto dropped to his knees. Isika stubbornly kept her feet. She refused to be on the ground before the priests ever again. The one in front wore the red edged crown and robe, and Isika knew that once again she was looking at the high priest.

Everything in her wanted to run, to shout for the others to run, but the air was thick, the wind howled like a thousand dogs, sucking the words out of her mouth. She could barely blink. *Keethior,* she called. *Keethior, please. This is more than we can fight on our own.*

28

Keethior, come! she called again. *We are going to die.*

Child?

There you are!

Coming, he said, but she could tell by the hollowness of his voice that he was very far away.

Then the howling wind stopped, and the black-robed priests were too close. There was a sudden crack of sound, and the waves of hatred shifted around them, so that the air rippled off their robes with malice and trapped the seekers, Isika, Ben, and the refugees. The dry air wicked the moisture out of their bodies. Isika strained to lift her arm and found that she could only move her eyes.

The little group stood in the cracked desert like a tableau of the stricken—parched and hollow. It seemed to Isika that they were shards of pottery, so fragile that if someone pushed them they might shatter. The six men stood around them in a ring. No one else fainted, no one fell. They were caught in the air, trapped, like ants in honey. The ground continued to crack, splits running to the horizon, shimmering with heat, as though the whole desert was a kiln, baking them to nothing.

Through the ripples in the air, Isika saw the burning eyes of the priests. Fear rolled over her in waves, until she could have drowned in it; she had never been so terrified. She saw Aria, bent nearly in half, rigid, paralyzed from the magic, her eyes shut tightly against some internal nightmare. It made Isika angry, and the bright spark of anger was enough to make her grind her teeth and force her body to move against the great weight, the horrible silence of the evil that went on forever and ever—not a bird, not a sound, no rushing of water or wind. Just heat and earth and dryness. She moved her tongue over her teeth and forced words out of her throat.

"You giant bullies."

The head priest laughed.

Helar, the man who had beaten her, turned toward her. Isika was pinned under his gleaming eye. He smiled a terrifying smile.

"Bullies throw power around because they are afraid they are powerless, my dear," said the head priest. "I am power." His eyes flashed and his head rolled on his neck in a way that didn't seem human. The air crackled.

If Isika wasn't paralyzed, she would have run far, far away from the man. She knew at that moment, she had been in this place before, on a ship, with another man whose head rolled strangely on his neck, whose voice was full of malice.

She was facing a demon. And the demon wasn't speaking

in metaphors; this was the goddess Power, whom Isika had bowed before in a red temple far away, in the Worker village.

She sighed and would have groaned if she could, but she forced hopelessness away from her.

"Mugunta," she ground out, cursing the sand in her throat.

"How dare you speak that name?" the head priest hissed. "You know nothing of me. You have always been weak. Your weakness is funny to me, little girl, how you run and cry and bleed."

He lifted a hand and the air grew heavier. They all twisted, like dolls, under the new weight. Aria bent farther, Jerutha sank lower, Jabari's back bowed in a way that didn't seem physically possible. There was a sound in the stillness; the faint cry of an infant. The baby in Ben's arms wailed, and Helar frowned and moved toward it. The cry seemed to vibrate through the air, striking true, deep into Isika's heart. *NO,* she said, but it was only in her mind and the man still walked toward the baby, though slowly, as though the magic was bothering him as well.

Close now, she heard Keethior say. *I am coming, hold on,* and she told him, *I can't hold on, there is no time.*

She watched helplessly as the priest, the same one who had shown her such violence, walked toward Benayeem and the baby. The other priests were like stone, holding their hands out, channeling the power that contained them all. Isika felt for the power, felt for cracks, she ran her senses over the web holding them, and realized it was like a net. She looked and looked, and she found the place she was looking for at the base of the net, close to the dry earth. A tiny crack, no more than a hair's breadth, and as Helar got closer and closer to the baby, Isika threw her spirit at the sliver of pure air and pulled, ripping it open, peeling the net of power off them. Everyone gasped and moved. Ben twisted back to normal and took a few steps away from the priest, the baby still in his arms.

The high priest bared his teeth at Isika. "Very good, little girl," he said. "The Desert King will love having you fight for him. Perhaps there is more power in you than he first thought."

"What does the Desert King have to do with any of this?" she asked, wishing her voice came out as more than a whine. "And why do you call him the Desert King? What is his name?"

"The Desert King is the chosen of Mugunta, child; you of all people should know that. And you aren't allowed to know his name. Very few are. But he wants you, for some reason known only to him. I don't understand what he could want with a weak, whimpering child, but I will enjoy pressing you before I deliver you to him." He looked at the other seekers. "He can always use more slaves." He grinned and moved toward Isika.

From the corner of her eye, Isika saw Abbas whirl. He lifted his staff and with more speed and strength than Isika had seen from him so far, whipped it through the air at the two priests nearest him, hitting them behind the knees, knocking their legs out from under them. When they were on the ground, he delivered two short jabs to the backs of their heads. Isika flinched as their eyes rolled back. But Abbas whirled again, almost as though he was dancing, and faced the large man who had beaten Isika. He grinned as he moved on light feet.

"Never the Desert King," he said. "I will never bow to him again. You can take my life first."

Aria sat on the ground beside Jerutha, who lay with her eyes closed, breathing shallowly. Jabari and Gavi pulled their own staffs out from behind them. Ben put the baby in Aria's arms, and then he and Ivy pressed forward as well, and soon the circle was filled with bodies fighting, limbs and staffs flying. Abbas and the large, cruel priest danced around one another.

Isika watched, not knowing what to do, not sure that fighting was their way out, because the priests were strong and pressed the tired group mercilessly. As she watched, she saw the head priest as he began to sneak over to Jerutha's crumpled body on the ground next to Aria and the baby.

Isika blew out a short, impatient breath. Enough of this. She heard the thundering of hooves with some distant part of her, heard Keethior calling out as he drew closer, and she lifted her own hands.

Everyone froze. It was almost comical, they were caught with their mouths open, or hands raised, halted on the spot. Even the head priest was like stone.

The Keerza came then, thundering into the camp, and there were many dozens more than before. The leader came to her.

Well done, daughter, he said.

We're not finished yet, she answered. *I need help.*

You have our help, he said.

Okay, great, she said, shuffling her feet and feeling suddenly shy. *Do you have any idea of what we're supposed to do now?* She smiled ruefully. *I've never had this happen before. I could set them free but it would be the same as before, with more fighting, and I don't think we will win.*

The answer is in the earth, daughter, said the Keerza. It cries out for its Shaper. The demon Power wants it, wants to warp and control it, but it can't be controlled forever. It calls to you because you are the Whisperer, in the hand of the Unmade one you can put things right. Begin child, we will collect your friends and put them out of the reach of the poisoned ones.

Isika watched them. *But what do I DO?* she asked. He didn't answer. The Keerza began to nudge at the seekers and refugees, pulling and pushing at them until they could toss them up onto their backs, which made Isika gasp. She couldn't believe the beautiful animals would allow people on them, but they didn't stop until they had every one of Isika's friends.

They were much stronger than their delicate bodies had led Isika to believe. In very little time, they carried Jerutha, the baby, Aria and the others outside of the circle that Isika was holding, placing them in the dubious shade of a withered tree. Isika was left alone with the priests in the circle.

The Keerza came back to her.

You still stand here, the leader said to her.

I don't know what to do, she said.

Have you listened to the earth? the female asked. *But we cannot tell you, because we know our work. We have more to do.*

As Isika watched, the Keerza began running in a large circle around herself and the priests, who were still frozen in place. She tried to watch, but their colors blurred together, and she felt dizzy. A hum rose as they ran, a haunting call that surrounded and lifted her. The priests fell to their knees as the music grew. Isika wondered if it was anything like the music Ben always heard. The priests fell all the way to the ground. She couldn't see them at all now, surrounded by a blur of color and light as they ran and ran. She could hear the beat of their hooves, and their music calling, longing, reaching for Nenyi. The priests disappeared. One minute they were there, the next, Isika stood alone in the circle of desert, surrounded by the high keening of the Keerza, colors flashing purple, blue.

She felt a tug toward the cracked earth and looked at her hands. They were peeling, still as dry as chalk, and she saw that the ground was aching for water. She knew what she needed to do.

She knelt on the ground and placed both hands in the dust. A golden tide began to break over her. She leaned down even farther, pressing her forehead to the sand. She could feel the poison that controlled the ground, forcing the life out of it, but beneath the poison, there was the hum, the rhythm of the earth far below. She called to the *naia*, the dolfina, far away, and then she called farther, to the heart that beat through the worlds. She remembered the sea, the rivers that had cradled her.

She wept then, remembering the waters of Lake Ayo, far from herself and anything that resembled a home. In the driest place, she cried for the broken earth. She wept for her mother and grandmother, stolen from their people. She cried for herself because her grandmother had been the queen, but she was gone and Isika didn't really know what to do in her place, and she didn't know who she was anymore. When her tears seemed like they were spent, Keethior came and spread his wings over her, and sang. She heard his song echoed in the humming of the earth and she sang the song with him.

Nenyi! She called, filled with an incredible longing.

"Nenyi love, Nenyi light, waters falling, washing, dying.
The rain said goodbye but it will be back.
The earth will be new
Light on the seas,
Green in our life, oh Nenyi.
Green is our love, oh Nenyi."

It was a song calling for water and for the healing of the earth, for Nenyi's life force to send the poison away from every grain of sand in the desert. As Isika sang, she began to feel as though she was swimming in a deep well of water, washed by golden light, lit from within.

She fell asleep, and she dreamed.

She dreamed that instead of being trapped in the desert, she was floating in a river with the *naia*. They were circling and flipping, throwing themselves out of the water, shimmering and gleaming in the sunlight, and she was with them.

She could swim like them. She laughed, and in an instant, she was airborne above the deltas that spread like a fan to the sea. She saw the great desert, far away, and she knew the people in the houses were crying out to her. They went to their wells and the wells were bone dry. Everywhere, everything she looked at was white-bleached and dying, and the people held out their hands. The demon, Power, had taken the life water away.

Then she dreamed she was in the sea again, but this time the *naia* were gone.

A giant, a great whale of the deep, turned in slow circles in front of her, his body glowing gold and green. She watched for a while before he turned and nudged her with his face, so that her whole body rang with joy. She shrieked with happiness and dove under his huge fins, clinging to his tail, nudging him back with her hands and face.

Nenyi! she called. She said his name over and over. *Nenyi. Nenyi. Nenyi.* Just the sound of it took the dread away from her, just being near him took away the horror of the priests and their fists.

Do you see yet? he asked.

You came when I called, she told him. It was all that mattered.

How many deserts are there? he asked her.

Oh, do there have to be deserts?

You can heal them, daughter.

I am just one girl, she told him again, the way she had the last time he appeared to her in a dream.

No, he said. *You are many.*

I'm afraid.

You never need to be afraid of Power, he said. *The demon cannot touch you.*

I am so small.

Being small is the only way to heal Power's evil.

But what do I do?

He swam and looked at her with one large, gentle eye. Her whole being was filled with light and happiness. She could have looked into that eye forever.

Call water, he said, then he turned as though he would swim away.

She quickly paddled until she could rest on his tail. All around them, thousands of tiny fish shone like lights against the blue of the deep.

Is this what you look like? she asked, and though they were in the water, she knew she was crying. Her voice sounded plaintive, like a kitten or a tiny child. She didn't want him to leave her again. She didn't want to be World Whisperer anymore. She wanted to swim with him, to stay in the water forever.

I'm not leaving you, he said, and she couldn't bear the kindness in his voice, or the emptiness she felt when he turned and went out into the blue, all the thousands of fish glowing on every side. But the *naia* came again, and they carried her to the shore, and she lay on the bank and wept. Finally, she turned and put her face to the ground, doing as the Shaper had told her.

She felt the water deep in the earth, and with everything

in her, every bit of joy the Uncreated One had given her, she called the water.

Come, she said. *We need you.*

SHE WOKE UP, finding herself back in the desert, back where she had been, but the land was changed. The Keerza stood in a loose circle around her, eating tall grass that grew in clumps. She sat up and looked around. In every direction, the desert was covered in the bright pink and yellow of flowers, green with patches of grass and plants.

She stared for a few long minutes, running her hand over a clump of soft pink flowers that seemed to smile at her, but she was desperately thirsty, so she crawled to a small spring that bubbled nearby. She cupped her hands and drank deeply of the sweet, cold water.

She looked up at a familiar sound, and saw that the horses were back. They stood nearby, nickering to each other between snatches of grass.

Where did you go? she asked, but they ignored her. Wind's hide shuddered with guilt and he cocked one ear in her direction. She knew he was trying to apologize, so she sent a stream of calm to the horses who had run when they felt they were in danger.

All around, her friends and family were lying curled in small depressions in the ground, wildflowers growing up around them as though they had been there a very long time. There were new trees, palms that swayed overhead. Was it the same place? Isika looked for the city in the distance and saw that it was right where it had been before, its shape perhaps more clear in the distance now because there wasn't any dust in the air.

Looking around, she saw Keethior, and beckoned him to her. Surprisingly, he complied, flying to drop down beside her. He was taller than her as she sat. The deep, rich calm of his presence comforted her.

What happened? she asked.

You called a clean sea out of the ground, said Keethior. *The water spread as far as our eyes could see, and when it soaked into the earth, plants grew.*

"How long have I been sleeping?" she asked aloud. "What did the Keerza do to the priests?"

They sent them back to the Worker city, Keethior told her, in his audible voice. *But I wish they had sent them away forever.* He didn't say more. Isika stood and went to her stepmother. The baby was curled up in Jerutha's arms, a sweet smile on his face. Isika scooped him up, and he awoke and blinked at her. She pulled him close, and he batted her on the chin with a dimpled hand. She laughed, and all around her, in that strange lush desert, her friends began to stir and open their eyes.

29

The journey back home took a long time. They walked, rather than running, and there were Jerutha and baby Mesu, the children, and the new foreigner, Abbas, to be concerned about, though Jabari thought perhaps they needed to worry about their new warrior less than Aria. She drooped after the scare in the desert, and he desperately wanted to get her to the healers, and to her family for good food and rest, far away from the troubles of the Worker priests.

He found that he was confused about everything they had been through, pulled into a city that had nothing to do with them, at the mercy of priests who screamed for their deaths but shouldn't have had any hold on them. In all his life, he had never touched the Great Waste so closely.

And somehow, instead of growing faster and going home more swiftly, they were taking all these people with them, adding to their load. He felt far away from the well-trained seeker journeys that were his way of life, he and Gavi running in stride. Was this how it was supposed to work with the World Whisperer? Dipping so close to the Great Waste, then emerging with a ragtag group of refugees?

He thought about it on and off for many days, watching Isika lead her tall horse by the reins while Aria and the two Maweel children swayed on its back, one in front of the other. Jerutha and the baby rode Ben's horse, and every once in a while, Jabari heard a whisper in his head; Isika murmuring to the horses, telling them what good horses they were, how brave and strong. He knew she didn't have to guide her horse, but she held onto the reins because she wanted to be close, checking for poison, ready to soothe both of the horses if she needed to.

Behind the horses, Jabari walked with Brigid and Gavi, sometimes Ben, then Ivy and Deto trailed behind. The Gariah man strode alongside Jerutha on the horse, as though he had been pronounced her personal guard.

The rescuers had pulled small children from the Workers' sending boats for many, many years. Now Jabari and Gavi had rescued two adults. Jabari shot a glance at the Gariah warrior. Was this going to be a new thing for the Maweel? Rescuing adults? He worried over it until one day Gavi poked him in the side.

"Growing walls, little brother?" Gavi asked. "What are you chewing on?"

Ben, walking beside Gavi, looked up as well. Jabari frowned. He wanted to talk to Gavi, but he didn't know how much of his mind Ben could read.

"Oh," Jabari said. "Just the way things have turned out. I'm not sure what any of this means for the future."

Isika looked back over her shoulder. "You can blame it all on me," she said, shrugging.

But as she turned back to lead Wind carefully over some difficult stones, he caught a glimpse of unease in her face, and there was something about the way her shoulder was hitched up, the way she walked as though she didn't have anything more to worry about than leading her horse. He recognized it as something he would do if he was trying to hide his fear.

When they stopped to camp at night, Abbas found them edible desert plants that even Gavi had never seen or heard of. There were spiny cactus that were delicate and full of flavor on the inside, small drinking flowers full of water that made their arms and legs tingle with energy, and roots that tasted like roasted nuts. Jabari and Ben also occasionally shot rabbits, or a slow blinking lizard that made a good soup. There were a lot of people to feed. Gavi was overjoyed at learning new plants to forage, and he and Abbas roamed the desert together, Gavi listening and watching while Abbas showed him what to look for. But, like Jabari, Gavi was eager to get home.

"I want to get back to my garden," Gavi said, and Jabari couldn't blame him. The desert food was good, but he wanted sliced tomatoes, fresh fruit, or a feast of everything there was to eat in Maween. He sighed just thinking of it.

So they followed Isika's path of springs out of the desert, and slowly, day by day, they drew closer to Azariyah. The travelers began talking about what they would do when they got home. Ben wanted to spend a day with the singers, Gavi would disappear into his gardens immediately, Aria didn't talk much but she wanted her own bedroom and her family. Brigid missed her dog, a tall fleethound who followed her everywhere. And she missed the sound of the looms in her family's house.

Jerutha traveled quietly, murmuring to her baby, and Isika became silent as they got closer to the sacred city. Neither seemed excited about their arrival, the way the others did. Jabari thought he understood Jerutha, who didn't know what she was being led into. He imagined she had very little reason to trust that it would be good. But he was puzzled and a bit hurt about Isika dragging her feet. He had believed that Isika loved the City and wanted to live there. She seemed to be doing so well in the pottery workshop. Dawit and Teru had been nothing but kind. Sure, she might gain some extra work for disobeying orders, but she had come from a Worker village, for the love of the sea! She knew how to work!

As the days went on, he grew increasingly irritated about it, more than he should be. Who cared if Isika loved the city or not? It didn't change things for him if she didn't like Azariyah, the place he'd been born and raised. But it upset him, it was a beautiful place to him, and there were so many more things he wanted to show her about the city. As he thought it over, he realized he himself might love his city more than he had believed. And he might be more drawn to Isika than he would let himself admit.

One night, as they sat around the fire, only two days

journey from Azariyah, he sat beside Isika. He meant to chat lightly about the day, but she was morose and silent again. He burst out in frustration.

"Why don't you want to go back?" he whispered, his voice fierce. Beside them, Aria and Ivy talked in low tones while Gavi, Deto, and Brigid cooked dinner.

Isika stared at him, her eyes flashing with surprise, then anger. Then she leaned forward until her face was close to his. He held himself still, refusing to move away.

"What are you talking about?" she asked. Her skin was the color of night. He leaned away, unable to think when she was so close.

"You seem so unhappy to be going home," he said. "Your feet drag more and more, the closer we get."

She sat back, her eyes still on his, tapping her long fingers on her knees as she watched him. She sat cross-legged, her eyes as still as water in a pond, focused on him with that strange, attentive way she had. He shivered and looked away. The night was chilly.

"You're so stupid sometimes that you don't deserve an answer," she said, and he stiffened, but softened at her next words. "I'm terrified they'll send me away," she said.

"They would never do that!" he said, shocked into looking at her again.

"Really? They told me not to go."

"They..." he stopped because he had no idea what they would do. He thought he knew his parents, but he had never known them in this role. They were regents. She was the World Whisperer.

"See? Even you don't know. You prance back to Azariyah without fear, with full assurance of your parents' love, and you know there is nothing you could do to change how they feel about you." She folded and pinched a piece of her tunic over and over, then smoothed it. "I, on the other hand, go back disgraced, on trial, an orphan who ran away. Our lives are very different."

She stood abruptly and walked out of the light of the fire.

"I never prance," he muttered under his breath, but he sat for a long time, thinking about how someone who pulled water out of the ground could be unsure of her welcome in a city that was supposedly her birthright.

It was like going back in time, Isika thought on the afternoon they reached the city. It was like last time, looking for Kital, not knowing whether the people of the city would help her or receive her. Except this time she knew exactly how much she loved Azariyah and how much she wanted to stay.

And yet I took horses and ran away, disobeying the high elders, she told herself. *But how could I not?*

She looked up at Jerutha, who sat tall on Isika's horse, baby Mesu sleeping in a piece of cloth tied around Jerutha's back. Although the journey had been hardest for Jerutha, a nursing mother and a recovering prisoner, she hadn't uttered one word of complaint. Isika had seen the admiring looks Gavi and Jabari sent her, as they stopped at night and she climbed down from the horse and went straight to helping gather wood for the fire. Isika thought that it had less to do with what an amazing person Jerutha was and more to do with how hard her life had been, right up to the point that she had been abducted by an evil priest occupied by a demon of power. The thought made Isika's heart hurt. No, she was glad that she had run away, glad that she had gone to get Jerutha. Even if it had been a trap.

Surely, even if they sent her away, they would allow her stepmother and the baby to stay. She would beg them to let Benayeem remain in the city as none of it was really his fault. He was loyal to her, that was all. It had been all her idea.

And now that she knew about the help she would have from creatures that could hear the Shaper in her, she knew she would be able to find a way to live in the wilderness. She sighed and looked down at her grimy hands.

Maybe they would at least let her have a bath at Auntie's before they sent her away.

The people who greeted them when they reached the city were the same as ever, coming to the road to call out welcome, staring at Isika, smiling shyly at Abbas and Jerutha. One woman came right to Jerutha and offered her flowers from her garden.

Isika looked at Jabari, who, ever since their conversation beside the fire, always seemed to be walking beside her.

"What was that about?" she asked.

"No idea," he answered, watching with a slight frown as the woman went back to her porch. Jerutha, on her horse, stared down at the flowers in her hands. Her baby cried, and she pulled him out of his sling with a motion she had practiced over the journey, feeding him easily, even on horseback.

They reached the point where the road was paved with wide stones. The horse's shoes clattered and the sound seemed unbearably loud after the thud of their hooves on sand and dirt. There were only minutes before they would be at the palace. Isika took a deep breath.

"I see why you wanted to rescue her," Jabari said, and Isika looked up at him in surprise. "She should never have been a prisoner."

Isika nodded, but couldn't keep herself from adding, "No one should," fiercely, under her breath.

Jabari quirked an eyebrow in her direction and she stopped worrying long enough to smile at him.

They were at the palace. Oh *deserts and dust*, she didn't want to leave Azariyah. And yet there was nothing she could do, no promises she could make to behave better, do a better job at being on trial. Because if it happened again, right now, if someone she loved was in danger, Isika would go, without hesitation.

Above her, Keethior let out a long, low cry, and Isika straightened her shoulders. He cried out again and then despite her fear and worry, she laughed as Nirral, Efir, and Eemia swooped through the sky toward him, diving at him until it seemed they would all tumble out of the sky. At the last moment, Keethior escaped them and flew up, straight up until he was only a speck. The three followed him and then, together, dove down, in a dance, twirling and tumbling and finally pulling up and flying lightly. Jerutha, from her horse, gave a small cheer, which startled Isika. She had never heard her stepmother make a sound like that before.

Then they were at the palace, and the meeting could not be put off for even one more second. Isika's heart was lighter because of the Othra, but the sight of Ivram, Andar, Karah, and Laylit almost drove the sense of well-being away. The four elders stood on the highest stair to receive the travelers, shiny and brilliant in their colorful robes. A cold lump of fear formed in Isika's stomach. The seekers and their fellow travelers clustered at the bottom of the stairs. Isika looked down at her dirty hands again, her grimy travel clothes. She was no queen. The elders were brilliant, royal, *clean*. She was just an orphan, parentless, no one to speak for her.

Isika couldn't look up, couldn't meet Ivram's eyes. She focused, instead, on Jerutha's leg, just in front of her, hanging at Wind's side. Jerutha was still on her horse. Wind nudged Isika's mind.

What's wrong?

Nothing I can explain right now, Isika told him, barely able to concentrate. She thought her heart might beat out of her chest. She took deep, unsteady breaths, vaguely aware of the murmurs and formal greetings around her. Because she was staring so intently at Jerutha's bare foot, she missed the approach, but jerked her head up as soon as she saw a slender, white, jeweled hand reach out and close around Jerutha's thin, dirty ankle.

It was Karah. She stood staring up at Isika's stepmother, holding onto her foot. Isika looked back and forth between the two of them, unable to comprehend what was happening. Isika reached up to take the baby as Jerutha handed him to her, then watched as Jerutha slid down the horse's flank to stand in front of Karah. The elder was half a foot taller than Jerutha, and for a moment, Isika didn't realize what she was seeing, but when she did, she gasped, and the baby in her arms whimpered as she accidentally tightened her arms.

Karah's hair was redder, a deep, rich copper color, and Jerutha's was brown, with only hints of red. And Jerutha was smaller, thinner, more worn. But their faces, in profile, looking at each other as they were, were nearly identical, mirror images of each other.

30

"Do I know you somehow?" Isika heard Karah ask Jerutha.

Memories floated through Isika's head.

Jerutha telling the sad story of her mother. *My sister was sent out before I was born. My mother went insane, she went out to the forest and never came back.*

Ivram telling of how they had begun rescuing the Worker children. *Karah was the first outcast we ever found. I found her myself—I was just a small boy and her boat had drifted to our shore. From then on we sent the boats to rescue the children who were given over.*

Ben after the first time they met the elders, whispering to her about Karah. *She looks familiar, doesn't she? As though we've known her in some other life.*

Jerutha stared up at the older woman in confusion.

"I don't know if I've ever met you, but you look just like my mother," she said.

"And who was your mother, child?" Karah asked, her voice very gentle, like rain on leaves.

"She was Hinnah," Jerutha whispered, "Of the fishers."

"Then you are my sister," Karah said, her face glowing in wonder. "And I never knew I had a sister."

"I knew about you," Jerutha said, still whispering, so that Isika thought she might be the only person nearby who heard, as she stood there protectively, not wanting to move away, patting the baby on his back, his little warm head nestled into her neck. She hummed under her breath, transfixed by what was happening, a new and unexpected miracle. Jerutha put her hands over her face, and Karah put an arm around her shoulder and pulled her close, so that Jerutha turned her face into the older woman's beautiful robe and sobbed.

"Welcome home, sister!" Karah called out, after Jerutha had calmed a bit, and the people all around them cheered.

THEN THEY STOOD TALKING and greeting one another. Jabari helped the two young children off the horse, and people came to offer the pair of them water and touch them gently on their heads. Isika heard a cluster of people discussing which village they might have come from, trying to untangle the directions from what the children could remember.

Karah and Ivram stood talking with Jerutha, who seemed stunned and overwhelmed, not far from the way Isika herself felt.

Bara slipped up to Isika and squeezed her arm, then

silently led the horses away. Isika felt and heard the happy noises the horses made over the prospect of food and rest.

Tomorrow, Wind told her, as he followed Bara, *I will stand under my favorite tree. Nothing else.*

Isika smiled. She felt a presence at her side and looked up to see Uncle Dawit standing beside her with Kital on his shoulders. A moment later, something heavy knocked into her side and she looked down to see Ibba, who threw her arms around Isika and squeezed as hard as she could. Isika squeezed her with her free arm, and Kital scrambled down from Uncle's shoulders to get in the hug. Ben ran over and it was a pile of hugging siblings.

Isika was close to tears. She looked around for Aria and saw her with her adopted parents. As she watched, Jabari approached Aria and her parents with a woman that Isika recognized as a healer. They spoke for a few moments, then all turned and walked in the direction of the healing tents. Isika let out a breath she hadn't known she'd been holding.

"Come on! Isika!" Kital said, hopping on one foot. "Auntie made cake and we can't have it till you come home!"

Isika blinked at her uncle and reached up an arm to hug him, still holding the baby in the other arm.

"Come on then, child," he said. "Let's get you some food and rest."

"But Jerutha," she said. "Where will she stay?" She went to her stepmother and friend. Jerutha's face was gray with exhaustion, but she reached out to take her baby.

"Karah says Mesu and I can stay in their rooms in the palace," she said. Isika wondered if Jerutha had ever said the word palace before that moment. From the fishing hut to the priest's prison, to the palace. Jerutha's face looked the way Isika felt.

"That's wonderful," she told her stepmother gently. Jerutha already knew that Isika had a home in Azariyah. They had discussed whether Jerutha would be able to fit as well, but it seemed there was no need. Isika stood watching as the three of them climbed the stairs to the palace. A little way away, Abbas stood watching as well. He looked wary and slightly lost. He stood alert, as though still ready to fight.

"Uncle," Isika said as Dawit walked to stand beside her. "Can I bring a new friend over?"

"Of course," he said.

She went to Abbas. "Would you like to eat with us?" she asked. And then she pretended not to see the look of relief that crossed his face.

THE HOUSE SMELLED OF BAKING, and after the desert its quiet coolness was like a cold cloth on a feverish face. Isika sighed with happiness as she walked into the house and straight into Auntie's arms. They hugged for a long time, then Auntie drew back to look at her. Isika knew there were no bruises or cuts to see, as her face had healed quickly once they stepped back into Maween, but still Auntie clicked her tongue and made unhappy noises.

"Thin again! After all the work I did to fatten you up! Come now, before dinner gets cold."

But then she turned to Abbas and held two hands out to

him. He took her two hands and pressed one after the other to his forehead.

"You are welcome in our tent," she said.

"Your welcome is water in the desert," he said in reply. He looked strange in the house, tall and warrior-like with his earrings and long black hair.

"What was that?" Ben asked as they all stood looking back and forth between the two of them.

"It is the Gariah greeting," Abbas replied.

"But how did you know it, Auntie?" Ibba asked.

"I know many, many things, young one," she said. "Now help me set the table." And Isika felt it, the warm, clean sense of home and welcome. It felt right, and beautiful, and precious.

LATER, Isika sat on a cushion mending her boots, bathed and changed into a new tunic and soft pants, exquisitely clean and smelling good for the first time since she had left home. Nearby, Ibba played cards with Uncle and Abbas, and Ben read a book. Isika was content and happy, but with that steady fear inside, like a sharp piece of metal that wouldn't stop jabbing at her. But the evening was quiet, the lamps were lit, and she was trying hard to ignore the fear.

There was a knock at the door, and Kital jumped up from where he was playing to answer it.

After a moment, Jabari stood at the entrance to the living space, looking sheepish.

"I'm here to tell you that the elders will be here for an audience in a moment," he said.

"Now?" Teru demanded, one hand on her hip. "Surely your parents haven't lost their minds."

"It won't take long. It's best this way, Isika," Jabari replied, looking only at her. "You won't need to wonder. You can rest tomorrow, knowing what will happen."

Isika's heart beat rapidly. She couldn't tell, from his words, whether he thought the news would be good or bad. But he was right. She nodded, eyes on his.

"They wanted you to come to the palace, but I told them Auntie should be there."

Auntie almost never left her home anymore. Her eyes softened, looking at him. "All right, son," she said. "There are spice cakes in the oven. Come help me cut them up."

Not too much later, a little crowd of people arrived: Andar, Laylit, Ivram, Karah, Ivy, and then Jerutha, and Gavi, who held baby Mesu.

Uncle Dawit stood up.

"Come in, friends, come in."

Teru went to put the kettle on. Her back was stiff with what Isika was beginning to recognize as protectiveness. Isika got to her feet and kissed Jerutha on the cheek, looking into her eyes to see how she was doing. She saw wonder, and a new thing; hope. Jerutha was dressed in a rose colored robe that hung a little too large on her, but transformed her face with its warmth.

Isika took the baby from Gavi, kissing him on his soft cheek. He too, was clean and sweet smelling. He smiled at

Isika and she put him on her hip and went to show him to Auntie. Isika was afraid of why they had come. Everyone settled on various cushions and couches, and Teru poured tea, a golden fragrant blend that was made for welcoming the end of day.

"Well?" Andar said. "Aren't you going to ask us why we came?"

Teru snorted. "I think we're waiting to see if you will explain," she said.

"We thought it would be too much to ask you to the palace again," Karah said. "But we wanted to talk about what has happened, and what has been decided, and quickly, so you don't have to wonder."

Isika looked at Jabari and caught his eye. He looked away innocently.

He had pushed for them to come quickly, then, knowing how she felt about waiting, knowing her fear. She felt a sudden rush of warmth toward him. He sat cross-legged on the mat, his spine tall yet relaxed. His dark skin glowed like a new pot out of the kiln. She dragged her eyes back to Karah.

"You have returned my sister to me," Karah said. "When we told you not to go to Jerutha, we didn't know just how much we risked."

Isika nodded, uncomfortable at the mention of her rebellion. However kindly Karah said it, she had chosen to go against the will of the elders. But she looked at Jerutha, sitting quietly, her hands in her lap, and she felt a sudden gladness that her stepmother would be fully welcomed into the palace family, treated as she should always have been treated.

"You went against what the elders said," Andar said.

"But your instincts were good," Ivram broke in, "and therefore we are again in a difficult position. What to do?" Ivram's eyes shone in the lamplight, and Isika bent her head and studied the rug thoroughly. "Not only that, Isika," he said gently, "but the kind of magic Jabari tells us you did hasn't been seen in these lands for thirty years. Since your grandmother was taken."

"And yet you have shown again that you don't respect our ways," Andar put in.

"Father, she turned a desert into a meadow!" Jabari cried. "And though I was powerless against the priests, she made them disappear. We opened our eyes and it was over. She did it herself."

Isika spoke up. "Actually, it was the Keerza who made the priests disappear. And Nenyi made the water appear. I didn't do it."

"You are the World Whisperer," Gavi said quietly. "You are the link between Shaper and Shaped Ones. Of course Nenyi does it, she is always the origin. But you are the reason it can happen."

There was silence. Andar opened and closed his mouth a few times. At a look from Ivram, he sat forward.

"What you did was amazing, Isika," he said. "It is not so simple for any of us. We do not have the power that you do. We haven't seen anything like this for years and years. But we have to deal with the fact that you didn't do as we said." Beside him, Laylit's lovely face glowed in the lamplight. She held Andar's hand, squeezing it gently at his words.

Isika thought of herself, back in that desert, broken and bruised and desperate. She wouldn't describe anything she had done as simple, and she was beginning to understand that her place came with a heavy weight. She looked at Teru and was surprised to see that Auntie's eyes shone with tears.

"We talked it over," Karah said. "And we have decided that it will be as though nothing happened for you, Benayeem and Isika. You will resume your work and learning here, but your trial will be restarted, you will again work a year. After that time, we will decide what to do with you, World Whisperer."

Even Ivram looked shocked when Karah spoke the title, but Karah gazed back at Isika with warmth and love in her eyes, and Isika understood a little of what Jerutha meant to her.

"Isika," Ivram said, and his voice was stern. Isika dragged her eyes away from Karah's kind eyes to look at him, her eyes resting briefly on the staff in his hand. It called to her again, and for a moment, she imagined what she would have been in the desert, if she had that staff with her. The tip flashed white, and Ivram glanced at it, then continued, his voice softer.

"You must understand. You are one of us now. There is a proper way to enter into your future. We require you to stay, and listen, and be as one of us. That means finishing your apprenticeship and not going on any more journeys against our wishes."

Isika nodded, but she was silent. She didn't know how she could promise not to help someone else if they asked.

Hopefully no one would send her any more messengers. Then she would be able to finish her trial without further disobedience.

The elders didn't stay long after that. Auntie passed around spice cakes, then they rose and stood to go. Isika let go of the sleeping baby reluctantly. "I'll come tomorrow to see you," she told Jerutha, and Jerutha smiled at her.

"I'm so thankful for you, my sister," she told Isika.

Isika kissed the baby one more time and watched the elders leave from the door. Beside her, Ibba slipped an arm around her waist.

"It just keeps getting better, doesn't it?" the little girl said.

As Isika heard Jerutha's rare laugh echo in the valley, she had to agree.

EPILOGUE

Three days later, Isika dragged herself out of sleep when she heard Ben calling her name.

"What?" she said. He stood in the doorway of her room.

"Auntie says get up, Tomas is going to have your head," he said, then left quickly.

Oh no! It was her first day back in the workshop and she could see that the sun was higher in the sky than it should be. She jumped up and dressed quickly, picking a soft pink tunic and winding her braids around her head.

"Why didn't you wake me earlier?" she moaned as she rushed into the kitchen.

"You need sleep," Auntie said. "No, no, don't even think about it. Come back here and eat your breakfast. Yes, he can wait a few more minutes."

The coffee was good, Isika had to admit. She ate Auntie's eggs and tomatoes, then jumped up to lace her soft boots, grab her satchel, and run out the door. She ran all the way to the workshop, breathless by the time she got there.

The door was open as usual, and she took a moment to compose herself before she went in. She soaked in the scene as she looked around, the building with its tall, bright windows, all the tables with pots in various stages. A couple of the other apprentices looked up and nodded, and Tomas looked up from where he sat at one of the pottery wheels.

"You're late," he said, then went back to throwing the pot he was working on. Isika waited. After a moment he looked up again.

"We have a big order from the school," he said. "You're on cups. Instructions are in the storage room."

Isika grinned and went to put her apron on, warmth filling her heart as she walked into the storage room to look over the plans. Someone was sweeping out the kiln room, and she paused as she tried to get by. The person looked up and Isika was suddenly breathless, looking into Jabari's deep brown eyes.

"What are you doing here?" she blurted, and he grinned.

"Hello to you, too," he said.

"No really, what are you doing here? You're a seeker."

He frowned and kept sweeping. "Well, my parents want me to take a little break from Seeking and they told me to pick a job. I find I want to be closer to the City anyway, get to know it a little more, and I've always been curious about pottery. So... here I am."

"You've always been curious about pottery."

"Yes!" he said, his eyes round and innocent.

Isika sighed and pushed by him to get into the storage room. No way. No way was Jabari going to be working in the pottery workshop! Why couldn't anything ever be simple? She ran her eyes over the instructions that were nailed on the wall, barely seeing what they said. She finally forced herself to focus, picked up a large slab of clay, and began to wedge it so she could throw it into hundreds of cups.

ACKNOWLEDGMENTS

Thanks again to Sara J Henry, who is the best kind of sharp-eyed reader. She doesn't let me get away with being confusing.

Thanks to Chinua, who is such a good first reader, and to Rowan, who encourages me with her love for these characters. Thanks to my kids, who inspire me endlessly.

Thank you to my dear friend Christy, who is the bravest, most inspiring person I know.

Thanks to my mom and her proofreading skills, to the readers of my blog, and to my Amazing Unicorn Readers' Group who read, correct, and review my words.

Thanks to Rowan, for her enthusiastic first readings, and to my beautiful, beautiful community, for your care and understanding. I love living with you!

Thanks to Cate for being simply amazing and so supportive.

I can't do anything without the love and support of friends in my life. So, thank you.

ABOUT THE AUTHOR

Newsletter

If you want to join Rachel Devenish Ford's Newsletter and learn about books and new releases, sign up here. Your address will never be shared!

∽

Bio

Rachel Devenish Ford is the wife of one Superstar Husband and the mother of five incredible children. Originally from British Columbia, Canada, she spent seven years working with street youth in California before moving to India to help start a meditation center in the Christian tradition. She can be found eating street food or smelling flowers in many cities in Asia. She currently lives in Northern Thailand, inhaling books, morning air, and seasonal fruit.

~

Works by Rachel Devenish Ford:

The Eve Tree

A Traveler's Guide to Belonging

Trees Tall As Mountains: The Journey Mama Writings-Book One

Oceans Bright With Stars: The Journey Mama Writings-Book Two

A Home as Wide as the Earth: The Journey Mama Writings: Book Three

World Whisperer : World Whisperer Book 1

Guardian of Dawn : World Whisperer Book 2

Shaper's Daughter: World Whisperer Book 3

Reviews

Recommendations and reviews are such an important part of the success of a book. If you enjoyed this book, please take the time to leave a review.

Don't be afraid of leaving a short review! Even a couple lines will help and will overwhelm the author with waves of gratitude.

~

Contact

Email: racheldevenishford@gmail.com
   Blog: http://journeymama.com
   Facebook: http://www.facebook.com/racheldevenishford
   Twitter: http://www.twitter.com/journeymama
   Instagram: http://instagram.com/journeymama

ALSO BY RACHEL DEVENISH FORD

Rachel has spent twelve years writing about life on her blog, Journey Mama. She has collected the best of these posts in the Journey Mama Writings series. If you love to know everything you wanted to know about authors and their children, you might like The Journey Mama Writing Series.

Book One: Trees Tall as Mountains

Book Two: Oceans Bright with Stars

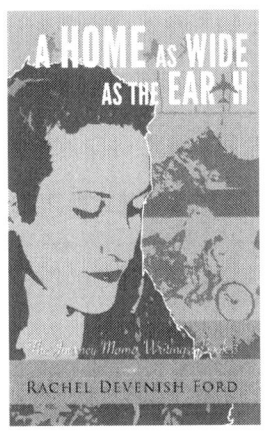

Book Three: A Home as Wide as the Earth

If you like literary fiction, you might like <u>A Traveler's Guide to Belonging</u>.

"A beautiful, beautiful book." -Sara J. Henry, Award-winning author of Learning to Swim

Twenty-four-year-old Timothy is far from his home country of Canada when his new wife dies in childbirth. Stunned, he finds himself alone with his newborn son in the mountains of North India and no idea of what it means to be a father. He begins a journey through India with his baby, seeking understanding for loss and life and the way the two intertwine.

Set among the stunning landscapes, train tracks, and winding alleys of India, *A Traveler's Guide to Belonging* is a story about fathers and sons, losing and finding love, and a traveler's quest for meaning.

Printed in Great Britain
by Amazon

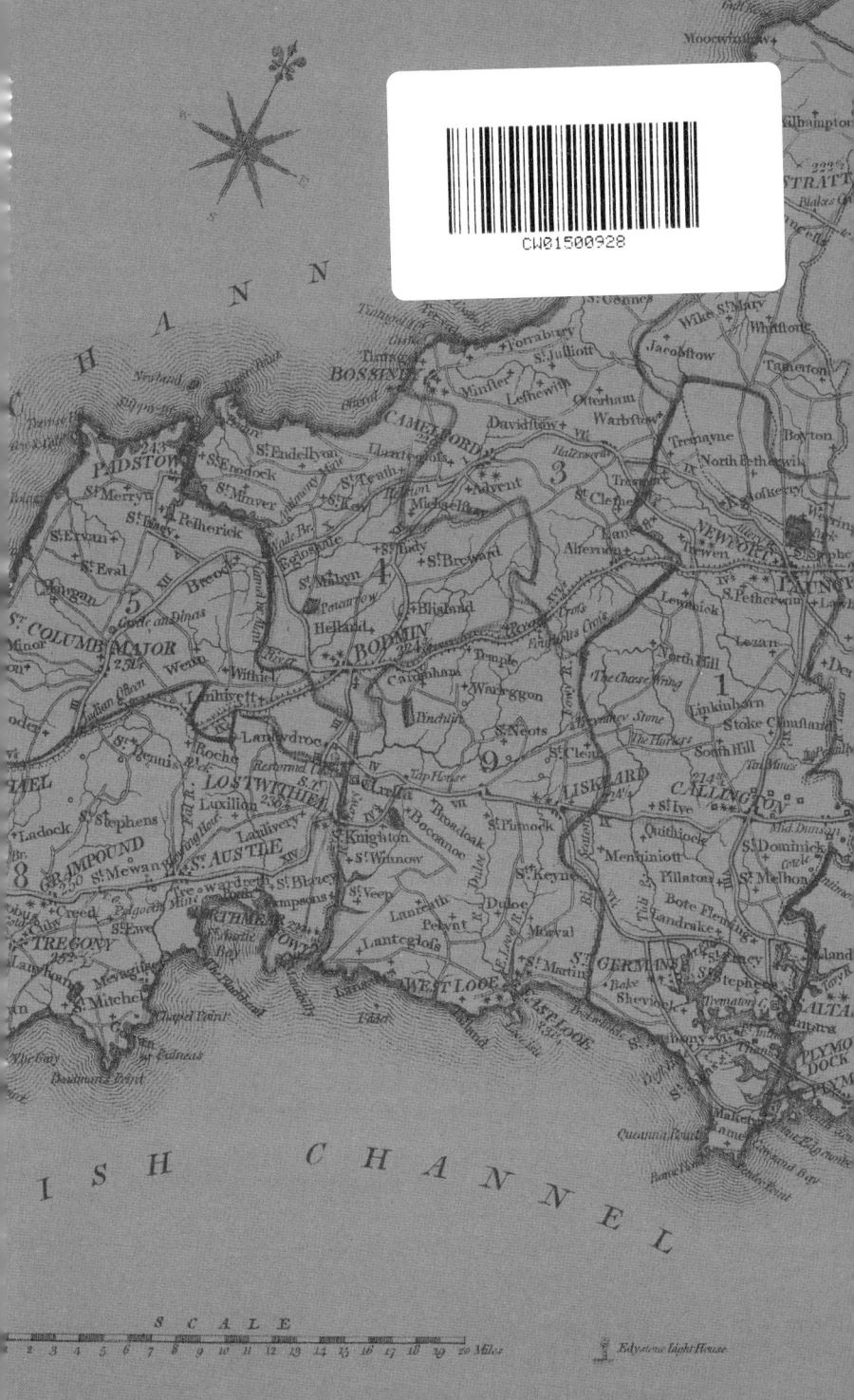

WILKIE COLLINS
ON
CORNWALL

WILKIE COLLINS
ON
CORNWALL

Foreword by Rick Stein

BODLEIAN
LIBRARY
PUBLISHING

This edition published in 2026 by Bodleian Library Publishing
Broad Street, Oxford OX1 3BG
www.bodleianshop.co.uk

ISBN 978 1 85124 656 4

Foreword © Rick Stein, 2026.

Rick Stein has asserted his right to be identified
as the author of the Foreword to this Work.

Illustrations by Henry C. Brandling from *Rambles Beyond Railways*,
1851, Bodleian Library, G.A. Cornw. 8° 5.
Front cover: John Samuel Lamorna Birch, *Pedn Vounder
and the Logan Rock, Land's End*, 1935. Photo: Alamy/Artepics.

First published as *Rambles Beyond Railways, or, Notes in Cornwall
taken A-Foot* in 1851 by Richard Bentley, London. The text
reproduced here is based on the second edition of 1861 but
omits the Postscript. Some spellings have been modernized.

Publisher: Samuel Fanous
Managing Editor: Susie Foster
Editor: Janet Phillips
Picture Editor: Leanda Shrimpton
Cover design by Dot Little at the Bodleian Library
Designed and typeset by Lucy Morton of illuminati
in 10.2 on 15 ITC New Baskerville
Printed and bound in China by C&C Offset Printing Co., Ltd
on 115 gsm Chinese Yulong Pure paper

British Library Catalogue in Publishing Data
A CIP record of this publication is available from the British Library

CONTENTS

FOREWORD

F ROM 2020 TO 2022, I made three programmes titled *Rick Stein's Cornwall*, a series which, for me, was made in heaven. I travelled through the "Delectable Duchy," so named by Arthur Quiller-Couch, remarking on the beauty of its seascapes, farmland and moors. I visited luscious valleys with tall deciduous trees and rich farms in the south and east, but then I also travelled to North Cornwall, romantic Jamaica Inn country, rugged and windswept, with stunted trees leaning away from the prevailing western winds. In West Penwith I found even sparser countryside, old farm houses, small farms, tiny prehistoric fields divided by stone walls and ancient sites everywhere, which really do make you feel we are all connected to the land in some way.

All the while I was cooking recipes from Cornwall or dishes inspired by Cornish produce. I also—and this was the part I really loved—looked at the history, folklore, art, literature and music of the county, often using such visitors to Cornwall as John Betjeman, Charles Dickens or Thomas Hardy as literary companions. My biggest regret is that only at the eleventh hour did I receive a copy of Wilkie Collins's book *Rambles Beyond Railways* from a good friend. Literally on the last day of filming, standing in the centre of Redruth by a sculpture of a tin miner, I read out a passage from the book which matched the clothing of the tin miner in the sculpture I was standing next to:

> The clothing consisted of a flannel shirt, flannel drawers, canvas trousers, and a canvas jacket— all stained of a tawny copper colour... A white night-cap and a round hat, composed of some non-hard substance, well calculated to protect the head from any loose stones that might fall on it.

Wilkie Collins had been given these to wear down the Botallack mine, which extends out under the sea between St Ives and St Just. He was told: "You'll be wet through with the heat and the work before you come up again." Collins had much respect for miners, "As a body of men, they are industrious and intelligent; sober and orderly; neither soured by hard work, nor easily depressed by harder privations," he wrote.

While down Botallack, witnessing first-hand the toughness of their work, he notes:

Lumps of ooze, of the most lustrous green colour, traversed by a natural network of thin red veins of iron, appear here and there in large irregular patches, over which water is dripping slowly and incessantly in certain places. This is the saltwater percolating through invisible crannies in the rock. On stormy days it spirts out furiously in thin, continuous streams. Just over our heads we observe a wooden plug of the thickness of a man's leg; there is a hole here, and the plug is all that we have to keep out the sea.

At the risk of concentrating too much on his extraordinary visit to Botallack, I am also going to quote his description of the view there—I do so because like so much in the book it seems to sum up the power of great descriptive writing, something Collins's mentor Charles Dickens was a master of, too. To me it is almost more powerful than photography, and I'm sure anyone who has been to Botallack will appreciate the power of the intellect to make an already spectacular view even more powerful.

Here, we beheld a scaffolding perched on a rock that rose out of the waves—there, a steam-pump was at work raising gallons of water from the mine every minute, on a mere ledge of land half way down the steep cliff side. Chains, pipes, conduits, protruded in all directions from the precipice; rotten-looking wooden platforms, running over deep chasms, supported great beams of timber and heavy coils of cable; crazy

little boarded houses were built, where gulls'
nests might have been found in other places.
There did not appear to be a foot of level space
anywhere, for any part of the works of the mine
to stand upon; and yet, there they were, fulfilling
all the purposes for which they had been
constructed, as safely and completely on rocks
in the sea, and down precipices in the land, as if
they had been cautiously founded on the tracts of
smooth solid ground above!

Collins was only twenty-six when he spent the summer
of 1850 "backpacking" (as we would call it now) through
Cornwall with an artist friend, Henry C. Brandling,
whose illustrations appeared in the first editions of the
book. He records a fascinating lost world before the
railways arrived. Some of his descriptions remind me of
days I spent filming in northern Bangladesh about twenty
years ago, and particularly waiting at a river crossing for
a ferry to take our minibus across one of the many wide
rivers there, along with a jumble of itinerant traders.
One was a dentist with a wire trolley with pliers, picks
and various types of what looked like old metal mouth
clamps, and another carried honeycombs for sale with
some bees still attached to them. The Cornwall in which
Collins travelled was similarly lost in time. Everywhere he
went on this trip the inhabitants were puzzled by what
on earth the two men were doing there:

Everybody asked whether we could pay for riding, and nobody believed that we preferred walking, if we could. So we soon gave up the idea of affording any information at all; and walked through the country comfortably as mappers, trodgers, tradesmen, guinea-pig-mongers, and poor back-burdened vagabond lads, altogether, or one at a time, just as the peasantry pleased.

The joy of the whole book is that it's so well written and feels so modern. I have shared similar experiences in Cornwall, good and bad, and I guess we have all spent a night in a terrible hotel, so his description of one in Liskeard is fabulous:

Not a human being appeared in the street where this tavern of despair frowned amid congenial desolation. Nobody welcomed us at the door—the sign creaked dolefully, as the wind swung it on its rusty hinges. We walked in and discovered a low-spirited little man sitting at an empty "bar," and hiding himself, as it were, from all mortal inspection, behind the full sheet of a dirty provincial newspaper. Doleful was our petition to this secluded publican for shelter and food; and doubly doleful was his answer to our appeal. Beds he believed he had—food there was none in the house, saving a piece of *corned beef*, which the family had dined on, and which he proposed that we should partake of before it got quite cold. Having said thus much, he suddenly retired behind his newspaper and spoke no word more.

Observation and writing like this are such a pleasure to read. I wish during all my filming I had a copy of *Rambles Beyond Railways* tucked into the glove box just so I could quote a line or two every time I went somewhere that Collins had visited. Even though he was writing about a world very soon changed by the arrival of the railways, it's still relevant to anyone who loves Cornwall, because for us, I think, it's a place still filled with echoes of the past.

Rick Stein

ONE

A LETTER OF INTRODUCTION

DEAR READER,

When any friend of yours or mine, in whose fortunes we take an interest, is about to start on his travels, we smooth his way for him as well as we can, by giving him a letter of introduction to such connexions of ours as he may find on his line of route. We bespeak their favourable consideration for him by setting forth his good qualities in the best light possible; and then leave him to make his own way by his own merit—satisfied that we have done enough in procuring him a welcome under our friend's roof, and giving him at the outset a claim to our friend's estimation.

Will you allow me, reader (if our previous acquaintance authorizes me to take such a liberty), to follow the custom to which I have just adverted; and to introduce to your notice this Book, as a friend of mine setting forth on his travels, in whose well-being I feel a very lively

St Michael's Mount

interest. He is neither so bulky nor so distinguished a person as some of the predecessors of his race, who may have sought your attention in years gone by, under the name of "Quarto," and in magnificent clothing of Morocco and Gold. All that I can say for his outside is that I have made it as neat as I can—having had him properly thumped into wearing his present coat of decent cloth, by the most competent book-tailor I could find. As for his intrinsic claims to your kindness, he has only two that I shall venture to advocate. In the first place he is able to tell you something about a part of your own country which is still too rarely visited and too little known. He will speak to you of one of the remotest and most interesting corners of our old English soil. He will tell you of the grand and varied scenery; the mighty Druid relics; the quaint legends; the deep, dark mines; the venerable remains of early Christianity; and the pleasant primitive population of the county of CORNWALL. You will inquire, can we believe him in all that he says? This brings me at once to his second qualification—he invariably speaks the truth. If he describes scenery to you, it is scenery that he saw and noted on the spot; and if he adds some little sketches of character, I answer for him, on my own responsibility, that they are sketches drawn from the life.

Have I said enough about my friend to interest you in his fortunes, when you meet him wandering hither

3

and thither over the great domain of the Republic of Letters—or, must I plead more warmly in his behalf? I can only urge on you that he does not present himself as fit for the top seats at the library table—as aspiring to the company of those above him—of classical, statistical, political, philosophical, historical, or antiquarian high dignitaries of his class, of whom he is at best but the poor relation. Treat him not, as you treat such illustrious guests as these! Toss him about anywhere, from hand to hand, as good-naturedly as you can; stuff him into your pocket when you get into the railway; take him to bed with you, and poke him under the pillow; present him to the rising generation, to try if he can amuse *them*; give him to the young ladies, who are always predisposed to the kind side, and may make something of him; introduce him to "my young masters" when they are idling away a dull morning over their cigars. Nay, advance him if you will to the notice of the elders themselves; but take care to ascertain first that they are people who only travel to gratify a hearty admiration of the wonderful works of Nature, and to learn to love their neighbour better by seeking him at his own home—regarding it, at the same time, as a peculiar privilege, to derive their satisfaction and gain their improvement from experiences on English ground. Take care of this; and who knows into what high society you may not be able to introduce the bearer of the present letter! In spite of his habit of rambling from subject to subject in his talk, much as he rambled from place to place in his travels, he may actually find himself, one day, basking on Folio Classics beneath the genial approval of a Doctor of Divinity, or trembling among Statutes and Reports under the learned scrutiny of a Sergeant at Law!

W.C.

HARLEY STREET, LONDON,
March, 1861

TWO

A CORNISH
FISHING TOWN

Tㅐㅌ TIME IS TEN O'CLOCK AT NIGHT—the scene, a bank by the roadside, crested with young fir-trees, and affording a temporary place of repose to two travellers, who are enjoying the cool night air, picturesquely extended flat on their backs—or rather, on their knapsacks, which now form part and parcel of their backs. These two travellers are the writer of this book and an artist friend who is the companion of his rambles. They have long desired to explore Cornwall together, on foot; and the object of their aspirations has been at last accomplished, in the summertime of the year eighteen hundred and fifty.

In their present position, the travellers are (to speak geographically) bounded towards the east by a long road winding down the side of a rocky hill; towards the west, by the broad half-dry channel of a tidal river; towards the north by trees, hills, and upland valleys; and towards

6

the south by an old bridge and some houses near it, with lights in their windows faintly reflected in shallow water. In plainer words, the southern boundary of the prospect around them represents a place called Looe—a fishing town on the south coast of Cornwall, which is their destination for the night.

They had, by this time, accomplished their initiation into the process of walking under a knapsack, with the most complete and encouraging success. You, who in these days of vehement bustle, business, and competition can still find time to travel for pleasure alone—you, who have yet to become emancipated from the thraldom of railways, carriages and saddle horses—patronize, I exhort you, that first and oldest-established of all conveyances, your own legs! Think on your tender partings nipped in the bud by the railway bell; think of crabbed crossroads, and broken carriage-springs; think of luggage confided to extortionate porters, of horses casting shoes and catching colds, of cramped legs and numbed feet, of vain longings to get down for a moment here, and to delay for a pleasant half hour there—think of all these manifold hardships of riding at your ease; and the next time you leave home, strap your luggage on your shoulders, take your stick in your hand, set forth delivered from a perfect paraphernalia of incumbrances, to go where you will, how you will—the free citizen of the whole travelling world! Thus independent, what may you not accomplish?—what pleasure is there that you cannot enjoy? Are you an artist?—you can stop to sketch every point of view that strikes your eye. Are you a philanthropist?—you can go into every cottage and talk to every human being you pass. Are you a botanist, or geologist?—you may pick up leaves and chip rocks wherever you please, the live-long day. Are you a valetudinarian?—you may physic yourself by Nature's own simple prescription, walking in fresh air. Are you dilatory and irresolute?—you may dawdle to your heart's content; you may change all your plans a dozen times in a dozen hours; you may tell "Boots" at the inn to call you at six o'clock, may fall asleep again (ecstatic sensation!) five minutes after he has knocked at the door, and may get up two hours later, to pursue your journey, with perfect impunity and satisfaction. For, to you, what is a timetable but waste paper?—and a "booked place" but a relic of the dark ages? You dread, perhaps, blisters on your feet—sponge your feet with cold vinegar and water, change your socks every ten miles, and show me blisters after that, if you can! You strap on your knapsack for the first time, and five minutes afterwards feel an aching pain in the muscles at the back of your neck—walk *on*, and the aching will walk *off*! How do we overcome our first painful cuticular reminiscences of first getting on horseback?—by riding again. Apply the same rule to carrying the knapsack, and be assured of the same successful result. Again I say it, therefore—walk, and be merry; walk, and be healthy; walk, and be your own master!—walk, to enjoy, to observe, to improve, as no riders can!—walk, and you are the best peripatetic impersonation of holiday enjoyment that is to be met with on the surface of this work-a-day world!

How much more could I not say in praise of travelling on our own neglected legs? But it is getting late; dark night-clouds are marching slowly over the sky, to the whistling music of the wind; we must leave our bank by the roadside, pass one end of the old bridge, walk along a narrow winding street, and enter our hospitable little inn, where we are welcomed by the kindest of landladies, and waited on by the fairest of chambermaids. If Looe prove not to be a little sea-shore paradise tomorrow, then is there no virtue in the good omens of tonight.

The first point for which we made in the morning, was the old bridge; and a most picturesque and singular structure we found it to be. Its construction dates back as far as the beginning of the fifteenth century. It is three hundred and eighty-four feet long, and has fourteen arches, no two of which are on the same scale. The stout buttresses built between each arch are hollowed at the top into curious triangular places of refuge for pedestrians, the roughly paved roadway being just wide enough to allow the passage of one cart at a time. On

Looe

some of these buttresses, towards the middle, once stood an oratory, or chapel, dedicated to St Anne; but no vestiges of it now remain. The old bridge, however, still rises sturdily enough on its ancient foundations; and, whatever the point from which its silver-grey stones and quaint arches of all shapes and sizes may be beheld, forms no mean adjunct to the charming landscape around it.

Looe is known to have existed as a town in the reign of Edward I; and it remains to this day one of the prettiest and most primitive places in England. The river divides it into East and West Looe; and the view from the bridge, looking towards the two little colonies of houses thus separated, is in some respects almost unique.

At each side of you rise high ranges of beautifully wooded hills; here and there a cottage peeps out among the trees, the winding path that leads to it being now lost to sight in the thick foliage, now visible again as a thin serpentine line of soft grey. Midway on the slopes appear the gardens of Looe, built up the acclivity on stone terraces one above another; thus displaying the veritable garden architecture of the mountains of Palestine magically transplanted to the side of an English hill. Here, in this soft and genial atmosphere, the hydrangea is a common flower-bed ornament, the fuchsia grows lofty and luxuriant in the poorest cottage garden, the myrtle flourishes close to the seashore, and the tender tamarisk is the wild plant of every farmer's hedge. Looking lower down the hills yet, you see the houses of the town straggling out towards the sea along each bank of the river, in mazes of little narrow streets; curious old quays project over the water at different points; coast-trade vessels are being loaded and unloaded, built in one place and repaired in another, all within view; while the prospect of hills, harbour, and houses thus quaintly combined together is beautifully closed by the English Channel, just visible as a small strip of blue water, pent in between the ridges of two promontories which stretch out on either side to the beach.

Such is Looe as beheld from a distance; and it loses none of its attractions when you look at it more closely. There is no such thing as a straight street in the place. No martinet of an architect has been here, to drill the old stone houses into regimental regularity. Sometimes you go down steps into the ground floor, sometimes you mount an outside staircase to get to the bedrooms. Never were such places devised for hide-and-seek since that exciting nursery pastime was first invented. No house has fewer than two doors leading into two different lanes; some have three, opening at once into a court, a street, and a wharf, all situated at different points of the compass. The shops, too, have their diverting irregularities, as well as the town. Here you might call a man a Jack of all trades, as the best and truest compliment you could pay him—for here one shop combines in itself a drug-mongering, cheese-mongering, stationery, grocery, and oil and Italian line of business; to say nothing of such cosmopolitan miscellanies as wrinkled apples, dusty nuts, cracked slate pencils and fly-blown mock jewellery. The moral good which you derive, in the first pane of a window, from the contemplation of memoirs of murdered missionaries and serious tracts against intemperance and tight-lacing, you lose in the second, before such worldly temptations as gingerbread, shirt studs, and fascinating white hats for Sunday wear, at two and ninepence apiece. Let no man rashly say he has seen all that British enterprise can do for the extension of British commerce, until he has carefully studied the shopfronts of the tradesmen of Looe.

Then, when you have at last threaded your way successfully through the streets, and have got out on the beach, you see a pretty miniature bay, formed by the extremity of a green hill on the right, and by fine jagged slate rocks on the left. Before this seaward quarter of the town is erected a strong bulwark of rough stones, to resist the incursion of high tides. Here, the idlers of the place assemble to lounge and gossip, to look out for any outward-bound ships that are to be seen in the Channel, and to criticise the appearance and glorify the capabilities of the little fleet of Looe fishing-boats, riding snugly at anchor before them at the entrance of the bay.

The inhabitants number some fourteen hundred; and are as good-humoured and unsophisticated a set of people as you will meet with anywhere. The Fisheries and the Coast Trade form their principal means of subsistence. The women take a very fair share of the hard work out of the men's hands. You constantly see them carrying coals from the vessels to the quay in curious hand barrows: they laugh, scream, and run in each other's way incessantly: but these little irregularities seem to assist, rather than impede them, in the prosecution of their tasks. As to the men, one absorbing interest appears to govern them all. The whole day long they are mending boats, painting boats, cleaning boats, rowing boats, or, standing with their hands in their pockets, looking at boats. The children seem to be children in size, and children in nothing else. They congregate together in sober little groups, and hold mysterious conversations, in a dialect which we cannot understand. If they ever do tumble down, soil their pinafores, throw stones, or make mud pies, they practise these juvenile vices in a midnight secrecy which no stranger's eye can penetrate.

In that second period of the dark ages, when there were High Tories and rotten boroughs in the land, Looe (containing at that time nothing like the number of inhabitants which it now possesses) sent Four Members to Parliament! The ceremony by which two of these members were elected, as it was described to me by a man who remembered witnessing it, must have been an impressive sight indeed to any foreigner interested in studying the representative system of this country. On the morning of the "Poll," one division of the borough sent *six* electors, and another *four*, to record their imposing aggregate of votes in favour of any two smiling civil gentlemen, who came, properly recommended, to ask for them. This done, the ten electors walked quietly home in one direction, and the two members walked quietly off in another, to perform the fatiguing duty of representing their constituents' interests in Imperial Parliament. The election was quite a snug little family affair, in these "good old times." The ten gentlemen who voted, and the other two gentlemen who took their votes, just made up a comfortable compact dozen, all together!

But this state of things was too harmonious to last in such a world of discord as ours. The day of innovation came: turbulent Whigs and Radicals laid uncivil hands on the Looe polling booth, and politically annihilated the pleasant party of twelve. Since that disastrous period the town has sent no members to Parliament at all; and very little, indeed, do the townspeople appear to care about so serious a deprivation. In case the reader should be disposed to attribute this indifference to municipal privileges to the supineness rather than the philosophy of the inhabitants, I think it necessary to establish their just claims to be considered as possessing public spirit, prompt decision, and wise fertility of resource in cases of emergency, by relating in this place the true story of how the people of Looe got rid of the rats.

About a mile out at sea, to the southward of the town, rises a green triangular shaped eminence, called Looe Island. Here, many years ago, a ship was wrecked. Not only were the sailors saved, but several free passengers of the rat species, who had got on board, nobody knew how, where, or when, were also preserved by their own strenuous exertions, and wisely took up permanent quarters for the future on the terra firma of Looe Island. In process of time, and in obedience to the laws of nature, these rats increased and multiplied exceedingly; and, being confined all round within certain limits by the sea, soon became a palpable and dangerous nuisance. Destruction was threatened to the agricultural produce of all the small patches of cultivated land on the island—it seemed doubtful whether any man who ventured there by himself might not share the fate of Bishop Hatto, and be devoured by rats. Under these pressing circumstances, the people of Looe determined to make one united and vehement effort to extirpate the whole colony of invaders. Ordinary means of destruction had been tried already, and without effect. It was said that rats left for dead on the ground had mysteriously revived faster than they could be picked up and skinned, or flung into the sea. Rats desperately wounded had got away into their holes, and become convalescent, and increased and multiplied again more productively than ever. The great problem was not how to kill the rats, but how to annihilate them so effectually as to place the reappearance even of one of them altogether out of the question. This was the problem, and it was solved in the following manner:—

All the available inhabitants of the town were called to join in a great hunt. The rats were caught by every conceivable artifice; and, once taken, were instantly and ferociously *smothered in onions*; the corpses were then decently laid out on clean china dishes, and straightway eaten with vindictive relish by the people of Looe. Never was any invention for destroying rats so complete and so successful as this! Every man, woman, and child who could eat could swear to the extirpation of all the rats they had eaten. The local returns of dead rats were not made by the bills of mortality, but by the bills of fare: it was getting rid of a nuisance by the unheard-of process of stomaching a nuisance! Day after day passed on, and rats disappeared by hundreds, never to return. What could all their cunning and resolution avail them now? They had resisted before, and could have resisted still, the ordinary force of dogs, ferrets, traps, sticks, stones, and guns arrayed against them; but when to these engines of assault were added, as auxiliaries, smothering onions, scalding stew pans, hungry mouths, sharp teeth, good digestions and the gastric juice, what could they do but give in? Swift and sure was the destruction that now overwhelmed them—everybody who wanted a dinner had a strong personal interest in hunting them down to the very last. In a short space of time the island was cleared of the usurpers. Cheeses remained entire; ricks rose uninjured. And this is the true story of how the people of Looe got rid of the rats!

It will not much surprise any reader who has been good-natured enough to peruse the preceding pages with some attention to hear that we idly delayed the day of departure from the pleasant fishing town on the south coast, which was now the place of our sojourn. The smiles of our fair chambermaid and the cookery of our excellent hostess addressed us in Siren tones of allurement which we had not the virtue to resist. Then, it was difficult to leave unexplored any of the numerous walks in the neighbourhood—all delightfully varied in character, and each possessing its own attractive point of view. Even when we had made our determination and fixed our farewell day, a great boat race and a great tea-drinking, which everybody declared was something that everybody else ought to see, interfered to detain us. We delayed yet once more, to partake in the festivities, and found that they supplied us with all the necessary resolution to quit Looe which we had hitherto wanted.

18

We had remained to take part in a social failure on a very large scale.

As, in addition to the boat race, there was to be a bazaar on the beach; and as fine weather was therefore an essential requisite on the occasion, it is scarcely necessary to premise that we had an unusually large quantity of rain. In the forenoon, however, the sun shone with treacherous brilliancy; and all the women in the neighbourhood fluttered out in his beams, gay as butterflies. What dazzling gowns, what flaring parasols, what joyous cavalcades on carthorses did we see on the road that led to the town! What a mixture of excitement, confusion, anxiety, and importance possessed everybody! What frolic and felicity attended the popular gatherings on the beach, until the fatal moment when the gun fired for the first race! Then, as if at that signal, the clouds began to muster in ominous blackness; the deceitful sunlight disappeared; the rain came down for the day—a steady, noiseless, malicious rain, that at once forbade all hope of clear weather. Dire was the discomfiture of the poor ladies of Looe. They ran hither and thither for shelter, in lank wet muslin and under dripping parasols, displaying, in the lamentable emergency of the moment, all sorts of interior contrivances for expanding around them the exterior magnificence of their gowns, which we never ought to have seen. Deserted were the stalls of the bazaar for the parlours of the alehouses; unapplauded and unobserved, strained at the oar the stout rowers in the boat race. Everybody ran to cover, except some seafaring men who cared nothing for weather, some inveterate loungers who would wander up and down in spite of the rain, and three unhappy German musicians, who had been caught on their travels, and pinned up tight against the outer wall of a house, in a sort of cage of canvas, boards, and evergreens, which hid every part of them but their heads and shoulders. Nobody interfered to release these unfortunates. There they sat, hemmed in all round by dripping leaves, blowing grimly and incessantly through instruments of brass. If the reader can imagine the effect of three phlegmatic men with long bottle noses, looking out of a circle of green bushes, and playing waltzes unintermittingly on long horns, in a heavy shower—he will be able to form a tolerably correct estimate of the large extra proportion of gloom which the German musicians succeeded in infusing into the disastrous proceedings of the day.

The tea-drinking was rather more successful. The room in which it was held was filled to the corners, and exhaled such an odour of wet garments and bread and butter (to say nothing of an incessant clatter of china and bawling of voices) that we found ourselves, as uninitiated strangers, unequal to the task of remaining in it to witness the proceedings. Descending the steps which led into the street from the door—to the great confusion of a string of smartly dressed ladies who encountered us, rushing up with steaming teakettles and craggy lumps of plum cake—we left the inhabitants to conclude their festivities by themselves, and went out to take a farewell walk on the cliffs of Looe.

We ascended the heights to the westward, losing sight of the town among the trees as we went; and then, walking in a southerly direction through some cornfields, approached within a few hundred yards of the edge of the cliffs, and looked out on the sea. The sky had partially cleared, and the rain had ceased; but huge fantastic masses of cloud, tinged with lurid copper colour by the setting sun, still towered afar off over the horizon, and were reflected in a deeper hue on the calm surface of the sea, with a perfectness and grandeur that I never remember to have witnessed before. Not a ship was in sight; but out on the extreme line of the wilderness of grey waters there shone one red, fiery spark—the beacon of the Eddystone Lighthouse. Before us, the green fields of Looe Island rose high out of the ocean—here, partaking the red light on the clouds; there, half lost in cold shadow. Closer yet, on the mainland, a few cattle were feeding quietly on a long strip of meadow bordering the edge of the cliff; and, now and then, a gull soared up from the sea, and wheeled screaming over our heads. The faint sound of the small shore waves (invisible to us in the position we occupied) beating dull and at long intervals on the beach, augmented the dreary solemnity of the evening prospect. Light, shade, and colour were all before us, arranged in the grandest combinations, and expressed by the simplest forms. If Michaelangelo had painted landscape, he might have represented such a scene as we now beheld.

This was our last excursion at Looe. The next morning we were again on the road, walking inland on our way to the town of Liskeard.

THREE

HOLY WELLS AND DRUID RELICS

RESH FROM THE QUAINT OLD HOUSES, the delightfully irregular streets, and the fragrant terrace gardens of Looe, we found ourselves, on entering Liskeard, suddenly introduced to that "abomination of desolation," a large agricultural country town. Modern square houses, barren of all outer ornament; wide, dusty, deserted streets; misanthropical-looking shopkeepers, clad in rusty black, standing at their doors to gaze on the solitude around them—greeted our eyes on all sides. Such samples of the population as we accidentally encountered were not promising. We were unlucky enough to remark, in the course of two streets, a nonagenarian old woman with a false nose, and an idiot shaking with the palsy.

But harder trials were in reserve for us. We missed the best of the many inns at Liskeard, and went to the very worst. What a place was our house of public entertainment for a great sinner to repent in, or for a melancholy recluse to retreat to! Not a human being appeared in the street where this tavern of despair frowned amid congenial desolation. Nobody welcomed us at the door—the sign creaked dolefully, as the wind swung it on its rusty hinges. We walked in, and discovered a low-spirited little man sitting at an empty "bar," and hiding himself, as it were, from all mortal inspection behind the full sheet of a dirty provincial newspaper. Doleful was our petition to this secluded publican for shelter and food; and doubly doleful was his answer to our appeal. Beds he believed he had—food there was none in the house, saving a piece of *corned beef*, which the family had dined on, and which he proposed that we should partake of before it got quite cold. Having said thus much, he suddenly retired behind his newspaper, and spoke no word more.

In a few minutes the landlady appeared, looking very thin and care-worn, and clad in mourning weeds. She smiled sadly upon us; and desired to know how we liked corned beef? We acknowledged a preference for fresh meat, especially in large market towns like Liskeard, where butchers' shops abounded. The landlady was willing to see what she could get; and in the meantime begged to be allowed to show us into a private room. She succeeded in incarcerating us in the most thoroughly private room that could be found out of a model prison.

It was situated far away at the back of the house, and looked out upon a very small yard entirely circumscribed by empty stables. The one little window was shut down tight, and we were desired not to open it, for fear of a smell from these stables. The ornaments of the place consisted of hymn books, spelling books, and a china statue of Napoleon in a light green waistcoat and a sky-blue coat. There was not even a fly in the room to intrude on us in our privacy; there were no cocks and hens in the yard to cackle on us in our privacy; nobody walked past the outer passage, or made any noise in any part of the house, to startle us in our privacy; and a steady rain was falling propitiously to keep us in our privacy. We dined in our retired situation on some rugged lumps of broiled flesh, which the landlady called chops, and the servant steaks. We broke out of prison after dinner, and roamed the streets. We returned to solitary confinement in the evening, and were instantly conducted to another cell.

This second private apartment appeared to be about forty feet long; six immense wooden tables, painted of a ghastly yellow colour, were ranged down it side by side. Nothing was placed on any of them—they looked like dissecting tables waiting for "subjects." There was yet another and a seventh table—a round one, half lost in a corner, to which we retreated for refuge—it was covered with crape and bombazine, half made up into mourning garments proper to the first and intensest stage of grief. The servant brought us one small candle to cheer the scene; and desired to be informed whether we wanted *two* sheets apiece to our beds, or whether we could do with a sheet at top and a blanket at bottom, as other people did? This question cowed us at once into gloomy submission to our fate. We just hinted that we had contracted bad habits of sleeping between two sheets, and left the rest to chance; reckless how we slept, or where we slept, whether we passed the night on the top of one of the six dissecting tables, or with a blanket at bottom, as other people passed it. Soon the servant returned to tell us that we had got our two sheets each, and to send us to bed—snatching up the landlady's mourning garments, while she spoke, with a scared, suspicious look, as if she thought that the next outrageous luxury we should require would be a nightgown apiece of crape and bombazine.

Reflecting on our lamentable situation the last thing at night, we derived some consolation from remembering that we should leave our quarters early the next morning. It was not Liskeard that we had come to see, but the country around Liskeard—the famous curiosities of Nature and Art that are to be found some six or eight miles away from the town. Accordingly, we were astir betimes on the morrow. The sky was fair; the breeze was exhilarating. Once past the doleful doorway of the inn, we found ourselves departing under the fairest auspices for a pilgrimage to the ruins of St Cleer's Well, and to the granite piles and Druid remains, now entitled the "Cheese-Wring" and "Hurler" rocks.

On leaving the town, our way lay to the northward, up rising ground. For the first two miles, the scenery differed little from what we had already beheld in Cornwall. The lanes were still sunk down between high banks, like dry ditches; all varieties of ferns grew in exquisite beauty and luxuriance on either side of us; the trees were small in size, and thickly clothed with leaves; and the views were generally narrowed to a few well-cultivated fields, with sturdy little granite-built cottages now and then rising beyond. It was only when we had reached what must have been a considerable elevation, that any change appeared in the face of the country. Five minutes more of walking, and a single turn in the road, brought us suddenly to the limits of trees, meadows, and cottages; and displayed before us, with almost startling abruptness, the magnificent prospect of a Cornish Moor.

The expanse of open plain that we now beheld stretched away uninterruptedly on the right hand, as far as the distant hills. Towards the left, the view was broken and varied by some rough stone walls, a narrow road and a dip in the earth beyond. Wherever we looked, far or near, we saw masses of granite of all shapes and sizes, heaped irregularly on the ground among dark clusters of heath. An old furze-cutter was the only human figure that appeared on the desolate scene. Approaching him to ask our way to St Cleer's Well—no signs of which could be discerned on the wilderness before us—we found the old fellow, though he was eighty years of age, working away with all the vigour of youth. On this wild moor he had lived and laboured from childhood; and he began to talk proudly of its great length and breadth, and of the wonderful sights that were to be seen on different parts of it, the moment we addressed him. He described to us, in his own homely forcible way, the awful storms that he had beheld, the fearful rattling and roaring of thunder over the great unsheltered plain before us—the hail and sleet driven so fiercely before the hurricane, that a man was half-blinded if he turned his face towards it for a moment—the forked lightning shooting from pitch-dark clouds, leaping and running fearfully over the level ground, blackening, splitting, tearing from their places the stoutest rocks on the moor. Three masses of granite lay heaped together near the spot where we had halted—the furze-cutter pointed to them with his billhook, and told us that what we now looked on was once one great rock, which he had seen riven in an instant by the lightning into the fragmentary form that it now presented. If we mounted the highest of these three masses, he declared that we might find out our own way to St Cleer's Well by merely looking around us. We followed his directions. Towards the east, far away over the magnificent sweep of moorland, and on the slope of the hill that bounded it, appeared the tall chimneys and engine houses of the Great Caradon Copper Mine—the only objects raised by the hand of man that were to be seen on this part of the view. Towards the west, much nearer at hand, four grey turrets were just visible beyond some rising ground. These turrets belonged to the tower of St Cleer's Church, and the Well was close by it.

Taking leave of the furze-cutter, we followed the path at once that led to St Cleer's. Half an hour's walking brought us to the village, a straggling, picturesque place, hidden in so deep a hollow as to be quite invisible from any distance. All the little cottage girls whom we met, carrying their jugs and pitchers of water, curtseyed and wished us good morning with the prettiest air of bashfulness and good humour imaginable. One of them, a rosy, beautiful child, who proudly informed us that she was six years old, put down her jug at a cottage gate and ran on before to show us the way, delighted to be singled out from her companions for so important an office. We passed the grey walls of the old church, walked down a lane, and soon came in sight of the Well, the position of which was marked by a ruined Oratory, situated on some open ground close at the side of the public pathway.

St Cleer or—as the name is generally spelt out of Cornwall—St Clare, the patron saint of the Well, was born in Italy, in the twelfth century—and born to a fair heritage of this world's honours and this world's possessions. But she voluntarily abandoned, at an early age, all that was alluring in the earthly career awaiting her, to devote herself entirely to the interests of her religion and the service of Heaven. She was the first woman who sat at the feet of St Francis as his disciple, who humbly practised the self-mortification, and resolutely performed the vow of perpetual poverty, which her preceptor's harshest doctrines imposed on his followers. She soon became Abbess of the Benedictine Nuns with whom she was associated by the saint; and afterwards founded an order of her own—the order of "Poor Clares." The fame of her piety and humility, of her devotion to the cause of the sick, the afflicted, and the poor, spread far and wide. The most illustrious of the ecclesiastics of her time attended at her convent as at a holy shrine. Pope Innocent the Fourth visited her, as a testimony of his respect for her virtues; and paid homage to her memory when her blameless existence had closed, by making one among the mourners who followed her to the grave. Her name had been derived from the Latin word that signifies *purity*; and from first to last her life had kept the promise of her name.

Poor St Clare! If she could look back, with the

thoughts and interests of the days of her mortality, to the world that she has quitted for ever, how sadly would she now contemplate the Holy Well which was once hallowed in her name and for her sake! But one arched wall, thickly overgrown with ivy, still remains erect in the place that the old Oratory occupied. Fragments of its roof, its cornices, and the mouldings of its windows lie scattered on the ground, half hidden by the grasses and ferns twining prettily around them. A double cross of stone stands, sloping towards the earth, at a little distance off—soon perhaps to share the fate of the prostrate ruins about it. How changed the scene here, since the time when the rural christening procession left the church, to proceed down the quiet pathway to the Holy Well—when children were baptized in the pure spring; and vows were offered up under the roof of the Oratory, and prayers were repeated before the sacred cross! These were the pious usages of a past age; these were the ceremonies of an ancient church, whose innocent and reverent custom it was to connect closer together the beauty of Nature and the beauty of Religion, by such means as the consecration of a spring, or the erection of a roadside cross. There has been something of sacrifice as well as of glory, in the effort by which we, in our time, have freed ourselves from what was superstitious and tyrannical in the faith of the times of old—it has cost us the loss of much of the better part of that faith which was not superstition, and of more which was not tyranny. The spring of St Clare is nothing to the cottager of our day but a place to draw water from; the village lads now lounge whistling on the fallen stones, once the consecrated arches under which their humble ancestors paused on the pilgrimage, or knelt in prayer. Wherever the eye turns, all around it speaks the melancholy language of desolation and decay—all but the water of the Holy Well. Still the little pool remains the fitting type of its patron saint—pure and tranquil as in the bygone days, when the name of St Clare was something more than the title to a village legend, and the spring of St Clare something better than a sight for the passing tourist among the Cornish moors.'

We happened to arrive at the well at the period when the villagers were going home to dinner. After the first quarter of an hour, we were left almost alone among the ruins. The only person who approached to speak to us was a poor old woman, bent and tottering with age, who lived in a little cottage hard by. She brought us a glass, thinking we might wish to taste the water of the spring; and presented me with a rose out of her garden. Such small scraps of information as she had gathered together about the well she repeated to us in low, reverential tones, as if its former religious uses still made it an object of veneration in her eyes. After a time, she too quitted us; and we were then left quite alone by the side of the spring.

It was a bright, sunshiny day; a pure air was abroad; nothing sounded audibly but the singing of birds at some distance, and the rustling of the few leaves that clothed one or two young trees in a neighbouring garden. Unoccupied though I was, the minutes passed away as quickly and as unheeded with me as with my companion who was busily engaged in sketching. The ruins of the ancient Oratory, viewed amid the pastoral repose of all things around them, began imperceptibly to exert over me that mysterious power of mingling the impressions of the present with the memories of the past, which all ruins possess. While I sat looking idly into the water of the well, and thinking of the groups that had gathered round it in years long gone by, recollections began to rise vividly on my mind of other ruins that I had seen in other countries, with friends, some scattered, some gone now—of pleasant pilgrimages, in boyish days, along the storied shores of Baiæ, or through the desolate streets of the Dead City under Vesuvius—of happy sketching excursions to the aqueducts on the plains of Rome, or to the temples and villas of Tivoli; during which I had first learned to appreciate the beauties of Nature under guidance which, in this world, I can never resume; and had seen the lovely prospects of Italian landscape pictured by a hand now powerless in death. Remembrances such as these, of pleasures which remembrance only can recall as they were, made time fly fast for me by the brink of the holy well. I could have sat there all day, and should not have felt, at night, that the day had been ill spent.

But the sunlight began to warn us that noon was long past. We had some distance yet to walk, and many things more to see. Shortly after my friend had completed his sketch, therefore, we reluctantly left St Clare's Well, and went on our way briskly, up the little valley, and out again on the wide surface of the moor.

It was now our object to steer a course over the wide plain around us, leading directly to the "Cheese-Wring" rocks (so called from their supposed resemblance to a Cornish cheese press or *wring*). On our road to this curiosity, about a mile and a half from St Clare's Well, we stopped to look at one of the most perfect and remarkable of the ancient British monuments in Cornwall. It is called Trevethey Stone, and consists of six large upright slabs of granite, overlaid by a seventh, which covers them in the form of a rude, slanting roof. These slabs are so irregular in form as to look quite unhewn. They all vary in size and thickness. The whole structure rises to a height, probably, of fourteen feet; and, standing as it does on elevated ground, in a barren country, with no stones of a similar kind erected near it, presents an appearance of rugged grandeur and aboriginal simplicity, which renders it an impressive, almost a startling, object to look on. Antiquaries have discovered that its name signifies The Place of Graves; and have discovered no more. No inscription appears on it; the date of its erection is lost in the darkest of the dark periods of English history.

Our path had been gradually rising all the way from St Clare's Well; and, when we left Trevethey Stone, we still continued to ascend, proceeding along the tram way leading to the Caradon Mine. Soon the scene presented another abrupt and extraordinary change. We had been walking hitherto amid almost invariable silence and solitude; but now, with each succeeding minute, strange, mingled, unintermitting noises began to grow louder and louder around us. We followed a sharp curve in the tramway, and immediately found ourselves saluted by an entirely new prospect, and surrounded by an utterly bewildering noise. All about us monstrous wheels were turning slowly; machinery was clanking and groaning in the hoarsest discords; invisible waters were pouring onward with a rushing sound; high above our heads, on skeleton platforms, iron chains clattered fast and fiercely over iron pulleys, and huge steam pumps puffed and gasped, and slowly raised and depressed their heavy black beams of wood. Far beneath the embankment on which we stood, men, women, and children were breaking and washing ore in a perfect marsh of copper-coloured mud and copper-coloured water. We had penetrated to the very centre of the noise, the bustle, and the population on the surface of a great mine.

When we walked forward again, we passed through a thick plantation of young firs; and then the sounds behind us became slowly and solemnly deadened the further we went on. When we had arrived at the extremity of the line of trees, they ceased softly and suddenly. It was like a change in a dream.

We now left the tramway, and stood again on the moor—on a wilder and lonelier part of it than we had yet beheld. The Cheese-Wring and its adjacent rocks were visible a mile and a half away, on the summit of a steep hill. Wherever we looked, the horizon was bounded by the long, dark, undulating edges of the moor. The ground rose and fell in little hillocks and hollows, tufted with dry grass and furze, and strewn throughout with fragments of granite. The whole plain appeared like the site of an ancient city of palaces, overthrown and crumbled into atoms by an earthquake. Here and there, some cows were feeding; and sometimes a large crow winged his way lazily before us, lessening and lessening slowly in the open distance, until he was lost to sight. No human beings were discernible anywhere; the majestic loneliness and stillness of the scene were almost oppressive both to eye and ear. Above us, immense fleecy masses of brilliant white cloud, wind-driven from the Atlantic, soared up grandly, higher and higher over the bright blue sky. Everywhere, the view had an impressively stern, simple, aboriginal look. Here were tracts of solitary country which had sturdily retained their ancient character through centuries of revolution and change; plains pathless and desolate even now, as when Druid processions passed over them by night to the place of the secret sacrifice, and skin-clad warriors of old Britain halted on them in council, or hurried across them to the fight.

On we went, up and down, in a very zigzag course, now looking forward towards the Cheese-Wring from the top of a rock, now losing sight of it altogether in the depths of a hollow. By the time we had advanced about halfway over the distance it was necessary for us to walk, we observed, towards the left hand, a wide circle of detached upright rooks. These we knew, from descriptions and engravings, to be the "Hurlers"—so we turned aside at once to look at them from a nearer point of view.

There are two very different histories of these rocks; the antiquarian account of them is straightforward and practical enough, simply asserting that they are the remains of a Druid temple, the whole region about them having been one of the principal stations of the Druids in Cornwall. The popular account of the Hurlers (from which their name is derived) is very different. It is contended, on the part of the people, that once upon a time (nobody knows how long ago) these rocks were Cornish men, who profanely went out (nobody knows from what place), to enjoy the national sport of hurling the ball on one fine "Sabbath morning," and were suddenly turned into pillars of stone, as a judgment on their own wickedness, and a warning to all their companions as well.

Having to choose between the antiquarian hypothesis and the popular legend on the very spot to which both referred, a common susceptibility to the charms of romance at once determined us to pin our faith on the legend. Looking at the Hurlers, therefore, in the peculiar spirit of the story attached to them, as really and truly petrified ball-players, we observed, with great interest, that some of them must have been a little above, and others a little below our own height, in their lifetime; that some must have been very corpulent, and others very thin persons; that one of them, having a protuberance on his head remarkably like a nightcap in stone, was possibly a sluggard as well as a Sabbath-breaker, and might have got out of his bed just in time to "hurl;" that another, with some faint resemblance left of a fat grinning human face, leaned considerably out of the perpendicular, and was, in all probability, a hurler of intemperate habits. At some distance off we remarked a high stone standing entirely by itself, which, in the absence of any positive information on the subject, we presumed to consider as the petrified effigy of a tall man who ran after the ball. In the opposite direction other stones were dotted about irregularly, which we could only imagine to represent certain misguided wretches who had attended as spectators of the sports, and had therefore incurred the same penalty as the hurlers themselves. These humble results of observations taken on the spot may possibly be useful, as tending to offer some startling facts from ancient history to the next pious layman in the legislature who gets up to propose the next series of Sabbath prohibitions for the benefit of the profane laymen in the nation.

Abandoning any more minute observation of the Hurlers than that already recorded, in order to husband the little time still left to us, we soon shaped our course again in the direction of the Cheese-Wring. We arrived at the base of the hill on which it stands, in a short time and without any difficulty; and beheld above us a perfect chaos of rocks piled up the entire surface of the eminence. All the granite we had seen before was as nothing compared with the granite we now looked on. The masses were at one place heaped up in great irregular cairns—at another, scattered confusedly over the ground; poured all along in close, craggy lumps; flung about hither and thither, as if in reckless sport, by the hands of giants. Above the whole rose the weird fantastic form of the Cheese-Wring, the wildest and most wondrous of all the wild and wondrous structures in the rock architecture of the scene.

If a man dreamt of a great pile of stones in a nightmare, he would dream of such a pile as the Cheese-Wring. All the heaviest and largest of the seven thick slabs of which it is composed are at the top; all the lightest and smallest at the bottom. It rises perpendicularly to a height of thirty-two feet, without lateral support of any kind. The fifth and sixth rocks are of immense size and thickness, and overhang fearfully, all round, the four lower rocks which support them. All are perfectly irregular; the projections of one do not fit into the interstices of another; they are heaped up loosely in their extraordinary top-heavy form, on slanting ground halfway down a steep hill. Look at them from whatever point you choose, there is still all that is heaviest, largest, strongest, at the summit, and all that is lightest, smallest, weakest, at the base. When you first see the Cheese-Wring, you instinctively shrink from walking under it. Beholding the tons on tons of stone balanced to a hair's breadth on the mere fragments beneath, you think that with a pole in your hand, with one push against the top rocks, you could hurl down the hill in an instant a pile which has stood for centuries, unshaken by the fiercest hurricane that ever blew, rushing from the great void of an ocean over the naked surface of a moor.

The Cheese-Wring

Of course, theories advanced by learned men are not wanting to explain such a phenomenon as the Cheese-Wring. Certain antiquaries have undertaken to solve this curious problem of Nature in a very offhand manner, by asserting that the rocks were heaped up as they now appear, by the Druids, with the intention of astonishing their contemporaries and all posterity by a striking exhibition of their architectural skill. (If any of these antiquarian gentlemen be still living, I would not recommend them to attempt a practical illustration of their theory by building miniature Cheese-Wrings out of the contents of their coal scuttles!) The second explanation of the extraordinary position of the rocks is a geological explanation, and is apparently the true one. It is assumed on this latter hypothesis that the Cheese-Wring, and all the adjacent masses of stone, were once covered, or nearly covered, by earth, and were thus supported in an upright form; that the wear and tear of storms gradually washed away all this earth, from between the rocks, down the hill, and then left such heaps of stones as were accidentally complete in their balance on each other, to stand erect, and such as were not to fall flat on the surface of the hill in all the various positions in which they now appear. Accepting this theory as the right one, it still seems strange that there should be only one Cheese-Wring on the hill—but so it is. Plenty of rocks are to be seen there piled one on another; but none of them are piled in the same extraordinary manner as the Cheese-Wring, which stands alone in its grandeur, a curiosity that even science may wonder at, a sight which is worth a visit to Cornwall, if Cornwall presented nothing else to see.

Besides the astonishment which the rock scenery on the hill was calculated to excite, we found in its neighbourhood an additional cause for surprise of a very different description. Just as we were preparing to ascend the eminence, the silence of the great waste around us was broken by a long and hearty cheer. The Hurlers themselves, if they had suddenly returned to a state of flesh and blood, and resumed their interrupted game, could hardly have made more noise, or exhibited a greater joviality of disposition, than did some three or four tradesmen of the town of Liskeard, who had been enjoying a picnic under the Cheese-Wring, had seen us approaching over the plain, and now darted out of their ambush to welcome us, flourishing porter bottles in their hands as olive branches of peace, amity, and goodwill. My companion skilfully contrived to make his escape; but I was stopped and surrounded in an instant. One benevolent stranger held a glass in a very slanting position, while a brother philanthropist violently uncorked a bottle and directed half of its contents in a magnificent jet of light brown froth all over everybody, before he found the way into the tumbler. It was of no use to decline imbibing the remainder of the light brown froth—"*There* was the Cheese-Wring (cried all the benevolent strangers in chorus), and *here* was the porter—*I* must drink all their good healths, and *they* would all drink mine—this was Cornish hospitality, and Cornish hospitality was notoriously the finest thing in the world! As for my friend there, who was drawing, they bore him no ill will because he wouldn't drink—they would buy his drawing, and one of the commercial gentlemen, who was a stationer, would publish a hundred, two hundred, five hundred, a thousand copies of it, on sheets of letter-paper, price one penny! What had I got to say to that?—If that wasn't hospitality, what the devil was?"

All this might have been very amusing, and our new friends might have proved excellent companions, under a different set of circumstances. But, as things were, we neither of us felt at all sorry when their manners subsequently exhibited a slight change, under the influence of further potations of porter. Soon, they began to look stolid and suspicious—suddenly, they discovered that we were not quite such good company as they had thought us at first—finally, they took their departure in solemn silence, leaving us free at last to mount the hill, and look out uninterruptedly on the glorious view from the summit, which extended over a circumference of a hundred miles.

Turning our faces towards the north-east, and standing now on the topmost rock of one of the most elevated situations in Cornwall, we were able to discern the sea on either side of us. Two faint lines of the softest, haziest blue indicated the Bristol Channel on the one hand, and the English Channel on the other. Before us lay a wide region of downs and fields, all mapped out in every variety of form by their different divisions of wall and hedgerow—while, farther away yet, darker and more indefinite, appeared the Dartmoor forest and the Dartmoor hills. It was just that hour before the evening, at which the atmosphere acquires a more mellow purity, a more perfect serenity and warmth, than at earlier periods of the day. The shadows of great clouds lay in vast lovely shapes of purple blue over the whole visible tract of country, contrasting in exquisite beauty with the sunny glimpses of landscape shining between them. Beneath us, the picturesque confusion of rocks, topped by the quaint form of the Cheese-Wring, seemed to fade away mysteriously into the grass of the moorland; beyond which, high up where the hills rose again, a little lake, called Dosmary Pool, shone in the sunlight with dazzling, diamond brightness. In the opposite direction, towards the west, the immediate prospect was formed by the rugged granite ridges, towering one behind the other, of Sharp Tor and Kilmarth—the long hazy outlines of

45

the plains and hilltops of southern and inland Cornwall closing grandly the distant view.

All that we had hitherto seen on and around the spot where we now stood had not yet exhausted its objects of attraction for strangers. Descending the rocks in a new direction, after taking a last look at the noble prospect visible from their summit, we proceeded to a particular spot near the base of the hill, where the granite was scattered in remarkable abundance. Our purpose here was to examine some stones which are well known to all the quarrymen in the district, as associated with an extraordinary story and an extraordinary man.

During the earlier half of the last century, there lived in one of the villages on the outskirts of the moor on which the Cheese-Wring stands, a stonecutter named Daniel Gumb. This man was noted among his companions for his taciturn eccentric character, and for his attachment to mathematical studies. Such leisure time as he had at his command he devoted to pondering over the problems of Euclid: he was always drawing mysterious complications of angles, triangles, and parallelograms, on pieces of slate, and on the blank leaves of such few books as he possessed. But he made very slow progress in his studies. Poverty and hard work increased with the increase of his family, and obliged him to give up his mathematics altogether. He laboured early and laboured late; he hacked and hewed at the hard material out of which he was doomed to cut a livelihood, with unremitting diligence; but times went so ill with him that, in despair of ever finding them better, he took a sudden resolution of altering his manner of living, and retreating from the difficulties that he could not overcome. He went to the hill on which the Cheese-Wring stands, and looked about among the rocks until he found some that had accidentally formed themselves into a sort of rude cavern. He widened this recess; he propped up a great wide slab, to make its roof: he cut out in a rock that rose above this, what he called his bedroom—a mere longitudinal slit in the stone, the length and breadth of his body, into which he could roll himself sideways when he wanted to enter it. After he had completed this last piece of work, he scratched the date of the year of his extraordinary labours (1735) on the rock; and then removed his wife and family from their cottage, and lodged them in the cavity he had made—never to return during his lifetime to the dwellings of men!

Here he lived and here he worked, when he could get work. He paid no rent now: he wanted no furniture; he struggled no longer to appear to the world as his equals appeared; he required no more money than would procure for his family and himself the barest necessaries of life; he suffered no interruptions from his fellow workmen, who thought him a madman, and kept out of his way; and—most precious privilege of his new position—he could at last shorten his hours of labour, and lengthen his hours of study, with impunity. Having no temptations to spend money, no hard demands of an inexorable landlord to answer, he could now work with his brains as well as his hands; he could toil at his problems, scratching them upon the tops of rocks, under the open sky, amid the silence of the great moor. Henceforth, nothing moved, nothing depressed him. The storms of winter rushed over his unsheltered dwelling, but failed to dislodge him. He taught his family to brave solitude and cold in the cavern among the rocks, as *he* braved them. In the cell that he had scooped out for his wife (the roof of which has now fallen in) some of his children died, and others were born. They point out the rock where he used to sit on calm summer evenings, absorbed over his tattered copy of Euclid. A geometrical "puzzle," traced by his hand, still appears on the stone. When he died, what became of his family, no one can tell. Nothing more is known of him than that he never quitted the wild place of his exile; that he continued to the day of his death to live contentedly with his wife and children, amid a civilized nation, under such a shelter as would hardly serve the first savage tribes of the most savage country—to live, starving out poverty and want on a barren wild; forsaking all things enduring all things for the love of Knowledge, which he could still nobly follow through trials and extremities, without encouragement of fame or profit, without vantage ground of station or wealth, for its own dear sake. Beyond this, nothing but conjecture is left. The cell, the bed place, the lines traced on the rocks, the inscription of the year in which he hewed his habitation out of them, are all the memorials that remain of Daniel Gumb.

We lingered about the wild habitation of the stonemason and his family, until sunset. Long shadows of rocks lay over the moor, the breeze had freshened and was already growing chill, when we set forth, at last, to trace our way back to Liskeard. It was too late now to think of proceeding on our journey, and sleeping at the next town on our line of route.

Returning in a new direction, we found ourselves once more walking on a high road, just as the sun had gone down, and the grey twilight was falling softly over the landscape. Stopping near a lonely farmhouse, we went into a field to look at another old British monument to which our attention had been directed. We saw a square stone column—now broken into two pieces—ornamented with a curiously carved pattern, and exhibiting an inscription cut in irregular, mysterious characters. Those who have deciphered them have discovered that the column is nearly a thousand years old; that it was raised as a sepulchral monument over the body of Dungerth King of Cornwall; and that the letters carved on it form some Latin words, which

may be thus translated:—"PRAY FOR THE SOUL OF
DUNGERTH." Seen in the dim light of the last quiet hour
of evening, there was something solemn and impressive
about the appearance of the old tombstone—simple
though it was. After leaving it, we soon entered once
more into regions of fertility. Cottages, cornfields, and
trees surrounded us again. We passed through pleasant
little valleys; over brooks crossed by quaint wooden
bridges; up and down long lanes, where tall hedges and
clustering trees darkened the way—where the stag beetle
flew slowly by, winding "his small but sullen horn," and
glow-worms glimmered brightly in the long, dewy grass
by the roadside. The moon, rising at first red and dull
in a misty sky, brightened as we went on, and lighted
us brilliantly along all that remained of our night walk
back to the town.

I have only to add that, when we arrived at Liskeard,
the lachrymose landlady of the inn benevolently offered
us for supper the identical piece of cold "corned beef"
which she had offered us for dinner the day before;
and further proposed that we should feast at our ease
in the private dungeon dining room at the back of the
house. But one mode of escape was left—we decamped
at once to the large and comfortable hotel of the town;
and there our pleasant day's pilgrimage to the moors
of Cornwall concluded as agreeably as it had begun.

FOUR

CORNISH PEOPLE

I T IS MY PURPOSE, in this place, to communicate some few facts relating to the social condition of the inhabitants of Cornwall, which were kindly furnished to me by friends on the spot; adding to the statement thus obtained, such anecdotes and illustrations of popular character as I collected from my own observations in the capacity of a tourist on foot.

If the reader desires to compare at a glance the condition of the Cornish people with the condition of their brethren in other parts of England, one small particle of practical information will enable him to do so at once. In the Government Tables of Mortality for Cornwall there are no returns of death from starvation.

Many causes combine to secure the poor of Cornwall from that last worst consequence of poverty to which the poor in most of the other divisions of England are more or less exposed. The number of inhabitants in the county is stated by the last census at 341,269—the number of square miles that they have to live on being 1327.[2] This will be found on proper computation and comparison to be considerably under the average population of a square mile throughout the rest of England. Thus, the supply of men for all purposes does not appear to be greater than the demand in Cornwall. The remote situation of the county guarantees it against any considerable influx of strangers to compete with the natives for work on their own ground. We met a farmer there who was so far from being besieged in harvest time by claimants for labour on his land that he was obliged to go forth to seek them himself at a neighbouring town, and was doubtful whether he should find men enough left unemployed at the mines and the fisheries to gather in his crops in good time at two shillings a day and as much "victuals and drink" as they cared to have.

Another cause which has contributed, in some measure, to keep Cornwall free from the burthen of a surplus population of working men must not be overlooked. Emigration has been more largely resorted to in that county than perhaps in any other in England. Out of the population of the Penzance Union alone, nearly five per cent left their native land for Australia, or New Zealand, in 1849. The potato blight was, at that time, assigned as the chief cause of the readiness to emigrate; for it damaged seriously the growth of a vegetable, from the sale of which, at the London markets, the Cornish agriculturalists derived large profits, and on which (with their fish) the Cornish poor depend as a staple article of food.

It is by the mines and fisheries (of both of which I shall speak particularly in another place) that Cornwall is compensated for a soil too barren in many parts of the county to be ever well cultivated except at such an expenditure of capital as no mere farmer can afford. From the inexhaustible mineral treasures in the earth, and from the equally inexhaustible shoals of pilchards which annually visit the coast, the working population of Cornwall derive their regular means of support, where agriculture would fail them. At the mines, the regular rate of wages is from forty to fifty shillings a month; but miners have opportunities of making more than this. By what is termed "working on tribute," that is, agreeing to excavate the mineral lodes for a percentage on the value of the metal they raise, some of them have been known to make as much as six and even ten pounds each, in a month. When they are unlucky in their working speculations, or perhaps thrown out of employment altogether by the shutting up of a mine, they still have a fair opportunity of obtaining farm labour, which is paid for (out of harvest time) at the rate of nine shillings a week. But this is a resource of which they are rarely obliged to take advantage. A plot of common ground is included with the cottages that are let to them; and the cultivation of this helps to keep them and their families, in bad times, until they find an opportunity of resuming work; when they may perhaps make as much in one month as an agricultural labourer can in twelve.

The fisheries not only employ all the inhabitants of the coast, but, in the pilchard season, many of the farm work-people as well. Ten thousand persons—men, women, and children—derive their regular support from the fisheries; which are so amazingly productive that the "drift," or deep-sea fishing, in Mount's Bay alone is calculated to realize, on the average, 30,000*l.* per annum.

To the employment thus secured for the poor in the mines and fisheries is to be added, as an advantage, the cheapness of rent and living in Cornwall. Good cottages are let at from fifty shillings to between three and four pounds a year—turf for firing grows in plenty on the vast tracts of common land overspreading the country—all sorts of vegetables are abundant and cheap, with the exception of potatoes, which so decreased in 1849, in consequence of the disease, that the winter stock was imported from France, Belgium, and Holland. The early potatoes, however, grown in May and June, are cultivated in large quantities, and realize on exportation a very high price. Corn generally sells a little above the average. Fish is always within the reach of the poorest people. In a good season, a dozen pilchards are sold for one penny. Happily for themselves, the poor in Cornwall do not partake the senseless prejudice against fish, so obstinately adhered to by the poor in many other parts of England. A Cornishman's national pride is in his pilchards—he likes to talk of them, and boast about them to strangers; and with reason, for he depends for the main support of life on the tribute of these little fish which the sea yields annually in almost countless shoals.

The workhouse system in Cornwall is said, by those who are well qualified to form an opinion on the subject, to be generally well administered; the Unions in the eastern part of the county being the least stringent in their regulations, and the most liberal in giving out-of-door relief.

Such, briefly, but I think not incorrectly stated, is the condition of the poor in Cornwall, in relation to their means of subsistence as a class. Looking to the fact that the number of labourers there is not too much for the labour; comparing the rate of wages with rent and the price of provisions; setting the natural advantages of the county fairly against its natural disadvantages, it is impossible not to conclude that the Cornish poor suffer less by their poverty, and enjoy more opportunities of improving their social position, than the majority of their brethren in many other counties of England. The general demeanour and language of the people themselves amply warrant this conclusion. The Cornish are essentially a cheerful, contented race. The views of the working men are remarkably moderate and sensible—I never met with so few grumblers anywhere.

My opportunities of correctly estimating the state of education among the people were not sufficiently numerous to justify me in offering to the reader more than a mere opinion on the subject. Such few observations as I was able to make inclined me to think that, in education, the mass of the population was certainly below the average in England, with one exception—that of the classes employed in the mines. All of these men with whom I held any communication would not have been considered badly informed persons in a higher condition of life. They possessed much more than a common mechanical knowledge of their own calling, and even showed a very fair share of information on the subject of the history and antiquities of their native county. As usual, the agricultural inhabitants appeared to rank lowest in the scale of education and general intelligence. Among this class, and among the fishermen, the strong superstitious feelings of the ancient days of Cornwall still survive, and promise long to remain, handed down from father to son as heirlooms of tradition, gathered together in a remote period, and venerable in virtue of their antiquity. The notion, for instance, that no wound will fester as long as the instrument by which it was inflicted is kept bright and clean still prevails extensively among them. But a short time since, a boy in Cornwall was placed under the care of a medical man (who related the anecdote to me) for a wound in the back from a pitchfork; his relatives—cottagers of respectability—firmly believe that his cure was accelerated by the pains they took to keep the prongs of the pitchfork in a state of the highest polish, night and day, throughout the whole period of his illness, and down to the last hour of his complete restoration to health.

Another and a more remarkable instance of the superstitions prevailing among the least educated classes of the people was communicated to me by the same informant—a gentleman whose life had been passed in Cornwall, and who was highly and deservedly respected by all those among whom he resided.[3]

A small farmer living in one of the most western districts of the county died some years back of what was supposed at the time to be "English Cholera." A few weeks after his decease, his wife married again. This circumstance excited some attention in the neighbourhood. It was remembered that the woman had lived on very bad terms with her late husband, that she had on many occasions exhibited strong symptoms of possessing a very vindictive temper, and that during the farmer's lifetime she had openly manifested rather more than a Platonic preference for the man whom she subsequently married. Suspicion was generally excited: people began to doubt whether the first husband had died fairly. At length the proper order was applied for, and his body was disinterred. On examination, enough arsenic to have poisoned three men was found in his stomach. The wife was accused of murdering him, was tried, convicted on the clearest evidence, and hanged. Very shortly after she had suffered capital punishment, horrible stories of a ghost were widely circulated. Certain people declared that they had seen a ghastly resemblance of the murder-ess, robed in her winding sheet, with the black mark of the rope round her swollen neck, standing on stormy nights upon her husband's grave, and digging there with a spade in hideous imitation of the actions of the men who had disinterred the corpse for medical examination. This was fearful enough—nobody dared go near the place after nightfall. But soon another circumstance was talked of, in connexion with the poisoner, which affected the tranquillity of people's minds in the village where she had lived, and where it was believed she had been born, more seriously than even the ghost story itself.

Near the church of this village there was a well, celebrated among the peasantry of the district for one remarkable property—every child baptized in its water (with which the church was duly supplied on christening occasions) was secure from ever being hanged. No one doubted that all the babies fortunate enough to be born and baptized in the parish, though they might live to the age of Methuselah, and might during that period commit all the capital crimes recorded in the "Newgate Calendar," were still destined to keep quite clear of the summary jurisdiction of Jack Ketch—no one doubted this, until the story of the apparition of the murderess began to be spread abroad. Then, awful misgivings arose in the popular mind. A woman who had been born close by the magical well, and who had therefore in all probability been baptized in its water like her neighbours of the parish, had nevertheless been publicly and unquestionably hanged. However, probability was not always truth—everybody determined that the baptismal register of the poisoner should be sought for, and that it should be thus officially ascertained whether she had been christened with the well water, or not. After much trouble, the important document was discovered—not where it was first looked after, but in a neighbouring parish vestry. A mistake had been made about the woman's birthplace—she had not been baptized in the local church, and had therefore not been protected by the marvellous virtue of the local water. Unutterable was the joy and triumph of this discovery throughout the village—the wonderful character of the parish well was wonderfully vindicated—its celebrity immediately spread wider than ever. The peasantry of the neighbouring districts began to send for the renowned water before christenings; and many of them actually continue, to this day, to bring it corked up in bottles to their churches, and to beg particularly that it may be used whenever they present their children to be baptized.

Such instances of superstition as this—and others equally true might be quoted—afford, perhaps, of themselves, the best evidence of the low state of education among the people from whom they are produced. It is, however, only fair to state that children in Cornwall are now enabled to partake of advantages which were probably not offered to their parents. Good National Schools are in operation everywhere, and are—as far as my own inquiries authorize me to report—well attended by pupils recruited from the ranks of the poorest classes.

Of the social qualities of the Cornish all that can be written may be written conscientiously in terms of the highest praise. Travelling as my companion and I did—in a manner which (whatever it may be now) was, ten years since, perfectly new to the majority of the people—we found constant opportunities of studying the popular character in its everyday aspects. We perplexed some, we amused others: here, we were welcomed familiarly by the people, as travelling pedlars with our packs on our backs; there, we were curiously regarded at an awful distance, and respectfully questioned in circumlocutory phrases as to our secret designs in walking through the country. Thus, viewing us sometimes as their equals, sometimes as mysteriously superior to them, the peasantry unconsciously exhibited many of their most characteristic peculiarities without reserve. We looked at the spectacle of their social life from the most searching point of view, for we looked at it from behind the scenes.

The manners of the Cornish of all ranks, down to the lowest, are remarkably distinguished by courtesy—a courtesy of that kind which is quite independent of artificial breeding, and which proceeds solely from natural motives of kindness and from an innate anxiety to please. Few of the people pass you without a salutation. Civil questions are always answered civilly. No propensity to jeer at strangers is exhibited—on the contrary, great solicitude is displayed to afford them any assistance that they may require; and displayed, moreover, without the slightest appearance of a mercenary motive. Thus, if you stop to ask your way, you are not merely directed for a mile or two on, and then told to ask again; but directed straight to the end of your destination, no matter how far off. Turnings to the right, and turnings to the left, shortcuts across moors five miles away, churches that you must keep on this hand, and rocks that you must keep on that, are impressed upon your memory with the most laborious minuteness, and shouted after you over and over again as long as you are within hearing. If the utmost anxiety to give the utmost quantity of good advice could always avail against accident or forgetfulness, no traveller in Cornwall who asks his way as he goes need ever lose himself.

When people possess the virtue of natural courtesy they are seldom found wanting in other higher virtues that are akin to it. Household affection, ready hospitality, and great gratitude for small rewards of services rendered are all to be found among the Cornish peasantry. Their fondness for their children is very pleasant to see. A word of inquiry or praise addressed to the mother makes her face glow with delight, and sends her away at once in search of the missing members of her little family, who are ranged before you triumphantly, with smoothed hair and carefully wiped faces, ready to be reviewed in a row. Both father and mother often wish you, at parting, a good wife and a large family (if you are not married already), just as they wish you a pleasant journey and a prosperous return home again.

Of Cornish hospitality we experienced many proofs, one of which may be related as a sample. Arriving late at a village, in the far west of the county, we found some difficulty in arousing the people of the inn. While we were waiting at the door, we heard a man who lived in a cottage near at hand, and of whom we had asked our way on the road, inquiring of some female member of his family whether she could make up a spare bed. We had met this man proceeding in our direction, and had so far outstripped him in walking that we had been waiting outside the inn about a quarter of an hour before he got home. When the woman answered his question in the negative, he directed her to put clean sheets on his own bed, and then came out to tell us that if we failed to obtain admission at the public house, a lodging for the night was ready for us under his own roof. We found on inquiry, afterwards, that he had looked out of the window, after getting home, while we were still disturbing the village by a continuous series of assaults on the inn door; had recognised us in the moonlight; and had thereupon not only offered us his bed, but had got out of it himself to do so. When we finally succeeded in gaining admittance to the inn, he declined an invitation to sup with us, and wishing us a good night's rest returned to his home. I should mention, at the same time, that another bed was offered to us at the vicarage, by the clergyman of the parish; and that after this gentleman had himself seen that we were properly accommodated by our landlady, he left us with an invitation to breakfast with him the next morning. Thus is hospitality practised in Cornwall—a county where, it must be remembered, a stranger is doubly a stranger, in relation to provincial sympathies; where the national feeling is almost entirely merged in the local feeling; where a man speaks of himself as *Cornish* in much the same spirit as a Welshman speaks of himself as Welsh.

In like manner, another instance drawn from my own experience will best display the anxiety which we found generally testified by the Cornish poor to make the best and most grateful return in their power for anything which they considered as a favour kindly bestowed. Such little anecdotes as I here relate in illustration of popular character cannot, I think, be considered trifling; for it is by trifles, after all, that we gain our truest appreciation of the marking signs of good or evil in the dispositions of our fellow beings; just as in the beating of a single artery under the touch, we discover an indication of the strength or weakness of the whole vital frame.

On the granite cliffs at the Land's End I met with an old man, seventy-two years of age, of whom I asked some questions relative to the extraordinary rocks scattered about this part of the coast. He immediately opened his whole budget of local anecdotes, telling them in a quavering high-treble voice, which was barely audible above the dash of the breakers beneath, and the fierce whistling of the wind among the rocks around us. However, the old fellow went on talking incessantly, hobbling along before me, up and down steep paths and along the very brink of a fearful precipice, with as much coolness as if his sight was as clear and his step as firm as in his youth. When he had shown me all that he could show, and had thoroughly exhausted himself with talking, I gave him a shilling at parting. He appeared to be perfectly astonished by a remuneration which the reader will doubtless consider the reverse of excessive; thanked me at the top of his voice; and then led me, in a great hurry, and with many mysterious nods and gestures, to a hollow in the grass, where he had spread on a clean pocket handkerchief a little stock-in-trade of his own, consisting of barnacles, bits of rock and ore, and specimens of dried seaweed. Pointing to these, he told me to take anything I liked, as a present in return for what I had given him. He would not hear of my buying anything; he was not, he said, a regular guide, and I had paid him more already than such an old man was worth—what I took out of his handkerchief I must take as a present only. I saw by his manner that he would be really mortified if I contested the matter with him, so as a present I received one of his pieces of rock—I had no right to deny him the pleasure of doing a kind action, because there happened to be a few more shillings in my pocket than in his.

Nothing can be much better adapted to show how simple and unsophisticated the Cornish character still remains in many respects than Cornish notions of organizing a public festival, and Cornish enjoyment of that festival when it is organized. We had already seen how they managed a public boat race at Looe, and we saw again how they conducted the preparations for the same popular festival, on a larger scale, at the coast town of Fowey.

In the first place, the dormant public enthusiasm was stimulated by music at an uncomfortably early hour in the morning. Two horn players and a clarionet player; a fat musician who blew through a very small fife and kept time with his head; and a withered little man who beat furiously on a mighty drum—drew up in martial array, one behind the other, before the principal inn. Two boys, staring about them in a stolidly important manner, and carrying flags which bore a suspicious resemblance to India pocket handkerchiefs sewn together, formed in front of the musicians. Two corpulent, solemn, elderly gentlemen in black (belonging, apparently, to the churchwarden type of the human species), formed in their turn on each side of the boys—and then the procession started; walking briskly up and down, and in and out, and round and round the same streets, over and over again; the musicians playing on all their instruments at once (drum included), without a moment's intermission on the part of any one of them. Nothing could exceed the gravity and silence of the popular concourse which followed this grotesque procession. The solemn composure on the countenances of the two corpulent civil officers who went before it was reflected on the features of the smallest boy who followed humbly behind. Profound musical amateurs in attendance at a classical quartet concert could have exhibited no graver or more breathless attention than that displayed by the inhabitants of Fowey, as they marched at the heels of the peripatetic town band.

But, while the music was proceeding, another adjunct to the dignity of the festival was in course of preparation, which appealed more strongly to popular sympathy even than the band and procession. A quantity of young trees—miserable little saplings cut short in their early infancy—were brought into the town, curiously sharpened at the stems. Holes were rapidly drilled in the ground, here, there, and everywhere, for their reception, at corners of house walls. While men outside set them up, women in a high state of excitement appeared at first-floor windows with long pieces of string, which they fastened to the branches to steady the trees at the top, hauling them about this way and that most unmercifully during the operation, and then vanishing to tie the loose ends of the lines to bars of grates and legs of tables. Mazes of long tight strings ran all across our room at the inn; broken twigs and drooping leaves peered in sadly at us through the three windows that lighted it. We were driven about from corner to corner out of the way of this rigging by an imperious old woman, who fastened and fettered the wretched trees with as fierce an air as if they were criminals whom she was handcuffing, and who at last fairly told us that she thought we had better leave the room, and see how beautiful things looked from the outside. On obeying this intimation, we found that the trees had absorbed the whole public attention to themselves. The band marched by, playing furiously; but the boys deserted it. The people from the country, hastening into the town, hot and eager, paused, reckless of the music, reckless of the flags, reckless of the procession, to look forth upon the streets "with verdure clad." The popularity of the Sons of Apollo was a thing of the past already! Nothing can well be imagined more miserably ugly than the appearance of the trees, standing strung into unnatural positions, and looking half dead already; but they evidently inspired the liveliest public satisfaction. Women returned to the windows to give a last perfecting tug to their branches; men patted approvingly with spades the loose earth round their stems. Spectators, one by one, took a near view and a distant view, and then walked gently by and took an occasional view, and lastly gathered together in little groups and took a general view. As connoisseurs look at their pictures, as mothers look at their children, as lovers look at their mistresses—so did the people of Fowey assemble with one accord and look at their trees.

After all, however, I shall perhaps best illustrate the simplicity of character displayed by the Cornish country people, if I leave the less amusing preparations for inaugurating the Fowey boat race untold, and describe some of the peculiarities of behaviour and remark which the appearance of my companion and myself called forth in all parts of Cornwall. The mere sight of two strangers walking with such appendages as knapsacks strapped on their shoulders seemed of itself to provoke the most unbounded wonder. We were stared at with almost incredible pertinacity and good humour. People hard at work left off to look at us; while groups congregated at cottage doors, walked into the middle of the road when they saw us approach, looked at us in front from that commanding point of view until we passed them, and then wheeled round with one accord and gazed at us behind as long as we were within sight. Little children ran indoors to bring out large children, as we drew near. Farmers, overtaking us on horseback, pulled in, and passed at a walk, to examine us at their ease. With the exception of bedridden people and people in prison, I believe that the whole population of Cornwall looked at us all over—back view and front view—from head to foot!

This staring was nowhere accompanied, either on the part of young or old, by a jeering word or an impertinent look. We evidently astonished the people, but we never tempted them to forget their natural good nature, forbearance, and self-restraint. On our side, the attentive scrutiny to which we were subjected was at first not a little perplexing. It was difficult not to doubt occasionally whether some unpleasantly remarkable change had not suddenly taken place in our personal appearance—whether we might not have turned green or blue on our travels, or have got noses as long as the preposterous nose of the traveller through Strasburgh, in the tale of Slawkenbergius. It was not until we had been some days in the county that we began to discover, by some such indications as the following, that we owed the public attention to our knapsacks, and not to ourselves.

We enter a small public house by the roadside to get a draught of beer. In the kitchen we behold the landlord and a tall man who is a customer. Both stare as a matter of course; the tall man especially, after taking one look at our knapsacks, fixes his eyes firmly on us and sits bolt upright on the bench without saying a word—he is evidently prepared for the worst we can do. We get into conversation with the landlord, a jovial, talkative fellow, who desires greatly to know what we are, if we have no objection. We ask him, what he thinks we are?—"Well," says the landlord, pointing to my friend's knapsack, which has a square ruler strapped to it, for architectural drawing—"well, I think you are both of you *mappers*—mappers who come here to make new roads—you may be coming to make a railroad, I dare say—we've had mappers in the country before this—I know a mapper myself—here's both your good healths!" We drink the landlord's good health in return, and disclaim the honour of being "mappers;" we walk through the country (we tell him) for pleasure alone, and take any roads we can get, without wanting to make new ones. The landlord would like to know, if that is the case, why we carry those weights at our backs?—Because we want to take our luggage about with us. Couldn't we pay to ride?—Yes, we could. And yet we like walking better?—Yes we do. This last answer utterly confounds the tall customer, who has been hitherto listening intently to the dialogue. It is evidently too much for his credulity—he pays his reckoning, and walks out in a hurry without uttering a word. The landlord appears to be convinced, but it is only in appearance. We leave him standing at his door, keeping his eye on us as long as we are in sight, still evidently persuaded that we are "mappers," but "mappers" of a bad order whose presence is fraught with some unknown peril to the security of the Queen's highway.

We get on into another district. Here, public opinion is not flattering. Some of the groups, gathered together in the road to observe us, begin to speculate on our characters before we are quite out of hearing. Then, this sort of dialogue, spoken in serious, subdued tones, just reaches us: Question—What can they be? Answer—*Trodgers!*

This is particularly humiliating, because it happens to be true. We certainly do trudge, and are therefore properly, though rather unceremoniously, called trudgers, or "trodgers." But we sink to a lower depth yet, a little further on. We are viewed as objects for pity. It is a fine evening; we stop and lean against a bank by the roadside to look at the sunset. An old woman comes tottering by on high pattens, very comfortably and nicely clad. She sees our knapsacks, and instantly stops in front of us, and begins to moan lamentably. Not understanding at first what this means, we ask respectfully if she feels at all ill? "Ah, poor fellows! poor fellows!" she sighs in answer, "obliged to carry all your baggage on your own backs!—very hard! poor lads! very hard, indeed!" And the good old soul goes away groaning over our evil plight, and mumbling something which sounds very like an assurance that she has got no money to give us.

In another part of the county we rise again gloriously in worldly consideration. We pass a cottage; a woman looks out after us, over the low garden wall, and rather hesitatingly calls us back. I approach her first, and am thus saluted: "If you please, sir, what have you got to sell?" Again, an old man meets us on the road, stops, cheerfully taps our knapsacks with his stick, and says: "Aha! you're tradesmen, eh? things to sell? I say, have you got any tea" (pronounced *tay*); "I'll buy some *tay*!" Further on, we approach a group of miners breaking ore. As we pass by, we hear one asking amazedly, "What have they got to sell in those things on their backs?" and another answering, in the prompt tones of a guesser who is convinced that he guesses right, "Guinea-pigs!"

It is unfortunately impossible to convey to the reader an adequate idea, by mere description, of the extra-ordinary gravity of manner, the looks of surprise and the tones of conviction which accompanied these various popular conjectures as to our calling and station in life, and which added immeasurably at the time to their comic effect. Curiously enough, whenever they took the form of questions, any jesting in returning an answer never seemed either to be appreciated or understood by the country people. Serious replies shared much the same fate as jokes. Everybody asked whether we could pay for riding, and nobody believed that we preferred walking, if we could. So we soon gave up the idea of affording any information at all; and walked through the country comfortably as mappers, trodgers, tradesmen, guinea-pig-mongers, and poor back-burdened vagabond lads, altogether, or one at a time, just as the peasantry pleased.

I have not communicated to the reader all the con-jectures formed about us, for the simple reason that many of them, when they ran to any length, were by no means so intelligible as could be desired. It will readily be imagined that in a county which had a language of its own (something similar to the Welsh) down to the time of Edward VI, if not later—in a county where this language continued to be spoken among the humbler classes until nearly the end of the seventeenth century, and where it still gives their names to men, places, and implements—some remnants of it must attach themselves to the dialect of English now spoken by the lower orders. This is enough of itself to render Cornish talk not very easy to be understood by ordinary strangers; but the difficulty of comprehending it is still further increased by the manner in which the people speak. They pronounce rapidly and indistinctly, often running separate syllables into one another through a sentence, until the whole sounds like one long fragmentary word. To the student in philology a series of conversations with the Cornish poor would, I imagine, afford ample matter for observation of the most interesting kind. Some of their expressions have a character that is quite patriarchal. Young men, for instance, are addressed by their elders as "my son"—everything eatable, either for man or beast, is commonly denominated "meat."

It may be expected, before I close this hasty sketch of the Cornish people, that I should touch on the dark side of the picture—unfinished though it is—which I have endeavoured to draw. But I have nothing to communicate on the subject of offences in Cornwall, beyond a few words about "wrecking" and smuggling.

Opinions have been divided among well-informed persons as to the truth or falsehood of those statements of travellers and historians which impute the habitual commission of outrages and robberies on sufferers by shipwreck to the Cornish of former generations. Without entering into this question of the past, which can only be treated as a matter for discussion, I am happy, in proceeding at once to the present, to be able to state, as a matter of fact, that "wrecking" is a crime unknown in the Cornwall of our day. So far from maltreating shipwrecked persons, the inhabitants of the seashore risk their lives to save them. I make this assertion on the authority of a gentleman whose life has been passed in the West of Cornwall; whose avocations take him much among the poor of all ranks and characters; and who has himself seen wrecked sailors rescued from death by the courage and humanity of the population of the coast.

In reference to smuggling, many years have passed without one of those fatal encounters between smugglers and revenue officers which, in other days, gave a dark and fearful character to the contraband trade in Cornwall. So well is the coast watched that no smuggling of any consequence can now take place. It is only the oldest Cornish men who can give you any account, from personal experience, of adventures in "running a cargo;" and those that I heard described were by no means of the romantic or interesting order.

Beyond this, I have nothing further to relate regarding criminal matters. It may not unreasonably be doubted whether a subject so serious and so extensive as the Statistics of Crime is not out of the scope of a book like the present, whose only object is to tell a simple fireside story which may amuse an idle, or solace a mournful, hour. Moreover, remembering the assistance and the kindness that my companion and I met with throughout Cornwall—and those only who have travelled on foot can appreciate how much the enjoyment of exploring a country may be heightened or decreased, according to the welcome given to the stranger by the inhabitants—remembering, too, that we walked late at night, through districts inhabited only by the roughest and poorest classes, entirely unmolested; and that we trusted much on many occasions to the honesty of the people, and never found cause to repent our trust—I cannot but feel that it would be an ungracious act to ransack newspapers and Reports to furnish materials for recording in detail the vices of a population whom I have only personally known by their virtues. Let you and I, reader, leave off with the same pleasant impressions of the Cornish people—you, whose only object is to hear, and I whose only object is to tell, the story of a holiday walk. There is enough to be found in them that is good, amply to justify a little inattention to whatever we may discover that is bad.

FIVE

LOE POOL

"Now, I THINK IT VERY MUCH AMISS," remarks Sterne, in *Tristram Shandy*, "that a man cannot go quietly through a town and let it alone, when it does not meddle with him, but that he must be turning about, and drawing his pen at every kennel he crosses over, merely, o' my conscience, for the sake of drawing it." I quote this wise and witty observation on a bad practice of some travel writers as containing the best reason that I can give the reader for transporting him at once over some sixty miles of Cornish high roads and footpaths, without stopping to drop one word of description by the way. Having left off the record of our travels at Liskeard, and taking it up again—as I mean to do here—at Helston, I skip over five intermediate market towns and two large villages, with a mere dash of the pen. Lostwithiel, Fowey, St Austell, Grampound, Probus, Truro, Falmouth, are all places of mark and note, and have all certain curiosities and sights of their own to interest the inquisitive tourist; but, nevertheless, not one of them "meddled" with me in the course of my rambles, and acting on Sterne's excellent principle, I purpose "letting them alone" now. In other words, the several towns and villages that I have enumerated, though presenting much that was generally picturesque and attractive in the way of old buildings and pretty scenery, exhibited little that was distinctive or original in character; produced therefore rather pleasant than vivid impressions; and would by no means suggest any very original series of descriptions to fill the pages of a book which is confined to such subjects only as are most exclusively and strikingly Cornish.

The town of Helston, where we now halt for the first time since we left the Cheese-Wring and St Cleer's Well, might, if tested by its own merits alone, be passed over as unceremoniously as the towns already passed over before it. Its principal recommendation, in the opinion of the inhabitants, appeared to be that it was the residence of several very "genteel families," who have certainly not communicated much of their gentility to the lower orders of the population—a riotous and drunken set, the only bad specimens of Cornish people that I met with in Cornwall. The streets of Helston are a trifle larger and a trifle duller than the streets of Liskeard; the church is comparatively modern in date, and superlatively ugly in design. A miserable altarpiece, daubed in gaudy colours on the window above the communion table, is the only approach to any attempt at embellishment in the interior. In short, the town has nothing to offer to attract the stranger, but a public festival—a sort of barbarous carnival—held there annually on the 8th of May. This festival is said to be of very ancient origin, and is called "The Furry"—an old Cornish word, signifying a gathering; and, at Helston particularly, a gathering in celebration of the return of spring. The Furry begins early in the morning with singing, to an accompaniment of drums and kettles. All the people in the town immediately leave off work and scamper into the country; having reached which, they scamper back again, garlanded with leaves and flowers, and caper about hand in hand through the streets, and in and out of all the houses, without let or hindrance. Even the "genteel" resident families allow themselves to be infected with the general madness, and wind up the day's capering consistently enough by a night's capering at a grand ball. A full account of these extraordinary absurdities may be found in Polwhele's *History of Cornwall*.

But, though thus uninteresting in itself, Helston must be visited by every tourist in Cornwall for the sake of the grand, the almost unrivalled scenery to be met with near it. The town is not only the best starting point from which to explore the noble line of coast rocks which ends at the Lizard Head; but possesses the further recommendation of lying in the immediate vicinity of the largest lake in Cornwall—Loe Pool.

The banks of Loe Pool stretch on either side to the length of two miles; the lake, which in summer occupies little more than half the space that it covers in winter, is formed by the flow of two or three small streams. You first reach it from Helston, after a walk of half a mile; and then see before you, on either hand, long ranges of hills rising gently from the water's edge, covered with clustering trees, or occupied by wide cornfields and sloping tracts of common land. So far, the scenery around Loe Pool resembles the scenery around other lakes; but as you proceed the view changes in the most striking and extraordinary manner. Walking on along the winding banks of the pool, you taste the water and find it soft and fresh, you see ducks swimming about in it from the neighbouring farmhouses, you watch the rising of the fine trout for which it is celebrated—every object tends to convince you that you are wandering by the shores of an inland lake—when suddenly at a turn in the hill slope you are startled by the shrill cry of the gull, and the fierce roar of breakers thunders on your ear—you look over the light grey waters of the lake, and behold, stretching immediately above and beyond them, the expanse of the deep blue ocean, from which they are only separated by a strip of smooth white sand!

Loe Pool

You hurry on, and reach this bar of sand which parts the great English Channel and the little Loe Pool—a child might run across it in a minute! You stand in the centre. On one side, close at hand, water is dancing beneath the breeze in glassy, tiny ripples; on the other, equally close, water rolls in mighty waves, precipitated on the ground in dashing, hissing, writhing floods of the whitest foam—here, children are floating mimic boats on a mimic sea; there, the stateliest ships of England are sailing over the great deep—both scenes visible in one view. Rocky cliffs and arid sands appear in close combination with rounded fertile hills, and long grassy slopes; salt spray leaping over the first, spring water lying calm beneath the last! No fairy vision of Nature that ever was imagined is more fantastic, or more lovely than this glorious reality, which brings all the most widely contrasted characteristics of a sea view and an inland view into the closest contact, and presents them in one harmonious picture to the eye.

The ridge of sand between Loe Pool and the sea, which, by impeding the flow of the inland streams spreads them in the form of a lake over the valley ground between two hills, is formed by the action of storms from the south-west. Such, at least, is the modern explanation of the manner in which Loo Bar has been heaped up. But there is an ancient legend in connexion with it, which tells a widely different story.

It is said that the terrible Cornish giant, or ogre, Tregeagle, was trudging homewards one day, carrying a huge sack of sand on his back, which—being a giant of neat and cleanly habits—he designed should serve him for sprinkling his parlour floor. As he was passing along the top of the hills which now overlook Loe Pool, he heard a sound of scampering footsteps behind him; and, turning round, saw that he was hotly pursued by no less a person than the devil himself. Big as he was, Tregeagle lost heart and ignominiously took to his heels: but the devil ran nimbly, ran steadily, ran without losing breath—ran, in short, *like* the devil. Tregeagle was fat, short-winded, had a load on his back, and lost ground at every step. At last, just as he reached the seaward extremity of the hills, he determined in despair to lighten himself of his burden, and thus to seize the only chance of escaping his enemy by superior fleetness of foot. Accordingly, he opened his huge sack in a great hurry, shook out all his sand over the precipice, between the sea and the river which then ran into it, and so formed in a moment the Bar of Loe Pool.

In the winter time the lake is the cause and the scene of an extraordinary ceremony. The heavy incessant rains which then fall (ice is almost unknown in the moist climate of Cornwall), increase day by day the waters of the Pool, until they encroach over the whole of the low flat valley between Helston and the sea. Then, the smooth paths of turf, the little streams that run by their side—so pleasant to look on in the summertime—are hidden by the great overflow. Mill wheels are stopped; cottages built on the declivities of the hill are threatened with inundation. Out on the Bar, at high tide, but two or three feet of sand appear between the stormy sea on the one hand, and the stagnant swollen lake on the other. If Loe Pool were measured now, it would be found to extend to a circumference of seven miles.

When the flooding of the lake has reached its climax, the millers, who are the principal sufferers by the overflow, prepare to cut a passage through the Bar for the superabundant waters of the Pool. Before they can do this, however, they must conform to a curious old custom which has been practised for centuries, and is retained down to the present day. Procuring two stout leathern purses, they tie up three halfpence in each, and then set off with them in a body to the Lord of the Manor. Presenting him with their purses, they state their case with all due formality, and request permission to cut their trench through the sand. In consideration of the threepenny recognition of his rights, the Lord of the Manor graciously accedes to the petition; and the millers, armed with their spades and shovels, start for the Bar.

Their projected labour is of the slightest kind. A mere ditch suffices to establish the desired communication:

and the water does the rest for itself. On one occasion, so high was the tide on one side, and so full the lake on the other, that a man actually scraped away sand enough with his stick to give vent to the waters of the Pool. Thus, after no very hard work, the millers achieve their object; and the spectators watching on the hill behold a startling and magnificent scene.

Tearing away the sand on either side, floods of fresh water rush out furiously against floods of salt water leaping in, upheaved into mighty waves by the winter gale. A foaming roaring battle between two opposing forces of the same element takes place. The noise is terrific—it is heard like thunder, at great distances off. At last, the heavy, smooth, continuous flow of the fresh water prevails even over the power of the ocean. Farther and farther out, rushing through a wider and wider channel every minute, pour the great floods from the land, until the salt water is stained with an ochre colour, over a surface of twenty miles. But their force is soon spent: soon, the lake sinks lower and lower away from the slope of the hills. Then, with the high tide, the sea reappears triumphantly, dashing and leaping, in clouds of spray, through the channel in the sand—making the waters of the Pool brackish—now, threatening to swell them anew to overflowing—and now, at the ebb, leaving them to empty themselves again, in the manner of a great tidal river. No new change takes place, until a storm from the south-west comes on; and then, fresh masses of sand and shingle are forced up—the channel is refilled—the Bar is reconstructed as if by a miracle. Again, the scene resumes its old features—again, there is a sea on one side, and a lake on the other. But now the Pool occupies only its ordinary limits—now, the mill wheels turn busily once more, and the smooth paths and gliding streams reappear in their former beauty, until the next winter rains shall come round, and the next winter floods shall submerge them again.

At the time when I visited the lake, its waters were unusually low. Here, they ran calm and shallow, into little, glassy, flowery creeks that looked like fairies' bathing places. There, out in the middle, they hardly afforded depth enough for a duck to swim in. Near to the Bar, however, they spread forth wider and deeper; finely contrasted, in their dun colour and perfect repose, with the flashing foaming breakers on the other side. The surf forbade all hope of swimming; but, standing where the spent waves ran up deepest, and where the spray flew highest before the wind, I could take a natural shower-bath from the sea, in one direction; and the next moment, turning round in the other, could wash the sand off my feet luxuriously in the soft, fresh waters of Loe Pool.

SIX

THE LIZARD

WE HAD WAITED throughout one long rainy day at Helston—"remote, unfriended, melancholy, slow"—for a chance of finer weather before we started to explore the Lizard promontory. But our patience availed us little. The next morning, there was the soft, thick, misty Cornish rain still falling, just as it had already fallen without cessation for twenty-four hours. To wait longer, in perfect inactivity, and in the dullest of towns—doubtful whether the sky would clear even in a week's time—was beyond mortal endurance. We shouldered our knapsacks, and started for the Lizard in defiance of rain, and in defiance of our landlady's reiterated assertions that we should lose our way in the mist, when we walked inland; and should slip into invisible holes, and fall over fog-veiled precipices among the rocks, if we ventured to approach the coast.

What sort of scenery we walked through, I am unable to say. The rain was above—the mud was below—the mist was all around us. The few objects, near at hand, that we did now and then see, dripped with wet, and had a shadowy visionary look. Sometimes, we met a forlorn cow steaming composedly by the roadside—or an old horse, standing up to his fetlocks in mire and sneezing vociferously—or a good-humoured peasant, who directed us on our road and informed us with a grin that this sort of "fine rain" often lasted for a fortnight. Sometimes we passed little villages built in damp holes, where trees, cottages, women scampering backwards and forwards peevishly on domestic errands, big boys with empty sacks over their heads and shoulders, gossiping gloomily against barn walls, and ill-conditioned pigs grunting for admission at closed kitchen doors, all looked soaked through and through together. Nothing, in short, could be more dreary and comfortless than our walk for the first two hours. But, after that, as we approached "Lizard Town," the clouds began to part to seaward; layer after layer of mist drove past us, rolling before the wind; peeps of faint greenish-blue sky appeared and enlarged apace. By the time we had arrived at our destination, a white, watery sunlight was falling over the wet landscape. The prognostications of our Cornish friends were pleasantly falsified. A fine day was in store for us after all.

88

The man who first distinguished the little group of cottages that we now looked on, by the denomination of Lizard *Town*, must have possessed magnificent ideas indeed on the subject of nomenclature. If the place looked like anything in the world, it looked like a large collection of farm outbuildings without a farmhouse. Muddy little lanes intersecting each other at every possible angle; rickety little cottages turned about to all the points of the compass; ducks, geese, cocks, hens, pigs, cows, horses, dunghills, puddles, sheds, peat stacks, timber, nets, seemed to be all indiscriminately huddled together where there was little or no room for them. To find the inn amid this confusion of animate and inanimate objects was no easy matter; and when we at length discovered it, pushed our way through the livestock in the garden and opened the kitchen door, this was the scene which burst instantaneously on our view:—

We beheld a small room literally full of babies, and babies' mothers. Interesting infants of the tenderest possible age, draped in long clothes and short clothes, and shawls and blankets, met the eye wherever it turned. We saw babies propped up uncomfortably on the dresser, babies rocking snugly in wicker cradles, babies stretched out flat on their backs on women's knees, babies prone on the floor toasting before a slow fire. Every one of these Cornish cherubs was crying in every variety of vocal key. Every one of their affectionate parents was talking at the

89

top of her voice. Every one of their little elder brothers was screaming, squabbling, and tumbling down in the passage with prodigious energy and spirit. The mothers of England—and they only—can imagine the deafening and composite character of the noise which this large family party produced. To describe it is impossible.

Ere long, while we looked on it, the domestic scene began to change. Even as porters, policemen, and work-men of all sorts gathered together on the line of rails at a station, move aside quickly and with one accord out of the way of the heavy engine slowly starting on its journey—so did the congregated mothers in the inn kitchen now move back on either hand with their babies, and clear a path for the great bulk of the hostess leisurely advancing from the fireside to greet us at the door. From this most corpulent and complaisant of women, we received a hearty welcome, and a full explanation of the family orgies that were taking place under her roof. The great public meeting of all the babies in Lizard Town and the neighbouring villages, on which we had intruded, had been convened by the local doctor, who had got down from London, what the landlady termed a "lot of fine fresh matter," and was now about to strike a decisive blow at the smallpox, by vaccinating all the babies he could lay his hands on at "one fell swoop." The surgical ceremonies were expected to begin in a few minutes.

This last piece of information sent us out of the house without a moment's delay. The sunlight had brightened gloriously since we had last beheld it—the rain was over—the mist was gone. But a short distance before us rose the cliffs at the Lizard Head—the southernmost land in England—and to this point we now hastened, as the fittest spot from which to start on our rambles along the coast.

On our way thither, short as it was, we observed a novelty. In the South and West of Cornwall, the foot-paths, instead of leading through or round the fields, are all on the top of the thick stone walls—some four feet high—which divide them. This curious arrangement for walking gives a startling and picturesque character to the figures of the country people, when you see them at a distance, striding along, not on the earth but above it, and often relieved throughout the whole length of their bodies against the sky. Preserving our equilibrium, on these elevated pathways, with some difficulty against the strong south-west wind that was now blowing in our faces, we soon reached the topmost rocks that crown the Lizard Head: and then the whole noble line of coast and the wild stormy ocean opened grandly into view.

On each side of us, precipice over precipice, cavern within cavern, rose the great cliffs protecting the land against the raging sea. Three hundred feet beneath, the foam was boiling far out over a reef of black rocks. Above and around, flocks of seabirds flew in ever-lengthening circles, or perched flapping their wings and sunning their plumage, on ledges of riven stone below us. Every object forming the wide sweep of the view was on the vastest and most majestic scale. The wild varieties of form in the jagged line of rocks stretched away eastward and westward, as far as the eye could reach; black shapeless masses of mist scowled over the whole landward horizon; the bright blue sky at the opposite point was covered with towering white clouds which moved and changed magnificently; the tossing and raging of the great bright sea was sublimely contrasted by the solitude and tranquillity of the desert, overshadowed land—while ever and ever, sounding as they first sounded when the morning stars sang together, the rolling waves and the rushing wind pealed out their primeval music over the whole scene!

And now, when we began to examine the coast more in detail, inquiring the names of remarkable objects as we proceeded, we found ourselves in a country where each succeeding spot that the traveller visited was memorable for some mighty convulsion of Nature, or tragically associated with some gloomy story of shipwreck and death. Turning from the Lizard Head towards a cliff at some little distance, we passed through a field on our way, overgrown with sweet-smelling wild flowers, and broken up into low grassy mounds. This place is called "Pistil Meadow," and is connected with a terrible event which is still spoken of by the country people with superstitious awe.

Some hundred years since, a transport ship, filled with troops, was wrecked on the reef off the Lizard Head. Two men only were washed ashore alive. Out of the fearful number that perished, two hundred corpses were driven up on the beach below Pistil Meadow; and there they were buried by tens and twenties together in great pits, the position of which is still revealed by the low irregular mounds that chequer the surface of the field. The place was named in remembrance of the quantity of firearms—especially pistols—found about the wreck of the ill-fated ship, at low tide, on the reef below the cliffs. To this day, the peasantry continue to regard Pistil Meadow with feelings of awe and horror, and fear to walk near the graves of the drowned men at night. Nor have many of the inhabitants yet forgotten a revolting circumstance connected by traditional report with the burial of the corpses after the shipwreck. It is said that when dead bodies were first washed ashore, troops of ferocious, half-starved dogs suddenly appeared from the surrounding country, and could with difficulty be driven from preying on the mangled remains that were cast up on the beach. Ever since that period, the peasantry have been reported as holding the dog in abhorrence. Whether this be true or not, it is certainly a rare adventure to meet with a dog in the Lizard district.

93

You may walk through farmyard after farmyard, you may enter cottage after cottage, and never hear any barking at your heels;—you may pass, on the road, labourer after labourer, and yet never find one of them accompanied, as in other parts of the country, by his favourite attendant cur.

Leaving Pistil Meadow, after gathering a few of the wild herbs growing fragrant and plentiful over the graves of the dead, we turned our steps towards the Lizard Lighthouse. As we passed before the front of the large and massive building, our progress was suddenly and startlingly checked by a hideous chasm in the cliff, sunk to a perpendicular depth of seventy feet, and measuring more than a hundred in circumference. Nothing prepares the stranger for this great gulf; no railing is placed about it; it lies hidden by rising land, and the earth all around is treacherously smooth. The first moment when you see it is the moment when you start back instinctively from its edge, doubtful whether the hole has not yawned open in that very instant before your feet.

This chasm—melodramatically entitled by the people "The Lion's Den"—was formed in an extraordinary manner, not many years since. In the evening the whole surface of the down above the cliff was smooth to the eye, and firm to the foot—in the morning it had opened into an enormous hole. The men who kept watch at the

Lighthouse heard no sounds beyond the moaning of the sea—felt no shock—looked out on the night, and saw that all was apparently still and quiet. Nature suffered her convulsion and effected her change in silence. Hundreds on hundreds of tons of soil had sunk down into depths beneath them, none knew in how long or how short a time; but there the Lion's Den was in the morning, where the firm earth had been the evening before.

The explanation of the manner in which this curious landslip occurred is to be found by descending the face of the cliff, beyond the Lion's Den, and entering a cavern in the rocks called "Daws Ogo" (or Cave). The place is only accessible at low water. Passing from the beach through the opening of the cavern, you find yourself in a lofty, tortuous recess, into the farthest extremity of which a stream of light pours down from some eighty or a hundred feet above. This light is admitted through the Lion's Den, and thus explains by itself the nature of the accident by which that chasm was formed. Here, the weight of the upper soil broke through the roof of the cave; and the earth which then fell into it was subsequently washed away by the sea, which fills Daws Ogo at every flow of the tide. It has lately been noticed that the loose particles of ground at the bottom of the Lion's Den still continue to sink gradually through the narrow, slanting passage into the cave already formed; and it is expected that in no very long time the lower extremity of the chasm will widen so far as to make the sea plainly visible through it from above. At present, the effect of the two streams of light pouring into Daws Ogo from two opposite directions—one from the Lion's Den, the other from the seaward opening in the rocks—and falling together, in cross directions on the black rugged walls of the cave and the beautiful marine ferns growing from them, is supernaturally striking and grand. Here, Rembrandt would have loved to study; for here, even *his* sublime perception of the poetry of light and shade might have received a new impulse, and learned from the teaching of Nature one immortal lesson more.

Daws Ogo and the Lion's Den may be fairly taken as characteristic types of the whole coast scenery about the Lizard Head, in its general aspects. Great caves and greater landslips are to be seen both eastward and westward. In calm weather you may behold the long prospects of riven rock, in their finest combination, from a boat. At such times, you may row into vast caverns, always filled by the sea, and only to be approached when the waves ripple as calmly as the waters of a lake. Then you may see the naturally arched roof high above you, adorned in the loveliest manner by marine plants waving to and fro gently in the wind. Rocky walls are at each side of you, variegated in dark red and dark green colours—now advancing, now receding, now winding in and out, now rising straight and lofty, until their termination is hid in a pitch-dark obscurity which no man has ever ventured to fathom to its end. Beneath is the emerald-green sea, so still and clear that you can behold the white sand far below, and can watch the fish gliding swiftly and stealthily out and in: while, all around, thin drops of moisture are dripping from above, like rain, into the deep quiet water below, with a monotonous echoing sound which half oppresses and half soothes the ear, at the same time.

On stormy days your course is different. Then, you wander along the summits of the cliffs; and looking down, through the hedges of tamarisk and myrtle that skirt the ends of the fields, see the rocks suddenly broken away beneath you into an immense shelving amphitheatre, on the floor of which the sea boils in fury, rushing through natural archways and narrow rifts. Beyond them, at intervals as the waves fall, you catch glimpses of the brilliant blue main ocean, and the outer reefs stretching into it. Often, such wild views as these are relieved from monotony by the prospect of smooth cornfields and pasture lands, or by pretty little fishing villages perched among the rocks—each with its small group of boats drawn up on a slip of sandy beach, and its modest, tiny gardens rising one above another, wherever the slope is gentle, and the cliff beyond rises high to shelter them from the winter winds.

But the place at which the coast scenery of the Lizard district arrives at its climax of grandeur is Kynance Cove. Here, such gigantic specimens are to be seen of the most beautiful of all varieties of rock—the "serpentine"—as are unrivalled in Cornwall; perhaps unrivalled anywhere. A walk of two miles along the westward cliffs from Lizard Town brought us to the top of a precipice of three hundred feet. Looking forward from this, we saw the white sand of Kynance Cove stretching out in a half circle into the sea.

What a scene was now presented to us! It was a perfect palace of rocks! Some rose perpendicularly and separate from each other, in the shapes of pyramids and steeples—some were overhanging at the top and pierced with dark caverns at the bottom—some were stretched horizontally on the sand, here studded with pools of water, there broken into natural archways. No one of these rocks resembled another in shape, size, or position—and all, at the moment when we looked on them, were wrapped in the solemn obscurity of a deep mist; a mist which shadowed without concealing them, which exaggerated their size, and, hiding all the cliffs beyond, presented them sublimely as separate and solitary objects in the sea view.

It was now necessary, however, to occupy as little time as possible in contemplating Kynance Cove from a distance; for if we desired to explore it, immediate

Kynance Cove

advantage was to be taken of the state of the tide, which was already rapidly ebbing. Hurriedly descending the cliffs, therefore, we soon reached the sand: and here, leaving my companion to sketch, I set forth to wander among the rocks, doubtful whither to turn my steps first. While still hesitating, I was fortunate enough to meet with a guide, whose intelligence and skill well deserve such record as I can give of them here; for, to the former I was indebted for much local information and anecdote, and to the latter, for quitting Kynance Cove with all my limbs in as sound a condition as when I first approached it.

The guide introduced himself to me by propounding a sort of stranger's catechism. 1st. "Did I want to see everything?"—"Certainly." 2nd. "Was I giddy on the tops of high places?"—"No." 3rd. "Would I be so good, if I got into a difficulty anywhere, as to take it easy, and catch hold of him tight?"—"Yes, very tight!" With these answers the guide appeared to be satisfied. He gave his hat a smart knock with one hand, to fix it on his head; and pointing upwards with the other, said, "We'll try that rock first, to look into the gulls' nests, and get some wild asparagus." And away we went accordingly.

We mount the side of an immense rock which projects far out into the sea, and is the largest of the surrounding group. It is called Asparagus Island, from the quantity of wild asparagus growing among the long grass on its summit. Halfway up, we cross an ugly chasm. The guide points to a small chink or crevice, barely discernible in one side of it, and says "Devil's Bellows!" Then, first courteously putting my toes for me into a comfortable little hole in the perpendicular rock side, which just fits them, he proceeds to explain himself. Through the base of the opposite extremity of the island there is a natural channel, into which the sea rushes furiously at high tide: and, finding no other vent but the little crevice we now look down on, is expelled through it in long, thin jets of spray, with a roaring noise resembling the sound of a gigantic bellows at work. But the sea is not yet high enough to exhibit this phenomenon, so the guide takes my toes out of the hole again for me, just as politely as he put them in; and forthwith leads the way up higher still—expounding as he goes the whole art and mystery of climbing, which he condenses into this axiom:—"Never loose one hand, till you've got a grip with the other; and never scramble your toes about, where toes have no business to be."

At last we reach the topmost ridge of the island, and look down upon the white restless water far beneath, and peep into one or two deserted gulls' nests, and gather wild asparagus—which I can only describe as bearing no resemblance at all, that I could discover, to the garden species. Then the guide points to another perpendicular rock, farther out at sea, looming dark and phantom-like in the mist, and tells me that he was the man who built the cairn of stones on its top: and then he proposes that we shall go to the opposite extremity of the ridge on which we stand, and look down into "The Devil's Throat."

This desirable journey is accomplished with the greatest ease on his part, and with considerable difficulty and delay on mine—for the wind blows fiercely over us on the height; our rock track is narrow, rugged, and slippery; the sea roars bewilderingly below; and a single false step would not be attended with agreeable consequences. Soon, however, we begin to descend a little from our "bad eminence," and come to a halt before a wide, tunnelled opening, slanting sharply downwards in the very middle of the island—a black, gaping hole, into the bottom of which the sea is driven through some unknown subterranean channel, roaring and thundering with a fearful noise, which rises in hollow echoes through the aptly named Devil's Throat. About this hole no grass grew: the rocks rose wild, jagged, and precipitous, all around it. If ever the ghastly imagery of Dante's terrible "Vision" was realized on earth, it was realized here.

At this place, close to the mouth of the hole, the guide suggests that we shall sit down and have a little talk!—and very impressive talk it is, when he begins the conversation by bawling into my ear (and down the

Devil's Throat at the same time) to make himself heard above the fierce roaring beneath us. Now, his tale is of tremendous jets of water which he has seen, during the storms of winter, shot out of the hole before which we sit, into the creek of the sea below—now, he tells me of a shipwreck off Asparagus Island, of half-drowned sailors floating ashore on pieces of timber, and dashed out to sea again just as they touched the strand, by a jet from the Devil's Throat—now, he points away in the opposite direction, under one of the steeple-shaped rocks, and speaks of a chase after smugglers that began from this place; a desperate chase, in which some of the smugglers' cargo, but not one of the smugglers themselves, was seized—now, he talks of another great hole in the landward rocks, where the sea may be seen boiling within: a hole into which a man who was fishing for fragments of a wreck fell and was drowned; his body being sucked away through some invisible channel, never to be seen again by mortal eyes.

Anon, the guide's talk changes from tragedy to comedy. He begins to recount odd adventures of his own with strangers. He tells me of a huge fat woman who was got up to the top of Asparagus Island, by the easiest path, and by the exertions of several guides; who, left to herself, gasped, reeled, and fell down immediately; and was just rolling off, with all the momentum of sixteen stone, over the precipice below her, when she was adroitly caught, and anchored fast to the ground, by the ankle of one leg and the calf of the other. Then he speaks of an elderly gentleman, who, while descending the rocks with him, suddenly stopped short at the most dangerous point, giddy and panic-stricken, pouring forth deathbed confessions of all his sins, and wildly refusing to move another inch in any direction. Even this man the guide got down in safety at last, by making stepping places of his hands, on which the elderly gentleman lowered himself as on a ladder, ejaculating incoherently all the way, and trembling in great agony long after he had been safely landed on the sands.

This last story ended, it is settled that we shall descend again to the beach. Stimulated by the ease with which my worthy leader goes down beneath me, I get overconfident in my dexterity, and begin to slip here, and slide there, and come to awkward pauses at precipitous places, in what would be rather an alarming manner, but for the potent presence of the guide, who is always beneath me, ready to be fallen upon. Sometimes, when I am holding on with all the necessary tenacity of grip as regards my hands, but "scrambling my toes about" in a very disorderly and unworkmanlike fashion, he pops his head up from below for me to sit on; and puts my feet into crevices for me, with many apologies for taking the liberty! Sometimes, I fancy myself treading on what feels like soft turf; I look down, and find that I am standing like an acrobat on his shoulders, and hear him civilly entreating me to take hold of his jacket next, and let myself down over his body to the ledge where he is waiting for me. He never makes a false step, never stumbles, scrambles, hesitates, or fails to have a hand always at my service. The nautical metaphor of "holding on by your eyelids" becomes a fact in his case. He really views his employer as porters are expected to view a package labelled "*glass with care.*" I am firmly persuaded that he could take a drunken man up and down Asparagus Island, without the slightest risk either to himself or his charge; and I hold him in no small admiration when, after landing on the sand with something between a tumble and a jump, I find him raising me to my perpendicular almost before I have touched the ground, and politely hoping that I feel quite satisfied, hitherto, with his conduct as a guide.

We now go across the beach to explore some caves— dry at low water—on the opposite side. Some of these are wide, lofty, and well-lighted from without. We walk in and out and around them, as if in great, irregular, Gothic halls. Some are narrow and dark. Now, we crawl into them on hands and knees; now, we wriggle onward a few feet, serpent-like, flat on our bellies; now, we are suddenly able to stand upright in pitch darkness, hearing faint moaning sounds of pent-up winds, when we are silent, and long reverberations of our own voices, when we speak. Then, as we turn and crawl out again, we soon see before us one bright speck of light that may be fancied miles and miles away—a star shining in the earth—a diamond sparkling in the bosom of the rock. This guides us out again pleasantly; and, on gaining the open air, we find that while we have been groping in the darkness, a change has been taking place in the regions of light, which has altered and is still altering the aspect of the whole scene.

It is now two o'clock. The tide is rising fast; the sea dashes, in higher and higher waves, on the narrowing beach. Rain and mist are both gone. Overhead, the clouds are falling asunder in every direction, assuming strange momentary shapes, quaint airy resemblances of the forms of the great rocks among which we stand. Height after height along the distant cliffs dawns on us gently; great golden rays shoot down over them; far out on the ocean, the waters flash into a streak of fire; the sails of ships passing there, glitter bright; yet a moment more, and the glorious sunlight bursts out over the whole view. The sea changes soon from dull grey to bright blue, embroidered thickly with golden specks, as it rolls and rushes and dances in the wind. The sand at our feet grows brighter and purer to the eye; the seabirds flying and swooping above us look like flashes of white light against the blue firmament; and, most beautiful of all, the wet serpentine rocks now shine forth in full splendour beneath the sun; every one of their exquisite varieties of colour becomes plainly visible—silver grey and bright yellow, dark red, deep brown, and malachite green appear, here combined in thin intertwined streaks, there outspread in separate irregular patches—glorious ornaments of the seashore, fashioned by no human art!—Nature's own home-made jewellery, which the wear of centuries has failed to tarnish, and the rage of tempests has been powerless to destroy!

But the hour wanes while we stand and admire; the surf dashes nearer and nearer to our feet; soon, the sea will cover the sand, and rush swiftly into the caves where we have slowly crawled. Already the Devil's Bellows is at work—the jets of spray spout forth from it with a roar. The sea thunders louder and louder in the Devil's Throat—we must gain the cliffs while we have yet time. The guide takes his leave; my companion unwillingly closes his sketchbook; and we slowly ascend on our inland way together—looking back often and often, with no feigned regret, on all that we are leaving behind us at KYNANCE COVE.

SEVEN

THE PILCHARD
FISHERY

IF IT SO HAPPENED that a stranger in Cornwall went out to take his first walk along the cliffs towards the south of the county, in the month of August, that stranger could not advance far in any direction without witnessing what would strike him as a very singular and alarming phenomenon.

He would see a man standing on the extreme edge of a precipice, just over the sea, gesticulating in a very remarkable manner, with a bush in his hand; waving it to the right and the left, brandishing it over his head, sweeping it past his feet—in short, apparently acting the part of a maniac of the most dangerous character. It would add considerably to the startling effect of this sight on the stranger, if he were told, while beholding it, that the insane individual before him was paid for flourishing the bush at the rate of a guinea a week. And if he, thereupon, advanced a little to obtain a nearer view of the madman, and then observed on the sea below (as he certainly might) a well-manned boat, turning carefully to right and left exactly as the bush turned right and left, his mystification would probably be complete, and the right time would arrive to come to his rescue with a few charitable explanatory words. He would then learn that the man with the bush was an important agent in the Pilchard Fishery of Cornwall; that he had just discovered a shoal of pilchards swimming towards the land; and that the men in the boat were guided by his gesticulations alone, in securing the fish on which they and all their countrymen on the coast depend for a livelihood.

To begin, however, with the pilchards themselves, as forming one of the staple commercial commodities of Cornwall. They may be, perhaps, best described as bearing a very close resemblance to the herring, but as being rather smaller in size and having larger scales. Where they come from before they visit the Cornish coast—where those that escape the fishermen go to when they quit it, is unknown; or, at best, only vaguely conjectured. All that is certain about them is that they are met with, swimming past the Scilly Isles, as early as July (when they are caught with a drift net). They then advance inland in August, during which month the principal, or "in-shore," fishing begins; visit different parts of the coast until October or November; and after that disappear until the next year. They may be sometimes caught off the south-west part of Devonshire, and are occasionally to be met with near the southernmost coast of Ireland; but beyond these two points they are never seen on any other portion of the shores of Great Britain, either before they approach Cornwall, or after they have left it.

The first sight from the cliffs of a shoal of pilchards advancing towards the land is not a little interesting. They produce on the sea the appearance of the shadow of a dark cloud. This shadow comes on and on, until you can see the fish leaping and playing on the surface by thousands at a time, all huddled close together, and all approaching so near to the shore that they can be always caught in some fifty or sixty feet of water. Indeed, on certain occasions, when the shoals are of considerable magnitude, the fish behind have been known to force the fish before, literally up to the beach, so that they could be taken in buckets, or even in the hand with the greatest ease. It is said that they are thus impelled to approach the land by precisely the same necessity which impels the fishermen to catch them as they appear—the necessity of getting food.

With the discovery of the first shoal, the active duties of the "look-out" on the cliffs begin. Each fishing village places one or more of these men on the watch all round the coast. They are called "huers," a word said to be derived from the old French verb, *huer*, to call out, to give an alarm. On the vigilance and skill of the "huer" much depends. He is, therefore, not only paid his guinea a week while he is on the watch, but receives, besides, a perquisite in the shape of a percentage on the produce of all the fish taken under his auspices. He is placed at his post, where he can command an uninterrupted view of the sea, some days before the pilchards are expected to appear; and, at the same time, boats, nets, and men are all ready for action at a moment's notice.

The principal boat used is at least fifteen tons in burden, and carries a large net called the "seine," which measures a hundred and ninety fathoms in length, and costs a hundred and seventy pounds—sometimes more. It is simply one long strip, from eleven to thirteen fathoms in breadth, composed of very small meshes, and furnished, all along its length, with lead at one side and corks at the other. The men who cast this net are called the "shooters," and receive eleven shillings and sixpence a week, and a perquisite of one basket of fish each out of every haul.

As soon as the "huer" discerns the first appearance of a shoal, he waves his bush. The signal is conveyed to the beach immediately by men and boys watching near him. The "seine" boat (accompanied by another small boat, to assist in casting the net) is rowed out where he can see it. Then there is a pause, a hush of great expectation on all sides. Meanwhile, the devoted pilchards press on—a compact mass of thousands on thousands of fish, swimming to meet their doom. All eyes are fixed on the "huer;" he stands watchful and still, until the shoal is thoroughly embayed, in water which he knows to be within the depth of the "seine" net. Then, as the fish begin to pause in their progress, and gradually crowd closer and closer together, he gives the signal; the boats come up, and the "seine" net is cast, or, in the technical phrase "shot," overboard.

The grand object is now to enclose the entire shoal. The leads sink one end of the net perpendicularly to the ground; the corks buoy up the other to the surface of the water. When it has been taken all round the fish, the two extremities are made fast, and the shoal is then imprisoned within an oblong barrier of network surrounding it on all sides. The great art is to let as few of the pilchards escape as possible, while this process is being completed. Whenever the "huer" observes from above that they are startled, and are separating at any particular point, to that point he waves his bush, thither the boats are steered, and there the net is "shot" at once. In whatever direction the fish attempt to get out to sea again, they are thus immediately met and thwarted with extraordinary readiness and skill. This labour completed, the silence of intense expectation that has hitherto prevailed among the spectators on the cliff is broken. There is a great shout of joy on all sides—the shoal is secured!

The "seine'" is now regarded as a great reservoir of fish. It may remain in the water a week or more. To secure it against being moved from its position in case a gale should come on, it is warped by two or three ropes to points of land in the cliff, and is, at the same time, contracted in circuit, by its opposite ends being brought together, and fastened tight over a length of several feet. While these operations are in course of performance, another boat, another set of men, and another net (different in form from the "seine") are approaching the scene of action.

This new net is called the "tuck;" it is smaller than the "seine," inside which it is now to be let down for the purpose of bringing the fish closely collected to the surface. The men who manage this net are termed "regular seiners." They receive ten shillings a week, and the same perquisite as the "shooters." Their boat is first of all rowed inside the seine net, and laid close to the seine boat, which remains stationary outside, and to the bows of which one rope at one end of the "tuck net" is fastened. The "tuck" boat then slowly makes the inner circuit of the "seine," the smaller net being dropped overboard as she goes, and attached at intervals to the larger. To prevent the fish from getting between the two nets during this operation, they are frightened into the middle of the enclosure by beating the water, at proper places, with oars, and heavy stones fastened to ropes. When the "tuck" net has at length travelled round the whole circle of the "seine," and is securely fastened to the "seine" boat, at the end as it was at the beginning, everything is ready for the great event of the day, the hauling of the fish to the surface.

Now, the scene on shore and sea rises to a prodigious pitch of excitement. The merchants, to whom the boats and nets belong, and by whom the men are employed, join the "huer" on the cliff; all their friends follow them; boys shout, dogs bark madly; every little boat in the place puts off, crammed with idle spectators; old men and women hobble down to the beach to wait for the news. The noise, the bustle, and the agitation increase every moment. Soon the shrill cheering of the boys is joined by the deep voices of the "seiners." There they stand, six or eight stalwart sunburnt fellows, ranged in a row in the "seine" boat, hauling with all their might at the "tuck" net, and roaring the regular nautical "Yo-heave-ho!" in chorus! Higher and higher rises the net, louder and louder shout the boys and the idlers. The merchant forgets his dignity, and joins them; the "huer," so calm and collected hitherto, loses his self-possession and waves his cap triumphantly; even you and I, reader, uninitiated spectators though we are, catch the infection, and cheer away with the rest, as if our bread depended on the event of the next few minutes. "Hooray! hooray! Yo-hoy, hoy, hoy! Pull away, boys! Up she comes! Here they are! Here they are!" The water boils and eddies; the "tuck" net rises to the surface, and one teeming, convulsed mass of shining, glancing, silvery scales; one compact crowd of tens of thousands of fish, each one of which is madly endeavouring to escape, appears in an instant!

The noise before was as nothing compared with the noise now. Boats as large as barges are pulled up in hot haste all round the net; baskets are produced by dozens: the fish are dipped up in them, and shot out, like coals out of a sack, into the boats. Ere long, the men are up to their ankles in pilchards; they jump upon the rowing benches and work on, until the boats are filled with fish as full as they can hold, and the gunwales are within two or three inches of the water. Even yet, the shoal is not exhausted; the "tuck" net must be let down again and left ready for a fresh haul, while the boats are slowly propelled to the shore, where we must join them without delay.

As soon as the fish are brought to land, one set of men, bearing capacious wooden shovels, jump in among them; and another set bring large hand barrows close to the side of the boat, into which the pilchards are thrown with amazing rapidity. This operation proceeds without ceasing for a moment. As soon as one barrow is ready to be carried to the salting house, another is waiting to be filled. When this labour is performed by night, which is often the case, the scene becomes doubly picturesque. The men with the shovels, standing up to their knees in pilchards, working energetically; the crowd stretching down from the salting house, across the beach, and hemming in the boat all round; the uninterrupted succession of men hurrying backwards and forwards with their barrows, through a narrow way kept clear for them in the throng; the glare of the lanterns giving light to the workmen, and throwing red flashes on the fish as they fly incessantly from the shovels over the side of the boat—all combine together to produce such a series of striking contrasts, such a moving picture of bustle and animation, as not even the most careless of spectators could ever forget.

Having watched the progress of affairs on the shore, we next proceed to the salting house, a quadrangular structure of granite, well-roofed in all round the sides, but open to the sky in the middle. Here, we must prepare ourselves to be bewildered by incessant confusion and noise; for here are assembled all the women and girls in the district, piling up the pilchards on layers of salt, at threepence an hour; to which remuneration a glass of brandy and a piece of bread and cheese are hospitably added at every sixth hour, by way of refreshment. It is a service of some little hazard to enter this place at all.

There are men rushing out with empty barrows, and men rushing in with full barrows, in almost perpetual succession. However, while we are waiting for an opportunity to slip through the doorway, we may amuse ourselves by watching a very curious ceremony which is constantly in course of performance outside it.

As the filled barrows are going into the salting house, we observe a little urchin running by the side of them, and hitting their edges with a long cane, in a constant succession of smart strokes, until they are fairly carried through the gate, when he quickly returns to perform the same office for the next series that arrive. The object of this apparently unaccountable proceeding is soon practically illustrated by a group of children, hovering about the entrance of the salting house, who every now and then dash resolutely up to the barrows, and endeavour to seize on as many fish as they can take away at one snatch. It is understood to be their privilege to keep as many pilchards as they can get in this way by their dexterity, in spite of a liberal allowance of strokes aimed at their hands; and their adroitness richly deserves its reward. Vainly does the boy officially entrusted with the administration of the cane strike the sides of the barrow with malignant smartness and perseverance—fish are snatched away with lightning rapidity and pickpocket neatness of hand. The hardest rap over the knuckles fails to daunt the sturdy little assailants. Howling with pain, they dash up to the next barrow that passes them, with unimpaired resolution; and often collect their ten or a dozen fish a piece, in an hour or two. No description can do justice to the "Jack-in-Office" importance of the boy with the cane, as he flourishes it about ferociously in the full enjoyment of his vested right to castigate his companions as often as he can. As an instance of the early development of the tyrannic tendencies of human nature, it is, in a philosophical point of view, quite unique.

But now, while we have a chance, while the doorway is accidentally clear for a few moments, let us enter the salting house, and approach the noisiest and most amusing of all the scenes which the pilchard fishery presents. First of all we pass a great heap of fish lying in one recess inside the door, and an equally great heap of coarse, brownish salt lying in another. Then we advance farther, get out of the way of everybody, behind a pillar, and see a whole congregation of the fair sex screaming, talking, and—to their honour be it spoken—working at the same time, round a compact mass of pilchards which their nimble hands have already built up to a height of three feet, a breadth of more than four, and a length of twenty. Here we have every variety of the "fairer half of creation" displayed before us, ranged round an odoriferous heap of salted fish. Here we see crones of sixty and girls of sixteen; the ugly and the lean, the comely and the plump; the sour-tempered and the sweet—all squabbling, singing, jesting, lamenting, and shrieking at the very top of their very shrill voices for "more fish," and "more salt;" both of which are brought from the stores, in small buckets, by a long train of children running backwards and forwards with unceasing activity and in bewildering confusion. But, universal as the uproar is, the work never flags; the hands move as fast as the tongues; there may be no silence and no discipline, but there is also no idleness and no delay. Never was threepence an hour more joyously or more fairly earned than it is here!

The labour is thus performed. After the stone floor has been swept clean, a thin layer of salt is spread on it, and covered with pilchards laid partly edgewise, and close together. Then another layer of salt, smoothed fine with the palm of the hand, is laid over the pilchards; and then more pilchards are placed upon that; and so on until the heap rises to four feet or more. Nothing can exceed the ease, quickness, and regularity with which this is done. Each woman works on her own small area, without reference to her neighbour; a bucketful of salt and a bucketful of fish being shot out in two little piles under her hands, for her own especial use. All proceed in their labour, however, with such equal diligence and equal skill that no irregularities appear in the various layers when they are finished—they run as straight and smooth from one end to the other, as if they were constructed by machinery. The heap, when completed, looks like a long, solid, neatly made mass of dirty salt; nothing being now seen of the pilchards but the extreme tips of their noses or tails, just peeping out in rows, up the sides of the pile.

Having now inspected the progress of the pilchard fishery, from the catching to the curing, we have seen all that we can personally observe of its different processes, at one opportunity. What more remains to be done will not be completed until after an interval of several weeks. We must be content to hear about this from information given to us by others. Yonder, sitting against the outside wall of the salting-house, is an intelligent old man, too infirm now to do more than take care of the baby that he holds in his arms, while the baby's mother is earning her threepence an hour inside. To this ancient we will address all our inquiries; and he is well qualified to answer us, for the poor old fellow has worked away all the pith and marrow of his life in the pilchard fishery.

The fish—as we learn from our old friend, who is mightily pleased to be asked for information—will remain in salt, or, as the technical expression is, "in bulk," for five or six weeks. During this period, a quantity of oil, salt, and water drips from them into wells cut in the centre of the stone floor on which they are placed. After the oil has been collected and clarified, it will sell for enough to pay off the whole expense of the wages, food, and drink given to the "seiners"—perhaps defraying other incidental charges besides. The salt and water left behind, and offal of all sorts found with it, furnish a valuable manure. Nothing in the pilchard itself, or in connexion with the pilchard, runs to waste—the precious little fish is a treasure in every part of him.

After the pilchards have been taken out of "bulk," they are washed clean in salt water, and packed in hogsheads, which are then sent for exportation to some large seaport—Penzance for instance—in coast traders. The fish reserved for use in Cornwall are generally cured by those who purchase them. The export trade is confined to the shores of the Mediterranean—Italy and Spain providing the two great foreign markets for pilchards. The home consumption, as regards Great Britain, is nothing, or next to nothing. Some variation takes place in the prices realized by the foreign trade—their average, wholesale, is stated to be about fifty shillings per hogshead.

As an investment for money, on a small scale, the pilchard fishery offers the first great advantage of security. The only outlay necessary is that for providing boats and nets, and for building salting houses—an outlay which, it is calculated, may be covered by a thousand pounds. The profits resulting from the speculation are immediate and large. Transactions are managed on the ready money principle, and the markets of Italy and Spain (where pilchards are considered a great delicacy) are always open to any supply. The fluctuation between a good season's fishing and a bad season's fishing is rarely, if ever, seriously great. Accidents happen but seldom; the casualty most dreaded being the enclosure of a large fish along with a shoal of pilchards. A "ling," for instance, if unfortunately imprisoned in the seine, often bursts through its thin meshes, after luxuriously gorging himself with prey, and is of course at once followed out of the breach by all the pilchards. Then, not only is the shoal lost, but the net is seriously damaged, and must be tediously and expensively repaired. Such an accident as this, however, very seldom happens; and when it does the loss occasioned falls on those best able to bear it, the merchant speculators. The work and wages of the fishermen go on as usual.

Some idea of the almost incalculable multitude of pilchards caught on the shores of Cornwall, may be formed from the following *data*. At the small fishing cove of Treen, 600 hogsheads were taken in little more than one week, during August 1850. Allowing 2,400 fish only to each hogshead—3,000 would be the highest calculation—we have a result of 1,440,000 pilchards, caught by the inhabitants of one little village alone, on the Cornish coast, at the commencement of the season's fishing.

At considerable seaport towns, where there is an unusually large supply of men, boats, and nets, such figures as those quoted above, are far below the mark. At St Ives, for example, 1,000 hogsheads were taken in the first three seine nets cast into the water. The number of hogsheads exported annually averages 22,000. In 1850, 27,000 were secured for the foreign markets. Incredible as these numbers may appear to some readers, they may nevertheless be relied on; for they are derived from trustworthy sources—partly from local returns furnished to me; partly from the very men who filled the baskets from the boat side, and who afterwards verified their calculations by frequent visits to the salting houses.

Such is the pilchard fishery of Cornwall—a small unit, indeed, in the vast aggregate of England's internal sources of wealth: but yet neither unimportant nor uninteresting, if it be regarded as giving active employment to a hardy and honest race who would starve without it; as impartially extending the advantages of commerce to one of the remotest corners of our island; and, more than all, as displaying a wise and beautiful provision of Nature, by which the rich tribute of the great deep is most generously lavished on the land most in need of a compensation for its own sterility.

Land's End

EIGHT

THE LAND'S END

SOMETHING LIKE WHAT JERUSALEM WAS to the pilgrim in the Holy Land, the Land's End is—comparing great things with small—to the tourist in Cornwall. It is the Ultima Thule where his progress stops—the shrine towards which his face has been set, from the first day when he started on his travels—the main vent, through which all the pent-up enthusiasm accumulated along the line of route is to burst its way out, in one long flow of admiration and delight.

The Land's End! There is something in the very words that stirs us all. It was the name that struck us most, and was best remembered by us, as children, when we learnt our geography. It fills the minds of imaginative people with visions of barrenness and solitude, with dreams of some lonely promontory, far away by itself out in the sea—the sort of place where the last man in England would be most likely to be found waiting for death, at the end of the world! It suggests, even to the most prosaically constituted people, ideas of tremendous storms, of flakes of foam flying over the land before the wind, of billows in convulsion, of rocks shaken to their centre, of caves where smugglers lurk in ambush, of wrecks and hurricanes, desolation, danger, and death. It awakens curiosity in the most careless—once hear of it, and you long to see it—tell your friends that you have travelled in Cornwall, and ten thousand chances to one, the first question they ask is:—"Have you been to the Land's End?"

And yet, strange to say, this spot so singled out and set apart by our imaginations as something remarkable and even unique of its kind is, as a matter of fact, not distinguishable from any part of the coast on either side of it, by any local peculiarity whatever. If you desire really and truly to stand on the Land's End itself, you must ask your way to it, or you are in danger of mistaking any one of the numerous promontories on the right hand and the left for your actual place of destination. But I am anticipating. Before I say more about the Land's End, it is necessary to relate how my companion and I got there, and what we saw that was interesting and characteristic on our road.

The reader may perhaps remember that he last left us scrambling out of reach of the tide, up the cliffs overlooking Kynance Cove. From that place we got back to Helston in mist and rain, just as we had left it. From Helston we proceeded to Marazion,—stopping there to visit St Michael's Mount, so well known to readers of all classes by innumerable pictures and drawings, and by descriptions scarcely less plentiful, that they will surely be relieved rather than disappointed, if these pages exhibit the distinguished negative merit of passing the Mount without notice. From Marazion we walked to Penzance, from Penzance to the beautiful coast scenery at Lamorna Cove, and thence to Treen, celebrated as the halting place for a visit to one of Cornwall's greatest curiosities—the Logan Stone.

This far-famed rock rises on the top of a bold promontory of granite, jutting far out into the sea, split into the wildest forms, and towering precipitously to a height of a hundred feet. When you reach the Logan Stone, after some little climbing up perilous-looking places, you see a solid, irregular mass of granite, which is computed to weigh eighty-five tons, supported by its centre only, on a flat, broad rock, which, in its turn, rests on several others stretching out around it on all sides. You are told by the guide to turn your back to the uppermost stone; to place your shoulders under one particular part of its lower edge, which is entirely disconnected, all round, with the supporting rock below; and in this position to push upwards slowly and steadily, then to leave off again for an instant, then to push once more, and so on, until after a few moments of exertion, you feel the whole immense mass above you moving as you press against it. You redouble your efforts—then turn round—and see the massy Logan Stone, set in motion by nothing but your own pair of shoulders, slowly rocking backwards and forwards with an alternate ascension and declension, at the outer edges, of at least three inches. You have treated eighty-five tons of granite like a child's cradle; and, like a child's cradle, those eighty-five tons have rocked at your will!

The pivot on which the Logan Stone is thus easily moved is a small protrusion in its base, on all sides of which the whole surrounding weight of rock is, by an accident of Nature, so exactly equalized, as to keep it poised in the nicest balance on the one little point in its lower surface which rests on the flat granite slab beneath. But perfect as this balance appears at present, it has lost something, the merest hair's breadth, of its original faultlessness of adjustment. The rock is not to be moved now, either so easily or to so great an extent, as it could once be moved. Six-and-twenty years since, it was overthrown by artificial means; and was then lifted again into its former position. This is the story of the affair, as it was related to me by a man who was an eyewitness of the process of restoring the stone to its proper place.

In the year 1824, a certain Lieutenant in the Royal Navy, then in command of a cutter stationed off the

The Logan Stone

southern coast of Cornwall, was told of an ancient Cornish prophecy, that no human power should ever succeed in overturning the Logan Stone. No sooner was the prediction communicated to him than he conceived a mischievous ambition to falsify practically an assertion which the commonest common sense might have informed him had sprung from nothing but popular error and popular superstition. Accompanied by a body of picked men from his crew, he ascended to the Logan Stone, ordered several levers to be placed under it at one point, gave the word to "heave"—and the next moment had the miserable satisfaction of seeing one of the most remarkable natural curiosities in the world utterly destroyed, for aught he could foresee to the contrary, under his own directions!

But Fortune befriended the Logan Stone. One edge of it, as it rolled over, became fixed by a lucky chance in a crevice in the rocks immediately below the granite slab from which it had been started. Had this not happened, it must have fallen over a sheer precipice, and been lost in the sea. By another accident, equally fortunate, two labouring men at work in the neighbourhood were led by curiosity secretly to follow the Lieutenant and his myrmidons up to the Stone. Having witnessed, from a secure hiding place, all that occurred, the two workmen, with great propriety, immediately hurried off to inform the lord of the manor of the wanton act of destruction which they had seen perpetrated.

The news was soon communicated throughout the district, and thence throughout all Cornwall. The indignation of the whole county was aroused. Antiquaries, who believed the Logan Stone to have been balanced by the Druids; philosophers who held that it was produced by an eccentricity of natural formation; ignorant people, who cared nothing about Druids, or natural formations, but who liked to climb up and rock the stone whenever they passed near it; tribes of guides who lived by showing it; innkeepers in the neighbourhood, to whom it had brought customers by hundreds; tourists of every degree who were on their way to see it—all joined in one general clamour of execration against the overthrower of the rock. A full report of the affair was forwarded to the Admiralty; and the Admiralty, for once, acted vigorously for the public advantage, and mercifully spared the public purse.

The Lieutenant was officially informed that his commission was in danger, unless he set up the Logan Stone again in its proper place. The materials for compassing this achievement were offered to him, *gratis*, from the Dock Yards; but he was left to his own resources to defray the expense of employing workmen to help him. Being by this time awakened to a proper sense of the mischief he had done, and to a tolerably strong conviction of the disagreeable position in which he was placed with the Admiralty, he addressed himself vigorously to the task of repairing his fault. Strong beams were planted about the Logan Stone, chains were passed round it, pulleys were rigged, and capstans were manned. After a week's hard work and brave perseverance on the part of every one employed in the labour, the rock was pulled back into its former position, but not into its former perfection of balance: it has never moved since as freely as it moved before.

It is only fair to the Lieutenant to add to this narrative of his mischievous frolic the fact that he defrayed, though a poor man, all the heavy expenses of replacing the rock. Just before his death, he paid the last remaining debt, and paid it with interest.

Leaving the Logan Stone, we next shaped our course for the Land's End. We stopped on our way to admire the desolate pile of rocks and caverns which form the towering promontory called "Tol-Pedn-Penwith," or "The Holed Headland on the Left." Thence, turning a little inland—passing over wild, pathless moors; occasionally catching distant glimpses of the sea, with the mist sometimes falling thick down to the very edges of the waves, sometimes parting mysteriously and discovering distant crags of granite rising shadowy out of the foaming waters—we reached, at last, the limits of our outward journey, and saw the Atlantic before us, rolling against the westernmost extremity of the shores of England.

Tol-Pedn-Penwith

I have already said that the stranger must ask his way before he can find out the particular mass of rocks geographically entitled to the appellation of the "Land's End." He may, however, easily discover when he has reached the *district* of the "Land's End," by two rather remarkable indications, that he will meet with on his road. He will observe, at some distance from the coast, an old milestone marked "I," and will be informed that this is the real original first mile in England; as if all measurement of distances began strictly from the West! A little further on he will come to a house, on one wall of which he will see written in large letters "This is the first Inn in England," and on the other "This is the last Inn in England," as if the recognised beginning, and end too, of the Island of Britain were here, and here only! Having pondered a little on the slightly exclusive view of the attributes of their locality, taken by the inhabitants, he will then be led forward, about half a mile, by his guide, will descend some cliffs, will walk out on a ridge of rocks till he can go no farther—and will then be told that he is standing on the Land's End!

Here, as elsewhere, there are certain "sights" which a stranger is required to examine assiduously, as a duty if not as a pleasure, by guidebook law, rigidly administered by guides. There is, first of all, the mark of a horse's hoof, which is with great care kept *sharply modelled* (to borrow the painter's phrase), in the thin grass at the edge of a precipice. This mark commemorates the narrow escape from death of a military man who, for a wager, rode a horse down the cliff to the extreme verge of the Land's End; where the poor animal, seeing its danger, turned in affright, reared, and fell back into the sea raging over the rocks beneath. The foolhardy rider had just sense enough left to throw himself off in time—he tumbled on the ground, within a few inches of the precipice, and so barely saved the life which he had richly deserved to lose.

After the mark of the hoof, the traveller is next desired to look at a natural tunnel in the outer cliff, which pierces it through from one end to the other. Then his attention is directed to a lighthouse built on a reef of rocks detached from the land; and he is told of the great waves which break over the top of the building during the winter storms. Lastly, he is requested to inspect a quaint protuberance in a pile of granite at a little distance off, which bears a remote resemblance to a gigantic human face, adorned with a short beard; and which, he is informed, is considered quite a portrait (of all the people in the world to liken it to!) of Dr Johnson! It is, therefore, publicly known as "Dr Johnson's Head." If it can fairly be compared with any of the countenances of any remarkable characters that ever existed, it may be said to exhibit, in violent exaggeration, the worst physiognomical peculiarities of Nero and Henry the Eighth, combined in one face!

These several local curiosities duly examined, you are at last left free to look at the Land's End in your own way. Before you stretches the wide, wild ocean; the largest of the Scilly Islands being barely discernible on the extreme horizon, on clear days. Tracts of heath; fields where corn is blown by the wind into mimic waves; downs, valleys, and crags mingle together picturesquely and confusedly, until they are lost in the distance, on your left. On your right is a magnificent bay, bounded at either extremity by far-stretching promontories rising from a beach of the purest white sand, on which the yet whiter foam of the surf is ever seething, as waves on waves break one behind the other. The whole bold view possesses all the sublimity that vastness and space can bestow; but it is that sublimity which is to be seen, not described, which the heart may acknowledge and the mind contain, but which no mere words may delineate—which even painting itself may but faintly reflect.

However, it is, after all, the walk to the Land's End along the southern coast, rather than the Land's End itself, which displays the grandest combinations of scenery in which this grandest part of Cornwall abounds. There, Nature appears in her most triumphant glory and beauty—there, every mile as you proceed offers some new prospect, or awakens some fresh impression. All objects that you meet with, great and small, moving and motionless, seem united in perfect harmony to form a scene where original images might still be found by the poet; and where original pictures are waiting, ready composed, for the painter's eye.

On approaching the wondrous landscapes between Treen and the Land's End, the first characteristic that strikes you is the change that has taken place in the forms of the cliffs since you left the Lizard Head. You no longer look on variously shaped and variously coloured "serpentine" rocks; it is granite, and granite alone, that appears everywhere—granite, less lofty and less eccentric in form than the "serpentine" cliffs and crags; but presenting an appearance of adamantine solidity and strength, a mighty breadth of outline and an unbroken vastness of extent, nobly adapted to the purpose of protecting the shores of Cornwall, where they are most exposed to the fury of the Atlantic waves. In these wild districts, the sea rolls and roars in fiercer agitation, and the mists fall thicker, and at the same time fade and change faster, than elsewhere. Vessels pitching heavily in the waves are seen to dawn, at one moment, in the clearing atmosphere—and then, at another, to fade again mysteriously, as it abruptly thickens, like phantom ships. Up on the top of the cliffs, furze and heath in brilliant clothing of purple and yellow cluster close round great white, weird masses of rock, dotted fantastically with patches of grey-green moss. The solitude on these heights is unbroken—no houses are to be seen—often, no pathway is to be found. You go on, guided by the *sight* of the sea, when the sky brightens fitfully: and by the *sound* of the sea, when you stray instinctively from the edge of the cliff, as mist and darkness gather once more densely and solemnly all around you.

Then, when the path appears again—a winding path, that descends rapidly—you gradually enter on a new scene. Old horses startle you, scrambling into perilous situations, to pick dainty bits by the hillside; sheep, fettered by the fore and hind leg, hobble away desperately as you advance. Suddenly, you discern a small strip of beach shut in snugly between protecting rocks. A spring bubbles down from an inland valley; while not far off, an old stone well collects the water into a calm, clear pool. Sturdy little cottages, built of rough granite, and thickly thatched, stand near you, with gulls' and cormorants' eggs set in their loop-holed windows for ornament; great white sections of fish hang thickly together on their walls to dry, looking more like many legs of many dirty duck trousers than anything else; pigsties are hard-by the cottages, either formed by the Cromlech stones of the Druids or excavated like caves in the side of the hill. Down on the beach, where the rough old fishing boats lie, the sand is entirely formed by countless multitudes of the tiniest, fairy-like shells, often as small as a pin's head, and all exquisitely tender in colour and wonderfully varied in form. Up the lower and flatter parts of the hills above, fishing nets are stretched to dry. While you stop to look forth over the quiet, simple scene, wild little children peep out at you in astonishment; and hard-working men and women greet you with a hearty Cornish salutation, as you pass near their cottage doors.

You walk a few hundred yards inland, up the valley, and discover in a retired, sheltered situation the ancient village church, with its square grey tower surmounted by moss-grown turrets, with its venerable Saxon stone cross in the churchyard—where the turf graves rise humbly by twos and threes, and where the old coffin-shaped stone stands midway at the entrance gates, still used, as in former times, by the bearers of a rustic funeral. Appearing thus amid the noblest scenery, as the simple altar of the prayers of a simple race, this is a church which speaks of religion in no formal or sectarian tone. Appealing to the heart of every traveller, be his creed what it may, in loving and solemn accents, it sends him on his way again, up the mighty cliffs and through the mist driving cloud-like over them, the better fitted for his journey forward here; the better fitted, it may be, even for that other dread journey of one irrevocable moment—the last he shall ever take—to his abiding-place among the spirits of the dead!

These are some of the attractions which home rambles can offer to tempt the home traveller; for these are the impressions produced, and the incidents presented during a walk to the Land's End.

NINE

BOTALLACK MINE

I HAVE LITTLE DOUBT that the less patient among the readers of this narrative have already, while perusing it, asked themselves some such questions as these:—"Is not Cornwall a celebrated mineral country? Why has the author not taken us below the surface yet? Why have we heard nothing all this time about the mines?"

Readers who have questioned thus may be assured that their impatience to go down a mine, in this book, was fully equalled by our impatience to go down a mine, in the county of which this book treats. Our anxiety, however, when we mentioned it to Cornish friends, was invariably met by the same answer. "Wait"—they all said—"until you have turned your backs on the Land's End; and then go to Botallack. The mine there is the most extraordinary mine in Cornwall; go down that, and you will not want to go down another—wait for Botallack." And we did wait for Botallack, just as the reader has waited for it in these pages. May he derive as much satisfaction from the present description of the mine, as we did from visiting the mine itself!

We left the Land's End, feeling that our homeward journey had now begun from that point; and walking northward, about five miles along the coast, arrived at Botallack. Having heard that there was some disinclination in Cornwall to allow strangers to go down the mines, we had provided ourselves—through the kindness of a friend—with a proper letter of introduction, in case of emergency. We were told to go to the counting house to present our credentials; and on our road thither we beheld the buildings and machinery of the mine, literally stretching down the precipitous face of the cliff, from the land at the top to the sea at the bottom.

This sight was, in its way, as striking and extraordinary as the first view of the Cheese-Wring itself. Here, we beheld a scaffolding perched on a rock that rose out of the waves—there, a steam pump was at work raising gallons of water from the mine every minute, on a mere ledge of land halfway down the steep cliff side. Chains, pipes, conduits protruded in all directions from the precipice; rotten-looking wooden platforms, running over deep chasms, supported great beams of timber and heavy coils of cable; crazy little boarded houses were built, where gulls' nests might have been found in other places. There did not appear to be a foot of level space anywhere, for any part of the works of the mine to stand upon; and yet, there they were, fulfilling all the purposes for which they had been constructed, as safely and completely on rocks in the sea, and down precipices in the land, as if they had been cautiously founded on the tracts of smooth solid ground above!

The counting house was built on a projection of earth about midway between the top of the cliff and the sea. When we got there, the agent, to whom our letter was addressed, was absent; but his place was supplied by two miners who came out to receive us; and to one of them we mentioned our recommendation, and modestly hinted a wish to go down the mine forthwith.

But our new friend was not a person who did anything in a hurry. He was a grave, courteous, and rather melancholy man, of great stature and strength. He looked on us with a benevolent, paternal expression, and appeared to think that we were nothing like strong enough, or cautious enough, to be trusted down the mine. "Did we know," he urged, "that it was dangerous work?" "Yes; but we didn't mind danger!"—"Perhaps we were not aware that we should perspire profusely, and be dead tired getting up and down the ladders?" "Very likely; but we didn't mind that, either!"—"Surely we shouldn't like to strip and put on miners' clothes?" "Yes, we should, of all things!" and pulling off coat and waistcoat, on the spot, we stood half-undressed already, just as the big miner was proposing another objection, which, under existing circumstances, he good-naturedly changed into a speech of acquiescence. "Very well, gentlemen," he said, taking up two suits of miners' clothes, "I see you are determined to go down; and so you shall! You'll be wet through with the heat and the work before you come up again; so just put on these things, and keep your own clothes dry."

The clothing consisted of a flannel shirt, flannel drawers, canvas trousers, and a canvas jacket—all stained of a tawny copper colour; but all quite clean. A white nightcap and a round hat, composed of some iron-hard substance, well calculated to protect the head from any loose stones that might fall on it, completed the equipment; to which, three tallow candles were afterwards added, two to hang at the buttonhole, one to carry in the hand.

My friend was dressed first. He had got a suit which fitted him tolerably, and which, as far as appearances went, made a miner of him at once. Far different was my case.

The same mysterious dispensation of fate, which always awards tall wives to short men, decreed that a suit of the big miner's should be reserved for me. He stood six feet two inches—I stand five feet six inches. I put on his flannel shirt—it fell down to my toes, like a bedgown; his drawers—and they flowed in Turkish luxuriance over my feet. At his trousers I helplessly stopped short, lost in the voluminous recesses of each leg. The big miner, like a good Samaritan as he was, came to my assistance. He put the pocket button through the waist buttonhole, to keep the trousers up in the first instance; then he pulled steadily at the braces until my waistband was under my armpits; and then he pronounced that I and my trousers fitted each other in great perfection. The cuffs of the jacket were next turned up to my elbows—the white nightcap was dragged over my ears—the round hat was jammed down over my eyes. When I add to all this that I am so nearsighted as to be obliged to wear spectacles, and that I finished my toilet by putting my spectacles on (knowing that I should see little or nothing without them), nobody, I think, will be astonished to hear that my companion seized his sketchbook, and caricatured me on the spot; and that the grave miner, polite as he was, shook with internal laughter, when I took up my tallow candles and reported myself ready for a descent into the mine.

We left the counting house, and ascended the face of the cliff—then walked a short distance along the edge, descended a little again, and stopped at a wooden platform built across a deep gully. Here, the miner pulled up a trapdoor, and disclosed a perpendicular ladder leading down to a black hole, like the opening of a chimney. "This is the shaft; I will go down first, to

145

catch you in case you tumble; follow me and hold tight;" saying this, our friend squeezed himself through the trapdoor, and we went after him as we had been bidden.

The black hole, when we entered it, proved to be not quite so dark as it had appeared from above. Rays of light occasionally penetrated it through chinks in the outer rock. But by the time we had got some little way farther down, these rays began to fade. Then, just as we seemed to be lowering ourselves into total darkness, we were desired to stand on a narrow landing place opposite the ladder, and wait there while the miner went below for a light. He soon reascended to us, bringing not only the light he had promised, but a large lump of damp clay with it. Having lighted our candles he stuck them against the front of our hats with the clay—in order, as he said, to leave both our hands free to us to use as we liked. Thus strangely accoutred, like Solomon Eagles in the Great Plague, with flame on our heads, we resumed the descent of the shaft; and now at last began to penetrate beneath the surface of the earth in good earnest.

The process of getting down the ladders was not very pleasant. They were all quite perpendicular, the rounds were placed at irregular distances, were many of them much worn away, and were slippery with water and copper-ooze. Add to this the narrowness of the shaft, the dripping wet rock shutting you in, as it were, all round your back and sides against the ladder—the fathomless darkness beneath—the light flaring immediately above you, as if your head was on fire—the voice of the miner below, rumbling away in dull echoes lower and lower into the bowels of the earth—the consciousness that if the rounds of the ladder broke, you might fall down a thousand feet or so of narrow tunnel in a moment—imagine all this, and you may easily realize what are the first impressions produced by a descent into a Cornish mine.

By the time we had got down seventy fathoms, or four hundred and twenty feet of perpendicular ladders, we stopped at another landing place, just broad enough to afford standing room for us three. Here, the miner, pointing to an opening yawning horizontally in the rock at one side of us, said that this was the first gallery from the surface; that we had done with the ladders for the present; and that a little climbing and crawling were now to begin.

Our path was a strange one, as we advanced through the rift. Rough stones of all sizes, holes here, and eminences there, impeded us at every yard. Sometimes, we could walk on in a stooping position—sometimes, we were obliged to crawl on our hands and knees. Occasionally, greater difficulties than these presented themselves. Certain parts of the gallery dipped into black, ugly-looking pits, crossed by thin planks, over which we walked dizzily, a little bewildered by the violent contrast between the flaring light that we carried above us and the pitch darkness beneath and before us. One of these places terminated in a sudden rising in the rock, hollowed away below, but surmounted by a narrow projecting wooden platform, to which it was necessary to climb by cross-beams arranged at wide distances. My companion ascended to this awkward elevation, without hesitating; but I came to an "awful pause" before it. Fettered as I was by my Brobdingnag jacket and trousers, I felt a humiliating consciousness that any extraordinary gymnastic exertion was altogether out of my power.

Our friend the miner saw my difficulty, and extricated me from it at once, with a promptitude and skill which deserve record. Descending halfway by the beams, he clutched with one hand that hinder part of my too voluminous nether garments, which presented the broadest superficies of canvas to his grasp. (I hope the delicate reader appreciates my ingenious indirectness of expression, when I touch on the unmentionable subject of trousers!) Grappling me thus, and supporting himself by his free hand, he lifted me up as easily as if I had been a small parcel; then carried me horizontally along the loose boards, like a refractory little boy borne off by the usher to the master's birch; or—considering the candle burning on my hat, and the necessity of elevating my position by as lofty a comparison as I can make—like a flying Mercury with a star on his head; and finally deposited me safely upon my legs again, on the firm rock pathway beyond. "You are but a light and a little man, my son," says this excellent fellow, snuffing my candle for me before we go on; "only let me lift you about as I like, and you shan't come to any harm while I am with you!"

Speaking thus, the miner leads us forward again. After we have walked a little farther in a crouching position, he calls a halt, makes a seat for us by sticking a piece of old board between the rocky walls of the gallery, and then proceeds to explain the exact subterranean position which we actually occupy.

We are now four hundred yards out, *under the bottom of the sea*; and twenty fathoms or a hundred and twenty feet below the sea level. Coast-trade vessels are sailing over our heads. Two hundred and forty feet beneath us men are at work, and there are galleries deeper yet, even below that! The extraordinary position down the face of the cliff, of the engines and other works on the surface, at Botallack, is now explained. The mine is not excavated like other mines under the land, but under the sea!

Having communicated these particulars, the miner next tells us to keep strict silence and listen. We obey him, sitting speechless and motionless. If the reader could only have beheld us now, dressed in our copper-coloured garments, huddled close together in a mere cleft of subterranean rock, with flame burning on our

149

heads and darkness enveloping our limbs—he must certainly have imagined, without any violent stretch of fancy, that he was looking down upon a conclave of gnomes.

After listening for a few moments, a distant, unearthly noise becomes faintly audible—a long, low, mysterious moaning, which never changes, which is *felt* on the ear as well as *heard* by it—a sound that might proceed from some incalculable distance, from some far invisible height—a sound so unlike anything that is heard on the upper ground, in the free air of heaven; so sublimely mournful and still; so ghostly and impressive when listened to in the subterranean recesses of the earth, that we continue instinctively to hold our peace, as if enchanted by it, and think not of communicating to each other the awe and astonishment which it has inspired in us from the very first.

At last, the miner speaks again, and tells us that what we hear is the sound of the surf, lashing the rocks a hundred and twenty feet above us, and of the waves that are breaking on the beach beyond. The tide is now at the flow, and the sea is in no extraordinary state of agitation: so the sound is low and distant just at this period. But, when storms are at their height, when the ocean hurls mountain after mountain of water on the cliffs, then the noise is terrific; the roaring heard down here in the mine is so inexpressibly fierce and awful that

150

the boldest men at work are afraid to continue their labour. All ascend to the surface, to breathe the upper air and stand on the firm earth: dreading, though no such catastrophe has ever happened yet, that the sea will break in on them if they remain in the caverns below.

Hearing this, we get up to look at the rock above us. We are able to stand upright in the position we now occupy; and flaring our candles hither and thither in the darkness can see the bright pure copper streaking the dark ceiling of the gallery in every direction. Lumps of ooze, of the most lustrous green colour, traversed by a natural network of thin red veins of iron, appear here and there in large irregular patches, over which water is dripping slowly and incessantly in certain places. This is the salt water percolating through invisible crannies in the rock. On stormy days it spirts out furiously in thin, continuous streams. Just over our heads we observe a wooden plug of the thickness of a man's leg; there is a hole here, and the plug is all that we have to keep out the sea.

Immense wealth of metal is contained in the roof of this gallery, throughout its whole length; but it remains, and will always remain, untouched. The miners dare not take it, for it is part, and a great part, of the rock which forms their only protection against the sea; and which has been so far worked away here that its thickness is limited to an average of three feet only between the water and the gallery in which we now stand. No one knows what might be the consequence of another day's labour with the pickaxe on any part of it.

This information is rather startling when communicated at a depth of four hundred and twenty feet under ground. We should decidedly have preferred to receive it in the counting-house! It makes us pause for an instant, to the miner's infinite amusement, in the very act of knocking away a tiny morsel of ore from the rock, as a memento of Botallack. Having, however, ventured on reflection to assume the responsibility of weakening our defence against the sea, by the length and breadth of an inch, we secure our piece of copper, and next proceed to discuss the propriety of descending two hundred and forty feet more of ladders, for the sake of visiting that part of the mine where the men are at work.

Two or three causes concur to make us doubt the wisdom of going lower. There is a hot, moist, sickly vapour floating about us, which becomes more oppressive every moment; we are already perspiring at every pore, as we were told we should; and our hands, faces, jackets, and trousers are all more or less covered with a mixture of mud, tallow, and iron drippings, which we can feel and smell much more acutely than is exactly desirable. We ask the miner what there is to see lower down. He replies, nothing but men breaking ore with pickaxes; the galleries of the mine are alike, however deep they may go; when you have seen one you have seen all.

The answer decides us—we determine to get back to the surface.

We returned along the gallery, just as we had advanced, with the same large allowance of scrambling, creeping, and stumbling on our way. I was charitably carried along and down the platform over the pit, by my trousers, as before; our order of procession only changing when we gained the ladders again. Then, our friend the miner went last instead of first, upon the same principle of being ready to catch us if we fell, which led him to precede us on our descent. Except that one of the rounds cracked under his weight as we went up, we ascended without casualties of any kind. As we neared the mouth of the shaft, the daylight atmosphere looked dazzlingly white, after the darkness in which we had been groping so long; and when we once more stood out on the cliff, we felt a cold, health-giving purity in the sea breeze, and, at the same time, a sense of recovered freedom in the power that we now enjoyed of running, jumping, and stretching our limbs in perfect security, and with full space for action, which it was almost a new sensation to experience. Habit teaches us to think little of the light and air that we live and breathe in, or, at most, to view them only as the ordinary conditions of our being. To find out that they are more than this, that they are a luxury as well as a necessity of life, go down into a mine, and compare what you *can* exist in there with what you *do* exist in, on upper earth!

On re-entering the counting house we were greeted by the welcome appearance of two large tubs of water, with soap and flannel placed invitingly by their sides. Copious ablutions and clean clothes are potent restorers of muscular energy. These, and a half hour of repose, enabled us to resume our knapsacks as briskly as ever, and walk on fifteen miles to the town of St Ives—our resting place for the night.

While we were sitting in the counting-house, we had some talk with our good-humoured and intelligent guide, on the subject of miners and mining at Botallack. Some of the local information that he gave us may interest the reader—to whom I do not pretend to offer more here than a simple record of a half hour's gossip. I could only write elaborately about the Cornish mines by swelling my pages with extracts on the subject from Encyclopædias and Itineraries which are within easy reach of every one, and on the province of which it is neither my business nor my desire to intrude.

Botallack mine is a copper mine; but tin, and occasionally iron, are found in it as well. It is situated at the western extremity of the great strata of copper, tin, and lead, running eastward through Cornwall, as far as the Dartmoor Hills. According to the statement of my informant in the counting house, it has been worked for more than a century. In former times it produced enormous profits to the speculators; but now the case is altered. The price of copper has fallen of late years; the lodes have proved neither so rich nor so extensive, as at past periods; and the mine, when we visited Cornwall, had failed to pay the expenses of working it.

The organization of labour at Botallack, and in all other mines throughout the county, is thus managed:— The men work eight hours underground, out of the twenty-four; taking their turn of night duty (for labour proceeds in the mines by night as well as by day), in regular rotation. The different methods on which their work is undertaken, and the rates of remuneration that they receive have been already touched on, in the chapter on the "Cornish People." It will be found that ordinary wages for mine labour are there stated as ranging from forty to fifty shillings a month—mention being made at the same time of the larger remuneration which may be obtained by working "on tribute," or, in other words, by agreeing to excavate the lodes of metal for a percentage which varies with the varying value of the mineral raised. It is, however, necessary to add here that, although men who labour on this latter plan occasionally make as much as six or ten pounds each, in a month, they are on the other hand liable to heavy losses from the speculative character of the work in which they engage. The lode may, for instance, be poor when they begin to work it, and may continue poor as they proceed farther and farther. Under these circumstances, the low value of the mineral they have raised realizes a correspondingly low rate of percentage; and when this happens, the best workmen cannot make more than twenty shillings a month.

Another system on which the men are employed is the system of "contract." A certain quantity of ore in the rock is mapped out by the captain of the mine; and put up to auction among the miners thus:—One man mentions a sum for which he is willing to undertake excavating the ore, upon the understanding that he is himself to pay for the assistance, candles, &c., out of the price he asks. Another man, who is also anxious to get the contract, then offers to accept it on lower terms; a third man's demand is smaller still; and so they proceed until the piece of work is knocked down to the lowest bidder. By this sort of labour the contracting workman— after he has paid his expenses for assistance—seldom clears more than twelve shillings a week.

Upon the whole, setting his successful and his disastrous speculations fairly against each other, the Cornish miner's average gains, year by year, may be fairly estimated at about ten shillings a week. "It's hard work we have to do, sir," said my informant, summing up, when we parted, the proportions of good and evil in the social positions of his brethren and himself—"harder work than people think, down in the heat and darkness under ground. We may get a good deal at one time, but we get little enough at another; sometimes mines are shut up, and then we are thrown out altogether—but, good work or bad work, or no work at all, what with our bits of ground for potatoes and greens, and what with cheap living, somehow we and our families make it do. We contrive to keep our good cloth coat for Sundays, and go to chapel in the morning—for we're most of us Wesleyans—and then to church in the afternoon; so as to give 'em both their turn like! We never go near the mine on Sundays, except to look after the steam pump: our rest, and our walk in the evening once a week, is a good deal to us. That's how we live, sir; whatever happens, we manage to work through, and don't complain!"

Although the occupation of smelting the copper above ground is, as may well be imagined, unhealthy enough, the labour of getting it from the mine (by blasting the subterranean rock in the first place, and then hewing and breaking the ore out of the frag-ments), seems to be attended with no bad effect on the constitution. The miners are a fine-looking race of men—strong and well-proportioned. The fact appears to be, that they gain more, physically, by the pure air of the cliffs and moors on which their cottages are built, and the temperance of their lives (many of them are "teetotallers"), than they lose by their hardest exertions in the underground atmosphere in which they work.

Serious accidents are rare in the mines of Cornwall. From the horrors of such explosions as take place in coal mines, they are by their nature entirely free. The casualties that oftenest occur are serious falls, generally produced by the carelessness of inexperienced or foolhardy people. Of these, and of extraordinary escapes from death with which they are associated, many anecdotes are told in mining districts which would appear to the reader exaggerated, or positively untrue, if I related them on mere hearsay evidence. There was, however, one instance of a fall down the shaft of a mine, unattended with fatal consequences, which occurred while I was in Cornwall; and which I may safely adduce, for I can state some of the facts connected with the affair as an eyewitness. I attended an examination of the sufferer by a medical man, and heard the story of the accident from the parents of the patient.

On the 7th of August 1850, a boy fourteen years of age, the son of a miner, slipped into the shaft of Boscaswell Downs Mine, in the neighbourhood of Penzance. He fell to the depth of thirteen fathoms, or seventy-eight feet. Fifty-eight feet down he struck his left side against a board placed across the shaft, snapped it in two, and then, falling twenty feet more, pitched on his head. He was of course taken up insensible; the doctor was sent for; and on examining him, found, to his amazement, that there was actually a chance of the boy's recovery after this tremendous fall!

Not a bone in his body was broken. He was bruised and scratched all over, and there were three cuts—none of them serious—on his head. The board stretched across the shaft, twenty feet from the bottom, had saved him from being dashed to pieces; but had inflicted at the same time, where his left side had struck it, the only injury that appeared dangerous to the medical man—a large, hard lump that could be felt under the bruised skin. The boy showed no symptoms of fever; his pulse, day after day, was found never varying from eighty-two to the minute; his appetite was voracious; and the internal functions of his body only required a little ordinary medicine to keep them properly at work. In short, nothing was to be dreaded but the chance of the formation of an abscess in his left side, between the hip and ribs. He had been under medical care exactly one week, when I accompanied the doctor on a visit to him.

The cottage where he lived with his parents, though small, was neat and comfortable. We found him lying in bed, awake. He looked languid and lethargic; but his skin was moist and cool; his face displayed no paleness, and no injury of any kind. He had just eaten a good dinner of rabbit pie, and was anxious to be allowed to sit up in a chair, and amuse himself by looking out of the window. His left side was first examined. A great circular bruise discoloured the skin, over the whole space between the hip and ribs; but on touching it, the doctor discovered that the lump beneath had considerably decreased in size, and was much less hard than it had felt during previous visits. Next we looked at his back and arms—they were scratched and bruised all over; but nowhere seriously. Lastly, the dressings were taken off his head, and three cuts were disclosed, which even a non-medical eye could easily perceive to be of no great importance. Such were all the results of a fall of seventy-eight feet.

The boy's father reiterated to me the account of the accident, just as I had already heard it from the doctor. How it happened, he said, could only be guessed, for his son had completely forgotten all the circumstances immediately preceding the fall; neither could he communicate any of the sensations which must have attended it. Most probably, he had been sitting dangling his legs idly over the mouth of the shaft, and had so slipped in. But however the accident really happened, there the sufferer was before us—less seriously hurt than many a lad who has trodden on a piece of orange peel as he was walking along the street.

We left him (humanly speaking) certain of recovery, now that the dangerous lump in his side had begun to decrease. I heard afterwards from his medical attendant that in two months from the date of the accident he was at work again as usual in the mine; at that very part of it, too, where his fall had taken place!

It was not the least interesting part of my visit to the cottage where he lay ill to observe the anxious affection displayed towards him by both his parents. His mother left her work in the kitchen to hold him in her arms, while the old dressings were being taken off and the new ones applied—sighing bitterly, poor creature, every time he winced or cried out under the pain of the operation. The father put several questions to the doctor, which were always perfectly to the point; and did the honours of his little abode to his stranger visitor, with a natural politeness and a simple cordiality of manner which showed that he really meant the welcome that he spoke. Nor was he any exception to the rest of his brother-workmen with whom I met. As a body of men, they are industrious and intelligent; sober and orderly; neither soured by hard work, nor easily depressed by harder privations. No description of personal experiences in the Cornish mines can be fairly concluded without a collateral testimony to the merits of the Cornish miners—a testimony which I am happy to accord here; and to which my readers would cheerfully add their voices, if they ever felt inclined to test its impartiality by their own experience.

161

TEN

THE MODERN DRAMA
IN CORNWALL

O<small>UR WALK FROM</small> B<small>OTALLACK</small> M<small>INE TO</small> S<small>T</small> I<small>VES</small>
led us almost invariably between moors and hills on
one side, and cliffs and sea on the other; and displayed
some of the dreariest views that we had yet beheld in
Cornwall. About nightfall, we halted for a short time at
a place which was certainly not calculated to cheer the
traveller along his onward way.

Imagine three or four large, square, comfortless-
looking, shut-up houses, all apparently uninhabited; add
some half-dozen miserable little cottages standing near
the houses, with the nasal notes of a Methodist hymn
pouring disastrously through the open door of one of
them; let the largest of the large buildings be called
an inn, but let it make up no beds, because nobody
ever stops to sleep there: place in the kitchen of this
inn a sickly little girl, and a middle-aged, melancholy
woman, the first staring despondently on a wasting fire,

the second offering to the stranger a piece of bread, three eggs, and some sour porter corked down in an earthenware jar, as all that her larder and cellar can afford; fancy next an old, grim, dark church, with two or three lads leaning against the churchyard wall, looking out together in gloomy silence on a solitary high road; conceive a thin, slow rain falling, a cold twilight just changing into darkness, a surrounding landscape wild, barren, and shelterless—imagine all this, and you will have the picture before you which presented itself to me and my companion when we found ourselves in the village of Morvah.

Late that night, we got to the large seaport town of St Ives; and stayed there two or three days to look at the pilchard fishery, which was then proceeding with all the bustle and activity denoting the commencement of a good season. Leaving St Ives, on our way up the northern coast, we now passed through the central part of the mining districts of Cornwall. Chimneys and engine houses chequered the surface of the landscape; the roads glittered with metallic particles; the walls at their sides were built with crystallized stones; towns showed a sudden increase in importance; villages grew large and populous; inns disappeared, and hotels arose in their stead; people became less curious to know who we were, stared at us less, gossiped with us less; gave us information, but gave us nothing more—no long stories, no invitations to stop and smoke a pipe, no hospitable offers of bed and board. All that we saw and heard tended to convince us that we had left the picturesque and the primitive, with the streets of Looe and the fishermen at the Land's End; and had got into the commercial part of the county, among sharp, prosperous, business-like people—it was like walking out of a painter's studio into a merchant's counting house!

As we were travelling, like the renowned Doctor Syntax, in search of the picturesque, we hurried through this populous and highly civilized region of Cornwall as rapidly as possible. I doubt much whether we should not have passed as unceremoniously through the large town of Redruth—the capital city of the mining districts—as we passed through several towns and villages before it, had not our attention been attracted and our departure delayed by a public notice, printed on rainbow-coloured paper, and pasted up in the most conspicuous part of the marketplace.

The notice set forth that "the beautiful drama of The Curate's Daughter" was to be performed at night, in the "unrivalled Sans Pareil Theatre," by "the most talented company in England," before "the most discerning audience in the world." As far as we were individually concerned, this theatrical announcement was remarkably tempting and well-timed. We were now within one day's journey of Piran Round, the famous amphitheatre where the old Cornish Miracle Plays used to be performed. Anything connected with the stage was, therefore, a subject of particular interest in our eyes. The bill before us seemed to offer a curious opportunity of studying the dramatic tastes of the modern Cornish, on the very day before we were about to speculate on the dramatic tastes of the ancient Cornish, among the remains of their public theatre. Such an occasion was too favourable to be neglected; we ordered our beds at Redruth, and joined the "discerning audience" assembled to sit in judgment on "The Curate's Daughter."

The Sans Pareil Theatre was not of that order of architecture in which outward ornament is studied. There was nothing "florid" about it; canvas, ropes, scaffolding-poles, and old boards threw an air of Saxon simplicity over the whole structure. Admitted within, we turned instinctively towards the stage. On each side of the proscenium boards was painted a knight in full armour, with powerful calves, weak knees, and an immense spear. Tallow candles, stuck round two hoops, threw a mysterious light on the green curtain, in front of which sat an orchestra of four musicians, playing on a trombone, an ophicleide, a clarionet, and a fiddle, as loudly as they could—the artist on the trombone, especially, performing prodigies of blowing, though he had not room enough to develop the whole length of his instrument. Every now and then great excitement was created among the expectant audience by the vehement ringing of a bell behind the scenes, and by the occasional appearance of a youth who gravely snuffed the candles all round, with a skill and composure highly creditable to him, considering the pertinacity with which he was stared at by everybody while he pursued his occupation.

At last, the bell was rung furiously for the twentieth time; the curtain drew up, and the drama of "The Curate's Daughter" began.

Our sympathies were excited at the outset. We beheld a ladylike woman who answered to the name of "Grace;" and an old gentleman, dressed in dingy black, who personated her father, the Curate; and who was, on this occasion (I presume through unavoidable circumstances), neither more nor less than—drunk. There was no mistaking the cause of the fixed leer in the reverend gentleman's eye; of the slow swaying in his gait; of the gruff huskiness in his elocution. It appeared, from the opening dialogue, that a pending lawsuit, and the absence of his daughter Fanny in London, combined to make him uneasy in his mind just at present. But he was by no means so clear on this subject as could be desired—in fact, he spoke through his nose, put in and left out his *h*s in the wrong places, and involved his dialogue in a long labyrinth of parentheses whenever he expressed himself at any length. It was not until the entrance of his daughter Fanny (just arrived from

166

London: nobody knew why or wherefore), that he grew more emphatic and intelligible. We now observed with pleasure that he gave his children his blessing and embraced them both at once; and we were additionally gratified by hearing from his own lips that his "daughters were the h'all on which his h'all depended—that they would watch h'over his 'ale autumn; and that whatever happened the whole party must invariably trust in heabben's obdipotent power!"

Grateful for this clerical advice, Fanny retired into the garden to gather her parent some flowers; but immediately returned shrieking. She was followed by a Highwayman with a cocked hat, mustachios, bandit's ringlets, a scarlet hunting coat, and buff boots. This gentleman had shown his extraordinary politeness—although a perfect stranger—by giving Miss Fanny a kiss in the garden; conduct for which the Curate very properly cursed him, in the strongest language. Apparently a quiet and orderly character, the Highwayman replied by beginning a handsome apology, when he was interrupted by the abrupt entrance of another personage, who ordered him (rather late in the day, as we ventured to think) to "let go his holt, and beware how he laid his brutal touch on the form of innocence!" This newcomer, the parson informed us, was "good h'Adam Marle, the teacher of the village school." We found "h'Adam," in respect of his outward appearance, to be a very short man, dressed in a high-crowned modern hat, with a fringed Vandyck collar drooping over his back and shoulders, a modern frock coat, buttoned tight at the waist, and a pair of jackboots of the period of James the Second. Aided by his advantages of costume, this character naturally interested us; and we regretted seeing but little of him in the first scene, from which he retired, following the penitent Highwayman out, and lecturing him as he went. No sooner were their backs turned than a waggoner, in a clean smock-frock and high-lows, entered with an offer of a situation in London for Fanny, which the unsuspicious Curate accepted immediately. As soon as he had committed himself, it was confided to the audience that the waggoner was a depraved villain, in the employ of that notorious profligate, Colonel Chartress, who had commissioned a second myrmidon (of the female sex) to lure Fanny from virtue and the country, to vice and the metropolis. By the time the plot had "thickened" thus far, the scene changed, and we got to London at once.

We now beheld the Curate, Chartress's female accomplice, Fanny, and the vicious waggoner, all standing in a row, across the stage. The Curate, in a burst of amiability, had just lifted up his hands to bless the company, when Colonel Chartress (dressed in an old *naval* uniform, with an opera hat of the year 1800), suddenly rushed in, followed by the Highwayman, who having relapsed from penitence to guilt had, as a necessary consequence,

168

determined to supplant Chartress in the favour of Miss Fanny. These two promptly seized each other by the throat; vehement shouting, scuffling, and screaming ensued; and the Curate, clasping his daughter round the waist, frantically elevated his walking stick in the air. Was he about to inflict personal chastisement on his innocent child? Who could say? Before there was time to ask the question, the curtain fell with a bang, on the crisis of the first act.

In act the second, the first scene was described in the bills as Temple Bar by moonlight. Neither Bar nor moonlight appeared when the curtain rose—so we took both for granted, and fixed our minds on the story. The first person who now confronted us was "good h'Adam Marle." The paint was all washed off his face; his immense spread of collar looked grievously in want of washing; and he leaned languidly on an oaken stick. He had been walking—he informed us—through the streets of London for six consecutive days and nights, without sustenance, in search of Miss Fanny, who had disappeared since the skirmish at the end of act the first, and had never been heard of since. Poor dear Marle! how eloquent he was with his white handkerchief, when he fairly opened his heart, and confided to us that he was madly attached to Fanny; that he knew he "was nothink" to her; and that, under existing circumstances, he felt inclined to rest himself on a door step! Just as he had comfortably settled down, the valet of the profligate Chartress entered, in the communicative stage of intoxication; and immediately mentioned all his master's private affairs to "h'Adam." It appeared that the Colonel had carried off Miss Fanny, had then got tired of her, and had coolly handed her over to a Jew,* in part payment of "a little bill." Having ascertained the Jew's address, the indefatigable Marle left us (still without sustenance) to rescue the Curate's daughter, or die in the attempt.

The next scene disclosed Fanny, sitting conscience-stricken and inconsolable, in a red polka jacket and white muslin slip. Mr Marle, having discovered her place of refuge, now stepped in to lecture and reclaim. Vain proceeding! The Curate's daughter looked at him with a scream, exclaimed "Cuss me, h'Adam! cuss me!" and rushed out. "H'Adam," after a despondent soliloquy, followed with his eloquent handkerchief to his eyes; but, while he had been talking to himself, our old friend the Highwayman had been on the alert, and had picked Fanny up, fainting in the street. And what did he do with her after that? He handed her over to his "comrades in villany." And who were his comrades in villany? They were the trombone and ophicleide players from the orchestra, and the "Miss Grace," of act first, disguised as a bad character, in a cloak, with a red pocket

---

* Prejudiced portrayals such as this were not uncommon on the stage and in literature at this time.

handkerchief over her head. And what happened next? A series of events happened next. Miss Fanny recovered on a sudden, perceived what sort of company she had about her, rushed out a second time into the street, fell fainting a second time on the pavement, and was picked up on this occasion by Colonel Chartress—in the interests, it is to be presumed, of his friend, the Jew moneylender. Before, however, he could get clear off with his prize, the indefatigably vicious Highwayman, and the indefatigably virtuous Marle, precipitated themselves on the stage, assaulting Chartress, assaulting each other, assaulting everybody. Fanny fell fainting a third time in the street; and before we could find out who was the third person who picked her up, down came the curtain in the midst of the catastrophe.

Act the third was opened by the heroine, still injured, still inconsolable, and still clad in the polka jacket and white slip. We thought her a very nice little woman, with a melodious, genteel-comedy voice, trim ankles, and a habit of catching her breath in the most pathetic manner, at least a dozen times in the course of one soliloquy. While she was still assuring us that she felt the most forlorn creature on the face of the earth, she was suddenly interrupted by the entrance of no less a person than the Curate himself. We had seen nothing of the reverend gentleman throughout the second act; but "h'Adam" had casually informed us that his time had been passed at his parsonage, "sittun with his 'ed between his knees, sobbun!" Having now wearied of this gymnastic method of indulging in parental grief, he had set forth to seek his lost daughter, and had accidentally stopped at the very inn where she had taken refuge. Nothing could be more piteous than his present appearance; he was infinitely more tipsy, infinitely more dignified, and infinitely more parenthetical in his mode of expressing himself than when we last beheld him. A streak of burnt cork running down each side of his venerable nose showed us how deeply grief had increased the wrinkles of age; and our pity for him reached its climax when he cast his clerical hat on the floor, sank drowsily into a chair, and began to pray in these words: "Oh heabben! hear a solemn and a solid prayer—hear a solemn heart who wants to embrace his darling Fanny!"

All this time, the lost daughter was hiding behind the forlorn father's chair; an awful and convenient darkness being thrown on the stage by the introduction of a plank between the actors and the tallow candles. In this striking situation, Miss Fanny told her sad story, and pleaded her own cause as a stranger, under disguise of the darkness. Useless—quite useless! The reverend gentleman, having never turned round to see who it was that was speaking to him, and having therefore no idea that it was his own daughter, received in dignified silence the advances of a young person unknown to him.

What course was now left to the unhappy Fanny? The old course—a rush off the stage, and a swoon in the street. As soon as her back was turned, the Parson, forgetting to take away his hat with him, staggered out at the opposite side to continue his journey. He uttered as he went the following moral observation:—"No soul so lost to Nature, but must be lost eternally—my 'art is broken!"

The next moment we were startled by a long and elaborate trampling of feet behind the scenes, and the villain Chartress ran panic-stricken across the stage, hotly pursued by "good h'Adam Marle." In the eloquent language of virtue, thus did Adam address him:—"Stay, ruffian, stay! Inquiring for Chartress at the bar of this inn, I found indeed that you was the very identical. You foul, venomous, treacherous, voluptuous liar, where is the un'appy Fanny? where is the victim of your prey?—Ha! 'oary-'edded ruffian, I have yer!" (*Collars Chartress.*) "But no! I will not *strike* yer; I will *drag* yer!" It was interesting to see Adam exemplify the peculiar distinction in the science of assault implied in his last words, by hauling Chartress all round the stage. It was awful to observe that the Colonel lost his temper at the second round, murderously snapped a pistol in "h'Adam's" face, and rushed off in hot homicidal triumph. We waited breathless for the fall of Marle. Nothing of the sort happened. He started, frowned, paused, laughed fiercely, exclaimed—"The villain 'as missed!" and followed in pursuit.

173

In the interim, Miss Fanny had been picked up in the street, for the fourth time, by a benevolent "washerwoman," who happened to be passing by at the moment; had been conveyed to the said washerwoman's lodgings; and now appeared before us, despoiled, at last, of all the glories of the red polka, enveloped from head to foot in clouds of white muslin, and dying with frightful rapidity in an armchair. In the next and last scene, all that remained to represent the unhappy heroine was a coffin decently covered with a white sheet. With slow and funereal steps, the Curate, Miss Grace, "h'Adam," the Highwayman, and the "venomous and voluptuous liar," Chartress, approached to weep over it. The Curate had gone raving mad since we saw him last. His wig was set on wrong side foremost; the ends of his clerical cravat floated wildly, a yard long at least over his shoulders; his eyes rolled in frenzy; he swooned at the sight of the coffin; recovered convulsively; placed Marle's hand in the hand of Miss Grace (telling him that now one daughter was dead, nothing was left for him but to marry the other); and then fell flat on his back, with a thump that shook the stage and made the audience start unanimously. Marle—well-bred to the last—politely offered his arm to Grace; and pointing to the coffin, asked Chartress, reproachfully, whether that was not *his* work. The Colonel took off his opera hat, raised his hand to his eyes, and doggedly answered, "Indeed, it is!" The Tableau thus formed was completed by the Highwayman, the coffin, and the defunct Curate; and the curtain fell to slow music.

Such was the plot of this remarkable dramatic work, exactly as I took it down in the theatre, between the acts; noting also in my pocketbook such scraps of dialogue as I have presented to the reader, while they fell from the actors' lips. There were plenty of comic scenes in the play which I leave unmentioned; for their humour was of the dreariest, and their morality of the lowest order that can possibly be conceived. I can only say, as the result of my own experience at Redruth, that if the dramatic reforms which are now being attempted in the theatrical byways of the metropolis succeed, there would be no harm in extending the experiment as far as the locomotive stage of Cornwall. Good plays are good missionaries; and, like missionaries, let them travel to teach.

And now, having seen enough of the modern drama in Cornwall, without waiting for the songs, the dances, and the farces which are to follow the "Curate's Daughter," let us go on to Piranzabuloe, and look at the theatre in which the Cornish of former days assembled; endeavouring to discover, at the same time, by what sort of performances the people were instructed or amused some two hundred and fifty years ago.

ELEVEN

THE ANCIENT DRAMA
IN CORNWALL

W E FOUND THE MODERN CORNISH THEATRE situated in a populous town; built up, as a temporary structure, with old canvas and boards; and opened to audiences only at night. We found the ancient Cornish theatre placed in a perfect desert; constructed permanently, though rudely, of mounds of turf—the sky forming its only roof, the flat plain its only stage, the broad daylight its only means of illumination. Nothing of the kind could be more strongly marked than the difference between the theatre of the past and the theatre of the present day in the far West of England.

In like manner, the country about Piran Round (such is the name of the Old Cornish amphitheatre) offers a startling contrast to the country about Redruth. You are at once powerfully impressed by its barren solitude, its dreary repose, after the fertility and populousness of the great mining districts through which you have just passed. Now, the large towns and busy villages disappear, the mines grow rarer, the roads look deserted, the wide pathways dwindle to the merest foot track. Again you behold the spacious moor rolling away in alternate hill and dale to the far horizon; again you pass through the quaint coast villages; and see the few simple cottages, the few old boats, the little groups talking quietly at the inn door, as they have already presented themselves along the southern and western shores of Cornwall. Soon, however, your onward road towards Piran Round becomes yet more desolate. Ere long, not even a solitary cottage is in sight, not a living being appears: you find yourself wandering along the uneven boundary of a wilderness of sandhills heaped up from the seashore by the wind. You look over a perfect desert of miniature mountains and valleys, in some places overgrown with thin, dry grass; in others, dotted with little pools of mud and stagnant water. Year by year, this invasion of sand encroaches on the moorland—year by year, it is ever shifting, ever increasing, ever assuming newer and more fantastic forms, now in one direction and now in another, with each fresh storm.

When you leave this dreary scene, you only leave it for the wild flat heath, the open naked country once more. You follow your long road, visible miles on before you, winding white and serpent-like over the dark ground, until you suddenly observe in the distance an object which rises strangely above the level prospect. You approach nearer, and behold a circular turf embankment; a wide, lonesome, desolate enclosure, looking like a witches' dancing ring that has sprung up in the midst of the open moor. This is Piran Round. Here, the old inhabitants of Cornwall assembled to form the audience of the drama of former days.

A level area of grassy ground, one hundred and thirty feet in diameter, is enclosed by the embankment. There are two entrances to this area cut through the boundary circle of turf and earth, which rises to a height of nine or ten feet, and narrows towards the top, where it is seven feet wide. All round the inside of the embankment steps were formerly cut; but their traces are now almost obliterated by the growth of the grass. They were originally seven in number; the spectators stood on them in rows, one above another—a closely packed multitude, all looking down at the dramatic performances taking place on the wide circumference of the plain. When it was well filled, the amphitheatre must have contained upwards of two thousand people.

Such is this rude, yet extraordinary structure, in our time. It has not lost its patriarchal simplicity since the far distant period when the populace thronged its turf steps to welcome the strolling players of their age. The antiquity of Piran Round dates back beyond the period of the earliest and rudest dramatic performances on English ground. It was first used for popular sports, for single combats, for rustic councils. Then, plays were acted in it—miracle plays—some translated into the ancient Cornish language, some originally written in it. The oldest of these are lost; but one of a comparatively late date has been preserved and translated into English. We will examine this book while we sit within the deserted amphitheatre; and thus, in imagination at least, people the simple stage before us with the rough country actors who once trod it—thus pry behind the scenes at all that is left to us of the ancient drama in Cornwall.

The play which we now open is called by the comprehensive title of "The Creation of the World, with Noah's Flood." It was translated in 1611, from a drama of much earlier date, for performance in Cornish, by William Jordan; was then rendered into English by John Keygwyn, in 1691; and was finally corrected and published by Mr Davies Gilbert, in 1827. The Cornish and English versions are printed on opposite pages, so we can compare the two throughout, as we go on.

The play is in five acts, and is written in poetry—in a rambling octosyllabic metre, often varied by the introduction of longer or shorter lines, and sometimes interspersed (in the Cornish version) with a word or two of English. It occupies a hundred and eighty pages, containing on the average about twenty-five lines each.

This would be thought rather a lengthy manner of developing a dramatic story in our days; but we must remember that the time embraced in the plot of the old playwright extends from the Creation to the Flood, and must be astonished and thankful that he has not been more diffuse.

The *dramatis personæ* muster by the legion. In the first act we have the whole heavenly host: in the second, are superadded Adam, Eve, "Torpen, a devil," Beelzebub, the Serpent, and Michael the Archangel; in the third, besides these, Death, Cain and his wife, Abel and Seth; in the fourth, we have the addition of Lamech, a servant, a Cherubim, and a first and second devil; and in the fifth, Enoch, Noah and his wife, Shem, Ham, Japhet, Seth, Jaball, and Tubal Cain.

The author manages this tremendous list of mortal and immortal characters with infinite coolness and dexterity. Nothing appears to embarrass him. He follows history in a negligent, sauntering way, passing over a hundred years or so, whenever it is convenient; and giving all his personages their turn of talking in orderly and impartial rotation. His speeches are wonderfully moral and long; even his worst characters have, for the most part, a temperate and logical way of uttering the most violent language, which must have read an excellent lesson to the roistering young gentlemen among the audiences of the time.

We will now examine the play a little in detail, quoting the stage directions (the most extraordinary part of it) exactly as they occur; and occasionally presenting a line or two of the dialogue from the old English translation wherever it best illustrates the author's style.

The first act comprehends the fall of the angels— the introductory stage direction commanding that the theatrical clouds, and the whole sky to boot, shall open when Heaven is named! All is harmony at the outset of the play, until it is Lucifer's turn to speak. He declares that he alone is great, and that all allegiance must be given to him. Some of the angels glorify him accordingly; others remain true to their celestial service; the debate grows warm, and some of the disputants give each other the lie (but very calmly). At length, the scene is closed by Lucifer's condemnation to Hell, which, as the directions provide, "shall gape when it is named." The faithful angels are then told to "have swords and staves ready for Lucifer," who, we are informed, "voideth and goeth down to Hell apparelled foul, with fire about him, turning to Hell, with every degree of devils and lost spirits on cords running into the plain." With this stirring scene the act ends.

The second act comprises the creation and fall of man. Here, again, we will consult the stage directions, as giving the best idea of the incidents and scenes. We find that Adam and Eve are to be "apparelled in white leather in a place appointed by the conveyor" (probably the person we term stage manager now); "and are not to be seen until they be called; and then each rises." After this, we read:—"Let Paradise be finely made, with fair trees in it, and apples upon a tree, and other fruit on the others. A fountain, too, in Paradise, and fine flowers painted. Put Adam into Paradise—let flowers appear in Paradise—let Adam lie down and sleep where Eve is, and she, by the conveyor, must be taken from Adam's side—let fishes of all sorts, birds and beasts, as oxen, kyne, sheep, and such like, appear."

Then, we have the preparations for the temptation, ordered thus:—"A fine serpent to be made with a virgin's face, and yellow hair on her head. Let the serpent appear, and also geese and hens." Lucifer enters immediately afterwards, and goes into the serpent, which is then directed to be "seen singing in a tree" (the actor who personated Lucifer must have had some gymnastic difficulties to contend with in his part!)—"Eve looketh strange on the serpent;" then, "talketh familiarly and cometh near him;" then, "doubteth and looketh angrily;" and then eats part of the apple, shows it to Adam, and insists on his eating part of it too, in the following lines:—

Sir, in a few words,
Taste thou part of the apple,
Or my love thou shalt lose!

See, take this fair apple,
Or surely between thee and thy wife
The love shall utterly fail,
    If thou wilt not eat of it![4]

The stage direction now proceeds:—"Adam receiveth the apple and tasteth it, and so repenteth and casteth it away. Eve looketh on Adam very strangely and speaketh not anything." During this pause, the "conveyor" is told "to get the fig-leaves ready." Then Lucifer is ordered to "come out of the serpent and creep on his belly to hell;" Adam and Eve receive the curse, and depart out of Paradise, "showing a spindle and distaff"—no badly conceived emblem of the labour to which they are henceforth doomed. And thus the second act terminates.

The third act treats of Cain and Abel; and is properly opened by an impersonation of Death. After which Cain and Abel appear to sacrifice.

Cain makes his offering of the first substance that comes to hand—"dry cow-dung"(!); and tells Abel that he is a "dolthead" and "a frothy fool" for using anything better. "Abel is stricken with a jawbone and dieth; Cain casteth him into a ditch." The effect of the first murder on the minds of our first parents is delineated in some speeches exhibiting a certain antique simplicity of thought, which almost rises to the poetical by its homely adherence to nature, and its perfect innocence of effort, artifice, or display. The banishment of Cain, still glorying in his crime, follows the lamentations of Adam and Eve for the death of Abel; and the act is closed by Adam's announcement of the birth of Seth.

The fourth act relates the deaths of Cain and Adam, and contains some of the most eccentric, and also some of the most elevated, writing in the play. Lamech opens the scene, candidly and methodically exposing his own character in these lines:—

> Sure I am the first
> That ever yet had two wives!
> And maidens in sufficient plenty
> They are to me. I am not dainty,
> I can find them where I will;
> Nor do I spare of them
>   In anywise one that is handsome.
> But I am wondrous troubled,
> Scarce do I see one glimpse
>   What the devil shall be done!

In this vagabond frame of mind Lamech goes out hunting, with bow and arrow, and shoots Cain, accidentally, in a bush. When Cain falls, Lamech appeals to his servant, to know what is it that he has shot. The servant declares that it is "hairy, rough, ugly, and a buck-goat of the night." Cain, however, discovers himself before he dies. There is something rudely dreary and graphic about his description of his loneliness, bare as it is of any recommendation of metaphors or epithets:

184

Deformed I am very much,
And overgrown with hair;
I do live continually in heat or cold frost,
   Surely night and day;
Nor do I desire to see the son of man,
With my will at any time;
But accompany most time with all the beasts.

Lamech, discovering the fatal error that he has committed, kills his servant in his anger; and the scene ends with "the devils carrying them away with great noise to hell."

The second scene is between Adam and his son Seth; and here the old dramatist often rises to an elevation of poetical feeling, which, judging from the preceding portions of the play, we should not have imagined he could reach. Barbarous as his execution may be, the simple beauty of his conception often shines through it faintly, but yet palpably, in this part of the drama.

Adam is weary of life and weary of the world; he sends Seth to the gates of Paradise to ask mercy and release for him, telling his son that he will find the way thither by his father's footprints, burnt into the surface of the earth which was cursed for Adam's transgression. Seth finds and follows the supernatural marks, is welcomed by the angel at the gate of Paradise, and is permitted to look in. He beholds there an Apocalypse of the redemption of the world. On the tree of life sit the Virgin and Child; while on the tree from which Eve plucked the apple, "the woman" is seen, having power over the serpent. The vision changes, and Cain is shown in hell, "sorrowing and weeping." Then the angel plucks three kernels from the tree of life, and gives them to Seth for his father's use, saying that they shall grow to another tree of life, when more than five thousand years are ended; and that Adam shall be redeemed from his pains when that period is fulfilled. After this, Seth is dismissed by the angel and returns to communicate to his father the message of consolation which he has received.

Adam hears the result of his son's mission with thankfulness; blesses Seth; and speaks these last words, while he is confronted by Death:—

Old and weak, I am gone!
To live longer is not for me:
Death is come,
Nor will here leave me
  To live one breath!

I see him now with his spear,
Ready to pierce me on every side,
There is no escaping from him!
The time is welcome with, me—
  I have served long in the world!

So, the patriarch dies, trusting in the promise conveyed through his son; and is buried by Seth "in a fair tomb, with some Church sonnet."

After this impressive close to the fourth act—impressive in its intention, however clumsy the appliances by which that intention is worked out—it would be doing the old author no kindness to examine his fifth act in detail. Here, he sinks again in many places, to puerility of conception and coarseness of dialogue. It is enough to say that the history of the Flood closes the drama, and that the spectators are dismissed with an epilogue, directing them to "come tomorrow, betimes, and see very great matters"—the minstrels being charged, at the conclusion to "pipe," so that all may dance together, as the proper manner of ending the day's amusements.

And now, let us close the book, look forth over this lonesome country and lonesome amphitheatre, and imagine what a scene both must have presented, when a play was to be acted on a fine summer's morning in the year 1611.

Fancy, at the outset, the arrival of the audience—people dressed in the picturesque holiday costume of the time, which varied with every varying rank, hurrying to their daylight play from miles off; all visible in every direction on the surface of the open moor, and all converging from every point of the compass to the one common centre of Piran Round. Then, imagine the assembling in the amphitheatre; the running round the outer circle of the embankment to get at the entrances; the tumbling and rushing up the steps inside; the racing of hot-headed youngsters to get to the top places; the sly deliberation of the elders in selecting the lower and safer positions; the quarrelling when a tall man chanced to stand before a short one; the giggling and blushing of buxom peasant wenches when the gallant young bachelors of the district happened to be placed behind them; the universal speculations on the weather; the universal shouting for pots of ale—and finally, as the time of the performance drew near and the minstrels appeared with their pipes, the gradual hush and stillness among the multitude; the combined stare of the whole circular mass of spectators on one point in the plain of the amphitheatre, where all knew that the actors lay hidden in a pit, properly covered in from observation—the mysterious "green room" of the strolling players of old Cornwall!

And the play!—to see the play must have been a sight indeed! Conceive the commencement of it; the theatrical sky which was to open awfully whenever Heaven was named; the mock clouds coolly set up by the "property man" on an open-air stage, where the genuine clouds appeared above them to expose the counterfeit; the hard fighting of the angels with swords and staves; the descent of the lost spirits along cords running into the plain; the thump with which they must have come down; the rolling off of the whole troop over the grass, to the infernal regions, amid shouts of applause from the audience as they rolled! Then the appearance of Adam and Eve, packed in white leather, like our modern dolls— the serpent with the virgin's face and the yellow hair, climbing into a tree, and singing in the branches—Cain falling out of the bush when he was struck by the arrow of Lamech, and his blood appearing, according to the stage directions, when he fell—the making of the Ark, the filling it with livestock, the scenery of the Deluge, in the fifth act! What a combination of theatrical prodigies the whole performance must have presented! How the actors must have ranted to make themselves heard in the open air; how often the machinery must have gone wrong, and the rude scenery toppled and tumbled down! Could we revive at will, for mere amusement, any of the bygone performances of the theatre, since the first days of barbaric acting in a cart, assuredly the performances at Piran Round would be those which, without hesitation, we should select from all others to call back to life.

The end of the play, too—how picturesque, how strik- ing all the circumstances attending it must have been! Oh that we could hear again the merry old English tune piped by the minstrels, and see the merry old English dancing of the audience to the music! Then, think of the separation and the return home of the populace, at sunset; the fishing people strolling off towards the seashore; the miners walking away farther inland; the agricultural labourers spreading in all directions, wherever cottages and farmhouses were visible in the far distance over the moor. And then the darkness coming on, and the moon rising over the amphitheatre, so silent and empty, save at one corner, where the poor worn-out actors are bivouacking gipsy-like in their tents, cooking supper over the fire that flames up red in the moonlight, and talking languidly over the fatigues and the triumphs of the play. What a moral and what a beauty in the quiet night view of the old amphitheatre, after the sight that it must have presented during the noise, the bustle, and the magnificence of the day!

Shall we dream over our old play any longer? Shall we delay a moment more, ere we proceed on our journey, to compare the modern with the ancient drama in Cornwall, as we have already compared the theatre of Redruth with the theatre of Piran Round? If we set them fairly against one another as we now know them, would it be rash to determine which burnt purest—the new light that flared brilliantly in our eyes when we last saw it, or the old light that just flickered in the socket for an instant, as we tried to trim it afresh? Or, if we rather inquire which audience had the advantage of witnessing the worthiest performance, should we hesitate to decide at once? Between the people at Redruth and the people at Piran Round there was certainly a curious resemblance in one respect—they failed alike to discern the barbarisms and absurdities of the plays represented before them; but were they also equally uninstructed by what they beheld? Which was likeliest to send them away with something worth thinking of, and worth remembering—the drama about knaves and fools, at the modern theatre, or the drama about Scripture History at the ancient? Let the reader consider and determine.

For our parts, let us honestly confess that though we took up the old play (not unnaturally) to laugh over the clumsiness and eccentricity of the performance, we now lay it down (not inconsistently), recognising the artless sincerity and elevation of the design—just as in the earliest productions of the Italian School of Painting we first perceive the false perspective of a scene or the quaint rigidity of a figure, and only afterwards discover that these crudities and formalities enshrine the germs of deep poetic feeling, and the first struggling perceptions of grace, beauty, and truth.

TWELVE

THE NUNS OF MAWGAN

ABOUT THREE MILES from the large market town of St Columb Major, in the direction of the coast, is situated the Vale of Mawgan. The village of the same name occupies the lower part of the valley, and includes a few cottages, an old church, a yet older manor-house, and a clear running stream, crossed by a little stone bridge, all nestling close together on a few hundred yards of ground enclosed by some of the most luxuriant wood foliage in Cornwall. The trees bound each side of the stream, tinging it in deep places where it eddies smoothly, with hues of lustrous green; and dipping their lower branches into it, where it ripples on white pebbles or glides fast over grey sand. They cluster thickly about the old churchyard, as if to keep the place secret, throwing deep shadows over the graves, and hiding all outer objects from the eye. The small cottage garden and the spacious manor house enjoy their verdant shelter alike; the byroads leading in and out of the village are soon lost to view amid outspread branches; and not even a peep of the land that leads on to the sea in one direction, and back to the town in the other, is to be obtained through the natural screen of leaves above, and mosses, ferns, and high grass below, which closely shut in this part of the Vale of Mawgan from the open country around.

There is an unbroken, unworldly tranquillity about this secluded place, which communicates itself mysteriously to the stranger's thoughts; making him unconsciously slacken in his walk, and look and listen in silence, when he enters it, as if he had penetrated into a new sphere. Slight noises, rarely noticed elsewhere, are always audible here. The dull fall of the latch, when an idle child carelessly opens the churchyard wicket, sounds from one end of the village to the other. The curious traveller who wanders round the walls of the old church, peering through its dusty lattice windows at the dark religious solitude within, can hear the lightest flap of a duck's wing in the stream below; or the gentlest rustle of distant leaves, as the faint breeze moves them in the upland woods above. But these, and all other sounds, never break the peaceful charm of the place—they only deepen its unearthly stillness.

Within the churchyard, the bright colour of the turf, and the quiet grey hues of the mouldering tombstones, are picturesquely intermingled all over the uneven surface of the ground, save in one remote corner, where the graves are few and the grass grows rank and high. Here, the eye is abruptly attracted by the stern of a boat, painted white, and fixed upright in the earth. This strange memorial, little suited though it be to the old monuments around, has a significance of its own which gives it a peculiar claim to consideration. Inscribed on it appear the names of ten fishermen of the parish who went out to sea to pursue their calling, on one wintry night in 1846. It was unusually cold on land—on the sea, the frosty bitter wind cut through to the bones. The men were badly provided against the weather; and, hardy as they were, the weather killed them that night. In the morning, the boat drifted on shore, manned like a spectre bark, by the ghastly figures of the dead—freighted horribly with the corpses of ten men all frozen to death. They are now buried in Mawgan churchyard; and the stern of the boat they died in tells their fatal story, and points to the last home which they share together.

But it is not from such a village tragedy as this; it is not from its retired situation, its Arcadian peacefulness, its embowering trees and hidden hermit-like beauties of natural scenery, that the Vale of Mawgan derives its peculiar interest. It possesses an additional attraction, stronger than any of these, to fix our attention—it is the scene of a romance which we may still study, of a mystery which is of our own time. Even to this little hidden nook, even to this quiet bower of Nature's building, that vigilant and indestructible Papal religion, which defies alike hidden conspiracy and open persecution, has stretched its stealthy and far-spreading influence. Even in this remote corner of the remote west of England, among the homely cottages of a few Cornish peasants, the imperial Christianity of Rome has set up its sanctuary in triumph—a sanctuary not thrown open to dazzle and awe the beholder, but veiled in deep mystery behind gates that only open, like the fatal gates of the grave, to receive, but never to dismiss again to the world without.

It is this attribute of the Vale of Mawgan which leads the stranger away from the cool, clear stream, and the pleasant, shadowy recesses among the trees, to an ancient building near the church, which he knows to have been once an old English manorial hall—to be now a convent of Carmelite nuns.

The House of Lanhearne, so it is named, comprises an ancient and a modern portion; the first dating back before the time of the Conquest, the second added probably not more than a century and a half ago. The place formerly belonged to the old Cornish family of the Arundels; but about the year 1700, their race became extinct, and the property passed into the possession of the present Lord Arundel. However, although the manor house has changed masters, there is one peculiar circumstance connected with it, which has remained unaltered down to the present time—it has never had a Protestant owner.

Thus, whatever religious traditions are connected with it are Roman Catholic traditions. A secret recess remains in the wall of the old house, where a priest was hidden from his pursuers, during the reign of Elizabeth, for eighteen months; the place being only large enough to allow a man to stand upright in it. The skull of another priest who was burnt at the same period is also preserved with jealous care, as one of the important relics of the ancient history of Lanhearne.

About the commencement of this century, the manor house entirely changed its character. It was at that time given to the Carmelite nuns, who now inhabit it, by Lord Arundel. The sisterhood was originally settled in France, and was removed thence to Antwerp, at the outbreak of the first French Revolution. Shortly afterwards, when the affairs of the Continent began to assume a threatening and troubled aspect, the nuns again migrated, and sought in England, at Lanhearne House, the last asylum which they still occupy.

The strictness of their order is preserved with a severity of discipline which is probably without parallel anywhere else in Europe. It is on our free English ground, in one of our simplest and prettiest English

Lanhearne

villages, that the austerities of a Carmelite convent are now most resolutely practised, and the seclusion of a Carmelite convent most vigilantly preserved, by the nuns of Mawgan! They are at present twenty in number: two of them are Frenchwomen, the rest are all English. They are of every age, from the very young to the very old. The eldest of the sisterhood has long passed the ordinary limits of human life—she has attained ninety-five years.

The nuns never leave the convent, and no one even sees them in it. Women even are not admitted to visit them: the domestic servants, who have been employed in the house for years, have never seen their faces, have never heard them speak. It is only in cases of severe and dangerous illness, when their own skill and their own medicines do not avail them, that they admit, from sheer necessity, the only stranger who ever approaches them—the doctor; and on these occasions, whenever it is possible, the face of the patient is concealed from the medical man.

The nuns occupy the modern part of the house, which is entirely built off, inside, from the ancient. Their only place for exercise is a garden of two acres, enclosed by lofty walls, and surrounded by trees. Their food and other necessaries are conveyed to them through a turning door; all personal communication with the servants' offices being carried on through the medium of lay sisters. The nuns have a private way, known only to themselves, to the chapel choir, which is constructed in the form of a gallery, boarded in at the sides and concealed by a curtain and close grating in front. The chapel itself is in the old part of the house, and occupies what was formerly the servants' hall. The officiating priest who undertakes the duties here lives in this portion of the building, and leads a life of complete solitude, until he is relieved by a successor. He never sees the face of one of the nuns; he cannot even ask one of his own profession to dine with him, without first of all obtaining (by letter) the express permission of the Abbess; and when his visitor is at length admitted, it is impossible to gain for him—let him be who he may—the additional indulgence of being allowed to sleep in the house.[5]

The chapel is the only part of the whole interior of the building to which strangers can be admitted: those who desire to do so can attend Mass there on Sundays. The casual visitor, when permitted to enter it, is not allowed to pass beyond the pillars which support the gallery of the choir above him; for if he advanced farther, the nuns, who might then be occupying it, might see him while they were engaged at their devotions. The chapel exhibits nothing in the way of ornament, beyond the altar furniture and a few copies from pictures on sacred subjects by the old masters. Some of the more valuable objects devoted to its service are not shown. These consist of the sacred vestments and the sacramental plate, which are said to be of extraordinary beauty and value, and are preserved in the keeping of the Abbess. The worth of one of the jewelled chalices alone has been estimated at a thousand pounds.

Much of the land in the neighbourhood belongs to the convent, which has been enriched by many valuable gifts. The nuns make a good use of their wealth. Neither the austerities and mortifications to which their lives are devoted, nor their rigid and terrible self-exclusion from all intercourse with their fellow-beings in the world around them, have diminished their sympathy for affliction, or their readiness in ministering to the wants of the poor. Any assistance of any kind that they can render is always at the service of those who require it, without distinction of rank or religion. No wandering beggar who rings at the convent bell ever leaves the door without a penny and a piece of bread to help him on his way.

But the charities of the nuns of Mawgan do not stop short at the first good work of succouring the afflicted; they extend also to a generous sympathy for those human weaknesses of impatience and irresolution in others, which they have surmounted but not forgotten themselves. Rather more than twelve years since, a young girl of eighteen applied to be admitted to share the dreary life-in-death existence of the Carmelite sisterhood. She was received for her year of probation: it expired, and she still held firmly to her first determination. But the nuns, in pity to her youth, and perhaps mournfully remembering, even in their lifelong seclusion of mind and body, how strong are the ties which bind together the beings of this world and the things of this world, gave her more time yet to search her own motives, to look back on what she was abandoning, to look forward on what she desired to obtain. Mercifully refusing to grant her her own wishes, they forebore the performance of the fatal ceremony which irrevocably took her from earth to give her up only to Heaven, until she had undergone an additional year of probation. This last solemn period of delay, which Christian charity and sisterly love had piously granted, expired, and found her still determined to adhere to her resolution. She took the veil; and the dreary gates of Lanhearne have closed on all that is mortal of her for ever!

The convent has two burial places. The first is in an ancient recess within the village church, and was given to the nuns with the manor house. Those among them who first expired on English ground lie buried here—the Catholic dead have returned to the once Catholic edifice, where the Protestant living now worship! When the Carmelite funeral procession entered this place, it entered at the dead of night, to avoid the chance of any intrusion. But as the nuns have no private entrance to their burial vault, and have been by law prohibited from making one; as they are obliged to pass through the public door of the church and walk up the nave, they are at the mercy of any stranger who can gain admittance to the building, and who may be led by idle curiosity to watch the ceremonies which accompany their midnight service for the dead. Feeling this, they have of late years abandoned their burial place, after first carefully boarding it off from all observation. No inquisitive eyes can now behold, no intruding footsteps can now approach, the tombs of the nuns of Mawgan.

The second cemetery, which they use at present, is situated in one of the convent gardens, and can therefore be secured, whenever they please, from all observation. A wooden door at one corner of the ancient portion of the manor house leads into it. The place is merely a small, square plot of ground, damp, shady, and overgrown with long grass. An old and elaborately carved stone cross stands in it; and about this appear the graves of the nuns, marked by plain slate tablets. But even here, the mystery which hangs darkly over the Carmelite household does not clear—the seclusion that has hidden the living in the Convent is but the forerunner of the secrecy that veils from us on the tombstone the history of the dead. The saint's name once assumed by the nun, and the short yet beautiful supplication of the Roman Church for the repose of the soul of the departed, form the only inscriptions that appear over the graves.

This is all—all of the lives, all of the deaths of the sisterhood at Lanhearne that we can ever know! The remainder must be conjecture. We have but the bare stern outline that has been already drawn—who shall venture, even in imagination, to colour and complete the picture which it darkly, yet plainly, indicates?

Even if we only endeavour to image to ourselves the externals of the life which those massy walls keep secret, what have we to speculate on? Nothing but the day that in winter and summer, in sunshine and in storm, brings with it year after year, to young and to old alike, the same monotony of action and the same monotony of repose—the turning door in the wall (sole indication to those within that there is a world without), moved in silence, ever at the same stated hour, by invisible hands—the prayer and penance in the chapel choir, always a solitude to its occupants, however many of their fellow-creatures may be standing beneath it—the short hours of exercise amid high garden walls, which shut out everything but the distant sky. Beyond this, what remains but that utter vacancy where even thought ends; that utter gloom in which the brightest fancy must cease to shine?

Should we try to look deeper than the surface; to strip the inner life of the convent of all its mysteries and coverings, and anatomising it inch by inch, search it through down to the very heart? Should we pry into the dread and secret processes by which, among these women, one human emotion after another may be suffering, first ossification, then death? No!—this is a task which is beyond our power; an investigation which, of our own knowledge, we cannot be certain of pursuing aright. We may imagine grief that does not exist, remorse that is not felt, error that has not been committed. It is not for us to criticise the catastrophe of the drama, when we have no acquaintance with the scenes which have preceded it. It is not for us, guided by our own thoughts, moved by the impulses of the world we live in, to decide upon the measure of good or evil contained in an act of self-sacrifice at the altar of religion, which is in its own motive and result so utterly separated from all other motives and results, that we cannot at the outset even so much as sympathise with it. The purpose of the convent system is of those purposes which are conceived in this world, but which appeal for justification or condemnation only to the next.

"Judge not, that ye be not judged!" Those words sink deep into our hearts, as we look our last upon the convent walls, and leave the living dead at old Lanhearne.

THIRTEEN

LEGENDS OF THE NORTHERN COAST

From the time when we left St Ives, we walked through the last part of our journey much faster than we walked through the first; faster, perhaps, than the reader may have perceived from these pages. When we stopped at the town of St Columb Major, to visit the neighbouring Vale of Mawgan, we had already advanced halfway up the northern coast of Cornwall. Throughout this part of the county the towns lay wide asunder; and, as pedestrian tourists, we were obliged to lengthen our walks and hasten our pace accordingly.

After we had quitted St Columb Major, our rambles began to draw rapidly to their close. Little more was now left for us to examine than the different localities connected with certain interesting Cornish legends. The places thus associated with the quaint fancies of the olden time were all situated close together, some fifteen or twenty miles farther on, along the coast. The first among them that we reached was Tintagel Castle, an ancient ruin magnificently situated on a precipice overhanging the sea, and romantically, if not historically, reputed as the birthplace of King Arthur.

The date of the Castle of Tintagel is as much a subject of perplexity among modern antiquaries as is the existence of King Arthur among modern historians. We may still see some ruins of the Castle; but when or by whom the building was erected which those ruins represent, we have no means of discovering: we only know that, after the Conquest, it was inhabited by some of our English princes, and that it was used as a state prison so late as the reign of Elizabeth. The rest is, for the most part, mere conjecture, raised upon the weak foundation of a few mouldering fragments of walls which must soon crumble and disappear as the rest of the Castle has crumbled and disappeared before them.

The position of the old fortress was, probably, almost impregnable in the days of its strength and glory. The outer part of it was built on a precipitous projection of cliff, three hundred feet high, which must have been wrenched away from the mainland by some tremendous convulsion of Nature. The inner part stood on the opposite side of the chasm formed by this convulsion; and both divisions of the fortress were formerly connected by a drawbridge. The most interesting portion of the few ruins now remaining is that on the outermost

Tintagel

promontory, which is almost entirely surrounded by the sea. The way up to this cliff is by a steep and somewhat perilous path; so narrow in certain places, where it winds along the verge of the precipice, that a single false step would be certain destruction. The difficulties of the ascent appear to have impressed the old historian of Cornwall, Norden, so vividly that he tries in his "Survey," to frighten all his readers from attempting it; warning "unstable man," if he will try to mount the cliff, that "while he respecteth his footinge he indaungers his head; and looking to save the head, indaungers the footinge, accordinge to the old proverbe: *Incidit in Scyllam qui vult vitare Charybdim.* He must have eyes,"—ominously adds the worthy Norden—"that will scale Tintagel."

The ruins on the summit of the promontory only consist of a few straggling walls, loosely piled up, rather than built, with dark-coloured stone. Some still remain entire enough to show the square loopholes that were pierced in them for arrows; and, here and there, fragments of rough irregular arches, which might have been either doorways or windows, are still visible. Those parts of the building which have fallen are concealed by long, thickly growing grass—the foot may sometimes strike against them, but the eye perceives them not. These are all the vestiges which remain of the once mighty castle; all the signs that are left to point out the site of the old halls, where the bold knights of Arthur gathered for the feast or prepared for the fight, at their royal master's command.

The Cornish legends tell us that the British hero held his last court, solemnized his last feast, reviewed his last array of warriors, at Tintagel, before he went out to the fatal battlefield of Camelford, to combat his nephew Mordred, who had rebelled against his power. In the morning the martial assemblage marched out of the castle in triumph, led by the king, with his death-dealing sword "Excalibur" slung at his shoulder, and his magic lance "Rou" in his hand. In the evening the warriors returned, fatally victorious, from the struggle. The rebel army had been routed and the rebel chief slain; but they brought back with them their renowned leader—the favourite hero of martial adventure, the conqueror of the Saxons in twelve battles—mortally wounded, from the field which he had quitted a victor.

That night the wise and valiant king died in the castle of his birth; died among his followers who had feasted and sung around him at the festal table but a few hours before. The deep-toned bells of Tintagel rang his death peal; and the awe-stricken populace from the country round, gathering together hurriedly before the fortress, heard portentous wailings from supernatural voices, which mingled in ghostly harmony with the moaning of the restless sea, the dirging of the dreary wind, and the dull deep thunder of the funeral knell. About the heights of the castle, and in the caverns beneath it, these sounds ceased not night or day, until the corpse of the hero was conveyed to the ship destined to bear it to its burial-place in Glastonbury Abbey. Then, dirging winds, and moaning sea, and wailing voices, ceased; and, in the intervals between the slow pealing of the funeral bells, clear child-like voices arose from the calmed waters, and told the mourning people that Arthur was gone from them but for a little time, to be healed of all his wounds in the Fairy Land; and that he would yet return to lead and to govern them, as of old.

Such is the scene—strange compound of fiction and truth, of the typical and the real—which legends teach us to imagine in the Tintagel Castle of thirteen centuries ago! What is the scene that we look on now?—A solitude where the decaying works of man and the enduring works of Nature appear mingled in beauty together. The grass grows high and luxuriant, where the rushes were strewn over the floor of Arthur's banqueting hall. Sheep are cropping the fresh pasture, within the walls which once echoed to the sweetest songs, or rang to the clash of the stoutest swords of ancient England! About the fortress nothing remains unchanged, but the sun which at evening still brightens it in its weak old age with the same glory that shone over its lusty youth; the sea that rolls and dashes, as at first, against its foundation rocks;

and the wild Cornish country outspread on either side of it, as desolately and as magnificently as ever.

The grandeur of the scenery at Tintagel, the romantic interest of the old British traditions connected with the castle, might well have delayed us many hours on these solitary heights; but we had other places still to visit, other and far different legends still to gossip over. Descending the cliff while the day gave us ample time to wander at our will; we strolled away inland to track the scene of a new romance as far as the waterfall called St Nighton's Kieve.

A walk of little more than half a mile brings us to the entrance of a valley, bounded on either side by high, gently sloping hills, with a small stream running through its centre, fed by the waterfall of which we are in search. We now follow a footpath a few hundred yards, pass by a mill, and, looking up the valley, see one compact mass of vegetation entirely filling it to its remotest corners, and not leaving the slightest vestige of a path, the merest patch of clear ground, visible in any direction, far or near.

It seems as if all the foliage which ought to have grown on the Cornish moorlands had been mischievously crammed into this place, within the narrow limits of one Cornish valley. Weeds, ferns, brambles, bushes, and young trees are flourishing together here, thickly intertwined in every possible position, in triumphant security from any invasion of billhook or axe. You win every step of your way through this miniature forest of vegetation, by the labour of your arms and the weight of your body. Tangled branches and thorny bushes press against you in front and behind, meet over your head, knock off your cap, flap in your face, twist about your legs, and tear your coat skirts; so obstructing you in every conceivable manner and in every conceivable direction that they seem possessed with a living power of opposition, and commissioned by some evil genius of Fairy Mythology to prevent mortal footsteps from intruding into the valley. Whether you try a zigzag or a straight course, whether you go up or down, it is the same thing—you must squeeze, and push, and jostle your way through the crowd of bushes, just as you would through a crowd of men—or else stand still, surrounded by leaves, like "a Jack-in-the-Green," and wait for the very remote chance of somebody coming to help you out.

Forcing our road incessantly through these obstructions, for a full half-hour, and taking care to keep our only guide—the sound of the running-water—always within hearing, we came at last to a little break in the vegetation, crossed the stream at this place, and found, on the opposite side of the bank, a faintly marked track, which might have been once a footpath. Following it as well as we could among the branches and brambles, and now ascending steep ground, we soon heard the dash of the waterfall. But to attempt to see it was no easy undertaking. The trees, the bushes, and the wild herbage grew here thicker than ever, stretching in perfect canopies of leaves so closely across the overhanging banks of the stream as entirely to hide it from view. We heard the monotonous, eternal splashing of the water, close at our ears, and yet vainly tried to obtain even a glimpse of the fall. Adverse Fate led us up and down, and round and round, and backwards and forwards, amid a labyrinth of overgrown bushes which might have bewildered an Australian settler; and still the nymph of the waterfall coyly hid herself from our eyes. Our ears informed us that the invisible object of which we were in search was of very inconsiderable height; our patience was evaporating; our time was wasting away—in short, to confess the truth here, as I have confessed it elsewhere in these pages, let me acknowledge that we both concurred in a sound determination to consult our own convenience, and give up the attempt to discover St Nighton's Kieve!

Our wanderings, however, though useless enough in one direction, procured us this compensating advantage in another: they led us accidentally to the exact scene of the legend which we knew to be connected with this part of the valley, and which had, indeed, first induced us to visit it.

We found ourselves standing before the damp, dismantled stone walls of a solitary cottage, placed on a plot of partially open ground, near the outskirts of the wood. Long dark herbage grew about the inside of the ruined little building; a toad was crawling where the leaves clustered thickest, on what had once been the floor of a room; in every direction corruption and decay were visibly battening on the lonesome place. Its aspect would repel rather than allure curiosity, but for the mysterious story associated with it, which gives it an attraction and an interest that are not its own.

Years and years ago, when this desolate building was a neat comfortable cottage, it was inhabited by two ladies, of whose histories, and even names, all the people of the district were perfectly ignorant. One day they were accidentally found living in their solitary abode, before any one knew that they had so much as entered it, or that they existed at all. Both appeared to be about the same age, and both were inflexibly taciturn. One was never seen without the other; if they ever left the house, they only left it to walk in the most unfrequented parts of the wood; they kept no servant, and never had a visitor; no living souls but themselves ever crossed the door of their cottage. They procured their food and other necessaries from the people in the nearest village, paying for everything they received when it was delivered, and neither asking nor answering a single unnecessary question.

Their manners were gentle, but grave and sorrowful as well. The people who brought them their household supplies felt awed and uneasy, without knowing why, in their presence; and were always relieved when they had dispatched their errand and had got well away from the cottage and the wood.

Gradually, as month by month passed on, and the mystery hanging over the solitary pair was still not cleared up, superstitious doubts spread widely through the neighbourhood. Harmless as the conduct of the ladies always appeared to be, there was something so sinister and startling about the unearthly seclusion and secrecy of their lives, that people began to feel vaguely suspicious, to whisper awful imaginary rumours about them, to gossip over old stories of ghosts and false accusations that had never been properly sifted to the end, whenever the inhabitants of the cottage were mentioned. At last they were secretly watched by the less scrupulous among the villagers, whom intense curiosity had endowed with a morbid courage and resolution. Even this proceeding led to no results whatever, but increased rather than diminished the mystery.

The expertest eavesdroppers who had listened at the door brought away no information with them for their pains. Some declared that when the ladies held any conversation together, they spoke in so low a tone that it was impossible to distinguish a word they said.

Others, of more imaginative temperament, protested, on the contrary, that their voices were perfectly audible, but that the language they talked was some mysterious or diabolical language of their own, incomprehensible to everybody but themselves. One or two expert and daring spies had even contrived to look in at them through the window, unperceived; but had seen nothing uncommon, nothing supernatural—nothing, in short, beyond the spectacle of two ladies sitting quietly and silently by their own fireside.

So matters went on, until one day universal agitation was excited in the neighbourhood by a rumour that one of the ladies was dead. The rustic authorities immediately repaired to the cottage, accompanied by a long train of eager followers; and found that the report was true. The surviving lady was seated by her companion's bedside, weeping over a corpse. She spoke not a word; she never looked up at the villagers as they entered. Question after question was put to her without ever eliciting an answer; kind words were useless—even threats proved equally inefficient: the lady still remained weeping by the corpse, and still said nothing. Gradually her inexorable silence began to infect the visitors to the cottage. For a few moments nothing was heard in the room but the dash of the waterfall hard by, and the singing of birds in the surrounding wood. Bitterly as the lady was weeping, it was now first observed by everybody that she wept silently, that she never sobbed, never even sighed under the oppression of her grief.

People began to urge each other, superstitiously, to leave the place. It was determined that the corpse should be removed and buried; and that afterwards some new expedient should be tried to induce the survivor of the mysterious pair to abandon her inflexible silence. It was anticipated that she would have made some sign, or spoken some few words when they lifted the body from the bed on which it lay; but even this proceeding produced no visible effect. As the villagers quitted the dwelling with their dead burden, the last of them who went out left her in her solitude, still speechless, still weeping, as they had found her at first.

Days passed, and she sent no message to anyone. Weeks elapsed, and the idlers who waited about the woodland paths where they knew that she was once wont to walk with her companion, never saw her, watch for her as patiently as they might. From haunting the wood, they soon got on to hovering round the cottage, and to looking in stealthily at the window. They saw her sitting on the same seat that she had always occupied, with a vacant chair opposite; her figure wasted, her face wan already with incessant weeping. It was a dismal sight to all who beheld it—a vision of affliction and solitude that sickened their hearts.

217

No one knew what to do; the kindest-hearted people hesitated, the hardest-hearted people dreaded to disturb her. While they were still irresolute, the end was at hand. One morning a little girl, who had looked in at the cottage window in imitation of her elders, reported, when she returned home, that she had seen the lady still sitting in her accustomed place, but that one of her hands hung strangely over the arm of the chair, and that she never moved to pick up her pocket handkerchief, which lay on the ground beside her. At these ominous tidings, the villagers summoned their resolution, and immediately repaired to the lonesome cottage in the wood.

They knocked and called at the door—it was not opened to them. They raised the latch and entered. She still occupied her chair; her head was resting on one of her hands; the other hung down, as the little girl had told them. The handkerchief, too, was on the ground, and was wet with tears. Was she sleeping? They went round in front to look. Her eyes were wide open; her drooping hand, worn almost to mere bone, was cold to the touch as the waters of the valley stream on a winter's day. She had died in her wonted place; died in mystery and in solitude as she had lived.

They buried her where they had buried her companion. No traces of the real history of either the one or the other have ever been discovered from that time to this.

Such is the tale that was related to us of the cottage in the valley of St Nighton's Kieve. It may be only imagination; but the stained roofless walls, the damp clotted herbage, and the reptiles crawling about the ruins give the place a gloomy and disastrous look. The air, too, seems just now unusually still and heavy here—for the evening is at hand, and the vapours are rising in the wood. The shadows of the trees are deepening; the rustling music of the waterfall is growing dreary; the utter stillness of all things besides becomes wearying to the ear. Let us pass on, and get into bright wide space again, where the down leads back to happier solitudes by the seashore.

We now rapidly lose sight of the trees which have hitherto so closely surrounded us, and find ourselves treading the short scanty grass of the cliff top once more. We still advance northward, walking along rough cart roads, and skirting the extremities of narrow gullies leading down to the sea, until we enter the picturesque village of Boscastle. Then, descending a long street of irregular houses, of all sizes, shapes, and ages, we are soon conducted to the bottom of a deep hollow. Beyond this, the bare ground rises again abruptly up to the highest point of the high cliffs which overhang the shore; and here, where the site is most elevated, and where neither cottages nor cultivation appear, we descry the ancient walls and gloomy tower of Forrabury Church.

The interior of the building still contains a part of the finely carved rood loft which once adorned it. Its rickety wooden pews are blackened with extreme old age, and covered with curiously cut patterns and cyphers. The place is so dark that it is difficult to read the inscriptions on many of the mouldering monuments, fixed together without order or symmetry on the walls. Outside are some Saxon arches, oddly built of black slate stone; and the window-mouldings are ornamented with rough carving, which at once proclaims its own antiquity. But it is in the tower that the interest attached to the church chiefly centres. Square, thick, and of no extraordinary height, it resembles in appearance most other towers in Cornwall—except in one particular, all the belfry windows are completely stopped up.

This peculiarity is to be explained simply enough: the church has never had any bells; the old tower has been mute, and useless except for ornament, since it was first built. The congregation of the district must trust to their watches and their punctuality to get to service in good time on Sundays. At Forrabury the chimes have never sounded for a marriage: the knell has never been heard for a funeral.

To know the reason of this; to discover why the church, though tower and belfry have always been waiting ready for them, has never had a peal of bells, we must seek instruction from another popular tradition, from a third legend of these legendary shores. Let us go down a little to the brink of the cliff, where the sea is rolling into a black, yawning, perpendicular pit of slate rock. The scene of our third story is the view over the waters from this place.

In ancient times, when Forrabury Church was still regarded as a building of recent date, it was a subject of sore vexation to all the people of the neighbourhood that their tower had no bells, while the inhabitants of Tintagel still possessed the famous peal that had rung for King Arthur's funeral. For some years, this superiority of the rival village was borne with composure by the people of Forrabury; but, in process of time, they lost all patience, and it was publicly determined by the rustic council that the honour of their church should be vindicated. Money was immediately collected, and bells of magnificent tones and dimensions were forthwith ordered from the best manufactory that London could supply.

The bells were cast, blessed by high ecclesiastical authorities, and shipped for transportation to Forrabury. The voyage was one of the most prosperous that had ever been known. Fair winds and calm seas so expedited the passage of the ship that she appeared in sight of the downs on which the church stood, many days before she had been expected. Great was the triumph of the populace on shore, as they watched her working into the bay with a steady evening breeze.

On board, however, the scene was very different. Here there was more uproar than happiness, for the captain and the pilot were at open opposition. As the ship neared the harbour, the bells of Tintagel were faintly heard across the water, ringing for the evening service. The pilot, who was a devout man, took off his hat as he heard the sound, crossed himself, and thanked God aloud for a prosperous voyage. The captain, who was a reckless, vainglorious fellow, reviled the pilot as a fool, and impiously swore that the ship's company had only to thank his skill as a navigator, and their own strong arms and ready wills, for bringing the ship safely in sight of harbour. The pilot, in reply, rebuked him as an infidel, and still piously continued to return thanks as before; while the captain, joined by the crew, tried to drown his voice by oaths and blasphemy. They were still shouting their loudest, when the vengeance of Heaven descended in judgment on them all.

The clouds supernaturally gathered, the wind rose to a gale in a moment. An immense sea, higher than any man had ever beheld, overwhelmed the ship; and, to the horror of the people on shore, she went down in an instant, close to land. Of all the crew, the pilot only was saved.

The bells were never recovered. They were heard tolling a muffled death peal, as they sank with the ship; and even yet, on stormy days, while the great waves roll over them, they still ring their ghostly knell above the fiercest roaring of wind and sea.

This is the ancient story of the bells—this is why the chimes are never heard from the belfry of Forrabury Church.

Now that we have visited the scene of our third legend, what is it that keeps me and my companion still lingering on the downs? Why we are still delaying the hour of our departure long after the time which we have ourselves appointed for it?

We both know but too well. At this point we leave the coast, not to return to it again: at Forrabury we look our last on the sea from these rocky shores. With this evening, our pleasant days of strolling travel are ended. Tomorrow we go direct to Launceston, and from Launceston at once to Plymouth. Tomorrow the adventures of the walking tourist are ours no longer; for on that day our rambles in Cornwall will have virtually closed!

Rise, brother-traveller! We have lingered until twilight already; the seaward crags grow vast and dim around us, and the inland view narrows and darkens solemnly in the waning light. Shut up your sketch book which you have so industriously filled, and pocket your pencils which you have worn down to stumps, even as I now shut up my dogs-eared old journal, and pocket my empty ink bottle.

One more of the few and fleeting scenes of life is fast closing, soon to leave us nothing but the remembrance that it once existed—a happy remembrance of a holiday walk in dear old England, which will always be welcome and vivid to the last, like other remembrances of home.

Come! The night is drawing round us her curtain of mist; let us strap on our trusty old friends the knapsacks for the last time, and turn resolutely from the shore by which we have delayed too long. Come! Let us once again "jog on the footpath way" as contentedly, if not quite as merrily, as ever; and, remembering how much we have seen and learnt that must surely better us both, let us, as we now lose sight of the dark, grey waters, gratefully, though sadly, speak the parting word:—

FAREWELL TO CORNWALL!

Lamorna Cove

NOTES

1. I visited St Cleer's Well, for the second time, ten years after the above lines were written; and I am happy to say that two gentlemen, interested in this beautiful ruin, are about to restore it—using the old materials for the purpose, and exactly following the original design. (March, 1861.)

2. It may be necessary to remind the reader that this statement respecting the population of Cornwall was written in the year 1850. I have no means at my disposal of ascertaining what the increase in numbers may have been during the last ten years.—(March, 1861.)

3. The gentleman here referred to—whose kind assistance while I was writing these pages I can never forget—was Mr Richard Moyle, long resident as a medical man at Penzance. Since my first visit to Cornwall, death has removed Mr Moyle from the scene of his labours, to the lasting and sincere regret of all who knew him.—(March, 1861.)

4. In case any of my readers should feel desirous of seeing a specimen of the Cornish language at the date of the play, I subjoin the original text of the seven lines of John Keygwyn's translation, quoted above.

Syr, war nebas lavarow,
Tast gy part an avallow,
    Po ow harenga ty a gyll!
Meir, Kymar an avall teake,
Po sure inter te ha'th wreage
An garenga quyt a fyll
    Mar ny vynyth y thebbry!

Some of this looks like a very polyglot language. But the ancient Cornish tongue had altered and deteriorated; and was indeed changing into English at the period of our play. Why the author should have helped himself, in his literary emergency to the two Latin words in the fifth line (*inter te*) when English would have served his turn as well, it is difficult to discover, unless he wished to show his learning before the rustic audiences of Piran Round.

5. All the particulars here related of the convent discipline, were communicated to me by the resident priest. This gentleman was certainly not a prejudiced witness on the side of austerity—for he frankly complained of the lonely life which the rules of the Sisterhood inflicted on him, and unhesitatingly acknowledged that he was anxious for the time when his clerical successor would come to relieve him.

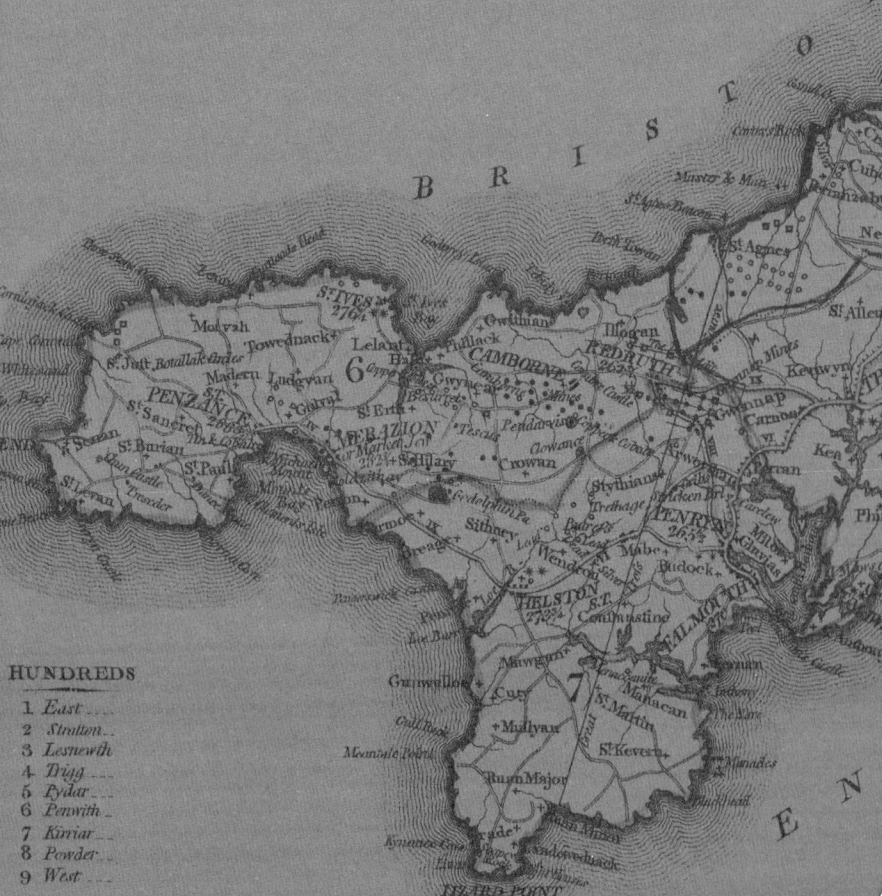

HUNDREDS

1 East ____
2 Stratton __
3 Lesnewith _
4 Trigg ____
5 Pydar ___
6 Penwith __
7 Kirriar __
8 Powder ___
9 West ____